ACCLAIM FOR THE BESTSELLING BOOKS OF KATHLEEN DRYMON:

PIRATE MOON

"A delicious adventure. Keeps you turning page after page!"

—*Romantic Times*

WARRIOR OF THE SUN

". . . an enthralling, passion-filled tale that will mesmerize you!"

—*Rendezvous*

CASTAWAY ANGEL

"A spirited heroine, a courageous hero, and a plot that will pull you in from the very first chapter. A winner!"

—*Inside Romance*

WHAT'S LOVE GOT TO DO WITH IT?

Everything . . . Just ask Kathleen Drymon . . . and Zebra Books

CASTAWAY ANGEL	(3569-1, $4.50/$5.50)
GENTLE SAVAGE	(3888-7, $4.50/$5.50)
MIDNIGHT BRIDE	(3265-X, $4.50/$5.50)
VELVET SAVAGE	(3886-0, $4.50/$5.50)
TEXAS BLOSSOM	(3887-9, $4.50/$5.50)
WARRIOR OF THE SUN	(3924-7, $4.99/$5.99)

KATHLEEN DRYMON
TIME'S ANGEL

ZEBRA BOOKS
KENSINGTON PUBLISHING CORP.

ZEBRA BOOKS are published by

Kensington Publishing Corp.
475 Park Avenue South
New York, NY 10016

First Printing: April, 1994

Printed in the United States of America

For Virginia Henley, Jill Jones,
and Maggie Davis.
Your friendship is more precious than gold.
Thanks for always being there and
for all the support you have all given me.

One

The rust-spot primed, red '68 Volkswagen van slowly made its way through the London streets. With a harsh curse, the balding, heavyset man sitting behind the steering wheel took his eyes off the road and glared over his shoulder as a paper missile hit him on the back of his head. The excited babble of children's voices in the cramped vehicle had him in an uncomfortable sweat.

"Hey, Mustafa, you are slow today! If you don't watch where you are driving, the morning will be over before you get us into the city!" a querulous voice shouted to the driver. The rest of the passengers called out their hearty agreement with the oldest boy's statement. His ebony eyes flashed with devilment, not only for the words he had shouted, but for the paper missile which moments before had hit Mustafa.

"Momma Leona will be hearing about your foul manners, Carlos! It is bad enough that I am forced to drive you bunch of ingrates into town every morning, let alone take your abuse!"

The man's threats did not affect young Carlos. He knew well his value to Momma Leona and knew also that when she received Mustafa's report, she would only threaten him. "Just be pushing the gas pedal a bit harder, Mustafa!" he shouted back at the bald head, and won the admiring glances of the other children and the nods of the young boys who dreamt of one day being exactly like their hero, Carlos.

Moments later Mustafa shouted, "Get yourselves out, and be quick about it!" He braked the van against the curb and Gypsy children began to clamber out the side door. "Be sure that you're all right here at this same spot this afternoon. Mateo will be picking you up." That said, he turned his heavy bulk back around on the seat, glad to be rid of the children, and started to drive away from the curb.

As the group of rough, good-natured children began to pair off and started walking toward the busiest parts of the city, two of the oldest girls stood at the curb for a minute longer. "Don't be forgetting what happened to Alex last night, Angela," the taller and apparently the older of the pair whispered in low, frightened tones. "Momma Leona has been in a foul mood of late. Make sure that you have a good day."

The girl called Angela slowly nodded her head, her long dark hair gleaming beneath the morning sun as the silver coins that had been braided into the thick mass of curls sparkled brightly. For a moment, her unusual blue eyes were shadowed with the silent remembrance of the evening before. Like the rest of the children, she had gotten little sleep as they had been forced to listen to the noises that had come from the small room that Mustafa and Mateo had built onto the back of the small motor caravan the children called their home. Alex was a soft-spoken, gentle girl who was more suited to cooking and caring for the smaller children than bringing in any profit to Momma Leona, and this fact had proven to be her undoing last night. Without a second thought or any regret, Momma Leona had sold Alex's body to two Gypsy men. Alex was only sixteen years old, and by the sounds which had come from the back room last night, she had not been treated kindly by the pair of ill-kempt brutes Momma Leona had chosen for her. There had been bruises on one of her cheeks, and both of her forearms had shown signs of her mistreatment this morning as she went about her usual task of preparing the morning meal of hot, thin cereal.

After breakfast, Alex had not climbed into the van as usual with the rest of the children. Momma Leona had singled her out and instructed her to go back into the trailer. "There just might be more need for you here today, Alex," the large Gypsy woman had declared, and all the children who were old enough to understand what was happening could well envision what kind of task Alex would be required to perform during the day.

"I will meet you back here later this afternoon, Penny," Angela called over her shoulder, with a touch of desperation in her tone as she started off on her own down the sidewalk. For a few more minutes, as Angela made her way toward Piccadilly Station, her thoughts were on the unfortunate Alex. She herself was a year older than Alex, and the other girl's plight brought home her own precarious situation under Momma Leona's charge. The cries coming from the small room had left chills of goose flesh upon her young body. Thank God she had only been able to imagine the horrors that Alex had been forced to endure and had not known their like herself.

Going down Lower Regent Street, Angela turned right onto Jermyn Street, and with an easy stride, her quick eyes darted about the busy London district. She easily picked out her first mark of the day. Standing in front of Wren Church, which faced Jermyn Street, she approached an elderly couple. They had the typical look of tourists. The man wore blue-and-yellow-checked casual pants and a yellow sport shirt, open at the throat. He had a large paunch that hung over his waistline and was nearly bald, wisps of gray hair barely covering his head. The woman at his side held a camera in her hand, and from time to time she took a picture. Upon one shoulder she carried a large, open purse, which more than likely contained numerous things besides her wallet. Angela studied them for another minute as they looked at the sights in the area and snapped pictures. They were easy prey.

"Why, look at that adorable little coffee shop, James. This is where they say that on weekends there is a street market. Right here on the grounds of the church!" the woman excitedly told her husband.

With a grin coming over her bow-shaped lips and her walk gaining a jaunty step which increased her momentum, Angela ran right into the surprised couple. Pushing her way between the man and woman, she nearly caused the woman to fall to the street.

"Look out here!" the man exclaimed as he tried to reach out a hand to steady his wife.

"Oh my, I am so sorry! I am so clumsy!" Angela cried as though not believing her own stupidity. "Let me help you, lady. Let me help you." She seemed in that moment to be all over the woman. Her hands were touching, petting, straightening out the woman's clothes, replacing the camera in her hand, and in the confusion the couple didn't know what was happening to them. Angela's slim hand reached into the large purse as quick as lightning and slipped the leather wallet into the deep pocket of her long black skirt.

"Get away from us!" the man at last shouted. If somewhat belatedly, he remembered something he had heard yesterday from a tour guide about the gypsies that roamed the London streets and had been known to converge upon unsuspecting tourists and within seconds rob their victims blind! Well, perhaps this was just a lone girl, but there was no question that she was one of that wild breed, what with her dark clothes and the glinting silver coins in her hair. He was not about to take any chances! Glancing about the street as though expect-

ing more of the ill-kempt creatures to converge upon him and his wife, he pulled his
wife away from the young girl's hands and
stated with some authority, "Get on your
way now before I call for the police!"

Making a sour face at the couple, Angela
murmured as she started to walk away, "I
was only trying to help." But the threat of
the man calling the authorities had its usual
effect upon her. She had been pinched too
many times in the past, and lately Momma
Leona had been warning her that she was
too old to be getting herself caught by the
bobbies. She was seventeen now; not that she
looked it with her small features and her
overlong skirts and blouses. She had the
look of a child in her early teens. With the
help of her clothing and her shabby appearance, she had hid all effects of being a
young woman thus far. She had known
many of her people who had been stuck in
jail because they had passed the age when
they could only be held for a few hours and
then released back to the street. A Gypsy
child had advantages in London. One of
them was the ability to practice thievery
without threat of punishment. They had no
permanent address when caught, and they
lied without a second thought when questioned. What choice did the authorities have

except to release the children after a few questions and warnings?

Until midday, Angela practiced her illegal occupation. Any unsuspecting person on the London streets was an easy victim for her deft hand. A few days earlier, Angela had ventured into the Burlington Arcade and had soon been ushered back out onto the streets by the Beadles. Wearing their gold-braided top hats and frock coats, they had explained that if caught in the Arcade again, she would be taken to the station. Today she passed Burlington Arcade without second thoughts. By lunchtime she found herself at Knightsbridge. Harrod's was more to her liking! It had over three hundred departments on five floors and tourists too numerous to count.

Begging a warm crust of bread from the good-hearted baker and filching an apple from the fruit and flower hall, Angela then found a bench to sit upon. She took a few minutes to rest and watch those passing by.

A discarded tabloid, the *Daily Mirror,* lay on the bench. While Angela munched the apple, she scanned the front page. The headlines of the scandal sheet announced that the descendants of the Duke of Westfield had placed a claim before Parliament to try to regain the lands and title that had been stripped from their family over two hundred years earlier. It appeared that the Duke of Westfield had been falsely accused of being involved in the conspiracy with the Jacobites to overthrow George II and put James Stuart on the throne. The duke had been stripped of title and lands and had been executed. Now years later, documents had been found at Hampsteed Castle giving conclusive proof that Royce St. James had been betrayed by a Lord Dunsely and several prominent men. Angela tossed the paper down on the bench as she finished her meal. She was not interested in anything that did not affect her own life.

She sat upon the bench and indulged her favorite pastime: watching other people. Men and women of wealth always fascinated her, and she admitted inwardly that she envied them. Their manners were always controlled and refined, and though they did not have the carefree manner of her own people, she knew they had all they wished to eat, and their clothing was always of the finest materials and styles. Her slender hand ran over her own long skirt, touching the pocket now filled with the morning's work. She felt the roughness of the material of the skirt that Momma Leona had given her one afternoon after a group of ladies had visited their trailer with a box of hand-me-downs and an odd assortment of canned foods. She could

15

not even imagine what it would be like to feel the coolness of silk against her thighs, and for a fleeting instant, Angela's body tingled with such a daring thought.

Momma Leona had often lectured Angela that she held her head too high in the clouds, aspiring to be better than the rest of her class. With the reminder of the old Gypsy woman's words, Angela left the bench, then wandered about the many shops at Harrod's As she passed a chocolate and confectionery shop, she eased a gentleman's wallet from his back pocket while he was busy trying to coax the young woman at his side to enter the shop.

Later, Momma Leona's words again came to mind. Why did the Gypsy woman think that Angela had high hopes for herself? How could the young woman forget the squalor of Momma Leona's trailer and the small ration of food that the children were allowed? Her life had always been one of drudgery, but she knew that things could be much worse. As she remembered the noises from the back room of the trailer, she quickened her steps. Her bright violet-blue eyes scanned the streets for her next mark. She could not allow herself to be put in the same position as Alex. She had to keep showing Momma Leona that her true worth was on the streets picking pockets!

She thought about running away from the large overbearing Gypsy woman, but before she could dwell upon these thought she was almost knocked from the sidewalk as a small, darkly dressed man rushed past her.

Quickly regaining her footing, Angela watched the retreating back of the little man. Why was he hurrying so? she wondered. As he rounded the street corner, her Gypsy blood began to throb with curiosity. Stepping up her pace, in too-tight shoes, she followed him down Beauchamp Place, a neat, narrow street of boutiques and restaurants, then trailed him down Pont Street, with its gabled buildings and terra cotta decorations. When the little dapper fellow entered a small shop, its wooden sign overhead stating, "Danning's Antique Shop and Bookstore," she stopped several doors down and waited for his return.

Peering into shop windows along the street as though she were an interested shopper, Angela worried as time passed and the little man did not leave the shop. She thought that she should be on her way as the afternoon was beginning to grow late, but there was something about the man that had drawn her, and she was loath to turn away. A strange quality about the little gentleman had intrigued her from the first moment. She desired, if nothing else, to have a closer look at him.

A half-hour passed before the little man left the antique shop. With determination, Angela decided that he would be her next mark. Too much time had been wasted waiting for him. She had to make some profit from him, she determined, knowing Momma Leona would be angry if she were to return to the trailer with little to show for a day's work. Again, the little man was hurrying as he left the antique shop, his hand tightly clutching a small bag. Angela fell in behind him, knowing that she would have to be quick. As he rounded Beauchamp Place, she took advantage of a simple opportunity that formed in front of her. A small group of people had gathered before a gold and jewelry shop. A mannequin had been set up and was wearing only the glitter of gold over her body. She appeared so lifelike that she was attracting the attention of all those that passed the window. To avoid the crowd, the little man had to slow his pace and step nearer to the curb.

Following upon his heels, Angela's proximity forced him to be pressed tighter into the crowd. As the man tried to escape the closing group, he did not feel her nimble fingers slide into his jacket pocket, nor did he see her grin as she transferred the small box from his pocket into her own.

Two

Making her way back to her group and to the spot where Mateo would be picking the children up, Angela again plied her trade. Her fingers were so nimble that none of the marks knew that they had been plucked clean. As she approached the appointed spot, she felt a tug on her shirt sleeve and turned.

"Come, Rawnie. What have you to give me? Make it be something of a little value and I will tell you of all your tomorrows." An old, bent Gypsy woman stood at her side, and immediately Angela knew her to be a *tacho rat:* one of the true blood. Her Rom features and dress told Angela more than anything that she should be on guard.

"I have nothing to give away, old mother." She pulled her arm from the woman's grip, knowing that even though this woman was one of her own race, her people were cunning tricksters. If she did not want to lose the day's large cache, she had best be wary.

"I leave London on the morrow with my good son, Jacob, Rawnie. It must be this day that I read the paths of your future. Give me your hand. Let me tell you of the days ahead of your steps." The gnarled old hand of the woman snatched at Angela's, and once she had her in her grip, she would not release her.

"I have already told you—I have nothing to give away!" Angela kept her other hand over the pocket of her skirt. "Why do you insist on calling me Rawnie? You can see that I am also a Rom." She decided that the old lady must be weak in the mind. She must be thinking to make an extra coin to take to her son, she reasoned as the old woman held to her hand.

"You must take this *diklo* then," the old woman proclaimed as she began to pull the bright yellow scarf from around her neck. "There must be an exchange before I can tell you what is upon your life path."

"But, old mother, I do not wish to take your scarf. I do not have time for this foolishness now." Angela had been raised around women like this one. She had seen many of their pranks on the *gorgios,* those that were not of the Gypsy blood. They told ladies and gentlemen what they most de-

20

sired to hear. She herself had been taught by her aunt how to read tea leaves and how to feel a pulse quicken in a hand in order to know what a person desired to be told as you questioned them. She did not have time for this old woman and her fortune-telling ways. Shortly the van would be back to pick up the children, and if she missed her ride, no one would be coming back for her. She would be forced to spend the night on the London streets.

But the old woman was persistent. She wrapped the garish scarf around Angela's throat, and clutching her hand, she continued as though the girl had not objected. "You will be known as Rawnie—a great lady. Your eyes are not the color of the Rom, but your blood is of your people. Your journey in this life will not be as others of your kind. You shall travel far and leave all those that know you. You shall lose your heart to a *gorgio*, but never will you lose yourself."

At last Angela was able to snatch her hand away. Scornfully she said, "I know your tricks, old one! You say that my blood is Rom, but I shall be lost to a *gorgio*? What talk is this? My father was a true Rom and his family before him. I shall ever be of the Rom! Here, take back your scarf!" She began hastily to untie the sash, but before she could do so, the old woman had turned

21

away and was hurrying off in the opposite direction.

For a moment Angela thought of following her and forcing her to take back the scarf, but with the sun beginning to lower, she decided against it. She would keep the scarf. If the old woman was stupid enough to give it away, why should she not enjoy it? Turning back down the sidewalk, she soon was encircled by the rest of the Gypsy children.

Standing silently on the sidewalk next to Penny, the old Gypsy's strange words returned to Angela's mind. The old woman was crazy, she told herself sternly. She had thought to gain something with crafty words, but Angela was not one to swallow any line that was handed out. The old woman must have thought to flee before Angela could berate her for her wild words. Why, though, had she given her the scarf? Angela felt it a strange action for a Rom. A Gypsy was not known for giving away bright-colored clothing, even to one of their kind.

She had little time to think upon the matter, for the van pulled to the sidewalk just then and Mateo hurried the children aboard. Angela sat quietly and watched the passing traffic as they traveled out of the city and back to Momma Leona's motor caravan.

* * *

The gay sounds of music and singing filled the area as the children descended from the van, then made their way into the small trailer. As they entered, each child seemed to find a corner in which to squeeze. The dim lighting of a kerosene lantern revealed Alex dancing in the small space of the front room. As she twirled about, she was aided in her endeavors by the lively music of a guitar and the loud claps, laughter, and shouts of Momma Leona and the two men that had been with Alex the night before, and one more man that was a stranger to their group.

The scene sickened Angela as she, like the other children, watched Alex's swirling, clapping performance. But Angela saw something that the others in the trailer had overlooked. A hollowness about Alex's features plainly exposed her fear of what the night would bring. Momma Leona's fat form, dressed in brightly colored shirt and skirt, sat upon a low stool. Her loud voice shouted, as her hands clapped in time with the three men, for the girl to spin faster and faster. As the flame red dress swirled around Alex's slender thighs and the men shouted louder with lustful glee, Angela slipped quietly out of the trailer and away from the rest of the noisy group.

Outside in the fresh evening air, she took in deep breaths of the country-sweet night breeze. It seemed Momma Leona had found another method for filling her purse. Angela could imagine the noises that would be coming from the back room of the trailer this night.

Wearily she began to make her way toward the small pond that was located on the property where the Gypsy motor caravans were camped. Her mind lingered upon thoughts of her own future as she reflected upon Momma Leona's large grin. Her two gold-capped teeth had shone in the lantern light as Angela had followed the children into the trailer and had quietly emptied her pockets into the wide expanse of the large woman's lap. But for how long would Momma Leona smile upon her? What if the older woman decided that Angela would share Alex's fate? The young woman held little doubt as to Momma Leona's greed. She had been with the woman since she was eight. Her father's aunt had been entrusted with her care after her beautiful Irish mother and her darkly handsome Gypsy father had been killed in an automobile accident. Less than six months later, her aunt Opal had run into Momma Leona and had, without regret, bargained a price for her small niece.

Angela had never protested her aunt's actions. She had been devastated by the loss of her parents and realized now that she must have been in a state of shock when her aunt had packed her bag and driven her out to the small, brightly colored trailer that had belonged to the slovenly woman whom she was told to call Momma Leona.

With a soft sigh, Angela threw herself down upon the soft grass near the pond's edge. She could not allow herself to be treated like Alex. Would she obey blindly anything that Momma Leona demanded of her? If the woman wanted her to sell her body to the men, what then? Instantly she knew the answer: no! She would fight and claw any man until he released her! But what, she wondered, would happen then? She had seen the punishment inflicted upon those that did not follow Momma Leona's will. Mustafa and Mateo were large brutes whom Momma Leona kept around for the sole purpose of keeping the dozen children in line. Angela herself had received many slaps and several harder assaults with Mustafa's unyielding paddle!

Snuggling deeply into the high grass, Angela decided that she would stay near the pond for the night. The small, crowded trailer was never comfortable for sleeping at night anyway, with all the children cramped upon the floor of the front room, but it was even more unbearable now, with what was taking place in the back room with Alex and the men that Momma Leona sent in to her.

Lying flat upon the earth, Angela allowed herself to feel every muscle in her slim body. Though almost eighteen, she was very small for her age, due, she felt, to the fact that she was allowed only the smallest portion of the morning meal, and then, in the evening, only a small bowl of stew. The only variation from this diet was the food that she was able to steal during the day. Momma Leona had started her off right away with this light diet, as she had insisted that Angela was too big for her age when she had first come into her charge. As Angela had begun to develop breasts, Momma Leona had taken over in this department also, insisting that the young girl keep a scarf tied about her bosom, confining the flowering buds so that no one would be able to see that she was maturing.

Pulling her dark shirt from the waistband of her skirt, Angela reached beneath the material and untied the constricting scarf. This confinement was becoming more unbearable with each passing day; her breasts had already grown far too large for such restrictions. Rolling over on her belly, she looked over the glittering water of the pond. The sun was lowering, and the pond and camp area were held in a yellowish haze that lent a peaceful quality to the early evening. There was usually a carefree humor about her people that was lost to Angela this day. She felt that life was slowly closing in on her, and there was but one way out. To survive, she would have to flee, then try to make it on her own! Each day brought the threat closer that she would soon find herself in Alex's circumstance. If not this fate, then eventually she would be caught by the authorities for stealing, then spend time in jail because her age could no longer be hidden. How would she be able to live within the confinement of walls and bars?

Rolling over once more, she tried to calm her turbulent emotions. As her hand brushed the pocket of her skirt, she realized that she had not given Momma Leona all the bounty of that day. She slowly withdrew the small box which she had stolen from the trim little man that afternoon. She had not as yet had a chance to look in the box. With a spark of excitement, she wondered at the priceless treasure she might find within. Sitting up, she lifted the lid of the box.

Within was no great jewel or fortune in gold. Instead Angela looked down upon an old, tarnished pocket watch. She would have to give this to Momma Leona when she returned to the trailer in the morning, she decided. Maybe a few coins could be gotten for the watch from the man who fenced her stolen goods. Perhaps the Gypsy woman would be reminded of how valuable Angela was to her, out on the streets.

Taking the old watch from the box's velvet interior, Angela turned it about in the palm of her hand. A picture of an Egyptian man and woman had been etched upon the facing. The pair were relaxing on a divan and were being fed fruit by a servant. Angela had once seen a book about an Egyptian woman named Cleopatra. Looking down at the pocket watch, she was reminded of the story. Her mother had loved books and had taught her daughter how to read at an early age. None of the other children that Momma Leona kept in her care could read, and Angela tried to keep her own abilities hidden. A true Rom always tried to remain like his family, never wishing to feel the outsider.

As she pushed a small clasp on the side of the watch, the lid popped open and Angela saw that the time was seven forty-three. She felt hungry, but pushed thoughts of food to the back of her mind as she examined the watch more closely.

There was a tiny inscription on the silver inside lid of the watch, and for a few moments she peered at the strange words. *Hold in your palm, set both hands to twelve. Move the small hand backward or forward if you desire the world at your feet. Your fate shall be set by the time of the watch. Close the lid and push the button.*

How peculiar, she thought as she set the watch back into the box. Lying back against the grass, her eyelids grew heavy as she waited for sleep. She thought of the old Gypsy woman from this afternoon. As her fingers absently fondled the yellow scarf around her neck, she reviewed the old woman's words. With a deep sigh of irritation, Angela sat up. If it wasn't one thing plaguing her this day, it was another, she decided. Looking down at the watch, she popped open the lid and again looked at the tiny hands as they slowly ticked the time.

Trying to take her mind from the old Gypsy woman, she read the instructions again. Slowly her fingers reached out and she did as the directions indicated. Holding the watch, she swept both hands to the twelve. So far the instructions had been simple, but now Angela was stumped: *Move the small hand backward or forward if you desire the world at your feet. Your fate shall be set by the time of the watch.* She wasn't sure what that meant, but slowly she moved the small hand back to the ten. Snapping the tarnished lid closed, she settled back down upon the cool grass. As she shut her eyes, she pushed the small button on top of the watch.

Three

Angela awakened to the feel of early morning sunlight caressing her face. Stretching her slender limbs, she felt damp and stiff from her night spent at the pond's edge. With a silent yawn, she pulled herself into a sitting position. With daybreak she knew that the occupants of Momma Leona's trailer would soon be stirring. Alex would be starting breakfast, and Mustafa and Mateo would be complaining as they poured their first cup of coffee.

Readjusting her clothing and again securing her breasts with the piece of material, Angela's blue gaze skimmed the surface of the pond. She noticed that the trailer that had been parked on the lot across from the pond was no longer there. It had been there last night, she reflected. The Gypsy family must have left quietly sometime during the night.

31

There was no schedule for the life of a Gypsy family, she thought, smiling inwardly. She relished that carefree lifestyle that was a part of their nature. When the mood struck, a Gypsy husband or father might order his family to move within a few hours. Without a word explained to neighbors, he might pack up belongings and family, then go to another city. The practices of her people held few restrictions. The law did try to bring changes in their nomadic way by forcing the children to attend school, but there was little attention paid to these demands—Gypsies lived as they saw fit. Like Momma Leona, Angela thought to herself. The Gypsy woman was constantly harassed by the authorities for not sending her large brood of children to school, but in her overbearing manner, she brushed aside such orders. She was a law unto herself. If things got too warm in one city, she would pack up her trailer and children and move on to the next.

Glancing around the camp area, a strange feeling came over Angela. The grass in the park appeared higher than yesterday. Picking up the yellow scarf the old Gypsy woman had given her, Angela tied it into a knot around the silver belt at her waist. She began to make her way back to Momma Leona's trailer, her step heavy because she dreaded facing Alex. Knowing what the girl must have experienced the night before, she felt the other girl's shame and embarrass-ment even before looking into her face. If only she had someplace that she could go; if only she had some other family besides Aunt Opal, perhaps then she would be able to ensure that her own fate would not be like Alex's.

Approaching the spot where Momma Leona's trailer had been parked for the past three months, Angela was brought up short. The motor caravan was no longer there, nor were the other trailers that had been parked nearby. She glanced quickly about the area. The park was stripped bare of any sign of the bright motor caravans. The tall grass around the area seemed to have grown several feet overnight. Even at the spot where Momma Leona's trailer had stood, the grass was not crushed or tram-pled where the children's feet had made paths over the past few months.

Standing in the empty field, Angela shook her head in confusion as she tried to make some sense of the disappearance of Momma Leona and the children. Of course, she reasoned, Momma Leona must have received word during the night that the authorities were coming to the park to harass her. Perhaps Mustafa had gotten into a knife fight with one of the locals in a pub. This had happened before in another town, and Momma Leona had had to leave the camp in a hurry. Perhaps this time she had only had enough time to gather belongings and children before being forced to flee during the quiet of the night. Other Gypsy families might have thought that they would encounter the backlash of abuse by the officers if they stayed behind, so they had also vanished before the light of morning. Looking around, still in a daze, Angela knew that Momma Leona must have had all the children working to make the park look as though no one had ever camped here before.

Brushing at a damp grass stain on her skirt, Angela knew that there was little that she could do except walk into the city to try and find one of the children on the streets. Her troubled gaze swept the area once again. Everything seemed strangely out of place. She wondered why Momma Leona had not sent one of the children down to the pond to find her before they left the park. The older woman knew that Angela often went to the pond to find solitude. Momma Leona must not believe her very valuable after all! Surely if she had thought of her as having any worth, she would have sent one of the children looking for her!

Cutting across the field that led to the main road, Angela could not find the road that led in and out of the park. She hoped that she would be able to find Penny or Carlos and learn if Momma Leona had stayed in or around London. Another thought followed; why should she not just avoid Momma Leona and the children? Could she not fend for herself? What was worse, being on her own or ending up like Alex? But as her stomach rumbled with hunger, Angela knew the answer. She had no money, no means to purchase a loaf of bread or pay for a place to rest her head for a night. She had to find Momma Leona, then she would start holding back a small portion of the daily cache that she turned over to her protector.

Forced to climb a low stone wall to gain the road, Angela was mystified as she gazed around. Nothing appeared as it had only the day before. She remembered no stone fence having been around the park. The road she now stood on was not paved but deeply rutted and dirt. She pinched herself sharply on the arm to make sure that she was not caught up in some wild dream, but she found no release for the moment's insanity. As she started out on the long trek that would take her into London, the signs, houses, and other landmarks that she had viewed daily had strangely vanished. The dusty road stretched through a portion of the countryside that Angela no longer recognized.

She passed several yards from the road, a small cottage that she had never noticed. The ugly glare she received from the large-bosomed woman frantically sweeping her front stoop forced Angela to keep to the other side of the road and not linger with any questions. The woman, she noticed, was strangely dressed in a long skirt, and a linen cap covered her head.

As Angela drew closer to the city, a large wagon passed her, pulled by four horses. The flat-bedded vehicle was stacked three crates high with geese and turkeys. She stood along the roadside, mesmerized. Another wagon passed a moment later, pulled by two large dray horses, piled high with bags of fruits and vegetables. Staring, she noticed two young boys in the back.

The scene seemed from another world, and as she stood to the side of the road gaping with amazement, one of the boys threw a potato at her. The children burst out in laughter, and even the driver, the children's father, smiled at his elder son's antics.

"She be no more than a stinking, dirty Gypsy!" she heard the boy who had thrown the potato at her pipe loudly. The smaller boy eagerly nodded in agreement.

What terrible manners! The vicious little *gorgio* brats, Angela railed to herself as she deflected the potato with a quick arm reflex. The farmer should tan the both of them! Reminded of the older man's smile, she knew that no such action would be forthcoming. The father was as ill-mannered as his children! Even though her anger had been pricked, Angela could not take her eyes from the wagon and its occupants until it slowly disappeared down the long, winding road. She could not remember encountering such sights before. Farmers usually took produce and animals into the city in trucks. Such a sight was unusual, but it was in keeping with all that had happened to her this morning.

Increasing her pace, she knew that she had to find Momma Leona or one of the children as quickly as possible. Nothing appeared as it should be. Soon another wagon, and then another, passed her. A carriage led by a handsome team of jet-black horses with a gold crest boldly displayed on the vehicle door raced past, sending Angela's skirts whipping about her thighs. The dust of the road rose up and threatened to choke her. "What on earth is going on?" she mumbled to herself. Was there some kind of event taking place in the city that she had not heard about? Were all of these people reenacting some historical era which used a primitive means of transportation? Why had Mustafa and Mateo not informed Momma Leona and the children of such an event? Any happening in the city that drew the attention of tourists or the rich was always ferreted out by the two men, then reported back to Momma Leona, who in turn ordered the children to cover the event area to ply their begging and thievery.

The city of London that Angela had known was no longer the one that she now viewed. The streets were cobbled or made of dirt, and very little attention was given for maintenance. On the outskirts of the city, she passed a tavern that she did not recognize, whose overhead, swinging sign stated, "Boar's Head Tavern." Outside of the large, wooden structure, there were two horses tied to a hitching rail, and toward the back of the yard was a large stable where Angela could see several boys scurrying around as they tended to their chores.

Angela's steps slowed as the morning wore on. She forced herself to travel down the Cambridge Heath Road toward Whitechapel. Her large, almost indigo eyes stared at the horses and carriages passing close by. The women were strangely dressed in long gowns. Some wore hats with flowers or feathers, others wore powdered wigs. The men were wearing outdated suits and jackets, with stockings encasing their legs, and many also wore wigs on their heads.

By early afternoon, when she had made her way to Fleet Street, Angela was truly mystified. It was completely inconceivable, and she repeatedly told herself that it was impossible, but she had to face the fact that somehow she had stepped back into time! She was no longer in the year 1994! There were no automobiles or buses. No busy men and women, in well-cut suits going about their daily business, no tourists, nothing that she recognized from her daily life, the life she had been living only yesterday! Trash lay in the street gutters, the houses and buildings in the area were run-down, and as she drew farther into the city, she passed two women who appeared to be prostituting themselves in public. One of the women wore a long, tattered, dirty gown with one sleeve hanging low over her shoulder, exposing the upper portion of her breast. The coarse vulgarity that left her mouth as a gentleman passed by left no doubt as to exactly what she would do for the required amount of coin.

Angela could see none of her people on the London streets, and as the minutes passed into long hours, she felt truly alone for the first time in her life. She wondered if perhaps somehow she was lost in a terrible nightmare from which she could not awaken. As her stomach began its rumbling protest, though, she knew that somehow all of this around her was real. She was *not* caught inside a nightmare! Nothing was the same, and for a few minutes, she truly wondered if she had gone insane. She remembered Aunt Opal saying that her sister, Angela's Aunt Sheila, had gone insane and that she had been put away in an institution because she had lost all grip upon reality. Could this be what was happening to her, Angela wondered, as her eyes swept the London streets. She then saw a small bent man pushing an ancient cart, calling at the top of his voice, "Rag man, rag man! Bring out your rags, good mothers, bring out your rags!" Rags? Angela wondered. What was her tortured mind concocting now?

A few minutes later when an adolescent girl passed her with a basket over her arm filled with fresh-baked loaves of dark bread, Angela told herself that she would worry about the stability of her mind at another time. It was much more important to get something to eat than to worry if she had inherited some dark defect from Aunt

Sheila. She couldn't continue on if she did not soon find something to fill her belly.

She silently approached the young bread girl. As Angela watched, the girl tucked a shiny coin into her skirt waist as a buxom woman with a small child purchased one of the loaves. Angela had been taught by Momma Leona how to beg for what she desired if there was no other way to get it, and that was what she set out to do now. "Please, girl, I have had nothing to eat in the past two days." She feigned weakness as the girl looked upon her. "Please may I have just a pinch of your delicious bread?"

The young bread girl looked with a cautious eye at the strange young woman who had approached her. "Me mum would skin me to an inch of death if'n I return without all the proper coins for her bread!" The girl quickly shook her head, her brown eyes suspicious of Angela's every movement. She clutched her basket tighter against her underdeveloped chest and observed the long dark curls braided down Angela's shoulders and the silver coins and gold hoop earrings which dangled in her ears. The dark skirt and blouse and the glitter of silver bracelets and a silver belt identified the girl as a Gypsy. Her skin was lighter than the Gypsies that the bread girl had seen in the past, but she knew her for what she was. Each year at

New Fair and also Derby Day, the Gypsies roamed about the grounds selling horses and their wares. It was widely known that they were swindlers and got their way with silvered tongues and sly manners. The bread girl, when going to such events as Derby Day, always had her mother at her side to watch out for her and had never been duped by the likes of this young woman. As she noticed the glitter in the blue eyes, she sensed that there was a wildness about this Gypsy girl that could easily prove very dangerous to her.

"Just one small bite, please. I have no coins. I truly fear that I am going to starve to death if you do not take pity upon me."

The bread girl was surprised by the Gypsy girl's manners and speech. The Gypsies she had heard had been barely understandable with their Romany language mixed with English. But even though she had found something to admire in the disheveled girl, she still could not give away her mother's bread, not even a tiny pinch! "I fear that I can't be giving away any of me mum's bread, girl." She vigorously shook her curls as she thought of the dire punishment she would receive at her mother's hand if she dared such an act.

As she felt the hollowness of her belly, Angela did not intend to be denied. The aroma from the breadbasket filled her nostrils, and she turned away as though she was giving up. A pair of women approached the bread girl, taking her attention from Angela. In that moment, Angela spun around, reached out, and snatched a loaf of the dark crusty bread. Racing down Fleet Street and around the corner, her ears were filled with the bread girl's angry cries. Angela ran down an alleyway, then up another long street until she could no longer hear the girl's outraged shouts.

A few breathless moments passed before Angela was able to slow down her pace. At last she slumped against the side of a building and began to bite off delicious chunks of the bread. She took precious minutes to rest and fill her belly, her blue gaze peering up and down the street for the bread girl or the authorities.

Now, with her stomach full, she tried to come to terms with her new situation. She was all alone, and London was no longer a city that she knew. There was no Momma Leona, nor the children for her to depend on. A tear slipped from her eye as she realized how much she had relied on all of them. They had given her a sense of belonging. Even though her life had been hard, at least she had had someone. She brushed away the tears with the back of her wrist.

She had been taught never to allow her inner feelings to show, and this moment was no different. She must go on until she could find her way back to her own time and life. She knew that she could make it. She had no other choice! She was strong and would survive, but knew that she would accomplish this only if she remained wary. She had been taught how to survive, and if she were here at this very moment, Momma Leona would be shaking her by the shoulders and shouting at her in her abrasive voice to be watching for her next mark! She should keep her guard up and take advantage of any opportunity that presented itself. The bread girl had been easy to dupe, but in this century or any other it took more than bread to survive. She could almost feel Momma Leona's eyes upon her, telling her that she needed to hear the jangle of money in her pockets to afford a place to lay her head and to have a bite of something to eat tomorrow!

Digging deeply into her soul, Angela's strong will forced her to pull herself upright against the side of the building. If indeed she were in the depths of a terrible nightmare, she would awake soon; if not, and everything around her proved to be real, she would have no choice but to survive as best she could! Finishing the loaf of bread, she felt a little bit stronger. The first thing she had to do was find some of her own people. She remembered stories about the treatment of Gypsies in early London and knew it was dangerous for her to be on her own in the city. Older Gypsies had told many tales about their ancestors as they had sat late at night around the bright campfire in front of Momma Leona's trailer. There had been stories about townships that had turned upon a single Gypsy man with the accusation that he had stolen a pig, horse, or even a child. The terrible things that the townspeople had done to the unfortunate Gypsy had been horrible for her young ears to hear. The fact that no one had taken the Gypsy's side now brought about a different kind of terror to Angela's wildly beating heart.

She must be on her guard in this strange time. Now she looked upon the streets and at those passing her by with a wary eye. She cringed when the *gorgios'* stares held upon her as though she were a strange thing to them. It might be for the best if she were to hide away somewhere safe until the cover of darkness could lend secrecy to her identity. She would head toward Piccadilly. Once there, she would find herself a spot to spend a few hours until she could find a rich mark. She would pocket some coins and leave London until she could understand better the situation that she was in. She could not afford to be caught stealing or begging in London, but once outside the city, she would find her own people. A Gypsy was a Gypsy in 1994 or 1745, which was the year, as she had asked an old woman earlier in the day. Her people would accept her and protect her, for she was one of the Rom.

Her only thoughts were of survival. Surviving in a city where only the day before she had felt safe and at ease roaming the streets. Finding an empty alley stacked with crates and boxes, Angela settled down between two empty crates and tried to sleep. She needed all the rest that she could get if she were to keep her wits and make it through this ordeal. As sleep began to dull her mind, her last thoughts were that when she would awaken, she would once again be with Momma Leona and the children. She smiled peacefully as she thought of telling Penny about the wild dream that she had had of being in a different century.

Four

Awakening, Angela was, at first, unaware of her surroundings. Feeling the light scurrying of a furry creature running across her ankles, she scrambled into a hasty, upright position as her enlarged eyes saw a large rat running away. The alley was quite dark, and finding herself still within the security of the crates, the shadows cast by the stacked boxes and crates loomed over her and caused her heartbeat to accelerate at an alarming rate.

As she came fully awake, she realized that she was still held within the clutches of the bad dream that had plagued her throughout the long day! She silently rose to her feet and brushed off her skirt. Returning to the streets, her wary eyes assessed her surroundings while taking in the lateness of the hour. She had slept a couple of hours longer than she had intended. The late afternoon hours had vanished, and the darkness of night had settled over the London streets. With an inward groan, she silently cursed herself for sleeping so long. She had depended upon early evening to pick the pocket of some unsuspecting lady or gentleman traveling on the streets. Now she would have to pick her victim with a cautious eye, for at this hour, there were few people on the streets, and she would be easily noticed.

Those people who were roaming about the streets at this time of the evening appeared to have much in common with Angela. There were few children about, mostly men and women of questionable character and dress. She passed a small group of gaudily dressed women. Their high-pitched laughter filled Angela's ears as she hurriedly made her way to the other side of the cobbled street. She passed by two pubs which seemed, by the sounds within, to be thriving with business this night. She tried to stay in the shadows. hoping to avoid notice. As Angela passed the second pub, a large, burly man rounded the upcoming corner and started walking down the cobblestone street in her direction. As he neared, Angela felt her heart beginning to beat a rapid tattoo. Her steps slowed considerably.

As he drew closer, she noticed that he wore the baggy dress of a mariner. A dark knitted cap was pulled low upon his fore-head. Glancing fearfully about, Angela could see no way of avoiding the man except to run. If he recognized her as a Gypsy girl and shouted for those in the pub to help him give chase, what then? The thought filled her mind with dread. Her breath clutched in her lungs as he came within a few yards.

"Hey, there ye be a sweet lass. What fur ye be doing over there in the dark shadows? Step on out now and give me a look." The sailor was more than a little surprised by a woman alone at this time of the night and in this section of the city. Assuming her to be one of the doxies that roamed about the London streets at all hours of the night, he called out again, "Come on over here, sweety, and bring old Albert a big kiss." He tottered closer toward her, his eyes squinting as he tried to make out something more of her features. He was not usually a picky man when it came to women, but the last time he had agreed to follow a doxie back to her shanty off Fleet Street, she had looked pretty good to his drunken gaze with the shadows of evening looming about, but when they had gained her room and she had lit a candle, he had viewed the ugly sight of a pock-ravished complexion. As much as he had tried, he had not been able to get his little willy up, even with all of her patient coaxing!

Not daring to even draw a breath of air into her lungs, Angela's steps stilled as the large man drew closer and his voice filled her ears. She feared that a scream of pure terror would escape her throat as she felt a hand reach out to ensnare her arm, but with the supple maneuver of a child of the street, Angela ducked beneath the large, hairy arm, and with a swift kick aimed at his baggy backside, her small figure toppled the drunken seaman onto the cobbled street.

With a loud grunt of surprise, the sailor found himself sitting flat on his bottom. As he turned his head, intending to call out that he only wanted to get a look at her, he saw only the fleeting image of a dark skirt rounding the corner on the wooden side-walk.

Overwhelming glee bubbling up within her depths, Angela ran down the street and around the corner. It had been a pleasure to topple the large man on his backside. The surprise upon his features when he lost his footing had in some strange fashion set her spirits spiraling skyward. It was too bad that Carlos was not at her side. The young Gypsy boy would have doubled over with laughter if he had been there to see Angela outmaneuvering such a large brute!

She continued to run a few minutes longer for safety's sake. As she slowed her pace, she knew she needed to be quick about picking out a rich mark, then get out of the city! She was asking for trouble if she lingered any longer than necessary. The sailor had been only the first of the many plagues that could easily beset her in this wild and untamed atmosphere.

Heading for that part of the city where in the past she had always had good luck in scoring a mark, she prayed that she would not find the whole of London as she had found the area around Fleet Street. She needed only a small bankroll to see her through until she could find some of her own people. Now with a more determined step, she made her way through the streets with a cautious study of the area.

The part of the city around Piccadilly appeared cleaner, but the number of pedestrians were fewer. Angela roamed the streets, and the best she could find was a gentleman's club with a bow-shaped front window. After passing the club twice, she decided to stay within the shadows to watch and await her victim. She tried to form a plan as she stood near the building, but far enough away from the glow of the street lamp to remain hidden.

The night air was a bit chilly, and several

times Angela rubbed her hands up and down her forearms to seek warmth, but she knew that much of her body temperature was due to nervousness. A short time after she had settled herself in to wait, the front double doors swung wide. Two gentlemen, both appearing in high humor, stepped out onto the wooden sidewalk, their talk loudly boisterous as they started toward their fancy carriages. Manservants hurried forward to give them each a hand. Angela considered the pair as unlikely victims, reasoning that it would be to her best advantage to try to approach a single gentleman. She would have a much better chance at fleeing if she were caught.

Finally a single man emerged through the front doors. He appeared to be a well-set-up young man, wearing a richly tailored suit of clothing. As he stumbled to the sidewalk and called loudly for his horse, Angela scornfully assumed he had spent hours consuming strong drink. This young man deserved exactly what he was going to get or, in truth, what he was going to lose! Calling aloud for his horse, indeed, as though the creature could hear him and come running up for him to mount! The rich always thought that life revolved around them. Today or two hundred years from now, they would still act in this same arrogant, imperious manner! She did not consider that she was judging him rather out of hand, that her hard life had shaped her beliefs. Because he was wealthy, she felt he must also be a "snob."

Angela silently approached the young man. As she left the darkened shadows, she was in the process of stepping to his side when he spied her. He almost fell full against her as he weaved about drunkenly.

"Pardon me, dear lady." The young man tried to right himself by holding on to her forearm with a firm grip. As he looked into the most incredibly large blue eyes that he had ever seen, he leaned even more upon her.

"Whatever are you doing out here on the streets all alone, at this ungodly hour?" he questioned as Angela slid her hand into his jacket pocket, withdrew his purse, and then proceeded to stash it into her skirt pocket. But, as though ill luck were her namesake, he shot out a hand and grabbed her slender wrist.

"Now what have we here, my fine beauty?" he sneered down at her, sobering up quickly. The young man's cold dark gaze held her penetratingly. In that moment, Angela knew true fear. She glimpsed the cruelty that was barely hidden beneath the surface of his scathing gaze. Belatedly she wished that she had waited for another mark.

"Why . . . I . . . I . . . am hungry!" Angela sputtered. With the confession she hoped that she would win his sympathy. She saw no warmth, though, filling the black eyes staring down at her, and without a second thought, she swiftly kicked him on the shin, hoping that he would release her and she would be able to get away with the purse that she had not released.

With a loud yell and a curse of outraged pain, the man's grip tightened upon her wrist with a viselike strength. Biting in its harshness, his voice declared, "Why, you're no more than a piece of Gypsy trash!" As his glaring gaze traveled over the dirty little urchin that had tried to relieve him of his purse, contempt was written upon his features.

Angela's chin rose at this insult upon her heritage. "Just release my hand, sir. I was hungry; that is the only reason that I tried to take your purse. I am sorry, so just let me go!" She tried to pull away, but found that her efforts to secure freedom were useless. The man's grip was unyielding, and there was not an ounce of understanding in his heartless stare.

Glancing from the young woman in his grip to the front double doors of the club and then down the street, the gentleman was not sure what he should do with this wild Gypsy girl, now that he had captured her.

At that moment, another gentleman stepped through the front doors of the club. "What on earth have you there, Damian?" A tall, wide-shouldered gentleman with his dark hair brushed back and held in a queue stepped closer, lazily pulling on a soft leather glove. "Are you attacking dirty little gutter-snipes now? Has London grown so boring to you that you have resorted to such actions?" Deep rich laughter followed this remark, and the sound falling upon Angela's ears intensified her fear.

"Why, Royce old boy, as a matter of fact I am not quite sure," came the reply from the one holding Angela's wrist.

As the gentleman was answering, Angela once again tried to earn her freedom. With a frantic jerk she tried to pull free; this maneuver not working, she pushed at the man's chest, thinking with any luck at all she might knock him off his feet and off his guard for a few seconds. As she gazed at the newcomer, she was even more frightened of the situation. She had to get away from these men quickly! She could not make out the other gentleman's features clearly, for the light from the front of the club and the street lamp were at his back and held his face in darkness, but his broad, tall frame bespoke of strength. Angela was more terrified of him than the man that was holding tightly to her wrist. "Let go of me!" she screamed.

"She was trying to steal my purse, Royce." The man holding Angela looked at his friend as though he could not believe that anyone would set upon him to try to pick him clean. "She claims hunger, can you believe that?" he added with an afterthought as he clutched tighter to her arm. He was not about to release her no matter how much she pulled and jerked for her freedom.

Slowly the dark-haired gentleman called Royce took another step closer. As though bored by the scene being played out before him, he said, "You have two options as I see it, Damian. Release the wench with a coin to purchase her dinner, or call the authorities and let them tend to the affair. I do warn you, though, it shall be you that the authorities will question and you that shall have to tend to any paperwork that they might request."

"As always, Royce, your logic is simple and to the point!" Though Damian considered the other man's advice, he was still loath to release the little baggage that had dared to affront his pride by attempting to pick his pocket.

The tall man appeared to be towering above Angela and the man called Damian. As he moved slightly to the side of the streetlight, Angela's eyes widened as she glimpsed his handsome visage.

Lord Dunsely not only saw the Gypsy girl's reaction to his friend's good looks, but he also felt her stiffening as Royce neared. "Damn, Royce, I can't believe this! Even this little, dirty Gypsy girl is not lost to that virile charm of yours!"

"Let the wench go, Damian." Royce had glimpsed the fear in the violet-blue eyes turn to surprise. As he looked down at her and his friend, he felt himself growing uncomfortable. Her look was not flattering as Damian was implying; after all, she was no more than a Gypsy brat who looked rather pitiful, with her dirty face and ragged clothing.

"Not so fast, Royce." Damian was not a man to let any slight to his person go unchallenged. This girl had not only affronted his pride, but also his purse!

"I will go behind the club and get our horses, Damian. Turn the girl loose. I will see you to your town house to insure that no other Gypsies set upon you," Royce chuckled as he began to turn away from the couple, believing the entire affair finished.

Damian was still loath to release the girl without some form of punishment. Frantically he searched for a solution besides calling the authorities. As Royce had pointed out, it would take tedious time to answer questions and fill out any reports that the authorities might require. Hearing his friend's mirth, suddenly an idea struck. His lips drew back into a wide grin as he called the other man's attention back to himself and the girl. "Royce, remember earlier in the club when Lord Bentley spilled his glass of port in the center of our table and you called out a bet on which side of the table the liquid might flow?"

"Aye, I remember the moment well, Damian." Another chuckle escaped the large man's throat and a wide smile slanted his sensual lips. He had won twenty pounds from Damian on that bet. "But what, pray tell, does that bet have to do with this moment or with the girl? I grow tired of standing on the sidewalk making small talk. Make it quick, man. What have you got on your mind?"

"Do you remember also how boring we both agreed that London town had become now that the season has passed?"

Once again, Royce St. James nodded.

"Well, I say, old man, why do we not liven things up somewhat with the events that have taken place here this evening?" Damian seemed to warm up to his plan as he looked from the girl and then back to his friend.

"Get on with it, Damian. I grow even more bored with your play of words." Royce absently brushed off a speck of lint from the waist jacket of his charcoal-colored suit.

"I propose to you a small wager, dear friend."

"Fine, Damian. Let us be on our way and we shall talk about whatever wager you care to make." At the moment Royce wanted only to be in bed. It had been a long evening of gaming and drinking with his friends, and to compound matters, his latest mistress, Belinda, had exhausted him earlier when she had pouted and wept in a womanly fashion that he was lacking attentiveness toward her. He would purchase a piece of expensive jewelry on the morrow to cure her feminine wailing, but at the moment sleep was the most important thing on Royce's mind, and Damian was not making things easy for him.

"You know my horse, Raven Boy, Royce?" Damian questioned. With the slight nodding of Royce's dark head, he continued, "How many times over the past year have you tried to purchase the stallion from me? And how often have I refused your offers?"

"Get on with it, Damian." The strong voice now held a touch of interest as his friend spoke about the stallion. It was true:

Royce had coveted Raven Boy for some time and had not been able to name the right price to whet his friend's appetite enough to sell the beast.

"This girl, Royce. She is the price for Raven Boy!" Damian's ebony eyes sparkled with amusement and cunning as Royce stared upon him without comprehension.

"Make sense, man. What has this Gypsy girl to do with anything between us?"

"I propose that the Duke of Westfield cannot take this stinking little Gypsy wench and made a presentable young lady out of her within an allotted time. Let me see." Damian appeared to reflect for a few seconds. "Shall we make it one year from today? If you can carry out the deed in the allotted time, Raven Boy will be yours!" He knew that the bait would be far too tempting for his friend to resist. Damian had to force himself not to burst out with laughter. He could imagine the effort and trials that Royce would go through over the course of the year. In the end, he would lose the wager. Looking at the dirty ragamuffin under his hand, he knew the feat would be impossible!

Angela gasped aloud as a deep breath was expelled from Royce St. James's wide chest. Not able to shout her outrage at such a proposal, she stood silently as the two men discussed her as though she were no more than a worthless piece of chattel.

"You say one year from this day?" One dark fine brow rose above a cool gray eye. For a few seconds, Royce St. James's gaze roamed over Angela. It was plain that he did not appreciate the sight as a frown tilted his lips.

"Exactly, my friend," Dunsely exclaimed. "One year! In that amount of time, we shall see if it is true what all of London says about the Duke of Westfield. If he can, in truth, tame any woman in the whole of the city with calculated charm and impeccable manners."

Dunsely could not help but laugh aloud at his friend's apparent discomfort. For the first time, he held Royce St. James at a disadvantage. He knew it would be practically impossible for Royce to turn down the bet.

Royce silently appraised the girl. Her features were deathly pale and her dark eyes held a hollow, frightened gaze that was not flattering to his masculinity. She looked for all the world as though she were a frightened rabbit who had been caught in a snare. "Done!" Royce slapped his thigh with the glove that he had not pulled onto his hand. He did not know why he had accepted Damian's bet, he only knew that it was hard for him to turn away from a challenge. "All that I will guarantee, Damian, is that at the year's ending you will be presented with a well-behaved young lady. No more than that can be wagered." He could not be expected to charm this Gypsy girl who was staring as though he had two heads. He would make certain that she could present herself well enough to satisfy, then he would be done with her and the bet!

Damian laughed as he remembered the feisty girl's sharp kick upon his shin. A few gypsies came every few years and camped on his father's property near Landcourt Hall. They were a wild lot, carefree and cunning in their ways, and not given to refined manners. His friend would have his hands full with this girl. He could have been given two years for all the good it would like do him! There would be no changing this girl under any gentleman's hand! "If a lady I am greeted with, then the stallion you will receive." Pulling Angela by the wrist, he gave her over to his friend's keeping. "I will go and get our horses, Royce. You had best hold to her tightly."

At long last he would best the Duke of Westfield. With a jaunty step he left the sidewalk. He was going to be looking forward to this year's ending!

Five

As Angela felt the firm grip of Royce St. James's large hand encircling her upper arm, she regained her senses. "Release me this moment!" She tried to jerk out of his grip. Who did these two louts think they were? Were they insane? How dare they hold her up as a part of their wager for something as stupid as a horse! She wouldn't allow it!

"Keep quiet, and keep still!" The tone directed at her was chilling, and the pressure on her arm increased, tightening around her forearm like a biting band of steel. The pain forced her to comply with his orders.

There was something ruthless about this man. Chills of apprehension danced up and down Angela's spine. His forceful, dominating tone allowed her no leeway for escape. She was overpowered and could not disobey him. She knew that she would have to use all of her cunning and strength to outwit this sinister man!

Damian brought the two horses around to the front of the club, and he was grinning widely as he handed over Royce's reins.

With ease Royce lifted Angela and set her atop the large black stallion that she assumed belonged to him. At that exact moment when he moved to pull himself up and behind her, Angela kicked out at the beast's sides, shouting for the animal to move, praying that she could throw off the brute of a man and win herself a few minutes' time to make good her escape.

All that she won was Lord Dunsely's raucous laughter and a fierce scolding from Royce St. James as he held tightly to the horse's bridle. Gracefully he jumped up behind her. "Do something like that again, and I will wear out your backside before I deliver you to the front gates of Newgate!" he said, seething.

The muscles in St. James's jaw throbbed as he endured his friend's laughter. He was beginning to regret accepting this insane bet! Royce could see that he was going to have a hard time gaining cooperation from this Gypsy brat. Drawing a deep breath, then exhaling sharply, he knew that it was too late for him to back out of the bet. He had given his word, and that was everything to him. He would do his damndest to win! When he got the grimy little street urchin home, he would be able to talk her into making life easier on both of them during the course of the next year. With a bit of persuasion, women usually did as he requested. This girl would be no different than any other. He would promise her a few pretty trinkets for her time, and at the end of the year, he would be the proud owner of one of the fastest horses in London, perhaps in the whole of Europe!

Nearing the outskirts of town, Damian bid his friend goodbye as he turned his horse toward the right fork in the road. Royce continued on the main road leading out of the city. It was a dark night, and the time passed in silence as the two on horseback held to their own thoughts. Royce was irritated. Plans to go to his town house and enjoy the comfort that was waiting there for him—a warm goblet of brandy and a comfortable bed—had been dashed. Instead he would have to ride out to Westfield Hall, and he pondered over what awaited him. He had not been to the Hall for a few weeks. There would be a pile of correspondence to answer, and he had put off working on the estate's ledgers far too long. Paramount, though, in his thoughts was the prospect of bending this wild Gypsy girl to his will.

Angela was busily making plans to escape this large beast of a man. His threats of taking her to Newgate prison had made her cautious: she should bide her time and flee him at the right moment, when recapture would be impossible! She would not be sent to prison, especially the infamous Newgate! If she escaped and found her own people, perhaps she would be able to understand how she had been thrown back into time and into this crazy situation. Somehow she had to return to the twentieth century and to Momma Leona and the children!

It had taken Angela forever to walk into London, but now, upon horseback, it seemed only a short time before the dark shadows of the park where Momma Leona and the children had camped was passed. Angela strained her eyes in the direction of the park: there were no glowing fires with embers of red and gold sparkling upward into the velvet night sky, nor were there any old men and women sitting around campfires telling stories of ancient days. The fields around the park were empty.

They rode for some time before Royce turned his mount off the main road and directed him down a long tree-lined lane. The horse's steps quickened as though he sensed that he was nearing a warm stable and food. From a distance Angela glimpsed a glimmer of light spilling from an upper story window. Swallowing nervously, she tried to calm her racing heart. She would escape the moment she was left alone, she tried to reassure herself. Or perhaps this madman would realize that he could not hold her against her will, and coming to his senses, he would release her. After all, he was committing a crime and could be punished harshly for kidnapping someone! Maybe the strong drink that she smelled upon his breath had made him agree to such a foolish bet, but he would soon realize the folly of his actions, and then she would be free to go on her way. She tried to concentrate upon this thought, but she felt smothered by the large man's presence. One of his hands gripped her waist as the other hand held the reins. His chest pressed tightly into her back, and Angela could feel the strong thumping of his heartbeat. With each movement her own heartbeat drummed out, *escape, escape, escape!*

The lane turned into a gravel drive which took them to the front of the sprawling mansion. As Royce St. James halted his mount, Angela stared, her mouth open in wonder. She could see that the house rose upward, seemingly to the very height of the

67

sky. There were lights in two of the second-story rooms and illumination coming from the third or possibly the fourth floor. After handing her down from the back of the stallion, Angela stood rooted to the spot as her gaze roamed over the expansive width of the manor house.

Before Royce had the chance to take Angela by the elbow and lead her up the front steps, a small middle-aged man with a scruffy cap pulled low upon his brow appeared. Without a word, he reached for the horse's reins. The little man's eyes lingered on the duke's guest for a second, but he turned back to his own business.

"Make sure that Satan is well-bedded with fresh hay after he eats his oats, Harry, Royce commanded in his husky, demanding tone. Angela saw that Harry seemed not to mind in the least; in fact, he bobbed his head, and with a smile for his employer, he turned to carry out the orders.

Still amazed by the strangeness of everything around her, Angela's arm was gripped again. In a brisk businesslike manner, the broad-framed man started up the steps which led to the front door of the manse. Before he could touch the gold-edged knob that rested beneath the impressive gold lion-headed knocker, the door was thrown wide, and a splendidly dressed butler stood to the side to allow the duke and Angela to enter the enormous, pale blue, marble and gold-trimmed foyer.

Pulling off his hat and leather riding gloves, Royce handed them into the keeping of the servant standing rigidly at attendance.

"Hawkins, bring some brandy to my study please," Royce ordered. The Duke of Westfield then grabbed Angela's arm and began to pull her down a long hallway which stretched through the main portion of the downstairs.

Nothing in Angela's life had ever prepared her for the incredible sights that now met her gaze. Wealth was abundant: glittering gold, crystal, antique tapestries, precious figurines, and statues of marble and bronze. Angela desired to wander through the long hallway and adjoining rooms of this fabulous mansion; it was a Gypsy's dream come true! Quickly she learned that this was not going to be the way of things for her this evening. Holding firmly to her wrist, Royce pulled her through the great room, and then down the imposing hallway that opened into a handsomely decorated study.

Silently shutting the intricately carved oak door, Royce released his grip upon her. In an irritated manner, he turned toward the hearth, and taking up a long, thin taper, he lit a candelabrum resting on the mahogany desk which sat in the middle of the chamber.

Angela's wide eyes rested upon the man who had circled the desk and was now sitting in the wine red leather chair behind it. He was more handsome than he had seemed earlier in the evening, she thought as her cobalt eyes studied his body. His eyes were the crystal cool color of silver-gray. His jaw was squarely cut, the nose almost aquiline, which lent him a devilishly intriguing look to an otherwise brooding visage. Angela's gaze lowered to the spot where his collar was unbuttoned, and traces of crisp dark hair could be glimpsed above the snow-white lawn shirt. As her gaze lowered farther, his voice drew her violet-blue regard back to his sensual lips.

"Sit over there on that stool near the hearth and allow me a few minutes. Then I will tell you how we will handle this situation for the coming year." He briskly ordered her about as though used to treating those around him in an authoritative fashion, then expecting them to do exactly as he instructed.

Angela eyed the red-leather stool which matched the rest of the furniture in the study with some distaste. She had understood his meaning, but as her temper began to flare, she straightened her backbone a bit more. Who on earth did this brute think he was, God almighty? He plainly did not think her worthy to be sitting on his expensive furniture, and clearly he believed that she would obediently respond to his every command! *Sit on that footstool indeed!* She had never easily complied to orders, and she certainly would not start now! She held no idea of how or why she had been brought to this century, but neither this man, nor any other, would treat her in such an arrogant manner, then witness her easy compliance! She would rather die first!

Impatiently, Royce's gaze rose from his desk as he saw that the Gypsy brat was still standing in the center of the room. Before he could instruct her on who the master of this house was, there was a hesitant knock on the door, and Hawkins brought in the requested brandy on a small silver tray. A pair of matching crystal goblets accompanied the decanter.

"Your brandy, your Grace." The servant remained rigidly straight as he set the tray down at Royce's elbow. "Will there be anything else, your Grace?" For a moment the butler's eyes went to the filthy girl, and with the realization that the girl was a wild Gypsy, his gaze quickly shifted back to his master, his features blank.

"Not now, Hawkins. I will call when I

need you further." Royce St. James glanced through the stack of correspondence on his desk and did not bother to look up at the butler again.

"Very well, your Grace." Hawkins turned stiffly and left the study. Most of the Hall had retired for the evening, believing that the master would be staying on in the city. With the Duke's appearance, Hawkins had awakened some of the staff and had set them about seeing to the master's comfort. He hurried away from the study to make sure that a fire had been built in the master's chamber and that water was being heated for a bath.

Quiet hung in the study for several minutes after the servant's leaving. Royce looked up from his desk and found that the girl was still standing in the center of the chamber. With some exasperation, he let out a soft sigh as his gray eyes held upon her face. His hasty agreement to Damian's bet might prove more tiring than he had expected after that incident with his horse. "I told you to sit upon that stool until I have the time to deal with you," he abruptly stated and watched the girl flinch at the chill in his tone. "We will start out on the right foot, girl. You will do as you're told. When the year is up, I will give you a handsome purse to take back to your family."

This would be how he would approach this situation, he told himself. He would pay for her services for the next year. What Gypsy was not willing to gain a fat purse? And what simpler job than to pretend for a year's time that she was a proper lady?

Angela's small chin jutted out as her frame straightened even more. "I don't know who the blazes you think you are!" she snapped as violet-blue eyes turned brilliant with lights of leaping flame sparkling in their depths. "But I do assure you that you cannot keep me here in this monstrous house against my will, nor can you inflict your domineering manners upon me any further!"

Royce St. James, the Duke of Westfield, had found in his twenty-seven years that he had seen just about everything that life had to offer, and rarely was he taken by surprise, but as the Gypsy brat railed at him, he leaned back in his chair, his gray eyes enlarging as he studied her with more interest. He hardly believed his own ears; this girl, standing in the center of his study, spoke better English than most of the ladies at court, and certainly better than his servants here at Westfield Hall, perhaps with the exception of Hawkins.

Critically his gaze swept over her once again, this time more slowly. He took in her Gypsy garb: the glittering, small coins braided in her long, thick, dark hair; the dusty worn skirt that reached to her ankles; and the shirt that was rolled carelessly up to her elbows. With the light from the candelabrum, he saw that her eyes were not Gypsy black, but a deep blue. Her skin, what was visible through the dirt and grime, was not swarthy, but was instead creamy ivory. "Who are you?" he finally blurted out after his close perusal. "Who are your parents, girl? What are their names?" Perhaps this girl was not a Gypsy at all, but an imposter. Perhaps she had run away from her family and her family might even hold some means. This could be the reason for her ease in conquering the English tongue so well.

"My parents were killed years ago, if it's any of your business." Angela tossed her head slightly as she related this small bit. She could not tell this *gorgio* the names of her parents. The belief of her people was that to speak the name of those that have died will bring bad luck, and as it was, she had all the bad luck she could take for one day!

As she refused to say any more, Royce asked, "Then what is your name? Can you not at least tell me this?" Royce rose from his chair, and stepping around his desk, he leaned a hip against the edge. "How is it that you look the part of a Gypsy in dress, but you do not speak, nor do you look like any Gypsy which I have ever seen before?" If she confessed to him that she had indeed run away from her family, he knew that he would be honor-bound to return her to them as soon as possible.

"Look, mister, I don't have to tell you anything! Let me be on my way, and I'll forget all about what has transpired this evening. I won't report this abduction to the authorities." All that Angela wanted was her release and then she would be free to find her own people. She was hungry, tired, and in no mood to play this rich man's strange games!

Swallowing a healthy draft of the dark liquid in his goblet, Royce felt his temper beginning to flare dangerously because of this brat's stubbornness. "So, if I do not release you, you will call the authorities on me, will you?" With the slight nod of her dark head, he noisily set the goblet on his desk. Taking a few steps in her direction, he intentionally towered over her. He spoke with a sharpened edge of impatience to his voice. "You will obey me, and you will do all that I instruct you to do for the next year! You are the one that will be handed over to the authorities if you disobey me in any fashion! It will be you, girl, who spends time in New-gate prison for your attempt at thievery, if you persist in this fashion!"

Clutching her hands tightly together in the folds of her skirt, Angela tried to appear brave in the face of his raging anger, but his words brought about the terror within her trembling heart which he had intended. For a few minutes she had almost forgotten about the attempt she had made to rob his fancy friend of his purse. She had heard horror stories all of her life about Newgate—that infamous prison of years long past! Stories wherein one of her ancestors or another Gypsy's relative had been locked away in the disease-infested prison and had never been heard from again! He could not truly mean to send her to such a place! But looking into his hard unyielding features, she knew that he was not one to make idle threats.

Taking a deep breath to try to steady her nerves, she looked directly into his gray eyes and wondered if there could not be some inner warmth to the man. Perhaps if she told him everything that had happened to her since she had awakened this morning, he would be willing to try to help her regain her own lifetime. Knowing that she had no choice but to agree to the imposed year of the bet, or to go straightway to Newgate prison, she drew in another deep, steadying gulp of air. "Sir, I will try and tell you what you wish to know. My name is Angela, and my people are Ro-many." How much of her story would he believe if she just blurted out everything, she wondered as words began to leave her lips. "I fear that my story may, at first, sound rather strange to you, but I have no one else to turn to."

Unwillingly Royce did feel for a few minutes some softening toward this Gypsy brat. She appeared so slight and frail standing bravely before him, childlike with those wide blue eyes framed with dark thick lashes. Slowly he nodded his head for her to continue.

"I really don't understand how any of this happened, but this morning when I awoke outside of London, I found that I had been somehow sent back in time. I don't belong here in this century: I belong in the future where there are automobiles and airplanes and condos and skyscrapers! I don't know how to get back to the future, nor how such a thing could be possible, but I do know that I have to find some of my own people. I know that they will be able to help me!" Angela felt the swift sting of tears in the back of her eyes.

"An automobile? An airplane?" Royce's dark brow rose in question as the edges of his lips quivered with humor after having listened to her incredible story.

"An automobile is . . . is something like a horseless carriage. Only it runs on gasoline instead of animals," Angela quickly supplied as she pinned all of her hopes on his believing her.

A large grin settled over Royce's lips. He didn't have to hear what this thing she called an airplane was. His deep masculine laughter filled the room. Royce had heard Gypsy stories and lies in the past. An old Gypsy man had even shown him a document of safe passage throughout Europe, which he claimed had been signed by Jesus himself. Because of the signature, he had demanded that he and his family had the right to camp on any property they saw fit. But this girl's story was certainly one of the most outlandish he had ever heard. Another century and a horseless carriage! As his mirth quieted, he grinned. "I'll say one thing for you, Angela—if that is your name—you certainly do have an extraordinary imagination!"

Angela felt her cheeks flaming. He had not believed a single word she had said! Had she truly expected him to, though? Why should a *gorgio*, and a rich one at that, believe a simple Gypsy girl?

Watching her face blushing brightly, Royce admitted that beneath the dirt and grime, the child was more than likely pretty. "Well then, Angela, we will start off on the right foot from the beginning, if you will conduct yourself like a little lady for the forthcoming year. Your speech proclaims that you are teachable, so I daresay that perhaps we shall not have such a hard time of it."

She was teachable, and perhaps he wouldn't have a hard time of it! "Didn't you hear one single word that I said to you?" Angela blurted out, her eyes glinting with impotent fury as this hardheaded man appeared to be ignoring everything that she had told him. "I am not from your time! I have to find some of my own people and try to return to the twentieth century! I can't stay here; I must leave as soon as possible!" As she glared at him, he tilted his head to better view her, and in so doing, the glitter of a tiny diamond stud in his right ear could be seen reflecting the candlelight.

"Oh, I heard all that you had to say," Royce replied casually, "but I don't believe a single word of your Gypsy lies! You will find that none of your wily nonsense will be appreciated here at Westfield Hall, so don't waste your time speaking of such fantasies to me or my servants. Do as you are told and all will go well for you. Your family will appreciate the purse that you will bring to them after I win Damian's stallion. I have offered him plenty of gold in the past for the beast. If you go along with what I offer, you will be the recipient of the purse."

"I will not stay here!" Angela declared, feeling panic rising up in her chest. Her gaze went to the study door as though seeking a route of escape. She had to find her own people! She could not be forced to stay here in this man's house for an entire year!

"Enough of your foolishness now!" Royce seemed to read her thoughts, and taking a step closer to her, he wished to ensure that she did not flee. "I will have Hawkins ready a chamber for you. If you are to act the part of a young lady, you had best live like one for the next year."

"But I have already told you, I can't stay here!" Her words were an anguished cry for release.

"Of course you can stay here at Westfield Hall. You will even find, in time, that you will begin to enjoy the life of a lady. You may even regret the ending of the year when you have to resume your old way of life and return to your family. Perhaps what you learn will further your future." Now what Gypsy had ever been offered such a generous opportunity? Royce asked himself.

"I told you that I no longer have any family. I truly doubt that I will hold a minute's regret when I leave this place!" Angela declared bluntly. She was regretting the fact that she had ever picked this arrogant, conceited man's friend as her mark. How dare this brute think that his way of life was so splendid that she would regret having to leave it!

Royce discarded her words as an annoyance. These Gypsies were crafty and known for playing on a person's sympathy. More than likely, her mother and father were both healthy and living, and she thought that he would be swayed into releasing her from the obligation of this bet if he believed her an orphan.

"Hawkins!" he shouted as his gray eyes studied her. Within moments, the butler, who had been anxiously pacing the hallway outside the study door in case the duke was in need of him, stepped into the room.

"Yes, your Grace?" His glance took in his master, then the girl, who appeared shaken.

"See that a chamber on the second floor is prepared for this young lady immediately."

"The second floor, your Grace?" Hawkins looked once again from his master to the dirty Gypsy girl and, for a moment, believed that he had heard the duke wrong. The second-floor chambers were used exclusively for the duke himself or his guests. Even long-time servants like himself did not use any chambers on the second floor but instead resided in small quarters on the fourth floor of the manse.

"Aye, you heard me right; the second floor, Hawkins. See that she is bathed and given clean clothing. Perhaps that undermaid, the small one, Clara, or Carey, perhaps she has something for the time being until Angela can have her own clothes brought out to the Hall." He made a mental note; the first thing he would do when he returned to the city would be to send a dressmaker to the Hall to see to the girl's needs. He would not be slack in any area which would help him to win the bet with Damian!

"Yes, your Grace," Hawkins agreed quickly, then silently turned to leave the study. He was not one to argue with the Duke of Westfield, even if it did appear that the duke had taken leave of his senses!

As soon as the door closed behind the servant, Angela rounded upon the dark-haired giant once again. "I am not staying here! I have already told you that, and I am not going to bathe either, nor will I wear anyone else's clothes!" Angela knew at that moment that her features had flamed with humiliation at having this terrible man tell his servant to ready her a bath and find her clean clothes!

Royce St. James had reached his limit of

patience with this girl. All he wanted was a few minutes of relaxation before he found his own bed and was able to put this night behind him. "Listen to me carefully, Angela, for I will not repeat myself again. You will do as you are told here at Westfield Hall, or I will have two of my most trusted footmen take you this very night to Newgate!"

Standing silently before his full wrath, Angela quickly took stock of her situation. At the moment there was no way out—except to comply with his wishes. She did not want to go to prison, since once there she would have no way of ever returning to her own life. "Well . . . perhaps I will stay here for the time being. The promise of a purse of gold does sound inviting."

She wanted to sound convincing, but the minute she had the opportunity she would run as fast and as far from Westfield Hall as possible, she swore to herself. "I will not bathe though, and I will not wear anyone else's clothes! I can wash off if someone will show me where the facilities are, and what I am wearing now will suit just fine. I can just wipe off a few grass spots, and I will be as good as new." She didn't want him to get the idea that she would give in to him completely, or he would more than likely have Hawkins scrub her down from head to foot!

Royce St. James did not reply. His gray eyes silently appraised her for several minutes until Hawkins returned to the study. "See that she is taken care of as instructed," the duke told his man before turning back to his desk, expecting that all would go as he wished.

Six

Relaxing in the comfortable winged chair
before the warm hearth, a good cigar in his
hand and a goblet of brandy resting on the
small table at his elbow, Royce St. James was
finally able to relax. Hawkins, his valued and
trusted servant would take in hand the
Gypsy girl, and at the end of the year, he
would have Damian Dunsely's treasured stallion. He blew a circle of smoke overhead as
he anticipated the horse races that he would
win with such a fine animal. He had never
seen a swifter horse than the black stallion
called Raven Boy. With the thought of adding such a fine beast to the Westfield stables, a smile settled over his sensual lips.
Though he and Damian had been good
friends for some years, it had become a con-
test of late for each to try to best the other.
It seemed that Royce, more often than not,
was the one to come out on top of their

contests, especially their bets, and at the moment Royce admitted to himself that he rather enjoyed the display of temper that Damian showed when he was the loser. Royce was confident that he would once again witness his friend's flushed face and silent stare as he handed over his stallion's reins.

Royce's self-indulgence came to a swift end. Without a knock, the study door was flung wide and Hawkins hurried into the room. "You had best come quickly, your Grace. The kitchen is in an uproar!"

Over a twenty-year span of serving at Westfield Hall, his employment beginning when the duke himself had been no more than a baby, Jerome Hawkins had held the very correct appearance of what a butler worthy of his station should maintain. At all times he was impeccably dressed, his stance straight, his manner correct. For the first time that Royce St. James could recall, the man was flustered; his dark cravat, usually neatly tied, was at odd lengths, and his suit of dark green velvet was stained with water.

"Well, take a breath, Hawkins, and explain yourself." A small grin flashed over Royce's lips as he took in the butler's bulging eyes and his thin cheeks flushed a deep scarlet.

Whatever the event, it must be a good one, he thought with amusement.

Hawkins drew in a few steadying breaths before continuing. "It is that Gypsy girl, your Grace."

Royce had known his few minutes of relaxation were too good to believe! He had hoped that the girl would behave herself, but given Hawkins's countenance things were not going to go as easily as anticipated. "What on earth has she done now?" For Hawkins to be ruffled it had to be extreme.

"Your Grace, she is wielding a butcher knife at the help out in the kitchen and is threatening to slice to ribbons anyone that tries to come near her!"

"She is doing *what?*" Royce was instantly on his feet.

"Yes, your Grace." This was more like the reaction that he wished from his master. "I did as you bid me, your Grace, and had Mrs. Biesely heat water for the young lady's bath. I also laid in Mrs. Biesely's hands the task of obtaining the girl clean clothes as you instructed." Drawing a deep breath before Royce could question him, the servant continued, "Mrs. Biesely was more than happy to do the task, your Grace, until the water was readied and she instructed the girl to get into the tub, which had been set up in the kitchen area." Anticipating his master's desire to interrupt him, he hurriedly continued, "The girl refused to comply with instructions, your Grace, and Mrs. Biesely brought in reinforcements—Agnes and Ethel, the upstairs maids. The two are sturdy young women, but they were no match for the girl! She set one on her backside in the tub of water, and the other fled the kitchen in tears with a bloodied nose! Hearing the commotion, I went to offer assistance. Upon entering the kitchen, the girl was holding a large butcher knife and waving it in the air in a threatening manner. I tried my best to take the knife and curb her willfulness, your Grace, but I fear that the knife had the desired effect of keeping me from carrying out my job."

Royce stood thunderstruck. How could such a young slip of a girl cause so much confusion as to ward off his entire staff? "I will tend to the matter myself," Royce muttered aloud and started out the study door. He had taken enough from the little brat. The sooner he set her straight on who she was taking orders from here at the Hall, the better off they were all going to be!

"As you wish, your Grace." Hawkins was only a few feet behind his master as they made their way down the long hall toward the back of the house where the kitchen was adjoined to the rest of the Hall. Hawkins

88

hated the fact that he had been forced to disturb the duke; this was a very rare occurrence for the servant. Usually Hawkins could handle any situation at the Hall, but he was relieved that he would not have to try once again to take the knife away from the wild Gypsy girl!

The scene which met Royce's gaze when he stepped foot into the kitchen held him immobile for a full minute. The kitchen was filled with Westfield servants standing around, and gawking at the deranged girl as she brandished a large knife in the air. She stood a few feet away from the brass hip tub, the steam from which was filling the air around her. She looked like a frightened child as she glared defiantly at all in the room.

"Hawkins, you can see the servants out of the kitchen. I will handle this alone." Royce's stormy gray gaze held Angela's eyes as the butler hurriedly rushed the rest of the servants out of the kitchen and set them about their duties.

Angela held the knife in front of her as though intent upon protecting herself from assault from any quarter. Her violet eyes dared even the duke to come near and taste the sharp edge of her weapon!

"What is the meaning of this Angela?" Royce softly questioned as he stepped farther into the room once all the servants had vacated. His tone was low and steady as he tried not to frighten her any further.

"I told you that I would not take a bath! And I certainly do not intend to strip down here in the kitchen in front of all your servants!" Angela's outrage was strong, but she was taken off guard by the sound of his gentle tone. She expected harsher treatment.

"The servants have left. Why don't you set the knife on that table before you hurt yourself? Then you can take a bath like a good child." Slowly advancing, Royce knew for a certainty that there was not a trace of a good child in this little hoyden that was glaring furiously at him.

Stubbornly she shook her head, the knife vigorously waving in his direction.

Royce was determined that the girl would take a bath whether she wanted to take one or not! He would not have a lice-ridden Gypsy running around in his home infesting everyone! Standing only a few feet away from her and the brass tub, he eyed the knife in her grasp warily. As his gaze rose up from the knife and locked with hers, his hand shot out and grabbed her wrist, the knife no longer a viable threat but still clenched between her fingers. "Drop it!" he demanded, and with more pressure upon her wrist, the weapon soon clattered to the floor.

A cry of pure rage spilled from Angela's lips. The unfairness that had been dealt her since waking up this morning swept over her in a heated rush. As another cry escaped her, she threw her slight form against the duke's broad chest, pounding the hard expanse for all she was worth. Her feet kicked whatever part of his legs she could reach as she twisted and turned in his embrace. While he tried to quell her attack, his large hand came near her face; upon sudden impulse, she bit down as hard as she could on the backside. She felt better as she heard his grunt of pain.

Having lost all patience with the little hellion, Royce took a firmer grip as he wrapped one arm around her waist and warded off her undiminished attack with the other hand. "You will do as you're told, and you will get in that bathtub right this minute!" Hearing her loud snort of defiance and feeling her limbs flail ineffectively, his grip tightened upon her. Though he believed he had her under control, her wriggling motions were making the job of undressing her difficult. With determination Royce began to attack the long row of buttons down the front of her blouse. Unlatching the silver belt at her waist with a deft movement of his free hand, he then unhooked her skirt and the material fell in a puddle around her ankles.

Angela no longer wasted strength trying to fight him off, but instead she fought to keep clothing on her body. "Take your stinking hands off of me, you cursed *gorgio!* Let me go!" Clutching her blouse together and trying to wriggle out of his hands at the same time to retrieve her skirt, she was out of breath and gasping loudly as she felt his hands tugging at the shirt.

Not in the least disturbed about being forced to bathe an unruly child, having in the past taken a hand in seeing that his cousin's twins, Julia and Jeffrey, were made presentable after the pair had wrestled in the mud next to the pond behind the stables at Westfield Hall, Royce clenched his jaw as he pried Angela's slender fingers from the material of her blouse. Soon he had stripped away the offending garment, casting it along with the skirt, to the floor.

Searing flames of embarrassment swept over Angela from head to toe as she tried to cover herself with her hands, standing completely naked in his embrace except for the scarf tied around her breasts. All she wanted was to escape; and the closest escape route from those coolly appraising eyes was the tub of steaming water in the center of the kitchen floor. Trying to break away, she made a lunge for the bathtub, desiring to gain the cover that the water could provide.

"What the hell is this for?" Royce kept a tight hold around her slender waist and took hold of the binding around her breasts. With a wide grin, he began to untie the small knot of the material centered on her back. Believing this a childish maneuver to hide the first budding signs of girlish breasts, he ripped away the material.

The only sound in the kitchen as the skimpy piece of material fell to the floor along with the rest of the clothes was Royce's gasp as Angela's full, luscious breasts were exposed to sight. As though grateful for their release, the creamy, tempting mounds rose to the occasion with rosy tips impudently straining.

Instantly Royce's hands fell to his sides, the stormy gray of his gaze turning a warm, metallic silver as his gaze took in her shapely curves. She hurriedly took the few steps to the tub and stepped within the warm depths to shield her body from his view.

"I . . . I . . ." he began. He tried to regain his composure but found that this was more of a task than his lagging brain could perform. Looking down at her and seeing the bright flush of scarlet on her cheeks, he tried once again. "I thought that you were a child. I had no idea. . . . How could I have known . . . ?" He was at a loss for words as the vision of womanly breasts assailed his thoughts. From the first moment he had set eyes upon her, there in front of the club, he had believed her a child; even Damian had shared this belief!

"I hope you bloody well got yourself an eyeful, your Grace! Now, if you will just leave the kitchen, I am able to wash myself!" Within the cover of the water, she tried to appear brave, even with him standing over her, but she knew that her tone did not carry her bravado as her words barely reached his ears. All she wanted was for him to leave her in her moment of shame. She should not have pushed him so far. She should have bathed when first instructed by that thin, pinch-faced woman, Mrs. Biesely. Now this man knew that she was not a child and Momma Leona's words of caution filled her head: *Never allow anyone to know that you are a woman grown!* She wondered what he would do with this information, though it mattered little in the seventeen hundreds whether she was a child or a woman; a Gypsy in this century was mistreated no matter his or her age!

"Why on earth would you try to appear a child? Whoever would wish to hide such perfection?" Royce stared down at the young woman in the tub, confused by what had just transpired. Her stunning features and form could earn her a king's ransom, he thought. Why did she engage in this charade?

Keeping her glance lowered to the water that rose to her chin, Angela knew that she could not explain her lifestyle with Momma Leona and the children to this man. She had tried to tell him that she was not from this century and the results had been cruel laughter. Why would he believe her now if she tried to explain, laws governing minors in late twentieth-century London? Slowly her violet-blue gaze rose upward. Worrying her bottom lip with her upper teeth, she chose to remain silent.

Held by the sparkle of candlelight reflected in her shimmering eyes, for a long moment Royce was lost to the strange alluring beauty of the woman whom only a short time ago he believed a child. It was Angela who first broke eye contact. As she looked down, the silver coins within her dark curls caught a reflection and enabled Royce to come to his senses. "Do you need help with your hair, Angela? Perhaps I should send for Mrs. Biesely or one of the maids to attend you." The steel warmth of his gaze traveled the long length of ebony hair that cascaded down her back and flowed like silken strands in the surrounding water; the sections of her hair that were entwined with silver coins had been braided.

"I have had enough help from the likes of you and your servants, thank you very much!" Angela's pert nose rose, but not daring to make any movement that could reveal any more of her body, she held her arms over her breasts.

"I could help you unbraid the coins if you like." Royce ignored her outburst and made his offer repentantly. Strangely, he wished to apologize for being so forceful. This offer of assistant was all that he could think to do.

Angela wondered if he took her for a complete fool! She was not about to let him unbraid the coins from her hair. They might not be very valuable, but they were hers, and what was hers, she had learned to protect! Stubbornly she shook her head, her blue eyes sparkling with newborn challenge if he dared to try and force her to comply with his demands! After all, what more did she have to lose? He had already discovered her secret and had glimpsed her naked body!

Not lost to the simmering heat in the glare she bestowed upon him, Royce reluctantly turned his back on the woman sitting in the brass tub. He would retreat and leave her to her privacy. The fact that his charge was not the young girl he had believed, but a woman full-grown put an entirely new light on the bet he had made with Damian. Leaving the kitchen, he looked for Hawkins. He would never have agreed to such a bet and brought the girl out to The Hall if he had known that the Gypsy girl was a woman. A small slip of a girl would have been easy to mold and train, but a fully grown woman was something else. One who held the enticing looks of Angela would be even more difficult!

Finding Hawkins not far from the kitchen, as though he had been listening for his master's call, Royce instructed the servant to have a tray sent to Angela's chamber as soon as her bath was completed. Making his way to his own chamber, the thought struck that perhaps it would not be as hard as he had feared to turn this Gypsy brat into a presentable young woman after all. He remembered her pure, refined voice and hoped that with a bath and plenty of good food perhaps she would become transformed into something more agreeable.

Though he knew deep within that the smartest thing would be to release the young woman in the morning and be rid of her, something within his stubborn nature would not let him concede the bet and release the girl. He would send word in the morning to Damian that he did not want anyone in London to know of his charge's origins, nor did he want anyone to know about the bet. He considered the bet personal business and desired no one else to know that the young woman under his roof was little more than a wild Gypsy wench who had been found on the streets of London picking pockets!

Seven

The moment that Royce St. James's large figure stepped from the kitchen, Angela's thoughts took flight. Escape was her top priority! She had to get out of this mausoleum of a house and as far away from the Duke of Westfield as possible! She had been threatened, manhandled, and shouted at. Now, to make matters even worse, the arrogant brute had glimpsed her nakedness! This had been the final insult, and feeling her face turning to flame, she wished that she could disappear! She knew, though, that she would not be snapped out of the eighteenth century so quickly.

Rising to her feet, she began to reach out to pick up her clothes, when the starkly thin, gray-haired Mrs. Biesely entered the kitchen with a nightgown thrown over one arm. "You surely are not finished yet with your bath! You have not even touched your hair!" the older woman admonished.

With quick, purposeful steps, the servant made her way to the bath tub and gave Angela an appraising look. Like the rest of the household, she had thought the Gypsy little more than a child. Seeing now the young woman's abundant charms, however, her stern features gave way to surprise as one gray brow rose over a warm autumn brown eye, her lips stretching into a tight grin.

Angela felt uncomfortable standing naked in the middle of the kitchen before the older woman. Instead of reaching out for her clothes, she decided to lower herself back into the tub of lukewarm water.

"Put this on when you finish with your washing. I will take these along to be washed." Before Angela could respond, the quick, angular woman retrieved her dark skirt and blouse and placed the nightgown upon the chair.

Angela would have stepped from the tub in order to retrieve her clothes from the woman, but she had had about all of the humiliation that she could stand for one night. Instead, she glared at the woman, then upon the nightgown lying across the back of the chair. "I can't wear that thing!" she blurted out as she looked at the soft cotton nightgown.

Mrs. Biesely wrinkled her nose at the clothes in her arms. She had told the young woman that they would be taken to the wash, but she had every intention of burning them! "And why on earth can you not be wearing them? Now, be a dear and don't be taking on so. We have had enough excitement for one evening. The gown will do for this eve, and if it's a touch too large, it will not be long before the duke will tend to the matter hisself." She nodded her gray head toward the lacy white nightrail, her face seeming to soften as she glimpsed the young woman's troubled features.

Did none of these *gorgios* know anything? Angela inwardly fumed as her glance went back to the nightgown. White was for mourning. No gypsy would ever be caught wearing something white! "I want my own clothes back!" she said more demandingly. She hoped that she could try and bully the kind-hearted servant into complying with her wishes.

"If you insist, I will have to call for the master and let him handle the affair of your clothing. It was his order that you were to be given the gown, and I, for one, would not dare to be going back on his Grace's orders."

Drat it, the woman was as impossible to deal with as the rest! Angela's gaze returned to the white nightgown, and with

101

that glance she wondered at the two evils which faced her. Finally Angela slowly nodded, her eyes lowered as though in defeat. She would wear the nightgown, and she would tell herself that she was in mourning. Was it not true that she was in mourning for a life that appeared lost to her? In mourning for Momma Leona and the children, and even for Mateo and Mustafa! After all, they had been the only family she had known for the past ten years. "I will wear the gown, Mrs. Biesely," she softly stated, her head still lowered. Better this than having to face Royce St. James again. She could not consider facing that beastly man again with another rebellion. If she ever set eyes upon him again, she would be able to read in those cool eyes everything that had taken place this evening between them here in the kitchen!

Slowly Angela reached up and began to unbraid the coins from her hair. She would bide her time until the house grew quiet, then she would find her clothes and she would flee, she told herself as she began to lather soap into her hair.

Mrs. Biesely nodded her head as she watched the young woman's actions. "Now that be a good lass. You finish up and slip into the nightrail. I'll be having Ethel show you to your chamber, and after fixing you a tray, Hawkins will bring it up to you." Looking at the young woman sitting in the tub, Sara Biesely did not see the defiant, wild-eyed creature that had been standing in the kitchen waving a butcher knife at the Westfield help. In her place sat a docile young woman who appeared defeated. But looking into the large blue eyes, she knew that this defeat would not be long lived! The duke had brought back a handful to Westfield Hall, whether he realized it or not!

Mrs. Biesely stepped through an adjoining room off the kitchen to rid herself of the clothes in her hands. Moments later, she returned to stoke the embers in the hearth. Angela finished washing her hair, and stepping out of the tub, she dried off with the fleecy towel that had been laid on the chair next to the nightgown. She heard Mrs. Biesely humming softly to herself as she went about her business of fixing Angela a tray. Angela pulled the nightgown over her head with some reluctance. The soft material felt heavenly upon her body, but years of superstitious beliefs kept Angela from appreciating the cloth against her flesh. While she stood in the center of the large kitchen, she wished she had the nerve to try to silently slip into the adjoining room and retrieve her clothes. As the older woman stirred a pot, her back toward Angela, she would have been able to slip out the back door and disappear into the dark night.

As she feared the duke's retaliation should she be caught, Angela stood where she was in the center of the kitchen. A few minutes later, Ethel, the upstairs maid, arrived. Eyeing Angela warily, the girl stood near the doorway and called for Mrs. Biesely. She had been the one that the Gypsy girl had pushed back into the tub of water. Her friend Agnes had been the unlikely victim of a bloodied nose, and Ethel did not want to take any more chances with this girl. She kept her distance.

"Oh, Ethel, you're here already!" Mrs. Biesely glanced up. "You're to show the duke's guest to her chamber."

Thus far, neither she nor Hawkins had been informed of the exact nature of the girl's visit. Hawkins had relayed the duke's order that she was to reside on the second floor, so, of course, Mrs. Biesely had imagined that the duke wanted the girl near his own chambers. Earlier the servant had instructed Agnes and Ethel to make ready the adjoining chamber to his Grace's. At the time, she had been somewhat surprised at his Grace, but now after having caught a glimpse of the Gypsy's bountiful curves, she told herself that there was little to be surprised about. The duke was a young, handsome man in his prime. He had brought few women in the past out to the Hall, but who was to know the mind of the gentry? She had heard gossip that Royce St. James was not averse to setting up a mistress in the city; why should any of them be surprised that he would bring one of his companions out here to the Hall? The only thing surprising was his choice of doxy.

"Yes, ma'am." Ethel bobbed her mob-capped head in a quick manner, but her gold-flecked, brown eyes remained fixed upon the Gypsy girl. Though the girl appeared calm in her nightgown, the maid could not put aside the image of the young woman waving the sharp butcher knife about in the air like a madwoman, nor could she forget her own encounter with the girl.

"Go along with you now, Angela. Ethel will take you to your room and then Hawkins will bring up your tray." Mrs. Biesely smiled warmly at the young woman, hoping to put her at ease and make Ethel's job easier. "Hawkins will report back to the duke later this evening that all has been carried out as he ordered." She threw this bit of information in, remembering earlier that the girl had only complied with her wishes after the servant had resorted to the threat of calling for the duke to settle the matter.

Angela did not respond. She knew a

threat when she heard one! Instead she picked up the coins for her hair and her silver bracelets. She started toward the kitchen door and stood before the girl that would show her to her chamber. Her blue eyes studied Ethel from head to toe. Angela knew that earlier when she had set the girl in the tub of water, she had caught her off guard. Quickly she discounted the other girl as any kind of threat. She would go along with the Duke's demands for now, but later this evening when the house was quiet, she would carry out her own plans, those of escaping from this house and the madman who owned it!

Ethel did not linger in the kitchen doorway for long. She turned and led the guest down the long hall that ran the length of the downstairs portion of the house. With a turn, she led the girl up the imposing stairway extending from the great room, which would take them to the second floor. Without a word, Ethel preceded Angela down the hallway of the second floor, which gave access to the elegantly furnished bedchambers at Westfield Hall. Halting before an ornately carved oak door, Ethel silently opened it and stepped aside for the girl to enter. "This is your chamber, miss. I hope you will be comfortable." Thus saying, and keeping a wary eye out for any attack upon her person, Ethel was more than happy to slip away from the bedchamber and retreat down the hall.

What a silly girl, Angela thought to herself as she watched Ethel's retreating back. The servant acted as though she feared that she would be set upon! Angela did not recognize the maid with her lacy little mobcap tied beneath her chin as one of the servants that she had attacked earlier in the kitchen. She had been far too upset while waving the knife to remember the faces of the servants that had come near. The only image she could remember was that of the Duke of Westfield!

With a soft sigh of pent-up nervousness escaping her bow-shaped lips, she entered the chamber. This beautiful room with mint green and peach decor would bring comfort to some, but as Angela looked around at the marble fireplace and the plush Persian carpet, her only heart's desire was to be as far away as possible from Westfield Hall! Everything that had transpired from awakening this morning to now quickly flashed through her mind. She knew that if she had any hope at all of regaining her old life, she had to find some of her people as soon as possible! They would be the only ones who would believe her; only her own kind could she trust!

Clearing his throat to announce his presence, Hawkins stood holding a dinner tray in hand. "I will just set this tray down over here before the hearth, miss." He did not direct his gaze upon her after the first glimpse of seeing her standing in the center of the bedchamber wearing only a nightrail.

Angela would have reached out for something in which to cover herself, but with a quick glance around the room, she spied only the satin peach coverlet draped across the fourposter bed in the center of the chamber. The coverlet would lend her the desired cover she needed, but the thought of hurrying across the room to gain the bedspread seemed a bit ridiculous at the moment. The action would draw more attention in itself!

Hawkins was gone soon, anyway. With the chamber once again empty and the door shut, she was soon drawn to the covered tray which held a savory assortment of foods that Mrs. Biesely had prepared as Angela's evening meal.

It was true that Angela would have wished to be anywhere besides Westfield Hall, but she was no one's fool. She had eaten only a loaf of stolen bread today, and listening to her stomach growl, she realized that long hours had passed since then.

Hawkins had set the tray on the small table which was centered between a pair of chairs before the fireplace. Without hesitation Angela sat down on one of the mint green chairs with satin pinstripes, and began to sample the fare laid out on the tray. A bottle of red wine accompanied the meal, and as Angela filled the goblet resting next to the bottle, a small smile of thanks for Mrs. Biesely's thoughtfulness settled over Angela's lips. She had rarely sampled such brew. Momma Leona, Mustafa, and Mateo had hoarded any alcohol that came into the trailer, not allowing any of the children the smallest taste. As she took a deep drink, the warming effects reminded her of the afternoon when Carlos had stolen a bottle of Mateo's wine and the older children had hidden away and passed the bottle amongst themselves. She sighed aloud as relaxation tingled throughout her body.

Putting the wine aside, she sampled the thick potato soup and the savory slices of roast beef that were covered with a delicious-tasting gravy. Angela did not stop until she had cleaned her plate. With a satisfied grin, she refilled the goblet with more of the rich wine, then leaned back in her chair. The fire in the hearth, as well as the wine, warmed her body and allowed the full weight of her weariness to be felt. There was comfort, after all, to be found here in this fancy chamber. She grinned as she wiggled bare toes before the warming fire in the hearth. Never could she remember a day in her life when she had felt so satisfied. She was clean and she had eaten a full meal! She could not remember a day when she had had both while living with Momma Leona! The slovenly Gypsy woman had on more than one occasion declared that a dirty child could outbeg a clean one any day, and a hungry Gypsy was a wary Gypsy, given to an appetite for thievery!

Angela was neither dirty, nor was she hungry, and Momma Leona should try and take a bath sometime! She giggled, amused by the thought, and the image of the overpowering, perfume-bathed, sweating body of Momma Leona instantly returned. Angela had despised the filth while living with Momma Leona. Taking another sip of the wine, she told herself it had been the abuse inflicted upon the children by the adult Gypsies that had been the worst. No, it had been the lack of food, she thought a moment later, and then shaking her head, she thought that the threat of imprisonment for stealing or begging, or the threat of Momma Leona selling one of the older girls' bodies had to be the very worst part of living under the old Gypsy woman's care. Angela couldn't make up her mind which had been the worst. As she stifled a yawn, her cobalt blue gaze rested on the fourposter bed. Imagining the softness, she hurriedly finished her glass of wine, then approached the bed. Tentatively she stretched out a hand and ran it across the soft satin coverlet, her breath exhaling at the feel. Dreamily she wondered what it would be like to be covered by such cool softness.

Looking around the chamber as though expecting her actions to be halted, Angela pulled back the coverlet. In awe she felt the silk sheets beneath. The bed was too tempting to resist. The pallet she had slept upon in the small front room in Momma Leona's trailer could not compare to such a luxury! Angela told herself that this one time in her life she would sleep on a real bed with silk sheets! Before climbing upon the large bed, she threw off the white nightgown that covered her body. She would only rest for a few minutes, she told herself. Just a few minutes until the house quieted, and she would find her clothes and make good her escape without fear of being caught!

The large bed with its silken sheets and coverlet were only something that a Gypsy girl like Angela could have dreamt about in the past. The cool silk welcomed her with a soft caress to her flesh. Her eyes closing as she rested her head upon the goose-down pillow, her hazy, wine-induced thoughts centered upon the caress of the man who had held her in his arms earlier this evening. She had been naked, and the luster of quickening passion that had leapt within his silver gaze had been disregarded then by Angela, but now she brought the reminder to her thoughts for inspection. Royce St. James, the Duke of Westfield, had been more of a threat to her than she had even realized, she now warned herself. With his handsome appeal and large, virile body, any girl's head could be easily turned. She again felt the tender strength in his hands as he had stripped away her clothes and had held her struggling body tightly against his own. No, she would not allow herself to think along these lines, she chided herself sternly as she turned over on her side to a more comfortable position. She would only rest for a few minutes. She would awaken in a couple of hours and flee Westfield Hall and the duke, and never would she again look back upon this night, nor would she give herself another opportunity to reflect over Royce St. James's good looks!

Royce St. James, the very one that Angela spurned in her dreams, was having a hard time finding sleep. Hawkins had reported to him after he had taken the girl her tray, stating that she had finished her bath, been given a clean nightrail, and had been shown to the chamber adjoining his own. Royce had not instructed the servant about which room on the second floor should be given to the Gypsy girl, but he had not expected that she would be given the one closest to his own. As he lay upon his bed, his eyes staring at the ceiling, he wondered why her sleeping arrangements disturbed him so much.

When Hawkins had left, Royce had sat before his hearth and had tried for a time to read. Now and then, he thought that he had heard the girl roaming about in the adjoining chamber, and he could not hold his mind upon the book in his hands. Setting the book aside, he had gone to his bed. Sleep was elusive as his thoughts centered upon the Gypsy wench. He wondered how she looked in the nightrail. With her long raven curls clean and free, he envisioned the sight of her delicate form wandering about in the bedchamber next to his own. He wondered if she had enjoyed her meal, remembering earlier that she had claimed that she was hungry and that was why she had tried to steal Damian's purse. Had she found the featherbed in the chamber inviting, and was she this very moment resting peacefully, unlike himself?

With an oath, he threw back the covers and pulled his dressing robe about his naked body. Telling himself that his only concern was to ensure that the girl had not slipped out of the chamber and fled the Hall, which would make him the loser of the bet, Royce silently made his way to the door that adjoined the two chambers. He silently listened at the closed door, and finding all silent on the other side, he turned the knob, inching the door open soundlessly.

His silent steps drew him to the side of the bed, silver-gray eyes roaming over the sleeping woman's naked back. The silken coverlet only covered the lower portion of her body, the edge draped carelessly over her rounded buttocks and shapely hips. She had not bothered to extinguish the candle that burned on the bedside table, so his view was not hindered as his gaze followed the ebony curls that wrapped around her body and flowed in silken strands over the peach sheets. Her face was turned away, but without walking around the bed, he knew that even in sleep she was the most beautiful woman he had ever seen in his life. Without a second thought, he reached out a hand, and between two fingers, he caressed a curling tress, bringing the piece of hair up to his face. He inhaled the lilac-fresh scent, the simple action bringing a tightening to his belly that stirred a quickening of hot blood rushing through his groin.

Stifling the groan that threatened to escape his throat, Royce dropped the curl as though he had been burned by the devil's own handmaiden! Good God, what was the matter with him? How could the sight of a sleeping Gypsy girl cause such a flow of desire to course over him? He, Royce St. James, who had seduced more eligible young women than he could remember by name and had had numerous mistresses in his past, was no callow youth given to bouts of uncontrol! He was a grown man, in his prime, a man who was master of his desires, or at least should be!

But there was something about this wild Gypsy brat that tempted his resolve. Before turning away from the bed, he decided that the first thing tomorrow morning he would have Hawkins move the girl to a chamber at the end of the hall. If that didn't work, he would have her moved to a different floor! As he bent to blow out the candle at her bedside, the glitter of her hair coins and jewelry caught his eye. Picking up the trinkets, he told himself that he would lock them away until the end of the year when the bet was up, believing this a form of insurance to keep the girl at Westfield Hall!

Eight

Bright morning sunlight streamed through the double-paned windows framed by thick velour draperies tied back on each side. A slight noise broke through Angela's deep slumber. She pulled herself out of the clutches of a bad dream and rising upright with her elbows, she peered groggily around the bedchamber. As she did so, she caught sight of a uniformed maid rushing through the chamber door. The soft colors of the room told Angela that the dream she had been fighting off had become a part of her reality. She was still locked within the unbelievable boundaries of a time long past, and looking around, she knew that she was still at Westfield Hall!

"Bloody hell!" she cursed aloud as she rubbed the sleep from her eyes and sat straight up against the pillows. She had slept the entire night away! She now cursed the soft bed, cursed the good food she had eaten and the wine that she had drunk. The combination of the three had caused her to sleep the sleep of the dead and had prevented her awaking during the night to make good her escape as she had planned. Dragging herself to the side of the bed, she pulled the sheet along with her, and without a second thought, she wrapped the length of peach silk around her body, knotting an edge over her breasts. Her clothes had not been returned, but a log had been placed upon the hearth, and Angela was drawn to its radiating warmth. It wasn't even winter yet and this mansion was freezing!

The maid she had glimpsed hurrying out of her chamber must have stoked up the fire and placed a large log on the hot coals, Angela reasoned. She could have at least brought her her clothes, so she could find her way out of this oversized museum.

Rubbing her hands along her forearms which were chilled with gooseflesh, Angela tried to calm her frayed nerves. If only she had forced herself awake during the night, she could have been a long way from Westfield Hall at this very moment! Spying the white nightgown lying on the floor, across the room, she instantly discarded the notion of putting the garment on and going downstairs in search of her own clothes. As she stood before the hearth and felt the warmth of the fire beginning to penetrate her cold limbs, her glance crossed to the bed and the nightstand beside it. Not seeing her hair coins and jewelry, her temper instantly soared. Her first thought was that the maid who had been in the chamber must have stolen them, pocketing them while she was sleeping! She should have been more cautious with her belongings, she fumed inwardly as she hurried across the room, making sure that she had not knocked the items to the floor during the night. Had she not learned anything over the years while living with Momma Leona? Had she not learned that she could not trust anyone?

It must have been everything that had happened to her since waking up yesterday morning and finding that reality had so drastically changed. This must be the reason that she had let her guard down. Finding neither her hair coins nor her jewelry on the floor next to the bed, she hurried to the chamber door. Intent upon finding the culprit who had stolen her property and then getting the bloody hell out of this house, she peered out into the hall before stepping foot upon the polished wood floor. There was no one around, not a servant or that fellow called Hawkins. Pulling the door closed behind her, she clenched her jaw as she started down the hallway, blue eyes flashing with dangerous lights of temper. She was going to find her possessions or she would find someone who would make the thief return them to her and now!

Just as she was about to start down the long staircase, a young girl wearing the starched uniform of a servant almost bumped into Angela as she was climbing the stairs to the second-floor landing.

"Oh, ma'am!" exclaimed the young girl, who was barely out of her teens, as she openly stared at the young woman draped in only a silk sheet. Her mouth gaped wide, and her apology was cut short as the young woman began to verbally assault her.

"Where are my things?" Angela demanded of the girl, believing her to be the perpetrator who had come into her chamber earlier.

"Your things, ma'am?" The maid took a step backward, intimidated by the young woman standing before her. Like the rest of the Westfield help, Abigail had heard about the incident in the kitchen the night before. She had gone to bed early in the evening with a headache and had not been awakened with the duke's return to the Hall. Therefore she had missed the scene in which the wild Gypsy girl had held the entire staff at bay with a butcher knife. This was all that was being talked about this morning by the servants; and at the moment, as the young woman stood glaring at her, she knew for a certainty that misfortune had surely come her way. She was facing the very woman that had dared to defy even the proper and resolute Hawkins! Quivering in her tracks upon the landing step, the girl softly stammered, "I . . . I . . . know nothing about your things, ma'am. The master, he told me to bring you these." She held out her hands and showed Angela the robe and slippers of white that matched the nightgown she had been given the night before.

"You can tell your master for me that I don't want any more hand-me-downs! I want what belongs to me, and I want my things immediately!" Angela's tone rose to a shout.

"But I don't be knowing anything about your things, ma'am." The undermaid drew back even further as though fearing that the woman would fly into a high rage.

"Did you not come into my chamber earlier this morning? My hair coins and jewelry were right there on the table beside the bed!" Angela was not about to let the girl off easily. She was going to make her return her property, even if she had to threaten her!

The girl shook her bright copper head in the negative, the curls falling from her hairpins bouncing up and down. "Oh, not I, miss. Perhaps it was Ethel or one of the other girls!" At that moment Abigail was glad that it had not been her job today of building up the morning fires!

"What kind of house has to have so many blasted servants roaming about anyways?" Angela demanded and would have pushed the girl aside and gone on down the stairs in pursuit of Ethel, but she was halted by a husky masculine voice and the tread of heavy footsteps coming up the stairs.

"What in God's name is going on now?" Royce demanded. He had heard the commotion as he was leaving his study to break his fast in the dining room. Remembering his houseguest and the uproar she had set his house into the night before, he made his way to find out what was amiss now. Seeing the undermaid cowering before Angela, he caught his breath in disbelief as he viewed the young Gypsy woman wearing only a silk sheet draped around her body and her hair in wild disarray. Swallowing hard to try and control the insistent thumping of his heart, he steadied himself for another confrontation with her.

"Someone in this house has stolen my belongings, and I want them back right now!" Angela drew herself up and glared from the girl to her master. With her temper so out of control, she forgot everything that had transpired between herself and the duke the night before. She also forgot that she wore only a sheet!

"What things were stolen from you, Angela? You were given a gown to wear." Surely she had not forgotten that her clothes had been left in the kitchen last night with Mrs. Biesely, and she could not be claiming that someone had stolen the nightgown that he had seen last night himself, discarded on the floor of her chamber. Royce held these thoughts, being confused by her announcement of thievery here at the Hall. "Abigail was sent to bring you a pair of slippers and a robe until something more presentable can be found for you to wear." He tried to keep his tone low and even, not wishing to display anger and begin another row. As Royce's cool gray gaze took in Angela's head of curling, ebony hair, he did not feel very angry, but he dared not allow his gaze to lower over her body. He was met with dark violet eyes glaring at him with cold fury, small chin jutting, and soft pink lips pouting invitingly toward him. He admitted that he was feeling more lust than anger for this incredibly beautiful young woman!

"If not this girl, then another under your employ stole my hair coins and jewelry, and I want them back this minute!" Angela's small naked foot tapped upon the polished

122

wood floor, eyes snapping back to the girl who stood trembling at the duke's side.

Royce sighed: so this was what all the ruckus was about. "Abigail, you can go about your duties. I can handle this affair." Royce reached out and relieved the frightened maid of the robe and slippers. As she turned and hurried back down the stairs, he turned his gaze upon Angela. "I suggest, Angela, that we retire to your chamber. I am sure that the servants have already gained an earful." And an eyeful, Royce thought to himself, frowning as he glimpsed the knot of silk tucked between her breasts.

"What do I care what your servants hear? All I want is my things and to get out of this madhouse!" Though Angela was angry, she did not fight off the hand that took her by the elbow and began to lead her back down the hall to her chamber.

As the door shut behind them, Angela swung around to face the man that was hell-bent on tormenting her life. Standing with the robe and slippers in hand, he appeared even more handsome in fawn-colored breeches and white shirt opened at the throat than she remembered him from the night before. With this silent admission, she was reminded of the scene in the kitchen. Instantly she thought of what she was wearing, and her hand went automatically to the knot of silk at her bosom.

Royce's silver gaze was involuntarily drawn to the tempting outline of her full breasts. As her alluring curves filled his vision, he sucked in a ragged breath. "Why did you not wear the gown that you were given by Mrs. Biesely?" he softly questioned, eyes still centered upon her hands which played with the silken knot.

"I don't want anyone else's clothes! I want my own!" she declared. She was not about to tell this brute about her people's belief that white is the color for mourning the loss of a loved one, nor would she admit to him that she couldn't sleep throughout the night with the gown on.

"I thought that we had decided last night that you would try to be a little more agreeable over the course of the next year."

"You mean that *you* decided that I would go along with whatever order you cared to dish out!" Angela snapped back.

"Be that as it may appear at this time," Royce relented, finding her language rather odd. "The bet I made with Damian is one that I confess I am loath to set aside. I have wanted that stallion since first setting eyes on him." He hoped that if he tried to be reasonable she would calm down.

"That's all that matters, isn't it, Lord High-and-mighty? You want a horse, so you think that you can hold me prisoner in this bloody cold mausoleum, whether I want to be here or not!"

Royce was at a loss for words. Her rejoinder confused him. All he could do was gaze upon her incredible beauty, almost forgetting the reason that had brought her to Westfield Hall.

It was Angela who broke the quiet that had settled around them. Drawing a deep steadying breath, she felt the sting of unshed tears in the back of her eyes. "If you will return my clothes and find my jewelry, I will leave here and find my own people. You can find something else to bet upon in order to gain the horse you seem so bent upon owning."

Royce was not about to admit that she was more than likely right, because the fact was, it was more than the bet and its outcome that drove him now. Perhaps it had become the challenge of seeing for himself this wild Gypsy beauty turned into a presentable young lady in a year's time. Perhaps it was her stubbornness that made him want to oppose her, but whatever it was, he was not about to hand over her clothes and jewelry and let her walk out of his life. "I have locked your trinkets away for the time being. They are secure, and at the end of the year, they will be returned to you with the promised purse filled with gold coins."

"You what?" Angela's cheeks flushed a bright red. *"You* took my things off the night table?" She groaned aloud, knowing that to have done so, he must have come into this chamber while she was sleeping. She could only pray that she had been covered with the satin coverlet, for her usual habit was to kick herself free of any coverings at night! She felt as embarrassed as the night before when he had stripped away the binding over her breasts.

But as swiftly, embarrassment turned to anger, and she began to shout, "You can't treat me like this! There are laws and I know my rights!" Her first thought was to run and find a telephone and call the police to report the theft and this man for trying to hold her here against her will!

A finely arched dark brow rose above one silver-gray eye. "And pray tell, what rights can a Gypsy thief have?" His words held a touch of humor. "Be assured, my little Gypsy brat, that Newgate still awaits you with open arms." Royce knew now that he was only making an idle threat. He would never be able to send such a beauty to that horrible prison! If a disease did not bring her low, then surely one of the guards or another prisoner would!

If nothing else held the power to shatter all of her illusions of having any rights, the name of the dreaded prison, Newgate, held such power! *A telephone, indeed!* She could have laughed aloud at her own lapse of time and place if she did not feel so like weeping. "I won't wear those clothes! I want my own things!" She tried to show him that his threat did not hold the power to frighten her, but her voice was not as strong as it had been earlier. For the time being, she was forced to go along with him, but there were certain limits to how far she would go! She was determined that at the first opportunity she would escape him and this Hall! In order to carry out this deed, she would need her own clothes!

"Your clothes have been disposed of, and until more can be made, you will have to make do with what there is at the Hall. I have sent Hawkins into the city this morning to bring a seamstress back here to start on your wardrobe. With any luck, they should be back by mid-afternoon." Royce knew that the letter of promised payment he had sent along with Hawkins would assure the finest dressmaker in London to hurry out to the Hall.

Jutting her chin stubbornly, Angela sat down in one of the chairs before the hearth. "Then this will have to do until the seamstress arrives." Holding the knot of silk above her bosom as though a shield of armor, her blue eyes clashed with gray. If he thought that she would wear that white garment, he had another thought coming!

"Then suit yourself!" Royce threw the robe and slippers onto the opposite chair. If the stubborn chit wanted to be locked in her chamber all day wearing a sheet, then far be it from him to try and change her mind! In fact the Hall would run far smoother with her out of sight! She held the rare talent of rubbing everyone the wrong way, including his servants!

"When the seamstress arrives, she will be brought directly here to your chamber." He turned without a backward glance and left the room.

As the door closed, a consuming anger overcame Angela, and without a second thought, she picked up the nearest object and sent it sailing toward the oak portal. A rare figurine shattered into a hundred tiny pieces, and still Angela felt no release to her fury. Slinging the robe and slippers to the floor, she stomped upon them with a heated display of temper, as she raged at her lack of freedom and at the man who imposed his demands upon her. How dare he dispose of her clothes! How could she flee this dreadful place without them? The life of a Gypsy was one that was carefree; how could she tolerate being caged in this pampered prison while being forced to do another's will?

The Duke of Westfield stood outside the chamber door, and hearing the crash, his breath released in a sigh. How on earth was he supposed to deal with such a wild, impetuous young woman? Perhaps in the letter he had penned to Damian this morning, which he had sent with Hawkins, he should have called off the bet instead of requesting his friend to keep quiet about the circumstances of his houseguest. Hearing her ranting and stomping on the other side of the door, he slowly started down the hall. Perhaps it would be for the best if he took himself away from the Hall entirely. Last night he had thought that he would have her removed to another chamber, but now he wondered if a greater distance was not required between them. He could easily conduct the wench's training from his London town house, and in this fashion, he would not be available for her ready temper, nor would he have to contend with his body's attraction to her. Going directly to his chamber, instead of the dining room where earlier he had intended to partake of a peaceful meal, he began to pack the few things that he would need to take with him from the Hall.

An hour later, Royce St. James stood once again in Angela's bedchamber. "I will be leaving Westfield Hall for my London town house. I wish for you to do what you are told by Hawkins. He will be sent instructions about your care. There will be tutors and instructors sent to the Hall, who will begin your education in the ways of a lady. I would wish for you to do all that you can to earn the purse of gold that you will be gaining at the end of the year."

Royce wanted to confront her this one last time before leaving Westfield Hall. He tried to ignore his body's response to her voluptuous beauty as she stood to the side of the fourposter bed wearing nothing but the silk sheet. Remaining businesslike, he told himself that she was only a Gypsy wench, and if not for the bet made with Damian, he would hand over her clothes this minute and be rid of her!

"My jewelry and the coins for my hair?" was the only response that Angela made to his announcement that he was leaving the Hall. The hair coins, though not valuable, had been a gift to her mother from her father. They were beyond any price to her, for they were all that Aunt Opal had allowed her to keep when she had been placed in Momma Leona's care.

"As I told you earlier, Angela, I have put them away where they will remain safe until the end of the year." Recognizing the glitter of anger coming into her blue eyes, he softly sighed, not wishing to go through another argument with this woman. "Listen, Angela, everything that you will need will be provided for you here at Westfield Hall. Everything that you came to the Hall with, except those foul clothes, you will leave with. You might realize that you are the one who will gain from this whole ordeal. You will have a fat purse, and I will also allow you to keep the clothes that will be fashioned for your use while you are here at the Hall."

Clothes that he will want her to wear when he would parade her around in front of his friend! Angela told herself, but at the moment she was wise enough to keep those thoughts to herself. If he was going to leave the Hall, perhaps things would not be so bad after all. If he were not here, there would be little reason for her to run away from this fancy estate. The two meals she had been given had been served on a silver tray, and there had been more food than she had been allowed to eat in a two-week period under Momma Leona's care. The room she was in held more comfort than anything she had ever known before. As she stood there, she knew she had no place else to go! She had no idea where she would find some of her own people and was not certain that she would be able to survive on her own in this

131

strange time period. She had believed herself capable of handling any situation in her own century, but she had already learned that the people in this time were more wary than those in her century. They were not so easily taken off their guard as those tourists and rich people of the twentieth century.

Taking a long, careful look at the man standing in front of her, her gaze roamed over the antiquated clothing that adorned his robust frame. Dark trousers were tightly molded over muscular thighs and hips, white stockings encased his calves, and diamond buckles glittered on his shiny, black shoes. His waistcoat was of black satin with silver shots running up and down the length. A snow-white shirt of fine linen boasted a row of ruffles down the front and at his wrists. His midnight hair was combed back and tied at the nape of his neck with a small length of ebony silk ribbon. Apparently he preferred this style to the numerous wigs of the day. Angela had to admit that even in this silly-looking getup, he was one fine specimen of a man.

A light blush flushed her cheeks. "It's a deal, Duke. You give me my possessions and a purse of gold at the end of the year, and I will endeavor to become the lady that you can flaunt in front of your fancy friend. In so doing, I will help you to win your coveted horse, than I will be free to leave."

If he wasn't going to be here at the Hall, then she would stay until a better opportunity presented itself. She held no guilt about making this promise knowing that she might break it any day. The first thing to do would be to find the safe where he had placed her jewelry and hair coins. Once finding it, she would see if her nimble fingers were as talented in this time period as they had been in her own. Mateo had taught her at an early age how to conquer a combination safe by listening to the tumblers. If the duke's safe was anything like those she had opened in the past, whenever she did decide to leave the Hall, she would have all of her possessions. For a moment she wondered if there even were combination locks in 1745!

Royce was surprised by her easy compliance. Though he knew that he should be happy at her agreeable response, a trail of anger began to burn within his chest as soon as he realized that she had only agreed to stay on here at the Hall because of his announcement that he would be taking his presence to his London town house. Why the hell would he care what her reason? As long as she was agreeable and he won Raven Boy at the end of the year, what did it matter how he won her acquiescence? As soon as he reached the city, he would go directly to Belinda's house and lose all thoughts of this Gypsy brat in the welcomed flesh of his mistress's body!

But even as he turned away from her and started toward the chamber door, he knew that her image would be forever imprinted in his brain. He also knew that even Belinda's talents of seduction would be hard-pressed to drive the vision of the Gypsy enchantress from his mind!

Nine

Within the hour, the gold-crested Westfield carriage was pulling away from Westfield Hall. Standing alone before her
chamber's double-paned windows, which
faced the front grounds of the vast estate,
Angela watched until the impressive vehicle
and matching team drove down the long
lane and disappeared from sight.

Left alone in the bedchamber, still adorned
in a sheet, Angela anxiously began to pace
the room. She was relieved that the overly
handsome Royce St. James had left Westfield
Hall. With his presence gone, she would be
able to concentrate on trying to find some way
to return to her own time and life. If she
could figure out what had sent her back to
this century, then perhaps she could reverse
the event.

It still seemed impossible that she was a
time traveler, but as each hour passed and she

remained at Westfield Hall, she was forced to admit that she was not dreaming. *No dream could possibly be this crazy!* Sitting before the hearth, she tried to remember what had taken place yesterday morning, from the moment she had awakened by the pond. So much had happened since, that everything was becoming jumbled in her mind. The realization that Momma Leona, the children, the trailer, and the other Gypsy families were no longer in the park, the long walk into the city. . . . As she searched her memory, she could not discover anything that could account for her departure from the twentieth century!

Later in the afternoon, Ethel entered the chamber carrying a tea tray and glimpsing Angela stretched out on the bed with her arm thrown over her eyes, she set the tray near the bedside on the night table. Without looking up, Angela knew that one of the servants had entered her chamber. "Lord, I would kill for an aspirin!" she murmured aloud, the pounding in her temples intensifying with her effort to speak and forcing a small groan from her lips.

"An aspirin, ma'am?" Ethel was unsure what the young woman was talking about, but she held little doubt that she was indeed capable of murder! She was not about to forget the blood lust in those dark blue eyes that she had seen last night as the girl had held the butcher knife in her fist.

Angela peeked out at the girl standing near the side of the bed. "I have a terrible headache and would love an aspirin or some Tylenol to try and get rid of it." She remembered then that aspirin hadn't been invented yet.

"Me mum always says that the best cure for such an ailment of the head is a bit of lilac scent mixed with water." Without a second thought, the undermaid went to the washbowl and began to prepare the mixture. Dipping a cloth into the bowl, she made her way back to the bed and nervously placed the damp cloth upon Angela's brow, her body tensed in case the young woman should strike her. "This should ease you, ma'am. When you feel up to it, your tea is right here. Also, Hawkins and the dressmaker have arrived downstairs. I expect that they will be coming up to your chamber shortly."

The soothing cloth felt good against Angela's brow. With a small smile, she thanked the maid for her kindness and assured her that she would be well enough to receive the dressmaker shortly. She didn't want to go about any longer than necessary with this sheet as her only covering.

Ethel smiled. Perhaps the young woman

had just gotten off on the wrong foot here at Westfield Hall, she reasoned.

When Angela once again opened her eyes and found herself alone in the chamber, she also realized that her headache had eased. As she was pouring herself a cup of tea, the chamber door once again was opened and Ethel entered the room.

"I'm so sorry to disturb you again, ma'am," the maid hastily said.

"Call me Angela," Angela invited with a smile. "Oh, by the way, thanks for the cloth you laid across my forehead. Amazingly, it worked!"

With a wide grin, Ethel nodded her head, pleased with herself for having a hand in helping this young woman. As for calling this young woman by her given name, she was not sure, but she reasoned that the duke had left the Hall without verifying the woman's position, so if the young woman wished for her to be called Angela, far be it to argue with her! "Hawkins sent me to tell you that the dressmaker and his entourage will be coming up to your chamber now. The original seamstress, Madam Devereux, was unable to come out to the Hall due to an illness. Instead she sent her brother to see to your wardrobe." Ethel then enquired if Angela needed more tea. When the young woman replied in the negative, the maid left.

A short time later, in a virtual whirlwind of color, attendants, boxes, and bundles, Blade Devereux entered Angela's bedchamber with the hustle and bustle of one who is in perpetual activity. Unable to take her eyes from the colorful figure, Angela watched as the tall, thin man, given to extravagant movements and mannerisms, hurried his workers into the chamber and issued rapid-fire instructions. "Set those bolts of cloth down over there to the side of the bed, Edna." "Those boxes can go in that corner." "You . . . you, Yvette. Wipe that stricken look off your face, my dear, and set those boxes of laces over here!"

As the young women hurried to do as instructed, the flamboyant dictator, hand resting upon one thin hipbone, mumbled heatedly under his breath, but so all could hear, "It is quite beyond me how my dear sister can abide such namby-pamby women around her all the time!"

It was some minutes before the bold character wearing a purple cape and scarlet short-waisted jacket and breeches appeared satisfied with the execution of his orders. Peering around the room, he turned his attention at last upon the woman standing before the hearth, who wore no more than a thin sheet.

Whipping off his flowing cloak and without a single thought to where it would land or who would pick it up, he slowly advanced upon the beautiful young woman with the cascading dark hair. With slow, purposeful intent, his sparkling black eyes roamed over every inch of her form. Exhaling, he spun around, and snapping his fingers together, he quickly called out, "You, shoemaker."

His high-pitched voice singled out the little man who was still standing near the doorway with Hawkins, peering into the chamber. "Come quickly, for goodness sake! What was the purpose of your being dragged along in the carriage during that godawful ride if you are going to stand across the room and gape like a dim-witted peasant? Come over here and trace Mademoiselle's tiny foot, then you can be gone! We have much work that must be done and have little time to idle around!"

The shoemaker ambled over to where Angela stood before the fireplace. "Please sit in the chair, mistress," he requested as he began to pull supplies from a small box which would allow him to make his tracings. His gaze went back and forth from his work to Blade Devereux, who now stood over him, intent upon watching his every movement for the slightest mistake.

With the tracings finished, the little shoemaker was relieved when Hawkins showed him out of the bedchamber, then took him to a room of his own where he would be able to set about his work. He had had more than enough of Blade Devereux on the ride out to the Hall! The man was in a never-ending hurry and expected those around him to be of the same nature! His watchful eye would ensure no shortcuts as the shoemaker had expected when first commissioned for the job of making shoes for the duke's houseguest.

"Now, my petite mademoiselle, let us have a look at what must be done to give you the most astounding wardrobe of any woman in all of Europe!" With both men out of the chamber, only Blade and his assistants remained.

He reached down a hand and pulled Angela to her feet. Angela felt her cheeks reddening under his close perusal as he turned her this way and that at arm's length. Turning her around one last time, he halted his inspection at last and declared, "Ah, loveliness indeed!"

He boldly kissed the tips of his fingers, his dark eyes lingering on the perfection of her heart-shaped face. "Hawkins told me very little about you when he visited my sister's shop, so I must make my own opinions. This is only possible through inspection." He boldly winked as his gaze lowered to her full breasts which were straining against the fabric of the sheet. "You are a very lucky mademoiselle, indeed. Many lesser endowed females would kill for a small portion of your charms." Turning her around once again, he murmured, "And such a nicely rounded posterior! Simply superb!"

Angela's cheeks flamed a bright scarlet at his pronouncements. Embarrassment was short-lived as he swept his fancy wide-brimmed hat, with its colorful peacock feather, off his head and bent with a courtly bow. "Truly, mademoiselle, this is your lucky day! My dear sister is very ill with the gout and was unable to come out to the Hall, but I, Blade Devereux, have most graciously agreed to take her place. You, my petite belle, can be assured of the most artful, most spectacular wardrobe in the whole of England!"

Angela held little doubt of the truth of his words. No man could be this boastful without good reason. A hesitant smile teased her lips. Her hand went to the knot between her breasts to ensure its security as her dark head lightly nodded.

"You and I, my dear, shall become great friends. You can call me Blade, instead of Monsieur Devereux, just like those closest to me!" It was not often that Blade Devereux had the opportunity to show off his amazing dressmaking talents. For the most part, he created gowns and an assortment of other ladies' apparel behind the closed doors of his sister's shop. With the invitation from the Duke of Westfield, he could not allow his sister Loretta to turn down the sizable purse that they would gain by creating an entire wardrobe for the duke's houseguest. He and Loretta had both been taught the art of fashioning and sewing women's clothing by their mother, who had owned a dress shop in Paris years before. Though Blade was the more talented of the pair of siblings, it had become his habit to stay in the background when it came to dealing with the many women customers who frequented the shop.

Stretching out her slender hand, Angela warmly invited in return, "You may call me Angela, Blade."

With formalities set aside, Blade, still holding tight to Angela's hand, began to pull her across the chamber toward the many boxes and bundles. "Oh, my dear Angela, you will be thrilled at all of the delightful bolts of cloth that I have brought!" he giggled. Angela glimpsed his assistants rolling their eyes heavenward.

"There is little daylight left, so we will not pull everything out of the containers, but girls," here he directed a pointed look at the four young assistants, having seen their lack of respect a minute earlier, "we will retrieve the nightrail and morning dress that was brought for Angela's use until more appropriate garments can be arranged."

The four assistants jumped to attention; they may be daring enough to roll an eye, but none were brave enough to openly rebel. Not one of them had ever worked directly for Blade Devereux, instead having been given their orders by Loretta, but as all valued their positions at the dress shop, they did not want to appear contrary. Hurrying to the numerous boxes, they began to rummage through the contents until they found the objects that their employer's brother desired.

"Yes, yes, yes!" With a flurry of hand motion, the man swept assistants aside as he gathered the flame red nightrail and the violet-sprigged morning dress with its white lace edging, into his own hands. "I knew that this would be the rage when that delightful fellow Hawkins described your coloring!" Blade beamed as he held up the satin nightrail for her inspection. "The gown may need a tuck here and a tuck there to fit properly, but we will worry over that in the morning."

Angela smiled her appreciation at the man and the clothing. It would be a delight to wear something other than this sheet!

Taking the bright red nightgown into her arms, she anxiously waited for the moment when she could put it on.

Spreading the morning dress over the back of a chair to allow the wrinkles to disappear, Blade Devereux turned around swiftly, his full weight upon a heeled purple shoe. Facing his attendants, he said, "Well, if you ladies are ready, I think we should find that nice Hawkins fellow and see where we retire for the evening. I fear that that horrible ride from London has about done me in, and I am absolutely famished!"

Pulling a large pink, lace-edged hanky from his inside vest pocket, he wiped an imaginary worry frown from his brow. Before heading to the door, he turned back toward Angela and bowed low. With a flashing grin he promised, "I always rise early, La Belle. Shall we meet here in your chambers at, say, nine of the morning!"

"That will be fine, Blade," Angela nodded, then watched as the group of women and their flashily dressed employer left her bedchamber.

After her supper, again brought to her chamber upon a silver tray, and a leisurely bath before the warm hearth, Angela put on the red satin nightgown, and then with little else to do, she climbed onto the large bed.

This was certainly the life of leisure! Never

had she ever felt so pampered. Perhaps she would remain here at the Hall for the full year, after all. As long as Royce St. James was not around badgering her, she rather enjoyed the attention and the luxurious lifestyle.

She remembered the duke as she had seen him last in her bedchamber. She did have to admit that he was indeed a handsome man. She envisioned his tight-fitting trousers and the width of the jacket across his broad shoulders. His glistening black hair appeared even more splendid as she saw him behind closed eyelids. It was too bad that the man was such an obnoxious, overbearing boor, she thought, recalling everything he had put her through since their first meeting. The humiliation, the condescension, the prejudice . . . A lone tear slipped from her closed eye and rolled down her smooth cheek. She punched the soft pillow trying to find a more comfortable position for her head, wishing it were the duke whom her small fists were pounding. She would show that damn man, and everyone else here at the Hall, that she was not someone for them to step on or look down upon!

She would learn all that she could! She would become the fine lady that they desired, Lord Dunsely would lose his treasured horse, and the Duke of Westfield, he would . . . What would he lose? she pondered silently.

What could such a stubborn, dominating man lose that would set him low?

Well, she would have plenty of time to find the answer to that question. But, with a full belly and feeling deliciously clean from her bath, she soon lost this train of thought and fell into a deep slumber.

It was within the balmy fold of her dreams that Angela was disturbed by the virile presence of the Duke of Westfield. In the hazy world of her deepest unconsciousness, he was not the sardonic blackguard that she had seen earlier. He stood before her handsomely imposing, hands reaching out, not to capture but to soothe the flesh of her upper bare arms. He was hypnotic in pursuit of her as his gray gaze held her blue eyes gently. As his dark head bent down to her and those sensual lips slanted over her own, she felt herself melting against him.

He drew her against his broad chest, the heavy thumping of his heart revealing his inner feelings as large hands caressed the upper length of her body. The fire of his touch seared through the satin material of her nightgown. As his hands gathered her buttocks and pulled her firmly to him, she felt his great need for her.

A soft moan of pent-up desire escaped Angela's lips and broke through her dream. Reaching out, she touched the imagined silken strands of midnight hair at the nape of his neck. Never had she felt anything so wondrously soft. His mouth moved against hers, his tongue pushing through her small, pearl white teeth and circling and plundering. His hands touched the outlined fullness of her breasts as her rose-hued nipples strained for attention. His touch lowered, fleetingly soft as the brush of a butterfly's wing, slipping across her ribs and belly as her breath clutched in her chest. She felt a strange, fiery need swelling and rising within her depths, and as his hand brushed against the heat of her womanhood, she clutched tightly to his broad shoulders. "Royce," she murmured.

He drew back, his handsome visage appearing darkly sinister as a sneer pulled back his sensual lips. "Did you think that a duke could enjoy the embrace of a dirty little Gypsy?" he questioned before he rose up before her and slowly, in a haze, drew farther away, until at last he disappeared into the dark shadows and mists of her dream world.

With his departure, the dream burst around her, and Angela awoke with a groan. "Damn his bloody soul to the fiery pits of hell!" she cried aloud as she thumped the pillow and rolled to her stomach. Tomorrow she would break into his safe and claim what belonged to her! The duke may think her of little importance, but he would realize upon his return to the Hall that she was not as insignificant as he believed!

Royce St. James was in a similar state, wishing nothing more than to be able to rid himself of the plaguing image of the Gypsy brat whom he had left behind at Westfield Hall. After arriving at his London town house, he had made the rounds at a few clubs which he frequented when in the city, but finding no release in drink from his troubled thoughts, he told himself that the best place to forget the Gypsy wench would be in the arms of his latest mistress.

Lying back on the satin pillows of her bed, his silver-gray gaze swept slowly over Belinda Thompson's lush form. There was no getting around it: Belinda was a very beautiful woman. Her blond hair was piled atop her lovely head instead of being be-wigged. Alone in her chambers, she wore only a see-through shift, which plainly revealed her womanly attributes. Her over-abundant breasts were straining against the lacy bodice of the shift, full hips curved and inviting to any male eye.

As she started toward him, two glasses of brandy in hand, his eyes took in the sultry sway to her walk—and he found himself not as sexually attracted to her as he had been.

Setting her glass of brandy down upon the small table at the side of the bed, she stretched out her body invitingly at his side as she handed him his drink. Her free hand brushed back a wayward lock of ebony hair from his forehead, as she purred, "I was so pleased that you decided to stay here in the city, Royce. I grow so bored and lonely when you take yourself to Westfield Hall!"

Royce heard her pouting tone, and for the first time since meeting her over four months ago, her actions and voice irritated him. Sitting up straighter against the headboard, he pulled her hand away from his head and slowly swallowed the amber brew.

His peevishness was not lost upon Belinda, and lowering her hand, she pulled herself away from his side and made her way to her dressing table. She had realized tonight when he had first entered the cozy little brownstone house, which he had rented for her, that something was bothering him. Picking up her hairbrush, she cautiously eyed the attractive man upon her bed. "You needn't be so abrupt with me, Royce dear."

She could not help the edge to her tone. She was used to men fawning over her wherever she went. She feared that Royce's treatment of her this evening could be the first signs that he was tiring of her. She had experienced a similar ordeal two years ago when she had given her favors to a married gentleman. Lord Selby had lavished her with expensive gifts, had rented her marvelous apartments near the palace, and then one day he had missed an engagement. Before long, one engagement ran into another. Then he was out of her life entirely, reunited with his plump little wife and living on his country estate. Upon reflection, Belinda knew that the other men in her life had never truly mattered. No man, present or past, mattered to her like Royce St. James. She had never known a lover with as much stamina as the Duke of Westfield!

"I should have returned to my town house this evening, instead of arriving here at your house, Belinda," Royce murmured in way of an apology as he finished his drink. "I fear that I am poor company, and do ask for your forgiveness." If only he could cast from his mind the image of that dark-haired vixen and those challenging blue eyes!

Belinda Thompson knew full well that she would forgive Royce St. James anything that he desired. He was the best catch in England, and she would not let him grow tired of her! Her nightly dreams were of becoming the Duchess of Westfield. Her aspirations were so high that she could overlook insults, endure implied slights, in order to achieve her goals.

"Why do you not tell me what is ailing you, my love?" She set the hairbrush down and approached the bed. Stretching out next to him, she pressed herself against his side. Her nails stole over broad shoulders and down his long muscular arms, anticipating the moment when he would not only remove his shirt, but also the rest of his clothing!

Royce turned to face her, his metallic gaze searing her entire length with an appraising regard. He was becoming quite angry with himself. As his gaze swept over Belinda's lush form, each feature he had been attracted to in the past, he now compared to the Gypsy wench back at Westfield Hall. Belinda's shoulder-length blond curls held little comparison to the long, lush, curling tresses of midnight black that he had silently caressed the night before when he had stolen into Angela's chamber. Belinda's warm, brown eyes, which were looking at him questioningly, were dull compared to the sparkling blue eyes of the Gypsy girl. Belinda's lips, whose soft, pouting petals had held the power to pull his inner control apart, now left him cool and emotionless as he wondered about the taste of the berry-red, full lips of the woman that plagued him to distraction.

"Damn!" he swore. Even here, in another woman's bed, she held the power to torment him! She must have cast some strange spell over him that he was having a hell of a time resisting!

"I am sorry, Belinda, but I must return to my town house. I . . . I have forgotten to take care of a matter of some importance," Royce said, pulling on his jacket. He would have to set his mind aright before he would be pleasant company for any woman, let alone of a mind to sample his mistress's inviting charms.

Belinda did not say a word as he stood next to her bed making himself ready to leave. Where Royce St. James was concerned, it would do little good to beg for his attentions. Her tempting form leaned into the satin pillows, watching his every movement. "You will return soon, won't you, Royce?" she softly questioned as he started toward the door without a word.

Turning around, as though only now remembering where he was, Royce stated more gently, "I will send you word upon the morrow, Belinda, as to when you might expect me. Perhaps we shall take a ride in the park soon."

Belinda brightened. Perhaps he was not

growing bored with her as she had feared, but, in truth, did have business matters on his mind. There was much intrigue going on at court. Perhaps Royce was embroiled in it. There was the rumor that the King would be enforcing the dismissal of the ministry soon. With people like the Pelhams and Granville holding the court, and George II in a constant uproar, it was more than possible that the Duke of Westfield was caught up in some dark politics.

Until this evening, she had believed herself having a tight hold upon the duke, but now she was not certain. If a problem at court or some quibble over one of his properties could so distract him as to force him to leave her bed, she would have to intensify her seduction of Royce St. James in order to ensure that she would one day become his duchess!

Ten

Over the next few days, Angela's bed-chamber became the center of activity at Westfield Hall. Each morning, Blade Devereux sailed into the room and issued harried orders. With the clap of his hands, he would order one of his assistants to fetch a width of lace; a snap of his fingers, and he would have another young woman jumping from her seat to cut a yard of material or send another to sew a fine seam. There were fashions to be looked over and decided upon, colors to be chosen, and long hours of fittings to be conducted. Angela was forced to endure many hours with arms outstretched and back ramrod straight as she was turned this way and that before Blade's searching inspection.

Near the end of the week, when the bolts of materials and lengths of lace and ribbons appeared at last to be taking shape as ladies' apparel, Angela stood in the center of her bedchamber, her breath indrawn after having been squeezed into a gown by two of Blade's assistants. "Oh, Blade, this is killing me! It is far too tight!" she cried. The gown was obviously too small, the bodice so constricting she was gasping for a breath of air.

Straightening from his kneeling position at the hem of the gown, Blade took one look at her and shrieked, "Yvette! Yvette! Come here, you mindless girl!"

Standing with both hands on his hips, he waited for the young woman to rush into the chamber from a nearby room that had been set up for stitching and assembling. "Just look what you have done to la belle Mademoiselle!" he seethed.

Yvette's slender hand rose to her throat as she saw the mistake. The material had been stitched too tightly in the bosom area. "It is a simple thing. I can quickly enough remedy the mistake," she assured him.

One of the other girls had done the stitching on this gown, but Yvette was not about to bring down Blade Devereux's wrath upon anyone else's head. She was the senior seamstress, and she should have checked the gown. Such a mistake would never slip past her eye again!

"It is a simple thing? Easily enough remedied?" Blade began to shout, and Angela could see Yvette visibly gulping back a gasp of fear. "The mademoiselle stands here with her bosom popping out of her gown, and you say 'tis a simple enough thing?"

"I . . . I certainly didn't mean to say . . ." Yvette tried to explain, but was given little chance.

"Out! Out of this chamber this minute!" Blade pointed a finger toward the chamber door, and as Yvette rushed to comply, his threat followed her out the door and down the hallway: "You had best hope that no more of Mademoiselle's gowns are in like condition, if you value your job!"

Blade hurriedly began to unbind the lacings that held the gown intact. "The whole lot of these silly chits that Loretta employs are absolutely impossible! They must believe that every woman is as flat-chested as themselves!" he fumed.

One again able to take in a deep breath, Angela found, to her surprise, that she was grinning widely. Only a few short days ago she had wished for all the world to believe that she also was flat-chested, but now she was gasping for breath and praying for a couple of more inches of material in the bodice of her gown! It was amazing how quickly her life was changing!

Blade caught her grin, and believing the moment of harm to have passed, he winked and simpered softly, "Perhaps our duke would not have minded so very much the sight of you spilling out of your gown, no, La Belle?"

Angela's grin slipped into a frown. Blade was quick to make amends for any unintentional offense. "Oh, but, Angela, I did not mean to imply—"

Angela did not allow him to finish. "I know what you mean, Blade, but the Duke of Westfield means nothing to me. I am here at the Hall only for a short time as his guest."

Though she and Blade Devereux had become friends in the past few days, Angela had not told the man what had brought her out to Westfield Hall. She could not tell him, or anyone else, that if not for the duke and his friend using her as their pawn, she would be this very moment sitting in Newgate!

Blade nodded his head, thinking it odd that the Duke of Westfield, or any man, would invest so heavily in a woman who claimed to be a mere guest, particularly one that was as beautiful as Angela. Ah well, he told himself, there was simply no understanding the way of the heart between a man and a woman.

By the end of the following week, the vast array of colorful gowns, riding habits, which Angela had helped to design with a split sewn between the full skirts, and every other mentionable and unmentionable portion of a lady's wardrobe had been completed.

As Angela stood surrounded by all her new finery, the wardrobe doors standing wide and articles of clothing, shoes, hats, parasols, and cloaks having yet to be put away, Blade Devereux, with attendants following behind, made his way into Angela's bedchamber to bid her farewell.

"When you come to London, La Belle, be sure that you visit me at my sister's dress shop. I know that all of Loretta's customers will be green with envy when they glimpse the beautiful gowns which I have fashioned for you. You and I will become the absolute rage!" The brightly bedecked dressmaker took her hand within his own and made a great show of kissing it, then set his emerald green hat, with its long ostrich feather, at a jaunty angle atop his bewigged head.

Angela doubted that she would ever have the opportunity to see Blade Devereux again, but all the same, she nodded. "I hope your sister is feeling better when you return, Blade. Please give her my best, and tell her that I am pleased with my new wardrobe." Though the gowns with their layers and layers of material were much more than Angela was used to and the whale-bone corsets more than a little impossible to bear, Angela had kept the gowns free of overmuch lace and ribbons, saying little about the corsets and farthingales that were stowed away in the wardrobe. She would wear the garments as she saw fit, and to her way of thinking, her waist was small enough!

For the next few days, Angela stayed mostly inside the large mansion that she now considered her shelter from the outside world, a world she no longer knew anything about. A tutor, Gerald Clemons, had arrived with a list of instructions from the duke. The stern-faced Mrs. Booth had also arrived at the Hall to take charge of Angela's everyday routine. With the first meeting of her charge, the older lady had boasted that she had held the privilege of teaching many a young lady the social graces.

Most of Angela's mornings were spent in the company of Mrs. Booth, who at every turn seemed to delight in admonishing Angela about her dress, her speech, her posture. There was little that Angela could say or do that did not draw the woman's attention, and the attention was always negative!

The afternoons with Gerald Clemons became a reprieve for Angela. In the study room, he always awaited her with a fresh supply of work. He was a kind, elderly man who had interesting stories to tell, along with bits of information to share about the time they were now living in. He had a simple knack for making her studies fun. Finding Angela an apt pupil who was willing to apply herself and listen to all that he could teach her, they got on quite well. The fact that Angela could read held the man's admiration. It was rare to find a woman who had been taught more than how to make her mark upon a piece of parchment.

This morning, Mrs. Booth entered Angela's chamber unannounced. Looking across the room at her charge, who was still stretched out on the fourposter bed, the deep frown lines across the older woman's forehead intensified. "Why have you not as yet left your bed and dressed, Angela?" At the sound of the strident voice, Angela kicked back the covers and made a sleepy attempt at rising. "A laggard gets nowhere in this world, miss, and mind you, a lady must not appear lazy or laggardly! It is enough, once married, to laze a morning away, but until that day, one must spend a morning readying oneself for the day!"

"Yes, Mrs. Booth," Angela murmured, knowing from past days under this woman's charge that it was no good arguing with this harridan! If she weren't so determined to show that damn duke that she could take whatever he could dish out, she would have left the Hall days ago.

Advancing upon the wardrobe across the room, Mrs. Booth pulled forth a rose-colored gown. "You will look quite comely in this gown today, miss, and after you finish your breakfast, we shall once again go over the proper use of cosmetics!"

Angela inwardly groaned. She had always been up and about early in the morning, but here at the Hall she saw little need to fret over the time that she arose, nor did she see much sense in spending hours of her day at her dressing table, being forced to apply the assortment of cosmetics that Mrs. Booth deemed proper for a lady to wear at all times!

"Did you say something, my dear?" Mrs. Booth looked sharply at her charge as she set the gown aside and began to pull from the wardrobe the undergarments and shoes that would accompany the dress. Left to her own devices, Mrs. Booth knew this young woman would go about the Hall like a hoyden, wearing the plainest of gowns without the proper undergarments! The first day of her arrival, when she had helped the young woman to disrobe that evening, she had been more than a little shocked at the sight of only a thin shift covering her form beneath her gown. She had quickly set out to

162

amend this outrage. Since then, she had faithfully arrived in Angela's chamber each morning to help her pick out her clothing for the day.

Angela grunted a response as she stepped to the commode and began to fill the bowl with fresh water from the pitcher.

"I asked you a question, Angela. When a question is put to you, you do not nod, grunt, or groan. Answer in a strong voice, girl. Now what was your reply?" Mrs. Booth found this young woman to be full of a strange vitality. Upon her arrival at the Hall, she had realized that she was going to have her hands full with the impossible task of turning this young woman into a proper young lady. It was beyond her reasoning why the Duke of Westfield would take it upon himself to be this young woman's guardian. She was being paid handsomely to teach this young woman all that she could, and she was beginning to realize that she was earning every coin to teach Angela the basics that most girls learned at an early age: How to sew a correct stitch, how to play a simple tune upon the spinet, how to dress properly for each occasion, and how to apply cosmetics correctly. With another long sigh, which she had been issuing more frequently of late, she stared hard at her charge.

"I heard you very well, Mrs. Booth." Angela knew that the old hag would not relent until she responded in the proper manner. She turned a becoming smile upon the battle-axe. "I will be more than delighted to wear this lovely gown that you have chosen for me, Mrs. Booth. I can't wait to sit through another one of those enjoyable cosmetic lessons." She cringed inwardly, wishing that she could let loose with her true feelings! She didn't dare, though, for fear that the old she-wolf would run screaming from her chamber for Hawkins to send word of her misbehavior to the duke.

Mrs. Booth wondered how she would be able to bear up to the ordeal of making a lady out of this rowdy creature. Even with the girl's sweet agreement, she could sense the rebellion that lay just beneath the surface.

By the time Angela finished dressing and ate her breakfast before the warm hearth, Mrs. Booth had arranged an assortment of cosmetics on the dressing table, for the lesson in application. "Now come along, dear, don't dawdle! The morning is almost at a finish, and Mr. Clemons will soon be waiting for you in the lesson room." Lord forbid she be forced to remain in the young woman's presence any longer than necessary, Mrs. Booth told herself as she thought of the pot of tea and pastry that would be waiting in her chamber at the end of the lesson.

Knowing that there was no way out of this, Angela was soon spreading full skirts over the Chinese silk-covered dressing table stool. Holding her hands folded in her lap, she dared not make the first move. She knew from experience that Mrs. Booth delighted in proclaiming her wrong.

"Before we begin with the cosmetics, Angela, I would like for you to tell me once again what this small box is used for and the contents within." She pointed to a small, gold-trimmed box sitting on the edge of the dressing table.

Angela could remember little about the box. Her interest had been elsewhere during yesterday's lesson. "Well, I believe that you said the box accompanied a lady when she went out without a servant at her side," she ventured, not sure if the box went along with the servant or without, but she took a chance.

"And the contents within the box?" Mrs. Booth's brow rose over a hawklike dark eye as though waiting to pounce on the smallest mistake. In fact, she was surprised that the girl had remembered this much. Yesterday she had been forced to pull the young woman away from the chamber window on more than one occasion; the girl seemed to have a most peculiar penchant for day-dreaming!

"The contents," Angela repeated, to gain some time. "Well," she at last remarked as she dredged her brain for any misplaced tidbit of information. "Well, I think that there are some bottles in the box."

"Bottles of what, my dear?" The arched brow had not yet lowered and the hard stare never wavered.

Lord God above, how was she supposed to remember all of this stuff? Bottles of what? It could have been alcohol that Mrs. Booth had said yesterday, but then on the other hand, it could have been medicine, or even poison, for all that she remembered! "Alcohol!" she said aloud, believing this her safest reply.

The brow instantly furrowed, and Mrs. Booth's dark eyes rose heavenward as though in supplication. She drew in a deep breath before she spoke again. "Pray tell, my dear, why on earth would a young lady go about with bottles of alcohol?" Jerking the lid off the box, Mrs. Booth pointed within. "There is no alcohol in the box! These small bottles contain an assortment of scents, these two at the top are aromatic vinegar. There is a pillbox, a snuffbox—if one is so inclined—and an extra fan if you have forgotten to carry one at your wrist."

Angela could hear the irritation in the older woman's voice, and looking down into the box, she dared not question her on the need for so many scents and the vinegar, but as a remembrance of the London streets came back to her, she told herself that she had answered her own question: the gentry could not be expected to go about enduring the odors from the open ditches of the London streets. A lady would be expected to douse her hanky with sweet scent and hold it up to her nose, while the rest of the populace went about their lives, used to the scent of living amongst the poor! Angela's own irritation surfaced with such thoughts of class separation.

Snapping the lid closed with a sharp clank, Mrs. Booth's attention was fully set upon her charge. "Let us hope that you do not forget again what is in the box! Now, why don't you show me what you remember about the cosmetics."

Was this another trap that the old woman had set? Angela wondered as she stared down at the assortment of cosmetics and the supply of bright red silk and black velvet paper that had been cut into circular or crescent shapes to form face patches. Gingerly her hand reached out and lifted the lid from the jar of foundation, which, unbeknownst to her, was made up of white lead.

167

Looking into the dressing-table mirror, she lightly applied this over her face. Next, she colored her high cheekbones with rouge—small strips of Brazilian red leather. There was an assortment of lipsticks in a variety of hues, some colored with carmine and others made from plaster of Paris. She chose a bright red, which made her own features appear even paler with the foundation. Her eyebrows had been trimmed the day before by Mrs. Booth, and now she darkened them with the lead combs that were placed in a small jar on the table.

As she finished, she gave herself an over-all look, and what she viewed brought on a small frown. She had never used cosmetics, Momma Leona believing them to be a wasted expense, and now, looking at the effect, she admitted that Momma Leona had been right! Not only were these cosmetics a waste of money, but they were also a waste of time to put on! She looked as pale as death with all this stuff smeared over her face, and the lipstick and dark eye makeup made her appear unnatural!

For the first time since meeting Mrs. Booth, the older woman smiled with genuine pleasure. "Why, my dear, you have done just perfectly! You look lovely, and that foundation covers that bit of darkness you have to your complexion!"

Good God, the woman must be blind or totally crazed to think that she looked becoming with this goop smeared on her face! Angela was wise enough to keep her thoughts to herself while the woman beamed.

"Well, if that is all, Mrs. Booth," she pushed the dressing-stool back away from the table, "I hate to keep Mr. Clemons waiting too long in the lesson room."

"Oh yes, of course, my dear. I had almost forgotten about Mr. Clemons and your lessons, so surprised was I at your ability to apply your cosmetics so well!" Looking down at the dressing table as the girl stood to her feet, the frown momentarily returned. "I guess you can do without the face patches. Many young women wear them as a means to hide the worst ravages of smallpox, but in your case, your skin is unblemished."

Angela could still remember the day when the state people had knocked upon Momma Leona's trailer door and had declared that all of her children had to go that afternoon for their smallpox vaccination!

"Tomorrow then, dear, we shall practice the art of wearing the proper wig for each occasion, and also how to powder and comb a wig. For now you may go. I am sure that Mr. Clemons is waiting."

On her way to the lesson room, Angela pulled out her handkerchief from her skirt

169

pocket and wiped away most of the makeup on her face. That godawful woman was driving her crazy, she told herself as she hurried away from the chamber. All *gorgios* were somewhat crazy, she knew, but this Mrs. Booth was a bit more so than the others she had met! It was too bad that all of these lessons would be a wasted effort. She would be gone from here when the year was up, and thank heaven for that! Wigs and makeup, what need did a Gypsy girl have for such things? Turning around to make sure that the old taskmistress was nowhere in sight, Angela hiked up her skirts over her knees and began to spring up the stairs and down the hallway on the third floor, where she would find Mr. Clemons waiting for her in the lesson room.

The main subject of today's lesson was Mr. Clemons's views on the government under the rule of George II. As Angela sat in her seat near the window, Gerald Clemons droned on and on about his favorite issue in this subject, that of the Tory back-benchers, to whom constant opposition in the government had become almost second nature, and the Whigs who held the upper hand. "As early as 1715, there has been a steady succession of defections from the Tory ranks, such as those for whom the attraction of office has become too much of a temptation. They

170

have forsaken their Tory heritage and have become Whigs."

Mr. Clemons pushed the wire spectacles back up the bridge of his slender nose as he looked at the young woman to insure that she was paying attention. She had a willing mind to learn, but oftentimes he found her attention far from the subject at hand. He should move her seat away from the window, where she was prone to peer out frequently and daydream. But at the moment she appeared to be paying attention. Perhaps as a reward he would call the lesson to a halt early this afternoon.

"As I told you, only days ago, the Young Pretender has already landed in Scotland. In fact last month shortly after his arrival on Scottish soil, the Stuart standard was raised at Glenfinnan, and Charles Edward began his march eastward, gathering support from the clans. Now, miss, you may mark my word that during our good King's absence—as you have already been informed, he left England for Hanover in May of this year—his three followers on the Regency Board, Bath, Tweeddale and Stair, are taking this matter of the Young Pretender far too lightly. I have been informed that there is rumor that the King is being beseeched to return to England, even at this hour!"

"And do you believe this Charles Edward

will get the support he desires from the High-landers?" Angela found the topic rather interesting.

"Aye, unfortunately, I think there will be many foolhardy souls throwing their lot in with the young Stuart." Mr. Clemons sadly nodded his head. "I am afraid that the Jacobites are in for a grand downfall." Gerald Clemons, like most good Englishmen, apart from a few Roman Catholic families in and around London, held scant enthusiasm for the Jacobite cause of setting James Stuart on the English throne.

"Jacobites?" Angela sounded the name upon her tongue and thought the word strangely familiar. Where had she seen that word before?

"I am content that George II will return to England and set the matter aright, but in the meantime I fear the damage that will be wrought on Scottish soil. With the King abroad and the ministry so bitterly divided, it appears that the efforts to organize resistance to the Stuart claims have been gravely impeded."

By the finish of her afternoon lessons, Angela was restless and her nerves were on edge. She went from the lesson room to her bedchamber, and finding little to hold her attention, she then made her way downstairs to the duke's study. Even though no one at the Hall besides Mrs. Booth ordered her about, she found that she was not used to the wealthy lifestyle. Looking at the numerous books on the shelves that lined one entire wall of the study, she stretched out her hand and ran it over a book that was covered in a rich, red moroccan leather binding. Like everything else in this house, these books were worth a fine fortune. A small smile settled over Angela's lips with the thought.

Her blue eyes were drawn across the room to the duke's desk. Her third evening here at the Hall, she had investigated the duke's study and had found where he kept his valuables.

The house had quieted, and Angela had, upon bare feet, silently made her way downstairs and into the duke's study. Entering the dark room, she had eased the door shut. Stepping to the fireplace, where dim coals burned in the grate, she had lit a candle.

Trying to keep as quiet as possible, she had started a diligent search for the duke's safe.

She was surprised not to find a wall safe behind any of the pictures, but then realized they might not have been invented yet. The answer to her search was easier than she thought: his desk.

One drawer was locked, and with a hairpin, it had taken her only a short time to open it. After listening at the door for footsteps coming down the hallway, she carelessly spilled the contents of the drawer atop the duke's desk. She had quickly removed her hair coins and jewelry, but she had not been able to avoid the temptation of admiring the duke's riches. There had been so many pieces of beautiful jewelry, she had lost count as she had gazed at the mounds of sparkling diamond and gem rings. There had been numerous pouches of coins and stacks of papers that looked like property deeds. The duke was more than wealthy, she thought to herself—he was fabulously rich!

Afraid to have Hawkins or another servant walk in and find her in the duke's study going through his desk, Angela had forced herself to return the contents to the drawer in the same order in which she had taken everything out, except for her own belongings. The hair coins and bracelets she had shoved into her skirt pocket and then had hidden them away in the farthest corner in the bottom of her wardrobe. If Momma Leona had seen her that night, the old, fat Gypsy woman would have clubbed her about the head for not taking the contents of the safe and running just as fast as her legs could take her away from Westfield Hall.

It was still not too late, Angela reminded herself as she stood caressing the books on the opposite wall. She could steal the Duke of Westfield blind and be gone from the Hall before he would realize that he had been wiped out!

Her thoughts were interrupted as Hawkins entered the study. Anyway, she told herself, she was in no hurry to flee the Hall. With Royce St. James gone, she had free run of the mansion. When she received word that he was going to return, perhaps she would think more on making off with the safe's contents.

Having had several weeks to adjust to this strange young woman roaming about the Hall, Hawkins was not quite as stern with her as before. There was something about this young woman, some strange quality of derring-do that oddly appealed to his strait-laced manner. "Is there anything that you would care for this afternoon, Miss Angela? Perhaps a tea tray brought in here to the study?"

His dark brow rose in question as he wondered if she had come to the duke's study to find a book. He had been told by Mr. Clemons that the young woman could read and write a legible hand, and being the only servant here at the Hall with such abilities, he was more than a little impressed with the Gypsy girl.

Angela declined the offer of a tea tray with a shake of her dark head. But remembering Mrs. Booth's stern admonishments about answering a question directly when spoken to, she lowered her hand from the bookshelf and softly replied, "I am fine for the time being, Hawkins. I think that perhaps I will take a walk in the gardens for a little while. I have been cooped up so long behind these walls, I do declare that I could use a bit of fresh air." Stepping through the study's French double doors, which had been standing wide, she felt the servant's eyes upon her as she made her way over the stone patio steps which led out into the back gardens behind the duke's study.

The gardens in the back of the estate were awash with brilliant colors. Many of the flowers were in bloom, the sculptured yews had been trimmed only the day before, and the lush fruit trees were hanging with fruit. Angela walked silently along the brick walkway, enjoying the feeling of the diminishing sunlight as she inhaled the late afternoon, cool breeze. Gazing at the gardens, she was impressed by the magnificence of Westfield Hall. The grounds around the gardens were immaculately kept: the lush green grass rolled on and on and then was met by dense forest on all sides. At the back of the estate were the large brick stables and paddocks, and on a sudden impulse, Angela ventured toward this area.

Approaching the large, double doors of the stable, Angela peered inside before venturing within. Seeing no one, she started to take a hesitant step into the dimly lit interior when a small elderly groomsman came up behind her.

Is there something I can be ahelping ye with, lass?"

Jumping in her tracks, Angela quickly turned around, blue eyes enlarging as her hand stole up nervously to her throat. "You all but scared the wits out of me!" she declared in a strangled voice.

"Now I be right sorry fur that, lass, but I spied ye peering into me stables and didn't know what ye were about."

"I was just curious!" Angela instantly took the defensive. "I thought that I would take a look at the duke's horses. No one told me that I couldn't."

"Ah now, lass, ye must be the duke's guest that be staying at the Hall. I've heard much talk about ye."

Angela could well imagine what the little man had been told. Though the servants about the Hall had warmed up to her, she doubted that any of them had forgotten her first night and the scene she had made on the second-floor landing her first morning at the Hall. Knowing that if this man had heard anything about her, it more than likely had come from one of the servants, she felt her cheeks beginning to blush.

"Well, lass, me name be Jamie, and I be the head groomsman fur the duke. He be a fine young fellow, the duke be. Why, I can be remembering when he was no taller than a pup and he would ride his little pony about the paddock fur hours on end."

Angela had not come to the stables to hear the merits of a man she so disliked. "Do you have any horses in the stables for riding?" she interrupted.

"Why, lass, the duke has fur himself one of the finest stables in all of England. King George himself has been out to Westfield Hall afore, and his Highness made comment right in front of me as how the duke has a fine stable of horseflesh!" There was pride in Jamie's words, and momentarily his thin chest puffed out. "Now if ye be wanting to go fur a ride, it be a bit late in the afternoon, but if ye decided at another time, ye come on out to the stables and give old Jamie a call. I be having one of the lads saddle ye a good mare that will take ye fur a pleasant-enough ride about the estate."

Angela beamed at the suggestion. As a young child, her father had worked on horse farms breaking and taming the wildest of beasts, and though it had been some years since Angela herself had ridden a horse, she had not forgotten the basics. Her dark feeling of confinement instantly fled as she looked forward to a long morning ride. "Perhaps tomorrow morning I could take a ride," she said, and a toothy smile split his face at her quick reply. "It will have to be early in the morning, though, for I have lessons every day, and that Mrs. Booth is not one to wait around while I go about the countryside upon horseback!" She would certainly report such an infraction to the duke, Angela thought to herself.

Jamie Templeton nodded his head in full agreement. As a widower these past ten years, Jamie had made it a point to meet Mrs. Booth after her arrival at the Hall. He was not averse to taking up a relationship with a likeable enough woman, but upon close inspection of the tight-lipped Mrs. Booth, he had immediately thought better of the notion. By all accounts, the woman held no patience for anyone or anything that was not exactly to her liking. She kept the servants hopping with her demands. It had been conveyed to him that more than once Hawkins himself had been at wit's end while dealing with the formidable matron. "I tell ye what, lass. I be having me stable boy, Gordon, ready Charmer fur ye. She will be ready at the first break of dawn."

Jamie grinned widely, pleased that he was

able to aid this young woman in passing an hour or so without being harassed and bullied by her teacher. To him, book learning was a waste of time; life was the best of teachers, he always said. Besides, with the girl around, the stables would be in use once again. Though Westfield Hall boasted some fine animals, they were seldom used. He could remember a time when the stables were a hub of activity. It would be like those early days when the duke's family was still alive!

"I shall be looking forward to the ride, Jamie." Angela smiled warmly upon the little man and watched as his ruddy cheeks flushed brighter.

Jamie had been told by Agnes, the upstairs maid, that this young woman was a bit touched in the head, but he saw no sign of such an affliction. He viewed only a true beauty. The duke was one lucky man, he thought as she turned and started back to the Hall.

Eleven

The Westfield stables became Angela's outlet for pent-up frustrations as the weeks passed into months. She rode early each morning if the weather permitted, before she had to face Mrs. Booth and her rigid drillings. Most days Mr. Clemons allowed her to finish her lessons early enough to have a second ride upon the back of the mare called Charmer. During these late-afternoon rides, she rode until she was exhausted, trying to drive plaguing thoughts from her mind. With each day that passed, they seemed to grow stronger. She was a captive in another lifetime, and she sought desperately for a way out; but all seemed a wasted effort as another day passed.

Angela held no illusions about her situation. The year would be up eventually, and she would be once again on her own. She tried not to think about the duke and the day when he would return to the Hall. She tried to make some kind of plan for her own future. She would have the purse of gold that he had promised her, and in the back of her mind, she thought that she could always steal a few trinkets from the duke's drawer. With so many baubles, he might not even miss a ring or two if she took them! But some fear, or newly found judgment of right and wrong, would not let her dwell on this thought of thievery. If she were not able to find some way to return to her own century, though, she would have to have the means to survive in an England that she no longer knew.

She would need all of the knowledge that she could possess by the year's end. Thanks to Royce St. James, she was learning a lot from Mr. Clemons. Grudgingly she admitted that Mrs. Booth had taught her much about the lifestyle and manners of those in this century. She knew that she had enough knowledge about manners and dress to fool anyone into thinking that she was a part of the gentry. Still, she was determined that she would find her way back to her own century! Being on her own with no family or friends left her feeling empty and afraid.

One day she had approached Gerald Clemons on the subject of traveling through time. Unaware that the young woman was being serious, the tutor had laughed uproariously. "Stepping back in time, indeed!" he had chortled as his spectacles steamed with moisture from tears of mirth. "You, young lady, have the most wonderful imagination of any young woman that I have ever had the privilege of meeting!" Never had he had another student as bright and inquisitive as this young woman!

This had not been the reaction that Angela had wanted, but what more could she have expected? Had she truly believed that a man in the seventeen hundreds would calmly discuss with a mere woman the possibility of someone traveling through time?

Occasionally a letter arrived at the Hall from the Duke of Westfield, and this day, another long list of instructions had come by messenger along with a box for Mr. Clemons containing a telescope, with instructions that he was to teach his pupil something about the stars. Why on earth would that insufferable man think that she should learn something about the stars? Angela questioned as she kicked Charmer's sides and set the mare into motion. Would she need to know such information when she left the Hall? She planned to find some of her own people, and a Gypsy didn't need a telescope to watch the stars to know in what direction to travel, or when the weather would turn foul. Gypsy children were taught such things, and she could probably teach Mr. Clemons a few things about the stars!

Feeling her irritation mounting with thoughts of spending some of her evenings bent over that damn telescope, Angela began to slow her mount near the edge of the dense forest that grew on the outer bounds of the pastures behind the Hall. Spying a path through the overgrown thicket that appeared to be little used, she slowly directed Charmer along the cool, tree-shaded passageway.

She had to admit that the duke had the strange ability, even without being around her, to keep her emotions in a state of turmoil. As the months had slowly passed, she had feared that Royce St. James would return to the Hall without word. This feeling of having to face the duke again kept her feeling unsure of herself and unsettled about her life and future.

After all this time, she still had no more clue about how she could return to her own life and time, than she had had that first night in London. The only hope that she clung to now was the promised purse of gold from the duke at the end of the year. She would be able to survive for a time once she left the Hall. As she pushed the mare deeper into the forest, she admitted that she was reluctant to give up the security and comfort that she had found at Westfield Hall. Everything would change once she left its confines. She could only hope that she would be able to return to Momma Leona and the children before the promised purse of gold was spent!

Sensing the mare pulling back and shying away from whatever lay ahead on the path, Angela forced her attention back to the forest which surrounded her. With some astonishment her violet-blue eyes looked up the trail, and she found herself staring at a small brightly colored, horse-drawn caravan. Looking further, she glimpsed the activity of a small Gypsy encampment. There were two other colorful caravan-wagons; all three having been unhitched, the horses were tied to a lead rope and grazing not far from camp. With an excited gasp, Angela nudged Charmer's flanks and sent her slowly forward. Hearing a shout sweeping through the camp that a stranger was approaching, Angela was soon encircled by a group of colorfully dressed men and women. A large smile split Angela's lips. "Hello!" she excitedly called out as she began to dismount, her blood pumping vigorously as she glimpsed the faces of her people.

Nervously the group around her stood

back a distance, none answering her friendly greeting. A tall, dark-skinned Gypsy man, perhaps in his early twenties, stepped forward at last. Another man, an older version of the young man, made his way to her side, too.

"What is it that you want of us, Rawnie?" the younger one said. "We have very little. We camp here on this property only for this night, and then we shall be on our way with the morning sun." He wore a bright scarlet shirt with flowing sleeves and a pair of black, tightly molded breeches which had been tucked into a pair of calf-high boots, having seen far better days. His words were spoken nervously as sharp black eyes searched the woman's features. Every once in a while, his glance went over her shoulder to the surrounding forest where she had come through the path, as though expecting to see more of the *gorgios*. "My people will harm nothing, we but need a few hours' rest for our animals and the children, and then we will be on our way."

In truth, the group had only just arrived in the forest a few hours previously. Outside of London, one of the younger men of their group had been caught trying to steal a horse. Last night, he had gone into the farmer's stable and had painted a white blaze down the dark animal's head and had also colored one of the horse's forelegs with the white paint. He waited until morning, after the farmer had gone off into the fields, and then had approached the barn. Taking the beast out of the stall, he had caught sight of the farmer's wife watching him from her stoop. He had called to her that the animal was his and had pointed to the streak of white that ran from forehead to nose.

The farmer's wife was not one to easily be misled, and coming as a surprise to the young Gypsy man, she had called to the house. Three large, strapping young men came outside and pointedly looked from their mother to the Gypsy man standing in their yard.

At first sight of the farmer's sons, the Gypsy knew that he had overplayed his hand. This same ploy had worked last month in another town, but this day, as the three young men began to approach him, he knew that the wisest thing he could do was to make tracks as far away from the farm as possible!

Turning on his heel, the Gypsy sprinted behind the barn, but not before he smacked the horse upon the rump to ensure that one or two of the young men would have to run after the animal.

By the time the young Gypsy had returned to camp, he was out of breath. It was not long before the wagons had been loaded and the entire camp was hurrying away from London. They escaped the bars of Newgate only because they were on the outskirts of the city and it took too long for the authorities to set upon them. There was no denying that the farmer and his sons might very well be looking for the Gypsy caravan right this moment! They had hoped to camp in this forest without notice, but this woman had come to force them off her lord's property. The Gypsy man standing before Angela could only hope to beg a few hours' rest.

"No!" Angela exclaimed. "I mean, you don't have to leave here on my account!"

The young man with his flashing jet eyes and shoulder-length ebony hair looked anew at the beautiful lady. His people had been chased from property to property. What did this woman mean when she said that they did not have to leave the forest? Stephan had never been one to look a gift horse in the mouth; what did it matter her meaning as long as his people gained their own end? The young man bent from the waist and imitated a courtly bow. He did not trust her kind, but he was glad that the tribe would be able to remain in the forest at least until morning, when they could set out refreshed by a good night's sleep. "We thank you,

Rawnie, for your generosity," he said loudly as the rest of the group began to softly murmur among themselves at this strange turn of events.

Listening to him, Angela hurriedly tried to explain herself. "I'm afraid that you still don't understand what I mean. I have been hoping to find a caravan such as yours for the past several months." She was so excited that she had at last found some of her own people; she knew that she wasn't saying everything quite right, but she told herself that given time she would make them understand how dire her plight truly was!

"What is it that you wish, Rawnie? Your fortune told? Or perhaps you are in need of a kettle mender or a basket weaver?" The young man appeared to be talking for the entire group. As he spoke, his dark brows arched over a sharp eye as he quickly took in not only her rare beauty, but also the fine cut of her fashionable riding gown and the rich trappings of her mount. If she desired some small service from his people, he would be more than willing to agree in order to gain her permission to camp here in the forest until they were ready to move on. Perhaps they would be able to camp through the long winter. Fall would shortly be on them, and it was always harder on the children and elders traveling through the winter months.

"Please don't call me Rawnie again. My name is Angela, and you must give me a few minutes to try and explain myself." Angela tried to pull her thoughts into order, knowing that the Gypsy people were a suspicious lot. If she told them her circumstances, they would not believe her; but what choice did she have? The words of the old Gypsy woman on the London streets came back to her from another century. She had called her Rawnie that day and had stated that she would be called a great lady by her own people one day.

The young man called Stephan sensed that the woman was becoming strangely upset. Graciously he offered, "Perhaps you would care to come to our fire and have a cup of strong tea?"

She would be easy pickings to their cunning ways, Stephan told himself as he led her to the fire. His large gold-hooped earring glimmered as his darkly handsome features studied the young woman thoughtfully. The rest of his group either watched silently or hurried to bring the desired cup of tea to their unexpected guest.

Without objection, Angela allowed the young man to lead her to the campfire. As the colorfully dressed group watched, she sat down upon the log that had been dragged close to the edge of the shallow fire pit. As her blue gaze swept over the men and women who had circled her, she told herself that though she had been born in another time, there was little difference between them and herself; they, as well as she, were of the Romany blood!

Several of the older men of the tribe, as well as Stephan, sat down before the fire as Angela was served a cup of tea. After taking the first sip of the strong brew, Angela took a deep breath and said, "I know that what I am about to say will seem strange to all of you, but please just listen."

Her cobalt eyes surveyed the group. After witnessing several heads nodding agreement, she began, "First of all, though you may think that I am of the gentry, I am the same as you. My own people are of the Rom." The faces around her showed disbelief as several of the older women began to whisper. "Please let me explain! It all began several months ago. I was raised by an old woman known as Momma Leona. She kept twelve children in her care, whom she taught at an early age to steal and to beg for her gain. The children and myself roamed about the streets of London plying our trade of picking pockets."

The young man sitting across from Angela held up a hand in order to halt her flow of words. He was finding her confession more than a little hard to believe. As he had listened to her, he wondered what she could possibly think to gain by telling them such an outrageous story. Did this *gorgio* woman believe that his people could so easily be taken in by her lies? What reason could such a lady have for claiming to be of the *tacho rat,* or of the true blood? Was she not sound in the head and wished to entertain herself with some strange day's excitement at the expense of his band? "But, Rawnie, why would you wish to tell us this tale? No Rom wears the fine clothes of the *gorgio,* nor do they speak in such a fine manner of voice."

He thought to stop her before she went any further with this wild story. Over the past year, Stephan had joined in with the older men of his tribe to help ensure that their band survived in this land where life was so hard for the Gypsy, and he did not take his obligations lightly. He was not about to allow his people to be taken in by a silver-tongued *gorgio,* even if she were as beautiful as this young woman sitting across from him!

"But I am not the rich lady that you believe me!" In desperation her tone rose. "These clothes, my manners, and voice are all due to the Duke of Westfield. I tried to relieve his friend of his purse. When that gentleman caught me, he made a wager with the duke that Westfield could not transform the Gypsy girl into a lady in a year's time! I am that same Gypsy girl! You must believe me!"

She knew that her only chance to get any help from this band was to convince them that she was one of them! It might be a long time before she found another band of Gypsies. "My mother was Irish, but my father was Rom. That is why my eyes are blue!" She knew that it was not only her dress and manners that held her in suspicion by these people, but it was also her features. They were not the swarthy dark ones of the Gypsy.

The group that had formed around her studied her a bit more closely after this new confession. Again, it was Stephan who spoke out. "Your story is a strange one, Rawnie." And then after a few seconds he added, "But our people have heard many strange tales in the past, and I am sure we will hear many more."

"Then you do believe me?" Tears sparkled in the violet depths of her eyes as she clutched this one slim hope. Perhaps they would take her in when the time came for her to leave Westfield Hall.

The young man did not comment upon her question, but instead he posed one of his own, "Do you know where your own band of people are now? This Momma Leona and the children, are they still in London?" He paused. "Perhaps we could help you to regain your place with this Momma Leona," he finally offered, knowing that the Gypsy people passed information from one tribe to the next by word of mouth. It took time, but it had always been efficient.

Taking another deep breath, Angela wondered how much she should tell them about herself; how much would they believe? "You see it is not as easy for me to return to Momma Leona and the children as one would think. As I have already told you, I have been at Westfield Hall under the care of the duke's staff for months, but what I did not mention is that I do not come from the London streets that you know today."

She brought her hand to her brow, feeling a headache coming on and not daring to reveal much more for fear they would think her mad. Crystal tears filled her eyes as she looked at those standing around her and read in their hard, worn features the disbelief of all she had told them. "You must believe me, I want only to return to my own people, and if not, I must remain with my own kind!"

"But how is it that we can help you, Rawnie, when you speak to us in these riddles?" Stephan's father for the first time spoke out, his dark gaze probing with such intensity Angela was forced to lower her own. "London is today as it was in my grandfather's day, and his before him."

She should confess all and allow them to think her insane, she thought as she looked up into the faces peering down at her. Before she could say anything further, an ancient bent-framed woman came to her side. Bending down, she picked up the chipped teacup that Angela had set to the side of the fire. Peering down at the leaves in the bottom of the cup, her dark eyes lifted, then held with Angela's. "You must find the treasure that ruled your fate. A stolen piece brought this turn to your destiny, and only with it once again in your palm can you know true peace."

"What are you talking about, old mother?" Angela gasped aloud as she shook her head, trying to understand the strange statement coming from the old woman. As the old crone held her gaze steadily, Angela looked deeply into the piercing black eyes, and an image came to her: the pocket watch she had stolen from the dapper little man her last day in the twentieth century—which now seemed an eternity ago.

"The pocket watch!" she softly gasped. She remembered that evening when she had lain by the pond and after reading the instructions on the inner facing of the watch, then had set the hands and pushed the button. She could remember the strange feeling of tiredness that had swept over her and how she had been unable to keep her eyes open.

"It must have been the watch!" she declared, and as the Gypsies stared in utter amazement, she jumped to her feet. Everything was falling into place! She had to regain the pocket watch. Once she had it in her possession, she would be able to return to her own time!

Halfway to her horse, she remembered the band of Gypsies. Turning around, she found them still staring after her. Her eyes went to the old woman, now standing beside the young man. "Thank you so much," she called, but then with an afterthought, she pulled off her forest green scarf and quickly made her way back to the old woman. Handing the piece of fine silk to the old woman, she said, "This is for you, old mother."

With a smile, Angela told the group that she would return and that they were free to stay on the Westfield property as long as they desired. What did she care, she would be gone as soon as she gained the pocket watch again! For the first time in months, she felt carefree and lighthearted as she mounted her horse and headed back down the forest path.

After the beautiful lady had ridden out of the camp, Stephan approached the old woman. "What were the meaning of the words that you spoke to her, Zela?"

"They were but words that came to my mind as I looked into her eyes. They were the words that she desired to hear, Stephan. Do you not like the *diklo* that your Rawnie rewarded me with? Does it not make me look much younger?" the old woman cackled as she patted the young man on the arm.

With a flashing of white teeth, Stephan murmured softly, "She is not my Rawnie, Zela." His people were very cunning and could easily enough discern what needed to be told to someone who sought out answers, and the proof of that lay about old Zela's throat. She had been rewarded with the expensive scarf, and their tribe had been assured that they could remain here in the forest for the time being. He didn't believe anything the beautiful young woman had told him and his people. But as his dark eyes went back to the path through the forest where she had disappeared, he warned himself to be on his guard. There had to be a reason for her attempt at getting close to his people, and envisioning her beauty once again, he knew for his own peace of mind, he had best be wary!

Twelve

Breaking through the enclosure of the forest, Angela sat in indecision as she looked toward the field of tall grass which would take her back to the Hall. She could go to the Hall, or she could turn Charmer in the opposite direction and go to the pond, where last she had seen the pocket watch. If she held any chance at all of returning to her own time, she had to find the pocket watch! Gazing up at the lowering sun, she tried to keep a tight rein on her wildly beating heart. It would be dark soon. She would never be able to find the pocket watch without the aid of a flashlight—which had not been invented!

She would have to return to the Hall, she decided. She would go in search of the pocket watch tomorrow, leaving early in the morning when she usually took Charmer out for a short ride before her lessons with

Mrs. Booth. A small smile graced her lips with the thought of Mrs. Booth's reaction when she did not return for her daily drillings. She would not worry herself a minute over that! Once she had the pocket watch, she would never have to worry about another rigid lesson given by that old bovine! Kicking Charmer's sides, she started back toward the Westfield stables, her heart singing with anticipation. She thought of what tomorrow would bring for her. At last, she could return to her old way of life!

As the mare slowly made her way through the belly-high grass, Angela wondered what she would be returning to once she set the hands on the face of the pocket watch in reverse. The life of drudgery and thievery had lost much appeal since living the life of luxury at the Hall. Perhaps she should wait until the year's ending before sending herself back to Momma Leona and the children. The promised purse of gold could be the only chance for a change in her future. With it she would not be forced to return to Momma Leona, but could go on to Paris or another city, wherever she desired to start anew. She could even stay in this time period! Why, she could convert the purse of gold into a business of some kind; this was something for her to think about.

Drawing nearer to the stables, her thoughts

of fancy disappeared. She had to return to her own time, she warned herself. There was nothing for her in this strange century. She had been little more than a pawn, a bet made between two rich gentlemen. What made her think that her life could be any better? She knew very little, beyond what Mr. Clemons had taught her about the world as it was today. The customs of the people were so different now, and the lifestyle of those that were without means was much harsher than in her own century. What if the business she were to choose did not succeed? No, her only choice was to return to the twentieth century, the promised purse dancing within her thoughts as an enticement not to return until the end of the year!

Arriving at the stables, Angela noticed that there was much more activity than usual, and dismounting, she wondered what grand event could have warranted the entire staff of stable boys to be scurrying around the stable and the surrounding yard. Over the past months here at Westfield Hall, only the arrival of the messenger from the duke had caused any change in activity among the staff. But the messenger had arrived and gone early this morning. She questioned Jamie as he approached and took the mare's reins. "Do we have a guest at the Hall, Jamie?"

"Aye, lass, it be the duke himself who has

at last returned home." The small man grinned widely, for the duke had always been good to him and he welcomed him back at the Hall. "It's been far too long that his Grace has tarried in London this time!"

"The duke? He has come back to the Hall today?" Angela could hardly believe her ears. Why had he not sent word of his forthcoming arrival? She inwardly cringed with thoughts of having to face Royce St. James once again. Somehow she had thought he was going to stay away the whole year.

"Aye, lass, it be himself that has returned to us, and ye had best take yerself back to the Hall. I'm sure the duke will be wishing to be seeing ye right soon enough."

Angela swallowed nervously, her throat going dry as the truth of his words hit her. Her dark head nodded as she left the stables and approached the outside servants' stairway, which led up to the second floor of the Hall. She needed time to think over this new turn. She had tried to put the Duke of Westfield out of her mind, but now his handsome visage filled her thoughts; the image was both frightening and tantalizing!

Gaining the second-floor landing, she opened her chamber door quietly, with the hope that no one would notice her presence back at the Hall. She noticed that Ethel had set up a bath before the hearth in expectation of her arrival. It would be best to face the master of Westfield Hall without the clinging smell of horse.

Looking to the bath of steaming water, her chin rose a bit. What reason had she to fear the coming confrontation with the duke? Perhaps he was just spending a night at the Hall and would be off again to London come morning. Perhaps the bet had been called in early! This thought brightened her up somewhat. If the bet had been called in earlier, she would gain the purse of gold. Once retrieving the pocket watch, she would be free to return to her own time period!

She would show the duke that she had indeed been transformed into the lady that he had desired! Pulling off her riding habit and calf-high kid boots, she quickly unbraided her long hair and allowed it to fall down her back before she stepped into the warm, lilac-scented water. She sighed with a catlike smile. If the duke could see her now, he would realize how much she had changed! Gone was the young woman who had fought not to take a bath. In her place was a young woman who welcomed the late-afternoon tub that always awaited her after a long ride.

Rinsing the last of the sweetly scented

soap from her hair, she rose out of the water. Sitting near the warm hearth, with only the fleecy towel wrapped about her, she began to brush out her long, dark tresses. Upon reflection, she admitted that she had learned much while being at the Hall. Her manners were above reproach as she sat at the dinner table, and she could sew and even sketch passably well. She was well-versed in current events, and she had learned a wealth of knowledge from Mr. Clemons. These months at Westfield Hall had not been a waste of time. She knew that she had changed more than superficially. She would not be returning to Momma Leona as the same young woman she had been when she had stepped through the door of time.

A small voice in her conscience began to intrude as she quickly set about carefully choosing her wardrobe for this evening. *Don't forget Alex and the men Momma Leona forced upon her. You might find yourself in a similar position!*

"No!" Angela said aloud. "I will not reveal the purse of gold until I am assured that my position with Momma Leona remains the same as before I left or has improved!" She was too old to roam the streets picking her marks and stealing them blind. Things would be different with her return.

She hoped that Momma Leona had softened over the past few months!

For now she would place her concentration on showing the duke that he had not wasted his coin by providing her with a wardrobe and hiring her teachers. She would deal with the duke first and encourage him to call in the bet early, if he had not already thought to do so. She would have plenty of time later to worry about the future with Momma Leona!

Going to her wardrobe, which was filled to overflowing with every color and style of gown imaginable, Angela pulled forth a shimmering blue taffeta creation that had been artfully stitched with gold embroidery. The sleeves puffed out from elbow to shoulders, the bosom was cut daringly low, and the waist was tightly molded, with a small farthingale extending the hip line. Blade Devereux had declared that this gown would make every woman in London faint with envy. This evening Angela cared not what any other woman might think of her apparel. She set her mind to dressing only to impress the Duke of Westfield.

Angela rang for Ethel, who came to help dress her. This night, above all nights, she was determined to look her best! As the image of the arrogant, high-handed Royce St. James came to mind, her cheeks warmed as she glanced in the pier glass and glimpsed the daring cut of the gown. The full, pale swelling of her breasts was plainly visible to the eye. Yards of material made up the skirt. An abundance of blue shimmering lace, stitched with a delicate hand, formed a cloudlike effect over the stiff taffeta. The matching shoes were studded with gleaming gold brilliants, and the tall heels were of the same bright gold as the stitching.

The overall effect of the gown, was most daring. There was a need to be daring this evening, she decided as Ethel began to arrange her hair. Entwining lustrous black curls with pieces of gold ribbon, the maid circled the mass at the crown of Angela's head, leaving wisps of dark curls to dangle freely at nape and temples.

Using a small amount of cosmetics that Mrs. Booth had harped so much about, Angela heightened her cheeks with a touch of rouge and traced a small amount of carmine on her lips. Looking at herself in the dressing-table mirror, she wondered what the duke would think of her.

Ethel clapped her hands and gushed, "You look beautiful in all of your finery, Miss Angela. When the duke gets an eyeful, he won't believe you're the same girl he left here at the Hall!"

As the dinner hour drew near, Angela left

her chamber a few minutes early. The best approach would be to try and take the upper hand right from the start. She made for the duke's study, knowing that she would find him in this sanctuary. With a silent tread, she halted a few feet from the slightly opened door. Taking a deep breath, she entered without knocking, hoping that she could take the duke off guard.

Royce St. James sat behind his large oak desk, thoroughly immersed in the stack of papers piled before him. At first he did not notice her.

Angela allowed herself time to slowly appraise the duke. He had changed little over the course of the past months. He was still as handsome as she had remembered; in fact, he was the most handsome man she had ever laid eyes on. Though she had dreamt of him often during the past months, nothing had prepared her for the sight of him and the stirring within her because of his mere presence. With a ragged breath, she warned herself to stay in control. The duke was just as ruthless and arrogant as he had been at their first meeting. She could not forget this fact! Men of his caliber thought that the world had been created for them, and if they desired to trample upon a small insignificant being, so be it!

Her deep breath must have penetrated

Royce's thoughts, for suddenly he realized that he was not alone in his study. His cool gray gaze rose to the woman standing in the doorway. Paralyzed and struck dumb, he stared at the vision of a goddess.

Angela felt the heat of his silver eyes and felt her cheeks flushing brighter than the painted rouge.

Slowly, as though breaking through a cloud which had entwined itself about his senses, Royce St. James rose to his feet and made his way around his desk. His work was now discarded without a thought. Clearing his the throat, he forced words from his mouth. "Please, excuse me for not seeing you sooner. Would you care to have a seat? I can have refreshments brought in, if you would like."

He had not been told by Hawkins that they had a guest at the Hall, and holding his warm gaze upon her lovely visage, he gained her side and offered her his hand. Who could she be? he wondered, and why was she standing in the doorway of his study? He cared not for the answer. Fortune had blessed him, and that was all that mattered!

"I believe that dinner will be served shortly," Angela murmured softly, surprised to be greeted by the duke with such graciousness. She had expected colder treatment from him.

"Of course, you are absolutely right, my dear." Royce was unable to think straight with her so near, and loath to release her hand, he drew her toward the comfortable burgundy-leather settee. Her delicate, musical voice had enchanted him, and her lilac scent filled his senses.

Angela allowed him to lead her to the small couch. His presence overwhelmed her. The feel of his warm gaze upon her evoked a trembling in the depths of her belly; the touch of his hand clasped over her own left her lightheaded.

Royce sat down at her side, reluctant to release her hand. He had little choice, though, as he searched his mind for some slim reason to hold it. Settling back against the soft cushions, he studied her intently in silence. Where had such a beautiful creature come from? he asked himself as he spied a slight blush on her creamy, smooth cheeks. She was new to London obviously, for he would have seen her at court or upon the arm of another gentleman if she resided in that town. Perhaps she was newly arrived in England, but if so, why was she here at Westfield Hall and apparently all alone? What reason did she have for being here? There were many things that he would like to ask her, but he only sat back and enjoyed the wonderful blessing of her presence.

Angela nervously sat on the edge of the settee. Those gray-silver eyes held her enthralled as they roamed over her every feature. She felt the searing heat of their touch upon the smoothness of her swelling bosom, and she felt her face flaming brighter.

A smile settled over Royce's sensual lips as he glimpsed the freshness of her innocent blush. It was invigorating to see such a rare beauty blush under the perusal of a gentleman, in this day and time. The women in his past had been fairly jaded. This woman intrigued him, and as he would have spoken aloud some inane remark, she spoke first, her words surprising him into a stunned silence.

"If I have passed the inspection, your Grace, I ask only for the promised purse of gold and permission to leave Westfield Hall." Angela decided to come straightforwardly to the subject.

The soft melody of her voice sent tingles dancing down Royce's spine, the sweet tremor filling his ears. But as the meaning of her words made their way into his brain, a fine dark brow rose above a glittering silver eye. "Pardon me?" He must have misheard. So enamored of her presence was he that he had thought she had claimed he owed her a purse of gold.

Clutching her hands in the folds of her lace and taffeta skirts, Angela avoided looking into his handsome features. "I said that the year is a few months shy, but already the wager is fulfilled. You have a lady to show to Lord Dunsely, and I wish for the promised purse of gold, so I can leave Westfield Hall as soon as possible." She despaired at the quiver in her voice.

Royce St. James looked more sharply at the stunning beauty sitting next to him. *The wager? A lady that he could show to Lord Dunsely? A purse of gold?* This gorgeous woman, outfitted and groomed to perfection, could not be the same Gypsy brat that he had left months ago here at the Hall! It was not possible that such a ravishing creature with a soft, cultured voice was the same wench that he had stripped down and thrown into the tub out in the kitchen! But even as these thoughts assailed him, he looked deeply into those same violet-blue eyes which had held the power, to send him from his mistress's bed, and he knew. Upon occasion over the past few months, her image had come to mind and disturbed his busy life. He was amazed, though, that her stay at Westfield Hall had brought about such a breathtaking transformation! She was so graceful, so totally alluring to the eye! Why, she had been no more than skin and bones when he had left the Hall! Her dark witch's locks had been unruly and unmanageable the last time

211

he had seen her in her bedchamber, but now they were lustrous and coiffed.

Royce was forced to face the results of his bet with Damian, and he was shocked by the outcome. The woman sitting next to him, Gypsy baggage or not, was the most beautiful woman he had ever seen!

Thirteen

"Is there something amiss, your Grace?" Angela softly questioned as she read the confusion on his handsome features. Had he truly forgotten all about the wager? she wondered to herself. How could that be possible when he sent out instructions for her care so frequently? Angela now was confused herself.

"No . . . no, there is nothing wrong. The wager . . ." Royce ran a hand through his dark hair, trying to come to grips with the consequences of his actions months ago.

"Then, your Grace, you do concede that the wager has been met and that I have earned the purse of gold?" Angela pushed him further, and inwardly she smiled at his lack of enthusiasm. She had sworn to show him that she was not a woman to be looked down upon. His uncharacteristic reaction to her made her chest swell with pride.

Royce tried to take control. He was sitting

with the most beautiful creature he had ever seen, and she was wanting no more than a purse of gold and freedom from his presence. He rose to his feet and for a few minutes roamed about the study, his gray gaze returning again to the woman upon the settee. From the crown of her glorious hair to the tips of her small slippered feet, she was perfection: poised and beautiful! "Damian will have to be witness to this transformation and agree to a shorter span of time than the agreed-upon full year," he said abruptly.

"Of course, your Grace," Angela relented, hoping that the ordeal would end quickly. He frightened her. He held the strange power to play havoc with her peace of mind, unlike any other man she had ever met. She had to get away from him as soon as possible!

There was a slight knock upon the outside study door, and Hawkins stepped into the room to announce that dinner was ready to be served in the dining room.

"The lady and I would prefer to be served here in the privacy of my study, Hawkins." Royce's gaze never left Angela. He believed that by studying her, some small sign of the Gypsy brat would be once again revealed. "We have some business to discuss and will find it more comfortable in here," he added as he glimpsed the young woman's blue eyes enlarging.

Hawkins nodded his bewigged head, and as his gaze went to the couch and settled upon Angela, a small smile came over his lips. The young Gypsy girl had certainly turned into a beauty. Like most of the servants here at the Hall, he had grown quite fond of her. Looking at the young woman dressed in all of her finery, it was hard to believe that she had appeared a filthy wench in tattered clothes. "I will have everything brought in here then, your Grace, as you wish."

The meal was set up before the fireplace on a small table, and after Hawkins had left the study, Royce pulled out a chair at the small table for Angela.

Approaching the table which held the savory-smelling food, Angela felt her hunger. Since being at Westfield Hall, she had not missed a meal. As if her body feared the return of those days of deprivation while under Momma Leona's care, at every meal she had a robust appetite. Sitting down in the comfortable, straight-back chair, she waited for the duke to do likewise before sampling the food on the plate.

In the few minutes it had taken Hawkins and the footmen to set up the table in his study, Royce had tried to regain his senses. He now filled the pair of crystal long-stemmed glasses with wine. As Angela's slender hand reached for the glass, her lilac scent again washed over him in a fragrant rush.

His manner toward her had much improved since their first meeting, Angela thought. Raising the wineglass to her lips, she wondered if she should welcome this or stay on her guard?

Relaxing in the chair across from her, Royce could not pull his gaze from the beauty of her features. "I hope that your stay at the Hall has not been too unpleasant, Angela," he said, cocking a brow and taking up his eating utensils. In London, he had not worried about her at all. Now, though, he wondered if she had been treated well. Had the servants treated her with respect? Had that prune-faced Mrs. Booth been too hard on her? And Gerald Clemons, had he used threats or punishment to achieve the results that he had claimed she had achieved?

Angela did not answer the question put to her, but instead took another sip of the fine wine. Now that she was sitting across from the handsome duke, she found that her appetite had deserted her. Lord, she wished he would just hand over the purse of gold and let her leave the Hall. It was agonizing to have to sit across from him and make small talk as though all that had transpired between them in the past had been a matter of course.

"It is a wonder that you have filled out as well as you have, Angela," Royce murmured.

"What?" Angela gasped aloud, knowing that he must be remembering that night when he had stripped her down and forced her to bathe! Crimson flushed her cheeks as her glance lowered.

Noticing the bright flush that graced her cheeks and was slowly creeping down her slender throat, Royce thought of that evening in the kitchen. Many nights he had reflected over that event in which he had discovered that she was no young child, but a woman full grown! "I meant nothing by such a statement, Angela. I . . . I only thought to say that you eat so little, I am surprised . . ." This was not going as he would have desired. He felt like a stumbling schoolboy trying to impress an innocent maid. The hell of it was, he could not take his eyes from the low cut of her gown. Her full breasts held his gaze as though they had been created for his perusal.

"I know what you meant." Angela gulped down the rest of the wine in her glass and stretched out her hand for him to refill the goblet. "I usually have a very good appetite." She wished they would get away from the subject of her appetite, or lack of it!

Looking at the outstretched hand holding the crystal glass, Royce longed to set aside the vessel and take that hand within his own. It was intriguing that this woman could have such an effect upon him, Royce thought as he forced himself to refill the glass. "Then perhaps it is I who have spoiled your desire this evening for food?"

Angela did not respond but instead clutched the wineglass tighter. Her face remained flushed from the wine as her bosom heaved invitingly with mounting anxiety.

Leaning back in his chair, his desire for food having vanished, Royce studied the woman closely as she cast her eyes down and sampled her wine. He still could hardly believe that this lovely young woman was the same Gypsy brat. "I am sure that Damian will not believe his eyes, no more than I, when he catches a glimpse of you, Angela."

Trying to shun his open looks and fighting the effect of the strong wine, Angela's midnight blue gaze rose and looked directly into his handsome face. She questioned softly, "Then you are ready to release me from your charge?"

The soft, breathless tone went straight to Royce's soul, but he was at a loss as how to answer her. Was he ready to call in the bet and release his little Gypsy brat? A small voice questioned, *What man in his right mind*

would ever want to release such a lovely treasure?
Instead of answering, he asked his own question: "What have you found with which to entertain yourself, Angela, while I have been absent from the Hall?"

Taking another long drink of the wine and feeling the warmth from the brew running swiftly through her body, Angela found it easier to relax in the duke's presence. After all, he was like any other man—well, not quite like the other men she had ever met, but all the same he appeared the gentleman. "You wish to know what I have been doing here at the Hall?"

As though her every move had not been reported to him, she thought, but still, she searched her mind for an answer. Making a sour face, she remembered Mrs. Booth and the daily drillings that the stern woman inflicted upon her. "It certainly is not Mrs. Booth's instructions or my lessons that give me pleasure! I would have to say that the best part of my day is when I get the chance to go riding." The wine had loosened her tongue, she realized with surprise.

Royce was delighted. Even the sour face she had made had gone to some secret portion of his heart. She was simply breathtaking. Without a second thought, he invited, "Would you care, then, to go for a ride with me upon the morrow, Angela?"

His silver-gray eyes never left hers. They seemed to devour her every movement; the simple lowering of her lashes, the dark fringe spreading delicately against her cheeks, sent his pulse racing.

"Tomorrow?" Surprised by the invitation, she knew that she had already planned something for tomorrow, but she could not remember what those plans had been. Her dark head began to slowly nod in agreement. "Perhaps sometime after my lessons." She felt her head spinning and her body felt strangely light. She should not have partaken of so much wine so quickly.

"Why don't we cancel your lessons for tomorrow?" Royce softly questioned, his full, sensual lips drawn back in admiration.

"Oh, could we truly?" Angela asked excitedly. This would be the first day that she would not have demands upon her. "You are sure that it will be all right?"

Royce was enchanted. Her pleasure with the small offering was so apparent, he could not help but smile. "Indeed, Miss, you may skip your lessons for a day. After all, I am the lord of the Hall." He winked boldly at her, in good humor.

"Indeed you are!" Angela's grin was as wide as his.

Her happiness warmed Royce as he was graced with her generous smile. With a strong will, he decided to end their little dinner party before things went too far. He knew that she had partaken of the wine a bit more than she should have. "Then we shall call it a date. Shall we say a ride after breakfast?"

Rising to his feet, he made his way to her side and would have pulled out her chair immediately, but for his gaze, of its own accord, roaming downward and taking in her pale bosom.

A strange current of energy that was completely alien to Angela moved through the room as he stood behind her chair, and for the moment, she was unable to move. As she felt the slight brush of his fingers against the indent of her collarbone, though, she fairly flew out of the chair. She stepped away from the touch of his heated hands, finding herself backing against the leather settee.

"I think that I should go to my chamber," she gasped aloud, not able to drag her gaze away from the silver eyes that burned with fire. She must be burning up with a raging fever, she told herself as she felt the trembling of her body. Her legs felt so heavy . . .

As though each movement was conducted in slow motion, Royce, with a pantherlike grace, made his way to stand directly before her. His hands reached out and caressed a fine silken strand of wispy curls. "Do you fear me, little Gypsy angel?" His words were husky, seductive, and set her bones to melting.

She wanted to scream out yes, but all she managed was, "I am not called Gypsy angel. My name is Angela," on a shaky whisper.

"Angela, Angela, I know the name well. It has circled within my brain more times over the past months than I can remember." The confession was made more to himself than for her benefit.

Nothing in her entire life had ever prepared Angela for such a moment, and especially not with a man like the Duke of Westfield. He seemed to steal breath from her body as she looked up into his handsome visage. Her heart raced. This meeting was not going as planned!

"I . . . I must go to my room!" she said breathlessly. She felt panic rising as she felt his heated silver regard hold her. Turning around to flee the study and the overly attractive duke, her own quickness entrapped her as her legs gave out and she tumbled in a seductive sprawl upon the upholstered leather settee.

Royce wore an appreciative smile as he looked upon the inviting display of taffeta and lacy petticoats and shapely legs encased in pale, silk stockings, all revealed as her skirts rose up about her thighs. With more will than he believed himself capable of possessing, the smile faded as a long sigh left him. His hands reached down to help her regain her footing.

Seeing his hungry gaze as it traveled over her length, Angela ignored his offer of help and tried to pull down the gown to cover her body as she attempted to stand. She was not getting very far until she felt the duke's hands around her waist. As he pulled her to her feet, he did not immediately release her, and she melted inside.

"Should I carry you to your chamber, Angela?" Royce asked softly as he held her in an embrace and stared down into her closed eyes.

Angela almost jumped out of his arms. "No!" she gasped aloud, and tried to pull herself out of his embrace.

Royce was loath to release the lush female in his arms. Drawing her even closer to his heart, he whispered, "Relax, little angel." His breath next to her ear sent rippling gooseflesh over her entire length.

How on earth was she supposed to relax, her brain cried out as his masculine power overcame her senses. His voice, scent, and breath combined to leave her a mass of putty.

His sensual lips slowly descended, their delicious taste covering her own. It was as though a ravaging beast was stealing the very substance from her body, ensnaring her being, and leaving her powerless but to clutch his broad shoulders. As his heated tongue slipped between her parted teeth and seductively circled and explored, she felt herself drowning in his embrace.

With a ragged breath, Royce forced himself to pull his lips away from Angela's. His senses spiraled as he, for one breathtaking moment, stared down into the simmering sapphire jewels that stared back at him. Had ever another woman felt so right, so comfortable in his arms?

With her mouth released from his plundering lips, Angela was able to regain a fraction of her senses. Heart hammering wildly in her breast, a small gasp escaped her kiss-bruised lips. She pulled away from his broad chest and rushed to the study door. Upon wobbly legs, she raced back to her room.

Entering her chamber, she slammed the door behind her. Her hand reached up and touched her soft lips. What had she done? She had never allowed any man to take such liberties! Had she truly allowed Royce St. James to hold her so familiarly and kiss her so heatedly when all she had wanted was the promised purse of gold and her release from Westfield Hall?

* * *

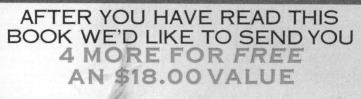

MORE PASSION AND ADVENTURE AWAIT... YOUR TRIP TO A BIG ADVENTUROUS WORLD BEGINS WHEN YOU ACCEPT YOUR FIRST 4 NOVELS ABSOLUTELY *FREE*
(AN $18.00 VALUE)

Accept your Free gift and start to experience more of the passion and adventure you like in a historical romance novel. Each Zebra novel is filled with proud men, spirited women and tempestuous love that you'll remember long after you turn the last page.

Zebra Historical Romances are the finest novels of their kind. They are written by authors who really know how to weave tales of romance and adventure in the historical settings you love. You'll feel like you've actually gone back in time with the thrilling stories that each Zebra novel offers.

GET YOUR FREE GIFT WITH THE START OF YOUR HOME SUBSCRIPTION

Our readers tell us that these books sell out very fast in book stores and often they miss the newest titles. So Zebra has made arrangements for you to receive the four newest novels published each month.

You'll be guaranteed that you'll never miss a title, and home delivery is so convenient. And to show you just how easy it is to get Zebra Historical Romances, we'll send you your first 4 books absolutely FREE! Our gift to you just for trying our home subscription service.

BIG SAVINGS AND FREE HOME DELIVERY

Each month, you'll receive the four newest titles as soon as they are published. You'll probably receive them even before the bookstores do. What's more, you may preview these exciting novels free for 10 days. If you like them as much as we think you will, just pay the low preferred subscriber's price of just $3.75 each. *You'll save $3.00 each month off the publisher's price.* AND, your savings are even greater because there are never any shipping, handling or other hidden charges—FREE Home Delivery. Of course you can return any shipment within 10 days for full credit, no questions asked. There is no minimum number of books you must buy.

GET
FOUR
FREE
BOOKS
(AN $18.00 VALUE)

ZEBRA HOME SUBSCRIPTION
SERVICE, INC.
120 BRIGHTON ROAD
P.O. Box 5214
CLIFTON, NEW JERSEY 07015-5214

Two hours later, with the finish of two more glasses of wine, Royce made his way to his own chamber, which were next to Angela's. The Duke of Westfield had not been able to get the dark-haired Gypsy angel out of his mind. How could he have foreseen that she would become the most beautiful woman he had ever set eyes upon?

With little control or careful thought, Royce found himself standing before the door that separated the two bedchambers. Reaching out a hand, he slowly tested the knob, but finding the portal locked from the other side, he reluctantly undressed and lay down upon his bed. If the door had been unbarred, he would have stolen into her chamber and tormented himself by viewing her sleeping form.

As he tried to shut his eyes and close out the sight of her shapely figure lying beneath the silken coverlet, his overactive imagination would not allow him the desired peace he sought. He imagined himself standing over her, his gaze traveling over each tempting curve. He envisioned her wearing only her chemise, which in his mind's eye was the same blue as the gown she had worn earlier to dinner, the sheer lace stitching of the undergarment leaving little to his imagination. Her full bosom, rose up and down, in her sleep, shapely limbs openly displayed for his viewing. Slowly Royce's glance went to her face. Her dark curls were fanned out over the peach coverlet, framing her creamy features in an alluring picture. Her pinkened cheeks and lips beckoned to him to partake of their sweetness. Within his own wine-sotted thoughts, he could imagine her sleek arms reaching out to enfold him within her embrace.

"Damn!" he cursed aloud to the empty room, jerking himself upright in bed, unable to stop remembering the sweetness of her taste in his study and how she had filled his arms in just the right fashion. *Could he so easily allow this woman to leave his Hall without first sampling the rest of her charms?* He pulled himself free from the comfort of his bed and made his way to the commode, where he began to splash water on his face and hair. Once he had sought out her hidden treasures, he would be ready to hand over her desired purse and wish her good luck. Straightening and shaking the droplets from his dark hair onto the carpet, a small voice in the back of his mind questioned, *And if this is not to be the way of things, would he then be forever tormented within the spell that the Gypsy wench had cast?*

Fourteen

With a soft moan, Angela awoke to a
piercing stream of sunlight coming through
the drawn draperies. "Aghhh," she groaned
aloud to the empty chamber, and as she
rolled away from the penetrating intrusion,
she pulled the silken coverlet up and over
her head. Now that her slumber had been
disturbed, she was hard-pressed to find that
peaceful state of unconsciousness again. Her
head throbbed unmercifully and her mouth
felt as dry as cotton, signs that she had
drunk far too much wine the evening before.

At last relenting and pushing back the
covers, Angela pulled herself up into a sitting position against the headboard of the
bed. Had that horrible man really kissed her
last night? This was the first rational
thought that pierced her roiling brain, and
with it, the entire evening came back to torment her in a heated rush. She had drunk

all that wine and then she had made a perfect fool of herself by falling onto the settee!

She slunk beneath the covers with another loud groan, her features flaming as she remembered everything that had happened in the duke's study. How was she ever going to face Royce St. James again? She recalled another time when she had asked herself this same question after the man had stripped her of her clothes. The duke seemed bent upon keeping her in a constant state of embarrassment!

She should have kept her wits about her last night and not have drunk so much wine. She should have stayed sober and demanded the promised purse of gold. Not only had she made a fool of herself, but she had also promised the duke that she would go riding with him this morning! Belatedly she remembered the pocket watch and the band of Gypsies camped in the forest. Her plans had been to retrieve the watch and to visit the encampment of gypsies before returning to her own century. Now her best-laid plans would have to wait until she could rid herself of Royce St. James!

As she tried to formulate a plan that would put the duke off for the rest of the day, Ethel brought up a tray of tea and toast. Setting the tray down near the side of the bed, the girl gave Angela one look and nodded her capped head. The duke had been right as rain, the undermaid thought to herself. It was plain to see that the young woman was suffering from a fierce hangover! She handed Angela a pewter mug from the tray. A soft steam was rising from the greenish brew within.

"What is this?" Angela groaned again; one glance at the contents of the mug had set her stomach turning upside down.

"His Grace mixed it for you and set it upon the breakfast tray. He said to instruct you to drink it all down and that in no time you're likely to be feeling better."

Could the man not even give her a moment's peace! Rising up on an elbow and looking once more into the goblet, Angela fiercely shook her head. "Take it away this minute!" As Ethel returned the mug to the tray, Angela slumped back down upon the bed.

"The duke told me to tell you that if the brew is left on the tray, he will be up to see that you drink it down." Ethel's brown eyes were filled with compassion, but her orders had come from the duke, and she aimed to see them carried out!

Not lost to the determined look, and not wishing to have Royce St. James barging into her chamber, she said with ill humor, "Drat it all, then give it to me!"

As soon as the mug was placed in her hand, she held her nose and drank until the bottom of the goblet was tilted high. Her belly lurched threateningly as she fell back against the pillows. "There. Now are you satisfied?" she muttered as she clasped her eyes tightly and tried to quell the pounding in her head. "I doubt that I will feel well for the rest of the day. You may tell the duke that I will be unable to ride with him this morning. I need to stay here in my chambers and rest."

Perhaps by nightfall she would be able to escape the Hall and that dreadful man! If she could retrieve the pocket watch, she would just have to do without the purse. Once back with Momma Leona and the children, she would work harder and put away a few coins, so eventually she could set out on her own!

"It be already past morning, Angela," Ethel said loudly, and the sound brought another moan from Angela's lips as the maid went over to the windows and pulled the draperies wide.

"Do you have to do that?" Angela laid her arm across her eyes to ward off the full glare of late-afternoon sunlight falling across her bed.

"You will be feeling fit enough soon. The potion that his Grace mixed for you is the

230

same that me own mum has fixed for me dad after he has stayed out all night with his friends. It be a promised cure, that's for sure!" As Ethel spoke, she went to Angela's wardrobe and removed a cinnamon brown riding habit with a lighter-hued, ruffled silk blouse. Laying the garments out at the foot of the bed, she retrieved the matching kid boots and found a small cinnamon-colored hat which boasted a saucy-looking feather on its side.

"What on earth are you doing, Ethel?" Angela, by now, felt well enough from the duke's brew to sit up without feeling as though her head were going to burst.

"His Grace told me to help you to dress to go riding with him within the hour."

"He could have at least had the courtesy to allow me this day to recover," Angela pouted. But her headache had fled and she was feeling somewhat better. Eyeing the tray with the pot of tea and plate of toast, she tentatively stretched out a hand. She had eaten little the night before, and now that her stomach was feeling right again, she bit off a small chunk of the toasted bread.

Ethel watched the young woman from the corner of her eye and grinned widely. "I told you that the potion would work right quick. Now let me dress you." Over the past months Ethel had found this young woman welcome relief to the otherwise boring routine of Westfield Hall. She always had some cheeky little comment to make, and the faces that Angela pulled behind staunch Mrs. Booth's back more than once had sent the undermaid rushing from a room with her hand covering her mouth to keep from bursting into peals of giggles.

Realizing that there was no way for her to get out of the ride with the duke, Angela finished her toast and tea, and let Ethel help her dress. When done and Ethel gone, she set the small hat at a sassy angle atop her head and allowed her waist-length dark hair to flow freely down her back. Giving herself one last glance in the mirror, she turned toward the chamber door. She had dared as much time as possible with her toilet, and fearful that the duke would begin to pound upon her door, she drew in a deep, steadying breath, determined to see this day out and swearing to herself that she would not be intimidated by the duke and the remembrance of what had taken place in the study the night before. Perhaps she could use this afternoon's ride with the duke to her own benefit. She would remind him to send for Lord Dunsely and be finished with the bet for once and for all. As she made her way downstairs, she kept her head high, determined to put from her mind the dinner last night, but with her determination followed the fleeting image of that handsome man holding her against his chest in those strong, capable arms! *Nay, do not let yourself dwell on this torment,* her inner mind rebuked sharply. *Such men as the Duke of Westfield are not for the likes of a Gypsy girl like yourself!* She must put such images of his sensual lips lowering over hers away. She would become no man's plaything! Like many young women her age, she held hopes of one day finding the man of her heart and marrying, and she did not fool herself into thinking that Royce St. James was that man! She was but a Gypsy girl, and he the Duke of Westfield!

Royce met his charge at the bottom of the stairway. His gray-silver eyes seemed to take in her every curve, then lingered upon her lovely features. Reaching out a hand, he softly murmured, "You look ravishing, Angela."

Angela felt her cheeks blush, from both the compliment and the heated look. Her response to the duke was one that Mrs. Booth had lectured was the proper response to be given by a young lady to a gentleman who has bestowed upon her a compliment. "Thank you, your Grace." She felt the words leaving her throat rather stiffly, but looking at the duke who wore snug-fitting, dove gray breeches and a white lawn shirt opened at the throat, she felt her heartbeat begin to accelerate.

"I hoped that you would not forget our appointed ride." Royce took her hand and eased it within the crook of his arm as he started to lead her to the front door.

As if she had had a choice, Angela thought as he led her through the door and across the yards to the stables.

"Jamie should already have our mounts readied," Royce stated. Nearing the stables, the two horses were waiting. The stable boy, young Harry, stood at attention holding their reins before the double doors of the stable. As Royce was about to give Angela a leg up, he stopped, looking at the saddle on the mare's back. "The boys must have made a mistake. It will only take a moment as they replace the saddle with an appropriate one." The duke gave Harry a dark frown.

"What is the problem with the saddle, your Grace?" Angela questioned with some confusion. "It is the same saddle that I have been using."

"But this is not a lady's saddle," Royce declared in surprise.

Angela smiled: her first thought was to remind the duke that she was not a lady! Thinking better of this, she declared instead, "Aye, your Grace, I have always ridden astride." Angela then slipped her foot into the stirrup without aid from the duke and lifted herself up and into the saddle, her long split skirt tending to her modesty.

Royce looked with amazement at the young woman upon horseback. He had rarely seen a woman riding astride, but looking upon her straight form, he had to admit that she was a beauty sitting upon Charmer's back. "You are certain that you are comfortable like that?" It was hard to believe that a woman could handle a mount like a man, but as she nodded her head, he told himself that the Gypsy brat had a wild spirit unlike any he had ever known in a woman before!

Angela smiled. "Most comfortable, your Grace, I assure you." With a nudge to Charmer's sides, she left the duke standing before the stable doors.

Royce watched as Angela rode away from him. She was a vision of beauty sitting atop the mare with her dark curls flowing out behind her. Quickly mounting his own stallion, he started after her.

Royce was as intrigued with his riding partner as he had been the evening before. She was breathtaking, every movement of her face or form drawing his attention as the afternoon swiftly passed. She sat the small mare as though she had been born to ride, her small chin firmly set and back straight.

There was little talk between the couple for the first hour of riding, and that satisfied Royce St. James. He received pleasure from merely looking upon Angela as his thoughts relived sampling her temptingly sweet lips.

As the ride progressed, Angela grew more comfortable with the duke's presence. She was not disappointed now that she had been forced to spend the afternoon riding over the Westfield properties with him. From the corner of her eye, she watched the duke's manly form atop his large black stallion. This afternoon she could find little in the man that portrayed him as the brute she had met that first night when he had brought her to the Hall. Nor had he displayed that arrogant, high-handedness with her last night or this afternoon. But she did not fool herself: she knew what he was capable of, even though he seemed bent upon charming her.

She was startled from her thoughts as he said, "You ride very well, Angela. Most ladies of my acquaintance are not as skilled." They had covered much of the Westfield back pastures and were now nearing a small ambling stream that ran a path through the south fields.

Angela smiled at the compliment, for she was proud of her skill as a horsewoman.

"Many of my people are trained from early childhood to ride and break horses. My father worked on a horse farm in Southampton near New Forest."

Her warm smile went straight to Royce's heart. "When you leave the Hall, will you return to your father?" He remembered vividly the first night he had brought her to the Hall and the wild story she had told him about being an orphan and a time traveler. He hoped that by now she might feel that she could trust him enough to tell him something about herself without resorting to such outrageous lies.

Her smile vanished. She knew that it would do her little good to try to explain her tale again. She slowly shook her dark head. "I have already told you that I have no family. When I leave the Hall, I plan to find some of my own people." Once she retrieved the pocket watch, she would indeed be able to return to her own people.

Something in her words gave Royce pause, and he looked at her a bit closer. Had he heard a touch of regret in her tone, perhaps loneliness? "When I found you in London, why were you not with some of your people? I am surprised that you were left alone in the city to make your own way."

It was on the tip of Angela's tongue to lie and tell him that she had gotten separated from her group, but something held her back. Instead she shouted over her shoulder, as she kicked Charmer's sides, "I'll race you to that stone fence!"

Without waiting to see if he accepted the race, she sped away through the field of tall grass and toward the fence.

Taken off guard, Royce stared after her retreating back, but quickly enough he regained his wits. With a shout of his own, he kicked the stallion's sides and, within seconds, was racing through the field after her. Though Royce was a practiced rider and his stallion much larger, Angela came only a hairsbreadth from winning.

With an engaging laugh and carelessly throwing the wild tangle of her dark hair from her shoulders, Angela was delighted by the frantic race, even though she had lost. "The next time, your Grace, I will give you little chance to beat me, so be on guard!" Her smile was enchanting as violet eyes sparkled and a healthy pink flush graced her cheeks.

Royce felt his breath sticking in his chest. There were a million things that he, given different circumstances and a different woman, would like to say, but, he could get nothing out of his mouth. All he could do was grin back, his hand automatically stroking the stallion's sleek neck as though imagining this to be Angela's tender flesh.

Charmer was also feeling exhilarated from the race. Prancing around Royce's stallion, the pert little mare whickered invitingly. "There, there, girl," Angela calmed, and then turned her about the meadow and cantered back from where they had just come.

Royce had little choice but to follow her lead, his silver gaze greedily drinking in every nuance of his charge's loveliness. "God grant me some much-needed strength!" he mumbled under his breath.

"When will Lord Dunsely be coming out to Westfield Hall?" Angela questioned as the pair stopped on a knoll which overlooked the Hall and the lush grounds.

"Damian?" So consumed by her radiance was he that Royce wondered what she could want of his friend. His memory then returned. "I suppose that I could have him out to the Hall soon enough." Royce felt disappointed that her only concern was to gain her purse and leave the Hall as quickly as possible.

Angela silently nodded as she tried to fight off the growing attraction that she was feeling for this man. As soon as possible, she had to find the pocket watch and return to her own century. She had to fight off these plaguing thoughts of the duke. Without a sideways glance in his direction, she started down the rise and toward the direction of the Westfield stables.

Royce followed, his mind in turmoil as he watched the shapely curve of her back. He would never have imagined that he could be so attracted to this young woman. The thought of inviting Damian out to the Hall and calling in the bet early left him feeling hollow inside.

Jamie met the pair outside the stable yard, and helping Angela from the back of her mount, he wore a wide grin. "I hope ye be having a fine day of it, lass," he ventured warmly before hurrying to the duke's side to offer his assistance.

"Indeed, Jamie, it was a wonderful ride!" Angela called out good-naturedly, always glad to converse with the head groomsman.

As she stood next to the mare, a small shaggy dog came to her side and stood wagging his tail as warm brown eyes looked up to her for attention. Bending down, Angela scratched the little mongrel behind the ears. "Who is this, Jamie?" she asked as Royce dismounted and handed over the reins to his stallion.

"He be called Denby, lass."

"Is he yours? I have never noticed him before now." Angela had always loved dogs and there was something about this skinny creature that immediately won her heart.

Jamie studied the young woman and the animal she was petting. "I reckon that old Denby be thinking that he be belonging to me now, lass." As she turned a questioning gaze upon him, he added, "It tweren't but a couple of weeks back, lass, that old Denby here belonged to old Mike Mailer. Mike, he lived in a little stone cottage some ways down the main road from his Grace's property. Twelve days ago, Mike's wee house just up and caved in, killing old Mike and his partner, Abner Bittner. He was helping Mike to work his dried-up piece of land. The only one to come out of the rubble was old Denby hisself."

"Oh, the poor thing!" Angela exclaimed. This time, she pulled the dirty little dog a bit closer as she petted his head and lavished him with attention.

"Now, lass, let me be afinishing me story before ye make any final judgments about Denby. As I told ye, Denby here made it out of the cottage, and then that same day he made his way to Bertha Winslow's house. She were a kindhearted widow lady, and taking pity on the little ragged creature, she took him in. It tweren't two days later that Bertha Winslow fell down in the middle of the village and broke her neck. Old Denby was right at her side, and not losing much time, he somehow made his way out here to the Hall and has sort of attached hisself to me. Now, don't be taking me wrong, lass. I ain't one to hold with superstitious ways, but there be something about this little old dog that rankles mighty strange at times. I just be ahoping that me own time ain't coming up soon and I be the next to meet up with an accident!"

Not lost to the edge of humor in Jamie's voice, Angela laughed softly. "I am sure that this little scamp's past has been a strange coincidence. He seems harmless enough to me."

"And if not, I wonder who his next master will be?" Royce joined in on the lively conversation, but he felt an ache in his heart as he watched Angela's tender touch being given to the little dog. He realized that it had been far too long since he had shared a carefree moment with one of his servants here at the Hall. The obligations of his title had distracted him from the enjoyment of life that was to be had here in the peaceful atmosphere at Westfield Hall.

Jamie snorted in feigned indignation over his master's comment. "It be too bad that old Denby here didn't attach himself to Pete Manning! Not a soul hereabouts would be missing the likes of that old sot!"

Fifteen

Having eaten dinner alone in her chamber as the hour grew late, Angela found herself prowling around the space of her bedchamber, trying somehow to fight off the boredom she had been feeling after the afternoon's activity. She was too keyed up with thoughts of Royce St. James to settle down upon the comfortable fourposter bed.

Arriving back at the Hall this afternoon, she found her usual bath waiting, and with its finish, she had dressed carefully, awaiting the anticipated summons from the duke to share dinner with him. When the summons did not come, but instead Hawkins brought her a dinner tray as usual, Angela only picked at her food. Finally she had given up all pretense of an appetite and had stripped off the shimmering ice-pink gown that she had donned for the evening.

Wearing only a thin shift, she paced about

the chamber, and with each minute's passing, she became more frustrated. Would the duke call his friend out to the Hall shortly? How soon would Damian Dunsely arrive here at Westfield Hall? The nagging thought that she was becoming far too comfortable in Royce St. James's presence tormented her. Why, she had even dressed in one of her finest gowns this evening with the hopes of spending more time in his company, and more than once this afternoon, she had found her gaze turned in admiration upon his masculine form! No, she had to get away from the Hall, and the sooner the better for her own peace of mind!

The small voice in the back of her mind questioned, *Then why don't you flee? Why linger at the Hall any longer than necessary? There is nothing holding you except the promised purse. Forget the gold and get yourself away from the Hall and Royce St. James as quickly as possible!*

But there was still the problem of regaining the pocket watch, Angela reminded herself. Unable to avoid Royce's presence this day, she had been unable to regain the watch as she had planned, and now once again, it was nighttime, too dark to search the bank of the pond.

Her pacing brought her up before her wardrobe, and without a second thought, Angela threw open the double doors and pulled forth a simple ruby dress. As she slipped the garment over her body, she delighted in the soft material. The sleeves were full, and the bodice fit snugly. She would wear the skirt without pannier or hoops. Pulling on the matching slippers which the shoemaker had designed with tiny ruby heels, she dug through the top bureau drawer in search of the right scarf. Pulling her hair back in a careless fashion, she tied the scarf over the crown of her head, capturing the mass of ebony curls.

Her mind was set, the outfit aiding her courage. She would go to the Gypsy encampment. She would have this evening to pay her last visit, and perhaps there in the forest among her own kind, she would be able to forget about Royce St. James for a few hours and be reminded of who she was! She left her bedchamber, silently making her way down the long hallway to the servants' stairway. Soon standing outside with the night breeze caressing her heated features, she drew in a ragged breath before starting toward the darkened stables.

Royce St. James was also finding the evening a restless one for him. He could not keep Angela from his mind! The vision of her enchanting blue eyes and glistening dark curls was burned within his brain, and as his hand lifted the brandy goblet once again, he gave up all pretense of working on the Hall's ledgers. He had deliberately instructed Hawkins to carry a dinner tray to Angela's chambers, and then one to him here in the study, hoping that this maneuver would clear his head of the seductive spell she had cast over him today while riding about the estate. All he could do was sample the food upon his plate, without an appetite, until at last he pushed the tray aside and began to sip at his brandy.

With the study's French doors standing open to capture the night breezes, the scent of late-blooming flowers from the gardens outside filtered through the air, and Royce was reminded of another scent: lilac. He found himself standing at the open doors, staring off into the night sky. As a cloud overshadowed the full moon, a fleeting image toward the back of the gardens caught his eye. It was a woman, and for a moment he wondered which of the servants could have an encounter planned for this night.

As the clouds scuttled across the sky, the fullness of the moon was revealed, and Royce was astonished to glimpse a horse and female rider leaving the entrance of the stables. Angela! Grabbing up his cloak, Royce left the house and made for the stables.

Angela was filled with a carefree exhilaration as she tried to force all thoughts of the Duke of Westfield out of her mind. She would once again visit the Gypsy people camped in the forest, and perhaps she would never return to the Hall! Perhaps she would go to the pond and wait until the first light of morning, then search for the pocket watch!

Making her way through the pasture and toward the forest, she was aided by the full moon which was riding high in the velvet night sky. As the mare neared the forest path, Angela caught her breath as she noticed the deep shadows about her. Determined to go on, she kept her mount on a steady path down the barely used trail through the forest. It was not long before she glimpsed the flickering orange glow of a campfire in the distance.

The Gypsy encampment was alive with activity even at this late hour. Angela reined Charmer in as she drew closer into the center of the camp, and she instantly felt the stares of the people around her. A few heads nodded in greeting, but for the most part, the people watched silently, wondering at her presence among them. It was the young man, Stephan, who came to her side and helped her dismount.

"So you have again returned to us," the young man said, his lively black gaze tinged with curiosity and caution.

Angela nodded her head. "I wanted to be with some of my own people this evening."

Stephan had never encountered a young woman quite like this one. None of the women of his tribe would dare what this one did. "And your lord? He allowed you to leave his Hall alone at this time of the night?"

Born to survive in a world that contained many threats to himself and his people, Stephan tried never to let down his guard. His dark eyes skimmed the outskirts of the encampment as though fearing the arrival of the powerful Duke of Westfield.

"The duke, as far as I know, is still at the Hall. I did not ask permission to leave!" Angela felt a spark of anger at the young man's questioning, but she knew that she could not blame him. These people had no reason to trust her.

"Come then." The young man surprised her by taking her hand and leading her toward the campfire, where most of the elders were standing or sitting as a brightly clad Gypsy man played a fiddle, those about him clapping and stomping their feet to the lively tune.

Angela silently watched the animated faces of those around her as she sat upon a log that had been pulled up near the fire. Two of the elder women of the tribe began to dance to the music.

"I did not think that you would return to us," Stephan said truthfully. Seeing her again, he was reminded of her incredible beauty. As her face tilted toward the dancing women, his gaze leisurely traced a path over her large blue eyes, high cheekbones, and full lips. "How is it that a beautiful woman such as yourself can ride unprotected at such an hour of the night?" He said nothing about her also riding alone in the daylight hours.

Angela did not believe it necessary for her to explain her actions to this young man. "I believe that I know the way back to my own people. I thought that I would return this one last time and thank you and your people." Especially the old woman called Zela, who had sparked the memory of the pocket watch, Angela reminded herself.

"Then you have found your Momma Leona?" Stephan questioned lightly, the flames of the fire dancing high in the night sky and filling his dark eyes with amber lights. He appraised her ruby dress, which molded itself seductively to her breasts.

"I have not found her, but I will now, I am sure." Angela smiled warmly into his olive face. She was finding him much easier to talk to than she had the day before, and with the added inducement of the lively music and the carefree manner of his people talking, laughing, and singing all around her, for the first time in almost a year, she felt as though she did indeed belong somewhere. These were her people, whether they admitted it or not, and she could remember many evenings like this one from her past.

Stephan made no further comment, but his dark eyes slowly went over to a voluptuous young woman who began to dance with wild gyrations. Her large, dark eyes seemed to pierce through the firelight as she held her gaze upon Stephan.

Angela's attention was also drawn to the young woman wearing a dark purple skirt and a scarlet, loose-fitting blouse. The rapid undulations of her abundant figure lifted her skirts to her thighs. The shouts of the onlookers encouraging her to dance even more frenziedly, Angela found her own feet tapping out a rhythm to the primitive beat of the music.

The Gypsy woman seemed to have eyes

only for the young man at Angela's side. With a catlike grace, she circled the fire and advanced upon the couple. Her slender arms, with their numerous bracelets jangling, reached out, and beckoned him to join her.

A wide grin spread over his handsome features, and Stephan rose from where he was sitting at Angela's side, his slim, muscular body stepping to the dancer's side. With sure steps, he boldly reached out and brought the young woman tightly against his chest. Releasing her, she swayed to the beat of the music alone, then joined him once again.

Her every curve molded to Stephan's length as the couple appeared joined as one, swaying and undulating before the campfire. Angela's breath caught in her throat as she watched them, so powerful were their movements. She could feel her own body moving to the music.

With the conclusion of the music, the young woman fell to the ground, her skirts flowing in an enticing puddle around her. As she looked up into the young man's face with hope in her dark eyes, Stephan stepped from her side. Going around the campfire, he nodded toward the one playing the fiddle, and instantly the music started up once again, this time the tune holding a livelier beat. Regaining Angela's side, he took her hand and pulled her to his side.

Angela felt all eyes upon her, including the glare of the Gypsy dancer. Nonetheless, Angela followed Stephan's movements. It did not take long to become one with the beat of the music, and soon she was swaying, her young ripe body picking up the rhythm, her feet turning and pausing, her skirts rising to her calves, then to her thighs. The firelight around the campfire enhanced the scene as sparks burst and flew into the velvet night sky and Stephan twirled her around to a breathless beat.

Her scarf, which had held back her willful curls, flew off, and her long tresses shimmered with highlights in the firelight. The entire Gypsy encampment stood breathlessly watching as the couple danced on. At the close of the music, instead of falling to the ground as the other woman had, Angela found herself held within Stephan's arms!

It took her a full moment to catch her breath, but when she did, she turned with a wide grin to face those standing silently by. She felt alive; but more than alive, she felt empowered! As though her life was finally falling into place and nothing could bring her low. The dance intensified every one of her emotions. By tomorrow she would be back where she belonged, but tonight she had danced the dance of life, of love, of strength!

After catching her breath, she pulled away from Stephan, his arm still wrapped around her shoulder. "I must be getting back to the Hall before I am missed," she lied, having no intention of ever returning to Westfield Hall, but as she gazed up into Stephan's face and was met with the warmth of his dark eyes, she knew that she had to leave. Throughout the dance, as the young man had drawn her against his lithe body, she had imagined herself dancing with Royce St. James!

"You will return?" Stephan was loath to release her. To him the dance had proven that she did belong here among his people. He could not just allow her to leave his camp; he might never see her again! When she did not answer quickly, he whispered, "If you do not return soon, I will come for you!"

Those around her, like Stephan, seemed more willing to accept her into their group. As she started to her horse, several voices called out for her to come back soon. Without answering, Angela mounted Charmer and started back down the forest path, Stephan's dark regard following her until she disappeared from sight.

* * *

By the time Royce St. James gained his stallion and left the Westfield stables, Angela had already cleared a large portion of the back pastures. Having glimpsed the direction she was taking, he followed at some distance with the hope of catching sight of her again by the light of the full moon. As she neared the forest's edge, he glimpsed the dark outlines of horse and rider before she disappeared down the forest path.

Thinking it strange that she would venture into the forest all alone, Royce became alert as he stayed his distance and followed her down the path. Did she have a lover that she was meeting here in the cover of the forest? With such thoughts, anger flared to life as he imagined her being held tightly in the arms of another man.

Royce noticed the flickering light of a campfire before seeing the Gypsy camp, and cautiously he drew close. At the edge of the camp, he stopped behind a tree and tied the stallion's reins securely to a low-hanging limb. Silently he kept to the shadows as he watched the activity in camp.

He watched as the young Gypsy man helped Angela to dismount, then saw her being led toward the campfire. He also saw the Gypsy woman begin her dance of seduction, but Royce had eyes only for Angela. As the young man left her side to dance with the woman, he studied Angela's features from where he stood hidden by the enclosure of the trees. Her beautiful face was alight as she watched the couple swaying and turning. When the young man drew Angela to her feet and began dancing with her, Royce wanted to charge forward and drag her back to the Hall with him!

With much self-control, he forced himself to remain still, gritting his teeth as he watched her shapely legs displayed beneath her ruby skirts. His silver eyes watched her as though he was a man bewitched; no one else in the area held any meaning for him. She danced only for him, and as her hair was released from the scarf and wound about her seductively, his heart hammered wildly in his chest.

Red-hot jealousy, the likes of which Royce had never felt before, seared his belly and boiled his blood as he watched Angela fall into the young man's arms at the finish of the dance. Opening and closing his fists, he swore savagely under his breath. If he were nearer to the couple, he knew that he would not be able to control the desire to strangle the young Gypsy man with his bare hands. The punishment he had in mind for Angela would not be that mild!

Stepping from the concealment of the trees, Royce was determined that he would confront the couple, for the lovers he believed them to be! He was pulled up short as he watched Angela pull away from the young man and mount her horse.

No one had noticed Royce St. James as he stood in the open on the outskirts of the camp. All eyes followed the young woman as she turned her mare back down the forest path. With a ragged breath, Royce once again disappeared into the forest, intent upon regaining his horse and then confronting Angela as being the deceitful little baggage that he now believed her to be. She had lied to him right from the start, he told himself. These were her people, the people that she claimed she no longer knew how to contact, and the Gypsy man was her lover! He did not remember in his madness that it had been he who had forced her to live at the Hall. That he and his friend had forced her to become the pawn in their wager over a horse! All he saw in his mind was the sight of her in the young man's arms!

Never had Angela felt so exhilarated! As the mare took her out of the forest, she pushed her hair back from her shoulders, the soft tendrils damp and clinging to her face from the exertion of dancing around the campfire. She had danced before in Momma Leona's camp with the other children, but never had she allowed herself to be so caught up, so totally lost within the spell of the Gypsy music! She felt her body shiver from the caress of the night breeze, as though a lover's touch, and without control, her thoughts again went to Royce St. James.

As the mare broke through the forest path, Angela's glance fleetingly turned to the path she had taken earlier. She could not return to the Hall, she knew, this night or ever. There was nothing there for her, only the torment of being near that which she could never possibly call her own. Royce St. James was not the man for her; he would always remain far beyond the reach of a mere Gypsy girl! Nudging the mare's sides, she set off through the pasture of tall grass, toward the London road which led to the pond. Not once did she think of Stephan or his whispered words. She would be gone from this century in a short time, and once back with Momma Leona and the children, she would put from her mind all thoughts of Royce St. James and Stephan!

Not far behind her on the forest path, Royce wondered at the direction she had turned the mare. Was she now going to meet another one of her lovers? His thoughts were not his usual rational ones, so jealous was he.

He boldly kicked the stallion's sides and set the large beast after the mare at a full gallop.

It was a few minutes before heavy hoof-beats broke through Angela's reflections. Glancing over her shoulder, Angela's heartbeat instantly accelerated. The large, dark shape of a horse and rider was only a short distance behind her. She kicked out at Charmer's flanks. Bending low over the mare's neck, she called out for her to race for all she was worth! It must be a highwayman, one of those ill-reputed thieves of the road that Mr. Clemons had told her about. Angela turned the little mare sharply to the right, realizing as her pursuer drew ever closer that this might be her only chance to avoid capture. Charmer's maneuvers were quick and sharp as she followed her mistress's instructions, but they were not fast enough to avoid the black stallion, which was, by the second, closing the distance.

Overtaking the fleet-footed little mare, Royce reached out a strong arm and swept Angela from Charmer's back. Amidst her struggles for release, he pulled her squirming form up before him on the stallion.

With a scream filled with outrage and a bold curse that would have made a sailor cringe, Angela fought the arm that had snatched her from her mount. Screams and curses bubbled out of her throat as her fists pummeled the dastardly villain's chest and upper body.

Royce knew that Angela had not recognized him, and realizing that she believed him some foul abductor of women gave him a small sense of retribution. She should be made to suffer, even if only for a few seconds, he told himself. Had he not felt his own soul torn to shreds as he had stood and watched her in the arms of her Gypsy lover?

At last he pulled her hands to her sides. Sharply he said, "Keep still, Angela. It is I, Royce."

Instead of complying, she fought him even harder. This was the very man that she had run away from! How on earth had he found her? Afraid that she would melt within his strong arms if she stayed there, she tried to pull away from him. "Let me go this minute!" she demanded.

If only it had been one of those infamous highwaymen instead of him! The irrational thought filtered through her mind as she tried to free herself from his embrace. With any other man she might have a chance of escaping. With another she could fight with a burning hatred, but this man, Royce St. James, was the one man who held the power to break through her defenses!

Not expecting such resistance, Royce was surprised by the fury of her fight. "I am sorry if I frightened you, Angela," he confessed, but he still believed her to be the deceiving little Gypsy he had witnessed earlier in the evening, and he was not about to release her to run into the waiting arms of another man!

"Why can't you just leave me alone?" Angela moaned softly, her defenses crumbling slowly as his gentle tone flowed over her. All he cared about was the bet. Nothing mattered to him but the treasured horse—not her feelings, or the fact that he was tormenting her soul by holding her so intimately against his broad chest. Her heartbeat thudded against her breasts and stirred her passion in directions other than anger.

"Why should I release you? So that you can run away with one of your lovers?" Royce was irrational, but he couldn't stop the accusation from leaving his mouth. He was overwhelmed by her nearness; her lush form made him mindless.

"My lovers?" Angela gasped aloud as she stilled at last in his arms. What was he talking about? She had no lovers!

"Your Gypsy lover back there. Lord only knows how many more you have!" Before she could say anything in her defense, he lashed out, "You can't deny it, because I saw you dancing with him!"

Angela felt herself blush and was thankful

that it was too dark for him to view her embarrassment. Her thoughts had been of him while she was dancing, but she would never reveal this. Knowing he had watched her body swaying so seductively increased her desire to be away from him! Instead of fighting him, she hissed, "How dare you follow me as though I were a common thief!"

"If the shoe fits, my dear," Royce chuckled. "You know that I must insure that you do not leave before the wager can be called in."

Angela could take no more from this cruel-hearted man. With a movement she caught him off guard, and pushing against his broad chest, she found herself slipping to the ground. The instant her feet touched earth, she was sprinting away from Royce and his stallion. If she could run the several yards to where Charmer was standing, perhaps she would be able to put some distance between them, then hide until he gave up the search.

She was not so lucky. Within seconds Royce was giving chase, his long legs covering a greater distance in a shorter amount of time. Before she grabbed the mare's reins, he caught hold of her and pulled her back into his arms. "You cannot flee me, Angela. I will never release you!"

Before she could do anything to ward him

off, his sensual lips covered hers in a joining that swept away all thoughts of anger and argument as they clung together in the pasture of tall grass with a full moon riding overhead!

Sixteen

Royce's mouth settled over Angela's passionately, his arms pulling her closely into his embrace as he molded her lush form fully against the length of his muscular torso. His first thought was to make her answer to his charges of deceit, but the tender womanliness of her form against his hard body tempered his harshness. His lips were as gently seductive as a butterfly's wing as it brushed against a dewy flower's petals.

Angela was lost within the spell of his kisses. She softly moaned as her mind issued a feeble warning: flee before it was too late. But it was already far too late! The touch of his mouth slanting over her own, the feel of his fingers across her cheek and along the slender column of her throat, even the strong inducement of his scent prevented her from breaking away! As the kiss intensified and her slim arms crept up and wrapped around the

263

broad expanse of his shoulders, her lips parted to receive the inviting warmth of his searching tongue.

For a magical moment the couple clung together beneath the star-bright night, surrounded by the tall grass as moonbeams shimmered down upon the earth. There was no future, no past, no right or wrong; all that mattered was this minute in the universe. This moment in time sealed their fate!

Royce was unable to get enough of her incredible taste. His searing tongue probed and plundered each secret place of her ambrosia-laced mouth. Her taste was like that of the sweetest honey, stirring within his depths a desire, a need, a want so great he trembled.

"Kissing you is like the drinking of a life-giving nectar." Royce finally pulled his inner senses together enough to speak, and as he did, his breath caressed the side of her face. "I have not been able to banish from my thoughts the taste of you and the feel of you in my arms since that night when I held you in my study."

Angela's head was reeling, her hands clutching tightly to the dark silk fabric of his shirt as she gazed into the swirling gray-silver depths of his eyes.

Slowly his thumb touched her mouth, making a light path down her chin to the creamy smoothness of her slender throat.

With a husky groan, he drew her tightly against him, his mouth capturing her lips in a scorching kiss that left them both gasping for breath. His sensual lips seemed to devour hers. His tongue slipped within and rhythmically plied her soft mouth. Then plunging deeply, both their souls ignited.

Royce's lips traversed a path from her mouth to her jawline, then down her neck. The fullness of her straining breasts tempted him as he felt the heavy pounding of her heart. With ease the bodice's tiny glass buttons parted and the sheer shift revealed the rose-tipped crests of her breasts swelling under the touch of his fingers as his hot kisses rained down upon her mouth, cheek, and then lowered to the erratic pulse of her throat.

"You are exquisite, my little Gypsy angel," Royce breathed against the flesh of her neck, the hot touch of his breath electrifying her entire body. Ever so tenderly, his hot tongue made tiny circles around the sheerly covered tip of one breast. As his ears filled with the sound of Angela's small gasps, his mouth took in the fullness of the delicate mound, sucking lovingly and with skill as his other hand lavished attention on the other rose-peaked nub.

In the distant recesses of Angela's mind, that small voice put forth an effort to bring her back to her senses. *This man is not for the likes of you, girl! He is a duke of the realm, a man used to taking that which he desires!* But, Angela was powerless to heed inner warnings. Her body strained toward Royce as her breasts swelled beneath his caresses and a burning heat began to grow in the depths of her body.

Perhaps it was the wild dance of seduction before the Gypsy encampment, or perhaps it was the gentle swaying of the tall grass which surrounded them, or the velvet-shrouded, star-brilliant night in which the song of life and love whistled softly upon the night breeze—perhaps all these pushed her to a point of no return. Angela was unsure. She knew only that all that mattered was Royce St. James. Only the thrilling touch of his mouth and hands as they roamed over her body was real! She was beyond the point of turning away. If she tried to quell the searing flames of desire that throbbed wantonly from the core of her being, she knew that she would perish from denial.

As Royce's mouth plied her with heated kisses and she lost all touch with reality within the whirling pleasure, his hands eased her dress from her body, and the shift next to follow. "God, you are even more beautiful than I remembered," he murmured.

He recalled the numerous times he had

relived that first moment when he had glimpsed her nakedness in the kitchen at the Hall, and a moan softly escaped his lips as silver eyes filled with her vision. The moonlight touched her with a golden stream of light, long ebony strands of hair flowing tantalizingly over smooth shoulders and down her back, enhancing her loveliness. He removed his cloak and spread it on the ground, then lowered Angela down to its silky folds.

As Angela writhed under his thrilling assault, she knew that she was completely out of control. She had never expected her first time with a man to be so beautiful or so breathlessly consuming. All she had to go by were the noises she had heard coming from the back room of Momma Leona's trailer and the sight of Alex the next morning after enduring the abuse that had been inflicted upon her by her lovers.

Royce's heated lips scorched a trail over a rounded hip, and his hand boldly touched the delicate crest of her womanhood. Sparkling sensations such as she had never before felt shot throughout every portion of her body. His touch was earth-shattering as he made contact with the nub of her very foundation. Angela was forced to clamp her teeth tightly together to keep herself from crying out.

As his mouth followed the trail blazed by his hand and his lips and tongue found that most treasured spot, a cry of incredible pleasure escaped her throat and filled his ears. With a penetrating, consuming fever he plundered her core, delving deeply into her, carrying her toward the highest pinnacle of pleasure's domain. She rose up and clutched the dark strands of his hair in her fists. What was he doing to her? She was on fire! She was a cauldron of hot, trembling desire! His mouth spiraled her soul into a vortex of impossible feelings. Swept heavenward, Angela met rapture's searing reward and could only hold on to him as her cries of release filled the air and her lover's ears.

Angela felt her body dissolving as a trembling started deep within her and raced throughout every portion of her body. Royce rose up, his dark hair hanging free about his shoulders as his rich, glittering silver eyes looked into her passion-laced features. Within seconds he was free of his clothes, and as Angela inhaled raggedly, trying to recapture her breath, he joined her again upon his cloak.

As his arms enclosed her young, lush body, a maelstrom of unquenchable passion swept over him. "From the first moment I looked upon you that night in the kitchen at the Hall, I have dreamed of this moment,

Angela. Your beauty is incomparable. You are all that any man could desire, all that I could ever wish for!" Royce's lips recaptured hers as he was seized with an urgency which only the taste of her sweet bounty could quell.

Angela moaned softly as his tender words deeply touched her heart. She welcomed his loving assault, not thinking of tomorrow, or the tomorrows that might follow. Wrapping her slender arms around his powerful neck, she pulled his naked body closer to her, wanting to be overcome, to be possessed by this man; only this man!

As his mouth covered hers, her lips opened to him, and as his tongue circled and plundered, her own lightly touched against his and was drawn into his mouth; tenderly he sucked it fully into his warm, moist depths. This sent her into deeper rapture! Every touch he bestowed kept her mindlessly aware of the new and powerful feelings storming through her body.

His mouth and hands seemed to be all over her. His mouth parted her lips, then sensuously drifted across her cheek, lightly kissing her soft creamy skin, then down the slim column of her throat. Tasting her flesh as though he could not get enough of her, he lingered over her full, straining breasts, tempting their hard tips with deft flicks of his heated tongue.

As his mouth reclaimed hers, she was swept to dazzling heights of desire. His large body rose atop hers as his hand roamed seductively over her form, lingering at her womanhood and evoking a heated response as Angela's body pushed against his probing fingers. Slowly he eased her thighs apart, and his body poised atop her as his large, pulsating length brushed against her velvet-soft warmth.

In some secret place within her heart, she was glad that he would be her first and not someone of Momma Leona's choosing. Even if she could but claim the Duke of Westfield only for this night, she would have these memories to hold when she returned to her rightful time. She felt the heated, blood-thickened tip of his lance touching her, and she craved him wantonly. As he slowly eased his great length into her moist depths, she gasped in surprised pain; her hands clutched the firm flesh of his sides, nails raking into his skin as the piercing pain chased away the earlier pleasure.

A virgin! The harsh bell of warning tolled within Royce's brain. The girl was untouched until this moment! He had deflowered her without a thought to the possibility of such a thing being possible! Not once had he even considered that he would find her chaste. With her figure, her beauty—she was a Gypsy for God's sake! He had watched her twirl and sway in a dance of seduction only a short time ago, a dance that, to his mind, had bespoken carnal knowledge. Her hips had undulated to a tempo that only a lover could have matched!

If only he had known, he thought as he looked down into her face and glimpsed a sparkling tear in the corner of her eye. His lips slowly lowered, and with a tender touch, he asked for her forgiveness. He knew as he kissed her that he would not have been able to change a moment of what had happened this evening!

Angela had never been one to shy from reality. She had not expected the sharp pain, but it was quickly diminishing, especially with Royce's gentle apology. As Momma Leona always said, "Girl, you made your bed, now lie in it." Well, her bed at this moment was a satin cloak, and as she wrapped her arms around Royce's neck, she was more than happy to be lying in it!

Her reaction startled him. He had expected harsh recriminations. But as her arms wrapped around his neck and her lips responded, her luscious body slowly began to move. Her hips then pushed against his own as though she were trying out this newfound fullness, and his emotions soared, skyrocketed, and exploded into a mighty tempest of scalding hot desire!

His body began to slowly move atop hers, and she welcomed the movement without any lingering pain, hips beginning to undulate temptingly in response. Her body rose up to his, keeping a steady movement that was breathtakingly pleasurable. From deep within, a small spark ignited and slowly grew into a towering blaze as her inexperienced body started to move and respond in the same rhythmic motions as Royce's. His manhood thrust within her sleek, hot passage, then drew back to the lips of her moist desire, leaving her panting. Over and over again, he continued to fill her, then ease out, and a glorious sensation grew in the very depths of Angela's being. Her body trembled and quivered as she was caught up in the blinding rapture of fulfillment. Her eyes enlarged as she moaned passionately, wave after wave of ecstasy's pleasure shuddering over her length.

Royce was caught up in her passion as he looked down into her face. Engulfed by the sensations her quivering sheath brought over him, he sampled all that she possessed, and with a deep, pleasurable moan, he was held for a timeless instant upon the brink of a towering climax. Another plunge within her wet, warm depths and wildfire shot through his loins, leaving him shuddering uncontrollably. Clutching her tightly, he rode out the full crest of his passions.

Gasping softly for breath, Angela marveled at all she had experienced during these past moments. She held no regrets. Deep within her body, she still experienced tremors of passion that this man had allowed her to discover.

Lying still, with his body braced atop hers, Royce regained his heartbeat. He wondered how she would receive him now, after the climax of their lovemaking. His anger and her resistance had led up to what had just taken place. He could only guess at the hurt and the anger that he would read upon her features when he dared to look into her eyes and brave the storm. Never had he found such delight in the arms of a woman, and this added to his guilt. Though he had not known her to be a virgin, he would not shrug off any of the blame for what had taken place this evening. She was an innocent. Though her kisses had been more responsive and sweeter than any he had ever tasted, her body more seductive and inviting, she was blameless!

He had avoided becoming entangled with virgins. Proclaiming himself a professed bachelor, he held no desire to be forced into a union with a woman just because he had been her first, and certainly he would not hold with the ties of matrimony before he was ready!

He was taken off guard as he looked down into the lovely violet-blue eyes and was held by the sheer wonder in their depths. There was no anger, nor was there any trace of regret in the dark blue jewels that looked up at him. There was amazement and fulfillment there, and for a breathless time, he was caught spellbound by their depths.

Royce lowered his head and kissed the savory sweetness of her mouth. She softly moaned and his lips released hers. Drawing her into his arms, he rose to his feet. "We should return to the Hall," he whispered huskily as he held her naked body against his powerful chest, overwhelmed with her nearness.

Angela nodded. Forgotten were all her plans to escape him and Westfield Hall. Also forgotten was the pocket watch and her desire to return to her own time. She was powerless but to cling to his magnificent body and go with him wherever he desired.

Having no wish to release her, even for the short time it would take her to dress, Royce bent and retrieved his cloak. This he draped around her shoulders as he set her atop his horse; his hands drew the folds of the cloak about her bountiful form, tucking the silk edges beneath a shapely thigh.

He retrieved his clothing, then drew on his trousers and pulled on his shirt. Gathering her dress and shift over his arm, he settled himself behind her on the stallion. He gathered the reins and tenderly drew her back against his chest. The mare followed behind the stallion as the couple started back in the direction of the Hall.

By the time they reached their destination, Royce St. James's head was clearer. No words had been spoken about what had taken place in the pasture. The only thing that Royce knew was that he could not let this woman go. Not yet anyway, he told himself. The wager be damned! There was more at stake here than a mere horse! Never had his passions soared to such heights of rapture as they had this evening. He was loath to let this Gypsy angel slip out of his arms until he had satisfied himself of her enough to put her from his mind. He could think of nothing else but carrying her up the stairs and into his chamber. He would teach her all that there was to learn between a man and a woman!

Angela shivered with renewed anticipation as his hands slid over her body beneath the silken cloak. One minute she felt as though she were burning with fever, the next as though she were taken with a chill.

The horses were left inside the stable as Royce gathered Angela once again into his arms and with bold strides made his way inside the Hall. Within the manse all was quiet, the servants already having retired for the evening. As Royce carried her up the stairs and opened his chamber door, Angela told herself that she would have this one night to claim him. Tomorrow she would retrieve the pocket watch and return to her own century. Tomorrow she would think about everything she had done this evening with the duke, and perhaps then her shame would be manifested, but now, she could feel no guilt.

With the tenderest care, Royce set Angela to her feet upon the thick Persian carpet before the fireplace in his chamber. For a lingering minute, his fingers traced the softness of the ebony curls that caressed her cheeks. Looking down on her, his regard gleamed with admiration as he studied her lovely face before the firelight. "Ahh, my little Gypsy angel, your beauty is simply breathtaking."

Each single feature that his hungry glance took in gave truth to these words. The delicate arch of her dark brows over the sparkling vibrance of her thickly lashed deep blue eyes; her high, fragile cheekbones; and the small, slender nose above pinkened lips— all attested to the fact that her beauty was not common, but perfection. No fault of feature or complexion could be seen.

As Royce searched her face, Angela, gazing at him, felt as though she were being cherished. Her life up until this point had been a struggle to survive; no one had ever taken the time to glimpse the beauty of her features or the tenderness inside her person. Royce St. James was the first to see her for who she really was, and she wanted to capture all the memories of their short time together. She reached up and unclasped the binding that held the cloak together at her throat. The mantle fell in a satin puddle at her feet; her naked body shone with the golden haze from the flickering firelight beyond the hearth. As her arms reached out to draw his head down to her, her lips pressed against his, and once again, her mind's warning tried to bring her to her senses. But Angela rebuked that more practical side of her nature. She would have this night with this man and nothing was going to stop her!

Seventeen

This woman was like no other that Royce St. James had ever known! Her silky smooth arms wrapped around his neck and drew him closer to her lush, ripe lips. Their all-consuming kiss left his mind swimming and feverish blood boiling in his veins. He wanted her this minute as much as he had earlier in the field of grass. When her tongue tentatively entered his mouth and hesitantly swirled around his own, he crushed her to his length with a groan of pure lust.

With the completion of the fiery kiss, Royce began to discard his clothing. As ravenous for him as he was for her, Angela's slender hands reached out to aid him. Pulling the dark shirt from his shoulders, her fingers ran a course over the bulging muscles of his upper torso, and with the contact, she felt a shiver run her length. As he stepped out of his trousers, her blue eyes enlarged. In the meadow, with the darkness of night to hinder her full vision, she had not been able to fully appraise his full measure, but here in his chamber with the firelight, there was nothing hidden.

His entire body was fit muscular from much activity outdoors. His broad chest and upper arms rippled with bulging muscles, and a crisp matting of dark hair centered on his chest, drawing her attention before her gaze lowered over his ribs and trim waist to tight hips and buttocks. His thighs and calves were muscular, but what drew her full attention was the blood-thickened, engorged length of his manhood. It appeared massive as it rose up from between his legs, and as a small gasp escaped her, she told herself that this had brought her so much pleasure earlier. Having lived in the cramped quarters of Momma Leona's trailer, Angela had seen a male body unclothed, but those few times she had come upon one of the older boys relieving themselves compared little with the sight of this bold, turgid lance!

Royce was not lost to her gaze's greedy appraisal. As it settled upon each portion of his body, he felt the heat of her blue eyes caressing him, until at last she feasted her full gaze upon his swollen manhood. Though she studied him for only a few seconds, he felt himself growing even harder, hungrier for the sampling of her tender flesh. Her regard was without guile as it rose back to his face and those violet-blue jewels locked with his own searching gaze. He read no fear in the eyes looking deeply into his own. There was a touch of surprise, even curiosity, but the fright that he had feared he would view was absent. What manner of woman was she, his little Gypsy brat? The question fleetingly flitted through his mind as his hands reached out and drew her back into his embrace.

Angela did not hold any fear; she was too full of this newfound daring nature to fear anything! Her lips met his in a scorching kiss that left her standing on her tiptoes to fully accommodate each masculine contour of his virile body.

The fire beyond the hearth heated their chilled flesh, the Persian carpet a soft bolster for their entwined bodies as Royce drew Angela downward. Her body opened to him, accepting his pulsating sword into her warm, moist sheath as she straddled her legs around his waist. His hands encircled her upper thighs and hips as he eased her up and down, setting the rhythm of their love play. Royce rocked his large body back and forth, her tight woman's depths wrapped around him and stroking him in a fashion that drove him wild.

The warm glow of passion flickered and kindled to a full blaze again as she was filled with Royce's hardness. With his arms encircling her body where she sat upon his lap, his hands on her hips, her mouth and tongue heatedly caressed his chest. Her lips trailed a moist path of fire along his broad neck and over the strength of his chest. Caught up with his passionate strokes, her entire body moved to a sensual, lustful beat. Undulating and seeking, her body rocked with a primal rhythm. Her breathing ragged and gasping, she moved up and down, up and down, until she lost all reason to the overwhelming feelings descending upon her. The rapturous sensations made by his love tool stoked the flames of her desire, leaving her breathless and slick with sweat as her body shuddered and trembled atop him.

"Let us drink more fully of this draft of passion," said Royce huskily as he laid her upon the cushion of the carpet, his body rising above hers.

As he entered her once again, she gasped, "Royce!" It was a caress, a plea, and as his eyes looked down on her beautiful face, he was held spellbound for a timeless period.

"Do not move, my angel. Keep your body still and enjoy the pleasure that I would give you," he whispered. As he slowly began to move the lower portion of his body, his lips and hands began to wander over the sensitive areas of her body. Chills of racing desire danced along her spine as she tried to obey his tantalizing command and forced herself to remain still beneath his titillating caresses.

Claiming a racing tempo of steaming desire, his manhood moved in and out of her velvet depths. As his mouth closed over one rose-tipped nipple, his tongue teased the ripe bud, teeth gently tugging as he suckled. She cried aloud from the sheer ecstasy of his actions. His mouth charted a damp path from one straining breast to the other as fingers roamed freely over her belly and ribs. As his body moved to the timeless beat of sensual pleasure, he was blessed with the sound of her musical voice calling out his name.

"Royce!" she cried. "Royce, please . . . !" She did not know at that moment whether she was begging him to stop or to continue with his divine torture. Her head was thrown back, her lips parted, her entire body aflame as she was consumed by a powerful vortex of passion.

Their rapture rose higher and higher until Angela felt a towering surge rippling, growing, as if a gigantic tidal wave washed over her, drowning her in its ecstasy as she pulled Royce into its glowing center. For a time, they floated in its magnificence.

Held within the throes of a raging climax, spasms quaking over her entire length. Angela cried aloud with the total force of the pleasure she was receiving as Royce also sought his own release. His manhood surged with one last mighty thrust, and with a spasm of release, his seed erupted into her.

As their heartbeats calmed, they clung together in the disbelief that their coming together could prove so wondrous. Royce's fingers gently plowed through the satin strands of Angela's hair as he turned her face to meet his. He kissed her gently. "God, you drive me wild, woman!" he growled. "Even this minute, with my body sated as it has never been before, you tempt me to my very soul with your soft, inviting flesh!"

Angela knew exactly what he meant: she felt the same! She had never experienced such overwhelming feelings as those she had shared with this man. Lying next to him, she shivered at his gentle touch, his lips holding her mindless as he softly whispered these words against her cheek.

Gathering her in his embrace, Royce made his way to the large bed in the center of the chamber. Placing her with care on it, he reclined next to her. "I would have you stay here next to my side throughout this night,

Angel." Royce looked down into her sleepy visage and a tender smile settled over his sensual lips.

"Hmm," Angela replied and snuggled deeper into the down mattress. She was more than content to share this great bed with him for one night. Tomorrow would be here soon enough, and with the rising of the sun, she might never know such pampering again. There were no down mattresses in Momma Leona's small trailer. As her eyes began to close, she thought to tell him that her name was Angela, not Angel, but she was too tired; perhaps tomorrow she would tell him.

As the flickering firelight cast shadows on the ceiling of the chamber, Royce pulled Angela's lush form tightly into his embrace. He heard her even breathing. Light tresses of her hair fell over his forearm and against his chest; the scent of lilac filled his nostrils. His being was fully attuned to this woman lying at his side. His senses had been ensnared in a fine web that she had cast. Everything about this woman enticed him. She fit so well in his arms, her every curve molding itself perfectly against his naked body and furthering Royce's desire to keep her at his side. He would not release her at the ending of the year. He would shower her with gifts and attention, and force her

284

to forget her desire to return to her own people. He would give her a town house in London; he would buy her a fancy carriage—two if she so desired! He would give her everything that a treasured mistress could ever desire! Yes, his Gypsy angel would become his mistress, he told himself. He would keep her at his side until this attraction that was between them vanished!

All of Angela's best-laid plans for the following day vanished when she opened her eyes and found herself lying next to Royce St. James in his large oak bed. She should flee his chamber this minute! If she had any sense at all, she would do exactly that and act as though last night had never happened! But as her head turned slightly and her eyes locked with those of sparkling silver, she was lost in his gaze. Her body shivered from the contact of his naked flesh molded against her.

"Good morning, my sweet." Royce's sensual voice warmed her to her toes as an arm tightened around her waist and pulled her closer against his loins. "I hope you slept well?" Royce could not remember a better night's rest.

Angela felt the heat of a blush staining her cheeks. She was powerless to answer, just as she was powerless to think clearly. She felt intoxicated by his closeness, his hands stealing over her body and reclaiming the intimacy which they had shared last night. His lips feathered little kisses along her slender neck and against her fragile jawline.

"Mmm, I could stay right here beside you for the rest of the day," Royce whispered tantalizingly against her cheek. Angela sighed her agreement.

There was a hesitant knock upon the door, and as Angela scurried below the covers, Hawkins entered the room bearing a covered breakfast tray. With two settings upon the tray, it was obvious that the servant was well-aware of Angela's whereabouts. Setting the tray down discreetly upon the side table next to the bed, Hawkins silently left the chamber after a single glance toward the master's bed.

Angela's embarrassment was keen, and after the servant closed the door behind him, a small moan escaped her as she began to pull herself toward the opposite side of the bed. "I should go to my chamber and get dressed," she whispered.

Sensitive to her feelings, and not having missed her hasty escape beneath the covers as Hawkins had entered the room, Royce was determined that she would not leave his bed. He drew her back to his side. "What we have shared together is beautiful, Angela. There is no reason to hide the attraction that we feel for one another. Hawkins is not such a prudish soul that he will look down upon you." His finger reached out and brushed away the frown line that was marring her soft brow.

His words of comfort did not salve the upset that Angela was feeling. She could imagine what Hawkins and the rest of the servants had thought of her when she arrived at the Hall months ago in her tattered clothes, holding them off at knife point. Now added to all their other not-so-very-pleasant thoughts of her was the fact that she was sleeping with their master! Last night had been the most wonderful night of Angela's life, but she had not thought of the consequences. She had told herself that she would leave the Hall today, but she was learning that this was going to be harder than she had anticipated. Looking into Royce's handsome face and feeling his tender arms around her did little to make her want to flee!

"I do not intend on letting you slip away from me, Angela. You will have to get used to the idea of others knowing my feelings toward you." With this he dipped his head, pressing his lips tenderly over hers. The kiss shared was as conductive as a match to dry timber, leaving Angela forgetful of everything but the heat racing through her limbs. As his mouth pulled away from hers, she wondered what these feelings that he claimed to hold for her were.

Placing a down pillow behind her, Royce leaned his large frame against the head-board as he brought the tray from table. Taking up the chalice which contained a cool drink, he first brought it to Angela's lips. " 'Tis the sweeter when shared, love." His silver regard watched with warm approval as she took a sip of the fruity nectar.

Breakfast was a sensual interlude as Royce fed Angela melon and pastry with his fingers. After the last bite, he was as hungry for her lush body as he had been for the food.

Some time later Angela left Royce's bed and made her way through the adjoining chamber door to her own room. Feeling languidly sated, the color in her cheeks heightened by the delicious bout of lovemaking, she swept across the room and stood before the wardrobe. Royce had told her that he had already informed Mrs. Booth and Mr. Clemons that they were no longer needed at the Hall. Her lessons had been terminated this very morning, and then with a wide grin, he had announced that the two of them would be leaving the Hall in less than an hour for a picnic lunch and an afternoon ride. He had received no argument from Angela. His words had hastened her from his side and hurried her to her own chamber. She would love nothing better than to spend a long afternoon out of doors. The prospect of spending the rest of the day with Royce St. James furthered her anticipation.

Opening the double doors of the wardrobe, she pulled out a riding habit with a matching hat boasting a wide brim and an embroidered ribbon to tie beneath her chin. Beginning to dress, her inner mind pricked her sharply with the reminder that she had planned this day to flee the Hall and the Duke of Westfield, retrieve the pocket watch, and then return to her own century. This life she was living, the attention she was now receiving from Royce, was little more than a dream that could shatter!

"But what a dream it was to give up!" Angela murmured aloud to herself as she began to dress, lacing her boots. Royce was no longer the same man who had brought her out to Westfield Hall. Gone now was the hardness in his tone when he spoke to her. There was no longer that glint of distrust in his gaze when she shared something of herself. He was the man of any woman's dreams: affectionate, attentive, very handsome, and bold! How could any woman be expected to give up such a man after only a sampling of the first fruits of his attentions? With the completion of her dressing, she stepped over to the vanity. She settled the hat upon her head, and looking into the dressing table mirror, she promised that tomorrow would be soon enough for her to make good her vows to leave the attraction that she had found here in the eighteenth century!

With one last glance in the mirror, she smiled at her own reflection. Aye, tomorrow would be soon enough to carry out her plans. Today she would share the precious moments that were left to her with Royce St. James.

But when tomorrow came, Royce and Angela spent the afternoon next to the pond behind the stables. Swimming naked in the chilly water, they frolicked and splashed like children, and then warmed each other by making love in the tall grass at the water's edge.

Royce was even more determined that he would not let Angela leave him. With the thought always lurking in the back of his mind that she might demand he call in the bet, allowing her to leave the Hall, he intensified his tender courtship of her!

Eighteen

A dim fire glowed beyond the hearth. Before it sat a brass tub with steam rising from the depths of the warm water. Candles had been arranged on two small tables, their golden light flickering sensuously over the gleaming tub and lending a silken hue to the bathwater. The scent of lilac delicately scented the chamber.

Entering the bedchamber, Angela smiled as she turned to Royce, who quickly stepped to her side. They had just shared a delightful dinner out in the gardens. The stars arrayed across the velvet-dark splendor cast a romantic spell over the couple as they had sat on the patio. With the aid of torchlight, they had shared a bottle of chilled champagne and sampled the savory fare that Mrs. Biesely had prepared.

Stepping farther into the room, Angela glimpsed another bottle of champagne and two crystal, long-stemmed glasses resting on the table next to the bedside.

"I thought this evening we could share our bath, sweet." Royce's husky voice seemed to physically caress Angela. He kissed her lightly, leaving her trembling as she stood in the center of the bedchamber.

Yesterday afternoon while they were out riding, Royce had had Ethel and Agnes move most of Angela's belongings into his chamber, but she had still taken her bath in the adjoining chamber after their return to the Hall. Royce St. James was a man not given to sharing that which he claimed for his own. He wanted his Gypsy angel to feel free to bathe in front of him, to dress in front of him, to share all those private things that lovers do without needing the privacy of another chamber. He not only desired this woman, but unlike any before, he wanted to share everything with her! "Let me pour us a glass of champagne, sweet." He broke away from her, and as he strode across the room, Angela stepped to the side of the tub.

Seeing several bottles of bath oils and an arrangement of scented soaps on one of the small tables holding the candles, and not lost to the scent of lilac drifting about the chamber, Angela softly said, "You seem to have thought of just about everything."

Royce grinned as he brought her a glass of the champagne. After she had taken a sip of the bubbly brew, he took the glass from her hand and set it down on the table near the tub. "If you will allow me, my heart, I would deem it an honor to play the part of lady's maid this night." Before she could voice any objections, he turned her around and started to undo the lacings that ran down the back of her ice blue silk gown.

Angela had stood naked in front of this man before, but for some reason, this slow stripping left her feeling a little embarrassed. Slipping her gown from her shoulders, his fingers lightly brushed against the soft flesh of her back. As he lowered the gown over her hips, his heated caress held her stock-still in his seductive spell.

Slowly the blue silk gown slipped to the floor, satin shift following, making a shimmering puddle around her ankles. Royce's hungry gaze took in the womanly curve of her perfection, and as she turned into his arms, her lips rose to meet his, eager for the feel of them against his own. A deep-throated laugh left his throat as he carried her to the tub. "We have the whole of the night before us, my sweet. Let us savor each delicious moment." He gently set her in the warm water.

Angela would have argued that the bath

could wait till later, but as he handed her the crystal glass containing the champagne, and then pulled the stopper from a bottle of lilac-scented bath oil, adding more to the water, she could only sit back and allow herself to enjoy this treatment.

Making his way back toward the bed, he lifted his glass of champagne and drank deeply, his silver gaze studying her where she sat so prettily in the brass tub. Aware that she was regarding him, he set the glass down and began to pull off his shirt. His eyes never left her face even as her gaze lowered and caressed the muscular strength of his upper body.

Taking another hasty gulp of the champagne to steady herself, Angela marveled at his raw power, her gaze lingering upon the rippling muscles of his flesh. She shivered with raging desire; she was intoxicated by the very sight of him!

With a stride that lent him a pantherlike grace, Royce went to the dressing table and gathered hairpins from the tabletop. Regaining the side of the tub, he bent down and, with gentle hands, gathered the mass of sable curls hanging over the rim, then fashioned the length of her hair at the crown of her head. For a few lingering moments, his hand caressed the nape of her neck. Angela could not resist the temptation to lean lovingly into his tender touch.

Reaching a hand over the tub, he trailed over the fullness of her bosom as he took up a soft sponge and the lilac soap. He began to wash her back, his hand roaming over her shoulders and the delicate line of her collarbone, then soaping the lengths of her upper arms. As he moved around to face her, Angela allowed her body to sink into the bathwater to rinse the soap away.

With a sigh, she leaned back against the rim. Sipping from her glass, she felt as liquid as the warm water. When Royce took her foot and slowly, sensuously roamed up her leg with the sponge, Angela surrendered herself completely to his attentions.

"You have such perfect little feet and the most beautiful legs," Royce murmured huskily. Rinsing the creamy soap from one shapely leg, his lips rained small kisses over the sole of her foot, and as his heated tongue streaked across a toe, shooting sparks of passion ignited deep within her being.

His ministrations were more sensual than Angela could bear, but as she would have reached out and drawn him to her breasts, he set the one foot down and very tenderly began to give the other the same adoring attention.

As he finished washing her, Royce's pale

gaze traveled to her face. She was positively the most beautiful woman he had ever set eyes upon, he thought, as he viewed her with her eyes closed and her head leaning back against the rim of the tub. "Here, let me refill your glass," he said with restrained desire as he rose to his feet and took her glass.

Angela's senses were overwhelmed by his lavish attention. Thoughts of what this would eventually lead to held her within the grip of passion-laced anticipation. She had gone through the past few days in a dream state, knowing that sooner or later reality would sweep over her, but she could not bear to let go of the illusion that this man truly held deep feelings for her and that what had happened was meant to be.

Returning with her glass full, Royce bent again and continued where he had left off. Taking up the sponge, he began to lather her arms, her slender neck, and the fullness of her tempting breasts. His silver eyes sparkled with amber lights of desire as he swirled the creamy white soap over her upper body. His other hand lightly caressed her soft mounds, with their hard-budded peaks.

Angela's heart fluttered beneath his hands. Appearing to finish with his washing, he dipped the sponge into the warm water and brought it up to rinse away the soap. His head bent toward her, his mouth following the same path that his hands had taken. The feel of his lips and tongue caressing her stirred her erotic senses to full wakefulness, and she entwined her fingers in the dark strands of his hair and drew him closer to her breasts. As his mouth covered a taut rose nipple, moans of pleasure filled the chamber.

His head rose after a while, and he stared into her gleaming violet depths. Raging passion leapt up as his mouth was drawn to her tender lips. "You may bathe me now, sweet," he whispered against the side of her mouth, leaving Angela feeling heady with the image of stroking his muscular body.

Within short seconds, Royce's breeches were lying discarded on the floor. Stepping into the brass tub, he sat down and pulled her onto his lap, her slender arms feeling weightless as they automatically wrapped around his neck. His large hands cupped the fullness of her rounded buttocks as he sat her over the pulsing heat of his loins.

Angela clung to him as though he were her only lifeline, more than ready to put an end to her fierce desires. But this was not to be the way of things, for Royce forced an iron band of control over his own body as he took up the sponge and soap. He would not rush this moment, he told himself, even though his body ached for him to do just that! "The moment will be better shared if prolonged to its fullest, my heart." He placed a tiny kiss against her lips and feathered a path down her jaw to her throat, his head drawing back as he handed her the sponge.

Angela would have liked nothing more than to throw the sponge from the tub. She ached inside with the sheer want of him, but looking into his face, she knew that he would have his way, even as her bottom squirmed hungrily against the length of his erection, her womanhood inviting as she tempted him into breaking his resolve.

With an animal growl from between clenched teeth, Royce's hand covered hers with the sponge and brought it to his chest, guiding the circular pattern of the soap across his upper torso. As the slender fingers from her other hand began to caress his chest and shoulders, he knew that he had lost control; he could take no more! "From this night forth you will not hide yourself away in another chamber to bathe. There is no longer aught between us that should be hidden from the other."

Angela nodded her head. Whatever he desired, she was ready to give, and with her slight movement, Royce released an audible sigh. He brought her legs up higher to fit closely about his hips. His body was braced to carry the full burden of their passion as he eased her up and drew her downward, her woman's jewel opening to the brush of his manhood. As he slowly moved into her tight opening, he felt the entire length of her body shudder as a gasp of excited desire filled his ears.

The water seemed to intensify Angela's sensitivity. She felt the strength of his large body, each curve and muscle, as her breasts pressed against the matting of dark, crisp hair on his chest and her nipples became even tauter. His hands caressing her buttocks and hips made her breathless. Gently moving downward and feeling the velvet smoothness of his lance touch the heart of her passion, she cried out. As he slid into her depths, an uncontrollable shudder traveled over her.

Rocking back and forth upon the throbbing hardness of his manhood, a scalding fire raged within the depths of her and at the same time was quenched. With each thrust of his body, she felt his surging passion.

Royce was lost to everything except the full measure of their passion. The tightness of her velvet sheath moving back and forth upon his love tool became the very center of his existence. He was consumed by the flaming cauldron of white-hot passion stirring in the depths of his loins. His hot seed erupted and raced upward at the very moment Angela cried out his name. Her body trembling with shudder after shudder, her head thrown back and her eyes closed, he met her release with his own storming climax as he clutched her tightly to his heart.

For a time, they did not move, did not dare to even breathe as their joining bodies slowly calmed. The fiery passion that had claimed them waned, and finally their lips joined in a tender kiss of communion.

Royce St. James could never have imagined that the lesson he had planned to teach his Gypsy angel could bind him that much closer to her. This woman more than met his passions! Instead of getting his fill of her, he was now finding that each time they made love it was a new experience to him. He wanted more of her; he wanted all of her! Her simple dark blue regard set off a coursing flow of hot blood within his veins. Gathering her into his arms, he rose and stepped out of the tub. He set her to her feet before the warm hearth, drying her body, then his own, with one of the fleecy towels that the undermaid had left for their use. Drawing her to the bed, the couple nestled side by side for a few minutes before Royce spoke. His fingers traced the smoothness of her upper arm as her head was cradled against his chest. "Tomorrow we leave for London, sweet."

He had made the decision earlier that day and looked forward to showing Angela off at court and to London society. He anticipated, too, taking her to the theater and to other events, having long rides in the park, and, in general, letting her see a side of London that she had never known.

Angela tensed in his arms, his words shaking her from the feelings of love and comfort. She had known that this day would come, when they would have to confront Damian Dunsely and call in the bet. She had tried to ignore the inevitable; there was no longer any sense in trying to fool herself. What was between herself and Royce was attraction, nothing more. "You're right. The sooner you give me the purse for my part in the bet with your friend, the sooner I will be able to return to my own people." The purse was no longer that important, but she was determined not to show him how hurt she was that he was so willing to end the relationship that they had just discovered. Even though she knew that she was being silly, she felt tears gathering in the back of her eyes. The sooner she returned to her own time, the better off she would be, she thought as she made the effort to try and harden her heart toward him.

Royce flinched at her response. He had not even considered the bet with Damian when he had made his plans to take her into the city; it had been the furthest thing from his mind. There was still a couple of months until the bet was up, and he would insist, if pushed, for the full time before calling in the bet. He could not lose Angela now. These feelings that he harbored for this woman were too overwhelming to even contemplate leaving her. Pulling her up closer against his body, he swore to himself that he would court her so splendidly in London, she would forget her wish to leave his side and return to her people. After all, what did she have to return to? What kind of life would she have had with a band of Gypsies? He remembered how she had looked that first night outside of the gentleman's club, with her frightened, thin features. Surely he could offer her much more than such a life!

Long into the night, Royce lay awake with his troubled thoughts. Angela's even breathing caressed the fine hairs upon his chest, making him aware of her slightest sigh. This woman was an enigma to him. He knew that the mysterious attraction that he had for her would disappear eventually, but for now, he was drawn to her like a moth to flame and could not release her!

Nineteen

Throughout the morning, the Westfield servants rushed about the manse packing clothes into luggage cases and strapping the baggage atop the Westfield carriage that was parked in front of the Hall. The lord of the manor watched all the proceedings with an anxious eye. Angela had been unusually quiet since rising this morning, and Royce could not dispel from his mind her response last night to his announcement that they would be staying at his London town house for a time. He was not ready to lose her, and as he watched her packing some articles of clothing into a chest, her beauty filled his every thought. He wondered if he would ever be truly ready to part with her company!

Two hours later, not long after the noon hour, the Westfield carriage lurched into motion and started down the long drive toward the main road that would lead them to the city.

Angela watched from the carriage window as the mansion slowly disappeared from view. She would never return to the Hall, nor would she ever see the servants who had befriended her during her stay. With a soft sigh, she leaned back against the plush velour squabs and forced herself not to give in to the despair that had taken hold of her when Royce had announced that they would be going to London.

Reclining upon the opposite seat, Royce leaned forward as he gathered her slender hand into his own. As though he were able to read her thoughts, he tried to liven her spirits. "It shan't be long before we will return to the Hall, sweet. Don't look so glum. It is a beautiful day, and once we reach London, perhaps we will go buy you a new hat." He would buy her anything her heart desired; she had but to say the word!

Angela gave him a small smile. Looking into his pale eyes, it could be so easy to believe him; but she knew better! There was no doubt that he would purchase her a new hat, but she knew she would never return to the Hall. Once the bet was called in, she would be on her own, and even if Royce was still enamored of her, she could not remain his plaything forever. Perhaps another woman would be well-satisfied to entertain such a lifestyle, but she had dreamed of marriage and a family of her own, and she would never be satisfied with less. Royce was a duke, she, a gypsy girl, and there was no future in their relationship. She could not fool herself into thinking that she could put off the inevitable. She had to retrieve the pocket watch and then return to her own time. Once back with Momma Leona and the children, she would try to forget Royce St. James. She felt the power of his silver regard and fought its pull. She had to leave before it was too late, before she was too lost to this man to care about anything but staying in his arms!

Wanting to lighten the moment, a teasing smile settled over Royce's lips. "I had Mrs. Beisely pack us a picnic lunch, and instructed the driver to halt the carriage halfway into the city. What say you that we forget about purchasing you a new hat until tomorrow and instead wile away the afternoon in a field of sweet-smelling flowers?"

Angela could not help smiling at the invitation. Reaching up a hand, she gently caressed his cheek and traced the lines of laughter near his mouth, as though she would commit to memory each feature of his handsome visage. "I wish for a lifetime to wile away in your arms, instead of an afternoon, your Grace." The truth broke her lips before she could prevent it.

Royce's grin enlarged with her proclamation. Perhaps he was softening her to his desires. "If it is a mere lifetime that my lady requests, than a lifetime she shall receive. There shall be no argument out of me." With a movement, he was sitting next to her, his long legs stretched out across the floor of the vehicle. "Come closer, my sweet, and show me what a lifetime might entail." His arm around her shoulders drew her closer to his chest.

He was such a daring rogue, Angela told herself. There was just no turning away from him! Her gaze swept over his lean, aquiline nose to the fullness of his sensual lips. Her hand reached out and brushed away a lock of raven hair that had fallen over his brow. "Can a lifetime be made to last a single afternoon?"

Her words were a breathless question, and Royce's reply was just as potent: "With you in my arms, a pair of lifetimes could pass by without notice. Only you matter, my little angel; you and these sweet, tempting lips." His dark head descended, lips hovering for the briefest second before they slanted over hers.

His mouth's touch chased away earlier thoughts of fleeing him. How could she think of anything except him when he was so near? "Your kisses make me forget everything else," Angela whispered as they broke apart.

"Do you find them satisfying then, my love?"

"Satisfying? Hmm, I don't know if that would be the exact word for them." As he drew back to look upon her better, she leaned toward him, her mouth only a few inches from his own. "They promise much, and only make me want more."

Chuckling softly, Royce pulled her tightly to his chest and gratified her questing lips with soft, lingering kisses that did indeed promise of much, much more! As his lips placed an enticing melody over hers, Royce reached across and pulled her onto his lap, adjusting his body so that he could lean back against the seats with Angela's skirts encircling them and her buttocks resting upon the manly boldness of his heated loins.

Angela was hardly aware of anything beyond his expert kisses. It was not until she drew back a moment later for a trembling breath that she realized her position.

"I should have thought over the matter further and instructed George to drive straight through to the city." The ride into London was not an overly long one, and stopping halfway left little time for even a short dalliance upon the carriage seat.

Angela was once again chagrined to find herself in this position. It was easy to make plans of escape while not in his arms. Now, though, as he plied her with loving kisses, his gentle hands lightly caressing her breasts, she knew it would be that much harder when the time came for her to leave him. She pulled back as though to leave his lap, but he cajoled her with sweet words.

"Don't leave me, sweetheart. I love the feel of you against me." Hoping to distract her, Royce kissed her again, this time holding nothing back. He gave without reserve, and in the process, he fully explored the mettle of her resistance. His parted lips ravished her and demanded that she answer him in kind. By degrees, Angela forgot her earlier objections and gave to him fully. Tentatively she allowed her tongue to be drawn into his moist mouth, then, with heated passion, she met his daring thrusts with equal fervor.

His silver passion-filled eyes smiled into hers as he lifted his head. His hand moved caressingly over her bosom, her hard nipples pressing against the satin material of her gown.

Once the flame caught, it was hard to extinguish. Angela pressed eagerly closer for more, her parted lips caressing his yielding mouth greedily.

With much reluctance, Royce pulled his head away, and his hand withdrew from the tempting feel of her bosom, though it took every measure of restraint. "Your response is more than pleasing, my love, but perhaps our timing is at a disadvantage."

Feeling the vehicle slow as it came to a stop along the side of the road, he drew in a deep breath and helped Angela to settle her skirts as she leaped from his lap to the opposite seat.

A soft grin graced Royce's lips when George pulled the carriage door open. Looking at Angela, she appeared as prim and proper as a graceful young virgin, with hands clutched sedately in her lap. No one would imagine that only short moments past she had been sprawled seductively across his lap with her lips pressed heatedly against his own. Only the telltale sign of a faint blush could be seen.

"To the best of me figuring, sir, this be about halfway to the city," George, the driver, announced.

"Thank you, George. I am sure that the lady is famished by now. Why don't you hand down the basket while I help Angela out of the carriage." Royce's silver eyes twinkled with amusement as the driver stepped away from the carriage door. After climbing out of the vehicle himself, Royce reached back in to help Angela from her seat. As she stood at the carriage door, he set both hands around her waist and entreated softly, "Watch your step, sweetheart." For a few lingering seconds, as he pulled her to the ground, he allowed her shapely curves to press fully against his length before releasing her.

Angela was flustered by Royce's treatment and could only hope that the driver had not noticed the duke's familiarity toward her. Angela was happy to receive Royce's attentions while in privacy, but she could not help feeling uncomfortable with the others bearing witness to their passion.

"I believe that there is a small pond over in that direction, sir." The driver pointed toward a field enclosed by a stone fence, after handing the picnic basket over to Royce.

His announcement had the effect of gaining Angela's full attention. The halfway mark from the city of London to Westfield Hall, Angela realized with some amazement, was where she had awoken and found herself in the eighteenth century. Fear and anticipation leaped within her breast. The pocket watch was nearby! The means to return to Momma Leona and the children was close at hand!

With the wicker picnic basket and blanket in one hand, Royce reached out and took

Angela's hand with the other. Following George's directions, he helped Angela to climb over the stone fence; then the couple made their way through the field of tall grass toward the pond, leaving the carriage driver to tend to the team of horses and to relax beneath the shade of a large oak as he awaited the couple's return.

The afternoon air held a touch of fall crispness, but the sun shining down upon the couple was warm as the glistening surface of the pond came into view. "I guess George was right about the pond." Royce smiled with anticipation at the inviting setting stretched out before them. "This looks like the perfect place for a picnic lunch to be shared."

Angela did not immediately respond, so busy was she looking around the area of the pond. Everything was as she remembered it, the grass a bit thicker perhaps, but other than that, all looked the same. Her steps quickened as they drew nearer to the pond. Royce would have spread out the blanket in the tall grass next to the edge of the water, but Angela led him father along.

Recognizing the area where she had fallen asleep after setting the hands of the pocket watch, she halted. As Royce spread out the blanket and began to set out the lunch which Mrs. Beisely had packed for them,

Angela's searching gaze traveled over the ground around the blanket.

Reaching out, Royce pulled Angela down to his side. "It is far more pleasant down here, sweet." He poured a goblet full of the wine that Mrs. Beisely had sent along, and pressing the vessel to Angela's lips, he watched with sparkling eyes as she took a sip of the savory liquid.

When Royce St. James lavished his full attention upon Angela, she was lost to everything else, and for the next hour, she was slowly hand-fed by her lover.

With the meal's completion, the utensils having been put away, Royce stretched his large body out upon the blanket and used Angela's soft lap as a pillow for his head. "I confess, I am enjoying pampering you, my love." He ran a lone finger along her jawline and down her slender throat to the neckline of her bodice.

Angela shivered at his touch, his words filling her heart with a soft ache, for she knew that this idyllic life could not last. As soon as the bet was done, she would be turned out. She felt the tears building behind her eyes and willed them not to flow. She was made of stronger stuff than that, she told herself. She had endured a harsh life, and she had learned that there were no guarantees. Happiness came only to the girls in fairly tales, not in real life. Not even in another century!

Sensing her pensive mood, Royce wondered about her thoughts. Was she thinking to that day when she would leave him and return to the people that she claimed as her family? An unsettling feeling gripped him and he tried to quell it by rising to his feet and pulling Angela along with him. He clutched her to his chest as though fearing that she was only an illusion, and then with a chuckle, he swung her high in the air. "You are going to love London, my little angel. I plan to show you everything!" He planned to keep her so busy she wouldn't have time to contemplate leaving him!

Breathless, Angela was set back to her feet, and with her head spinning, she clutched his jacket. Before she could catch her breath, Royce was kissing her parted lips and rendering her more dependent upon him in order to stand upright.

The kiss was as potent as the wine they had drunk earlier as Royce's lips plundered hers with a consuming intensity. Opening her mouth, Angela's tongue danced with his in a mating ritual that left her pressing her shapely length hungrily against the solid wall of his body. Her slim hands wrapped around his neck and tangled within the strands of dark hair that lay against his broad shoulders. She could no longer think; she could only feel! As he lifted her off her feet and carried her to the blanket, she moaned with anticipation.

With the tenderest of touches, Royce began to undress her, his sensual lips following each movement of his hand until she lay naked before him. "Your body was made to be worshiped," he said as he gazed upon her length hungrily. "Your flesh is as soft as thistledown, and I seem not to be able to get enough of your touch. Each time I look upon you, I want you with a hunger that is all consuming; I need only to lose myself within you to feel complete!"

As he had undressed her, his heated kisses had coursed over her entire body, lingering over her breasts, trailing over her ribs to the small indent of her navel, then delicately roaming over one shapely hip, then the other. As her gown was discarded at her feet, not a space upon her body was lost to the attention of his adoring lips, the effect leaving Angela clutching the blanket with both hands at her sides, her body shivering with the delicious effects of his love play. As his husky endearments touched her ears, she knew the spell in which this man held her.

In seconds Royce's clothes lay next to Angela's. Nothing mattered as they came together in a wordless fusion of minds, bodies, and souls. The entire world could have come to an end, the couple spiraled into the darkness of a deep, black abyss, but neither would have taken notice; they were too filled with the touch, the feel of each other!

As they lay naked, Royce rose above her, his searing gaze devouring her beauty with a bold glance that left nothing untouched and caused Angela's heartbeat to flutter wildly out of control. His mouth and tongue plied their magic over her body and left her gasping as he seared a path from her lips down to her breasts. He worshiped her creamy mounds, taking each rosy nipple into his mouth to suckle.

The canopy of trees overhead, the softly lapping water, and the sounds of songbirds building a nest overhead combined to heighten the couple's ardor to fever pitch.

Angela could not get enough of Royce's body as her hands reached out and caressed any part of him that she could reach and her body writhed beneath the onslaught of his wild seduction. As he leaned over her and feasted upon her breasts, her mouth met his muscular shoulder and her lips trailed tiny kisses down his chest. Her hands glided over the strong planes of his muscled body, outlining his broad sculpted back, narrow hips, and firm buttocks. His breath caught as one hand brushed against the length of his shaft.

With the slight touch of her hand, his manhood enlarged, expanding to mighty proportions as the blood rushed through his loins. He groaned deeply.

Feeling her power, Angela wrapped her slim fingers around his swollen member and slowly drew them up his length until she touched the heart-shaped head. Slowly, tantalizingly, her hand traveled back down the thick, throbbing organ, inch by slow inch.

Royce felt a tremendous shudder travel the length of his body. Pulling his mouth from her breasts and hungrily settling on her lips, he gasped, "I can take little more of your loving touch, my sweet. Your simplest caress brings home fully my great need for you." With these words, his hand gently drew hers away from his manhood. He pressed her thighs apart and settled the yearning fullness of his shaft against the heated portal of her womanhood.

As he rubbed the velvet tip of his manhood against her moist cleft, she moaned aloud, undulating beneath him and seeking the fullness she knew he would soon give her. Not willing to wait another moment, she placed her hands upon his firm buttocks and pulled him closer, rising up to meet him.

Heated, intoxicating pleasure flamed between them, their bodies seeking, thrusting, striving. Caught up in a wild frenzy of emotion, Angela hardly noticed when Royce drew her slim body over him. His passion-filled silver eyes blazed with branding flames of steaming desire as his hands roamed at will over her shapely curves, bringing her to passion's edge. She rose above him, her body writhing to a primal rhythm.

She felt a fierce craving throughout her entire being as her hands splayed across the broad, fur-matted chest, her lips seeking his as her body moved and sought all that he had to offer. The rapturous sensations of his thick, pulsing length moving in and out of her depths added to her raging fire. She was catapulted toward the outer bounds of no return and left breathlessly gasping as her womanhood contracted around his manhood and caused Royce to moan aloud.

Their passions rode out the full crest of trembling pleasure. As Angela was swept over the soaring edge, Royce also gave up control, and with mindless intensity, his body arched toward her as he rode out the blinding tempest of his climax.

Clutched tightly together, Angela's head resting against Royce's chest, it was moments before either could speak. Royce's hands roamed over Angela's body. Even after such satisfaction, he still wanted more. "I would that we could stay forever wrapped within each other's arms," he whispered against her neck. In that moment, he vowed that he would do everything in his power to make this come true.

Angela sighed softly as her breathing became regular and his tender words touched her heart. If only he were speaking from his heart and not his lust, she thought. If only he could truly care for her, a Gypsy girl, and not want her only for his pleasure.

Feeling her soft sigh stir the crisp hairs upon his broad chest, Royce tilted her face up to meet his. He covered her mouth with his own, drinking of the sweetness of her lips and feeling his body beginning to come to life as though she were food for a starving man! Controlling himself, he drew his lips away. There would be plenty of time to fully sate his desires once they reached his town house. Looking into her deep blue eyes, he smiled tenderly. "We should dress and return to the carriage. George might be wondering what has happened to us."

Angela had forgotten about the driver. Royce pulled her to her feet, then helped her to dress. When finally they both stood fully clothed, he smiled warmly down upon her as he viewed her full loveliness. With an affectionate hand he caressed her cheek. "Your beauty is beyond mere words. You blind these poor eyes with your fair radiance."

He meant his declaration. Indeed, this woman was the fairest of the fair. There was none that could compare in beauty or grace, and for now she was all his! His chest swelled with pride, but soon he remembered that she desired to leave him, and some of his pride diminished.

Angela was not unaware that his admiring glance had turned into a frown, and wishing to chase away any ill thoughts after the glorious time they had spent here at the pond, she grinned upon him. "You, sir, are truly a daring rogue! You think to flatter me with attention and kisses and render me mindless with my own self-image while Mrs. Biesely's delicious lemon tarts are still in the picnic basket!"

"I confess you caught me dead to right," Royce chuckled. Before bending down to retrieve the picnic basket, he placed an adoring kiss upon the tip of her upturned nose. "You have found me out, and I will be forced to share Mrs. Biesely's little treats after all."

"Indeed you will, your Grace." Angela grinned back and bent down to pick up the blanket. As she straightened, a glimmer of silver in the flattened grass caught her eye. Her breath caught in her chest as her glance stole back to Royce. Seeing him rummaging through the basket for the promised sweets, she quickly bent down and snatched up the watch in her palm. Her heartbeat accelerated as she looked back to see if he had noticed her actions. He hadn't, and she expertly slipped the watch into her skirt pocket.

The packet of lemon tarts had been at the bottom of the basket, and by the time Royce had retrieved them and turned back to Angela, she was folding the blanket and placing it over her arm. Holding out one of the sweets, he said, "A mere token in comparison to your own rare sweetness, my heart."

Angela's response was not as light as she took the offered tart. "You do know how to flatter a girl, dear Duke. I only wonder at the numerous others to whom you have professed such like words." With the knowledge that she soon would be leaving this century, Angela wondered how soon Royce would be sharing another picnic with a different young woman. She drew her chin up a notch in order not to start weeping.

There was little that Royce could offer in his own defense. He certainly could not deny his past, nor was he ready to swear off other women and make a declaration of his feelings at this time. He was not certain what his feelings for this woman were; he knew only that he did not want to give her up. He needed more time, and time was the one thing he feared he had little of!

During the rest of the carriage ride into London, the pocket watch seemed to burn through the material of Angela's skirt and sear her skin. As Royce held her to his side, his arm casually draped over her shoulders, she could not think of anything except that she now held the power to leave this time and return to her own century. At the first opportunity, she would slip away to examine the watch more closely. There was no sense in prolonging the inevitable. She was just hurting herself by remaining in this century!

The town house was much smaller than Westfield Hall, but there was no denying that it was as elegantly furnished and lavish in appearance. From the moment that the couple stepped through the front double doors, Angela found herself the center of Royce's attention. He showed her from room to room, introduced her to each servant personally, and then escorted her upstairs to the chamber that they would be sharing.

Having sent word to the town house yesterday of their expected arrival, the servants had prepared a warm fire in the bedchamber and had set up a steaming bath in the center of the room. They knew that the duke usually desired to wash away the travel dust before going about his duties in the city.

"I instructed Nathan to bring our dinner trays up to our chamber. I thought we should stay here at the town house this evening. Tomorrow will be soon enough for the whole of London town to catch a glimpse of the most beautiful woman alive." Royce had followed her into the bedchamber and now stood directly behind her, his hands resting upon her shoulders.

Just one more night alone with this man! Her conscience softly entreated her for this small favor. *What could one more night possibly matter when you will spend a lifetime with only your memories of what you have shared with Royce St. James?* Angela turned within his arms, and standing on tiptoe, she pressed her lips to his. "Then let us not waste a moment of this evening that is before us, your Grace."

Her fingers deftly began to unbutton his vest and the silk shirt beneath. The pocket watch and her own life and time would wait until tomorrow. She wanted this one last night in Royce St. James's arms!

Royce's mouth sought hers, and he kissed her hungrily. Their coming together was a wild, desperate thing; neither was sure what tomorrow would bring. They stood in the center of the chamber, naked flesh glowing from the fire beyond the hearth, and as

Royce's head lowered and his warm lips closed on her throbbing nipple, a small moan filled the back of her throat. He teased and licked the peak, tonguing it playfully before his hot mouth began to draw upon it in earnest.

With a womanly instinct, she pushed her breast fully against his loving mouth, and he drew hard, satisfying himself with the feel and taste of her silken flesh. His hand stole down the length of her body and felt her slippery moistness, his fingers teasing her velvety woman's jewel. As he pushed through the tightness of her sheath, he whispered as his mouth seared kisses against her jaw and throat, "Touch me, Angel. Feel the desire that only you can satisfy."

Unable to refuse him as she yielded to his questing fingers, she blindly reached out a hand to cup his maleness, stroking and fondling him as she spread her legs wider. As their passions reached a fever pitch, Royce drew his hand away from her tempting chamber of love. He slipped his hands over her shapely hips and drew her upwards, her hands releasing his love tool as he lifted her onto his shaft. "I love the way that you open to me like a flower."

With his enormous lance slowly filling her, Angela's legs wrapped around his hips, her arms clutching his neck as her mouth, tongue, and lips seared every inch of his flesh. She went wild as he filled her deeper, covering his throat and face with flaming kisses. Her mouth covering his, she plunged her tongue into his mouth, drawing his into her own. Sucking, she stirred Royce to depths of passion that he had never known before.

Clutched within the bounds of paradise as he filled her totally, he drew her up and down upon the searing boldness of his shaft, exciting her to such wildness that she screamed aloud, his tongue within her mouth muffling the sound as it filled the chamber. "Let's go to the bed, sweet," he raggedly gasped, and as he strode to the great, curtained bed with her still straddled about him, the motion drove Angela even further into rapture.

They toppled to the bed, Royce remaining within her. As he rose up above her, his silver eyes locked with hers, and a timeless promise was made. Royce's fingers entwined with hers as he drew her hands above her head, the fullness of her breasts pressing against his chest, the hard length of him pressing upon the enticing length of her. As her slender legs drew back around his hips and he once again fully explored the potent depths of her honeyed sheath, she knew total fulfillment!

Deep within the sanctioned dimensions of her innermost being, a flaming, passionate brilliance erupted and encompassed her entire body as her muscles constricted around his male organ and shudder after shudder caressed his pulsing erection.

Royce felt as though his entire being was being sucked within the sweet, tight folds of her womanhood, and with savage abandon his thrusts became deeper and harder as he, too, was swept toward earth-shattering splendor.

Long moments later neither could speak of what had just passed between them. Their relationship was too new, the trust between them just beginning to build.

Twenty

Bound within the clutches of a dream, Angela felt the intense quickening of blood as she moved down the London streets. Her nimble fingers lifted a wallet from a gentleman who passed by, and around the next corner she gained an expensive camera that had been left on a street bench unattended as the owner's attention was diverted. Her lithe figure slipped in and out of the busy street traffic, and as she entered Harrods', she quickly began to look around for her next easy mark.

Strangely, it was not a victim that drew her focus, but instead the bench which resided not far from the fruit and flower stall. Her steps seemed to glide across the floor, and looking down at the bench, she glimpsed a discarded *Daily Mirror*. Her fingers shook as she picked up the scandal sheet, her eyes not able to focus on the front-page article but picking out certain words which seemed to shake her very soul. *Descendants of the Duke of Westfield . . . their claim before Parliament . . . lands and title stripped . . . falsely accused . . . the Jacobites conspiracy to overthrow George II . . . Documents found at Hampsteed Castle . . . Royce St. James betrayed by a Lord Dunsely . . . executed by the scaffold after the Culloden Moor defeat in April 1746. Executed! Executed! Executed!*

"Nooooooo!" The cry was torn from her lips as she sat up in bed, her heartbeat racing as she reached out in the dark to make sure that Royce was still at her side. Tears streamed down her cheeks as the full realization of her dream swept over her. What she had read in the tabloid had been forgotten until this very moment! Now it all came back in a flood, everything she had read in the tabloid the day before she had traveled back in time.

"What is the matter, sweet?" Royce questioned. Sitting up, he pulled her into his strong arms. "You're trembling, love. You have nothing to fear: it was but a dream."

Angela could not speak; she could scarce catch a breath of air. All she could do was clutch Royce tightly to her, needing the assurance that he was truly there at her side.

Royce allowed her time to regain herself, believing that she had been caught unaware by some frightful nightmare. He soothingly held her, and as the trembling began to subside, he pulled her back down upon the bed, his arms still wrapped around her, her cheek pressed against his chest. "Do you want to tell me about the dream?" he softly questioned after several minutes of quiet.

Angela did not know how to tell him, but she could not keep the knowledge to herself. Royce's life was at stake! He had to be warned. "It was not a dream, Royce. It was a reminder of something I had read in the past."

"Don't tell me that your lessons with Mr. Clemons were so frightful that they have the power to wake you in the middle of the night and set you to trembling," Royce said lightly, hoping to pull her from her gloom.

However would she be able to make him understand? She would have to try and convince him that she was not from this time period, but a time two hundred years in the future. The possibility of someone stepping back in time seemed insane to her, so how could she make Royce believe her? She pulled herself out of his embrace, her head rising from his chest as she peered through the darkness to glimpse his features. "Royce, what I am going to tell you has nothing to do with Mr. Clemons's lessons. Oh, he did inform me of the present political situation, but my dream had nothing to do with my lessons. Do you remember the first night that you took me out to the Hall?" She glimpsed the flash of his white teeth as he smiled. His memories would be of those that had taken place between them in the kitchen, she thought, then quickly turned his thoughts away from that direction. "Do you remember the conversation that we had in your study? When I tried to explain to you who I was and where I came from?"

Royce could not recall her ever telling him exactly where she was from. She had made mention that her mother had been Irish, her father a Gypsy horse trainer, but other than that, there had been little talk about her past, except that nonsense about a horseless carriage and her not belonging in this century. As his silver regard held her, he was nonplussed.

She could tell that he was having difficulty grasping her meaning. "That first evening, Royce, I tried to explain to you that I was not from this time period, that somehow I have been sent back into your time." Before he could say anything to try and halt the flow of her words, she rushed on. "I didn't know then how or why such a thing could be possible, but I think now I am beginning to understand better the reason."

"You understand how one can be sent

back in time?" Royce pulled himself up a bit straighter against the pillows resting on the headboard. Looking at her, he wondered if the dream had so affected her that she had taken leave of her senses.

"No, not really how it happens." She pushed the instant image of the pocket watch from her mind. "I mean, why it happened; why I was sent to this time, to you, Royce. The day before I found myself in this century, I was reading a tabloid in a store. A tabloid is filled with information about prominent people. It's mostly gossip and scandal." Drawing a deep breath, she said, "That day the headline concerned you and your family, Royce."

Royce looked more keenly upon her, not understanding any of this.

"You see, in nineteen hundred and ninety-four, your descendants will put a claim before Parliament in order to try and reclaim your lands and your title."

"And pray tell, why would my family have to venture such an effort? Westfield Hall and the land it resides upon, and the numerous other properties that I hold have been in the St. James family since my grandfather, the first Duke of Westfield. He gained them through his services to his King. My title will pass to my son, as his will to his. In two centuries or five, these lands

330

and the title will remain the holding of a St. James!" Royce was beginning to become irritated at her insinuation that somehow what his family had held for years would be lost.

"It will happen, Royce. You have to believe me. I swear, though, it will be by no fault of your own. You will be betrayed as a Jacobite and declared to be a part of those who are aiding Charles Edward to put his father on the throne. The Jacobites will be defeated next April at Culloden Moor." She could not bring herself to tell him that he would be executed along with the other eighty traitors who would lend aid to a fruitless cause.

With her hand pressed against Royce's chest, she could feel the deep rumbling of his laughter before she heard it, and as it exploded from his lips, his arms wrapped more tightly around her body as he pulled her against his length. "You were only dreaming, sweetheart. There is no way on God's green earth that I could ever become involved with the Jacobite cause!"

The Young Pretender, as most Englishmen called Charles Edward, had already marched into Perth and proclaimed his father King and himself Regent. Traveling to Edinburgh, he had set up his court in Holyrood. After a brisk victory over Cope at

Prestonpans, he had boosted morale and had attracted further recruits. Last month he had held a force of between seven to nine thousand. This was sufficient to command respect in Scotland, but quite inadequate for any invasion against England, and Royce, ever a man to stand with honor, would give his life for his King! His name would never be linked with that of the Jacobites!

Angela could have screamed aloud with frustration. She knew that it would be futile to try and convince him that she was from another time. He would never believe her! But as she listened to his mirth dying down, she told herself that she couldn't give up! Surely he would pay with his life, and such a price was far too dear, even if he were the most bullheaded man she had ever met! "Listen to me, Royce. I didn't say that you will become involved with the Jacobite cause; I said that you will be accused falsely." She had almost to shout to make sure that he was hearing her clearly. She wanted no mistakes: he had to realize how dire the situation was!

"Who would dare to falsely accuse me?" Royce wiped away the moisture from his eyes with the back of his hand. He had once told himself that his little Gypsy brat had an extraordinary imagination, and he now reaffirmed those thoughts.

"Lord Dunsely is the man who will betray you, Royce." Angela's tone was soft as she exposed his friend for the blackguard she knew him to be.

His deep, husky laughter erupted. "Damian wouldn't have the nerve to betray anyone, heartling. You were dreaming, and in the morning you will forget this foolishness, I promise." He pressed her head back against the pillows and plied her with soft kisses until he felt her body melting against his own. Rising over her on an elbow, he brushed way a dark curl that caressed her smooth cheek. "Sleep now, my heart. I will hold you throughout the rest of the night in my arms. There is no reason to fear the morrow. Trust in my strength, for I will keep all harm at bay."

Aye, harm that he could see coming straight at him, Angela told herself as he stretched out next to her. How could he protect himself from someone he believed a friend, a friend who would accuse him falsely as a traitor to the Crown and allow him to be executed? Long into the night Angela worried over each word which she had read in the tabloid. She had to do something to save Royce, but what? How could she save a man who did not believe a single word she said?

The following day Royce took Angela, as promised, to Loretta Devereux's dress shop in order to purchase a new hat. Upon waking he had noticed the redness of her eyes, which he had rightfully assumed was caused from her wild dream and lack of sleep, but as the morning progressed and she remained unusually quiet, he took it upon himself to lighten her mood.

With Royce at her side in the carriage, Angela forgot her dream of the night before and enjoyed his entertaining company. As the vehicle left Eaton Square, the area of Royce's town house and not far from the palace, he eagerly pointed out sights of interest. Royce had instructed George to ride through Cheapside in the heart of the city and then go to Sloan Square, the shopping area centered chiefly around King's Road. The vehicle was halted in front of an attractive little shop which, according to its swinging sign, belonged to Blade and Loretta Devereux. Sloan Square was a cosmopolitan region of London where writers and artists congregated at the pubs or pastry shops. The buildings in this area held more of an upper class appeal than those they had spied earlier along Cheapside.

Handing Angela down from the carriage, Royce took her arm and led her through the front door of the dress shop. Within seconds of the little bell overhead tinkling out their arrival, several of the shop's assistants surrounded the couple. One young woman took Royce's hat and Angela's gloves and cloak; another offered refreshments; and still another, pointing toward the back of the shop, indicated two comfortable chairs for them to use at their leisure.

"M. Devereux will be with you shortly. Please make yourselves comfortable," said the tall, thin young woman who had pointed out the chairs.

As Royce began to lead Angela toward the back of the shop, her blue eyes were wide as they took in the abundance of bolts of material stacked on shelves and set up in every corner of the front room, as well as boxes of laces and bows and spindles of ribbons and embroidery material. Every available inch of space was utilized to its fullest advantage, and in the back of the shop, near the chairs and small table that held a tea tray, there was a dressing screen.

Angela suddenly heard a loud, piercing cry. "La Belle, you have at last arrived in London town!"

In a whirl of brilliant colors—mustard yellow, flaming red, and deepest purple—Blade Devereux sailed from the back room and hurried to Angela's side. Pulling her hand into his own, he lifted it high and twirled her around in a tiny circle, his eyes admiring the lavender gown embroidered with burgundy nosegays.

"Mademoiselle is *parfait*, yes, your Grace?" Blade's dancing dark eyes met Royce's, and he grinned widely, proud of his handiwork.

"Indeed, she is perfect!" Royce pulled Angela back to his side. The dressmaker's familiarity with Angela was making him rather grouchy.

"*Non, non*, your Grace. There is no reason for jealousy between you and I. La Belle and myself are the best of friends!" Blade was not lost to the duke's dark look.

"Don't be silly, Blade." Angela spoke up before Royce could make further comment. Of course Royce wasn't jealous! "We have come to purchase a new hat!" She smiled at the bold figure as Blade attentively stood before them.

Blade clapped his hands together as though her announcement brought him the greatest joy. "Oh, please have a seat. We can't have his Grace standing about, now can we?" He winked at Angela as he nodded his head toward the pair of chairs. "I will have the girls bring out some hats for your appraisal."

Within seconds, he was calling out orders, snapping his fingers sharply. One of the girls reached up to pull down a box of hats on a high shelf and dropped the box, spilling the contents across the shop floor. Blade's bright yellow heels stamped against the floor as he glared at the offending assistant. Turning back toward Angela and the duke, he simpered, "As you can see, Angela, I am still surrounded by incompetents!" He pulled out a lacy hanky and wiped at his brow.

"I had hoped to meet your sister Loretta," Angela grinned, having missed Blade's overdramatic actions these past months.

"Oh, dear Loretta is still laid up with the gout. I do fear that she might be enjoying her role as the invalid a little too much. Our clientele has taken on new life over these past months since her illness, and I am called on constantly by demanding women."

It seemed that Blade was no longer confined to the back room, Angela thought, and knew that for all of his complaining ways he was entirely in his element! He was gaining the recognition that he had always desired.

Sitting back in his chair rather stiffly, it was not long before Royce was also smiling at Blade's humor.

The chosen hat matched the gown that

Angela was wearing. Adding a small bunch of burgundy pansies to the brim, Blade set the hat atop her head and tied the violet bow at an angle beneath her chin.

Before leaving the dress shop, Royce instructed Blade to create a gown for Angela that was more striking than anything she now owned. "Something that she could wear at court, if she had a mind," Royce said as Angela's eyes widened.

That would be the day—when a mere Gypsy girl went to the court of George II on the arm of a duke, Angela thought, but held her tongue as Royce looked over some patterns with Blade and then chose the colors for the gown and cloak that would accompany it.

The theater in Covent Gardens that evening had a lively audience for *Love In A Village*, a comedic opera by Isaac Bickerstaffe. Sitting in the Westfield theater box with Royce, Angela was enraptured by the performance. With her eyes upon the actors on stage, she took little notice of the frequent stares from the ladies in attendance, as they fluttered their lashes behind their colorful fans and wondered who the Duke of Westfield's companion could be. Nor did Angela pay heed to the many admiring glances cast in her direction by the gentlemen.

Royce, though, was not lost to a single glance which settled upon the lovely young woman at his side. He had believed, while still at Westfield Hall, that he would be able to take a great deal of pride in her beauty, that he would be proud to escort her around London and show her off to his companions. But each look this evening from another man made the small muscle below his cheekbone clench. More than once he had reached over and drawn her cloak a bit closer about her lovely shoulders in order to conceal the daringly low cut evening gown which she had worn for this occasion.

The trip to the dress shop in the early part of the day had appeared to lift Angela's spirits, but by the time they had arrived back at his town house, she had become quietly reflective as they shared a small meal together in the gardens in the back of the house. With his announcement that they would go to the theater that evening, she had appeared willing enough, but had not displayed the excitement that he had expected. As they sat in the pair of elegantly upholstered chairs in the Westfield booth, he could hardly take his eyes from her. Her features were alight, enthralled, and Royce's enjoyment came from her; with each sigh or small laugh, he felt a tender pang assaulting his heart.

As the final act was completed, Angela sat back in her chair with a small sigh. For a full moment she held her eyes tightly shut. A small smile lingered over her lips as she envisioned the last few minutes of the play. The participants had been so colorful, so alive and carefree; and when she thought of the love between the main characters, she sighed. This had been her first play and what a wonderful event it had been!

Royce reached over and covered her hand with his own, delighting in her enjoyment and inquiring if she were ready to leave the theater box. Angela nodded her head, her hand warming beneath his. "Thank you for bringing me here tonight, Royce." If she had had her way this evening, they would have remained at Royce's town house with the doors tightly shut and the draperies drawn. Throughout the day, her only thoughts had been of how she could save Royce from Damian's foul plot!

As she had lain abed last night in Royce's arms after her dream, she had told herself that she could not possibly send herself back to her own time, not now when Royce would be left alone to face whatever fate Damian Dunsely had in store for him. When she had awakened this morning, she had hidden the pocket watch at the bottom of her clothes chest along with her hair coins and jewelry. During the rest of the day, she had nervously tried to plan some strategy that would prove Damian for the blackguard he was. Once Royce was made aware of Damian's plans to ruin him, she would no longer be needed in this century. She would then be free to return to Momma Leona and the children. But looking into Royce St. James's tender gaze, the thought of leaving his side chilled her. With every passing hour in his company, she was growing more dependent upon his gentle treatment.

With his hand lightly resting upon the small of her back, Royce began to lead her out of the crush of people making their way toward the front of the theater. Several of Royce's friends approached them with the hope of making the acquaintance of the beautiful woman who had accompanied him. Grudgingly Royce introduced Angela to the gentlemen who surrounded them in the main saloon of the theater.

Angela smiled warmly at each gentleman that approached. She was pleased that Damian Dunsely was not among those who slapped Royce upon the back in greeting and eyed her appreciatively. She needed more time in which to formulate a plan before coming face to face with Royce's foe again.

As yet another gentleman joined the small group that stood around her and Royce, Angela noticed out of the corner of her eye one of the numerous orange girls standing several feet away. The redhead seemed tense and calculating, traits she remembered in herself while living off the livelihood she had gained from the streets. The girl did not appear to be selling the goods in the small basket that was resting upon one hip, but as Angela watched, the girl sidled close to a few of the gentlemen. Angela studied the girl, she watched her extract a purse from a gentleman's jacket pocket. The young woman, with her pixie features, turned her gaze directly upon Angela.

Instant recognition sprang between the two. Angela saw a young woman, much like herself only short months before, and the young woman realized that she had been found out! With her lightly freckled face turning pale, the orange girl turned away from Angela's gaze, and without a backward glance, she hurriedly disappeared into the crowded saloon. Angela would have assured the young woman that she had nothing to fear from her, but before she could do anything, the girl was gone.

Without further incident, Royce led Angela

342

from the main saloon and out into the cool night. Once settled within the comfort of the Westfield carriage and with Royce's arm wrapped around her shoulders, Angela forgot all about the orange girl in the theater.

The following day Royce left the town house early, having business to attend and hoping to have a moment or two of Granville's time at court. He hoped to smooth the way for Angela to be presented at court. He knew that Granville held the King's ear, even though he no longer held the power of the ministry behind him, having lost that to the Pellhams. It was no secret that George II was well-advised behind closed doors by Granville, and Royce wanted to insure that the King would not object to his wishes of escorting Angela as the woman of his choice, for all to plainly view.

Angela gave no argument to Royce's announcement that he had to attend to business that morning. He assumed that she would occupy herself at the town house, but Angela had other plans. The moment he kissed her soundly and left through the front door, she was hurrying upstairs to their chamber and was pulling a warm, velvet day dress from her wardrobe.

If she had intentions of finding some way

to halt Damian Dunsely's plans to destroy Royce, she had better come up with something fast, she thought as she dressed in the dark blue gown. Fetching a matching cloak from within the wardrobe, she carried it over her arm as she made her way back downstairs. She would accomplish nothing by sitting here at Royce's town house, and every moment counted!

Being confronted by Mrs. Cambridge, the housekeeper, she quickly assured her that she was only going out for a short stroll and adamantly refused the kindly lady's offer to send a footman along with her for protection.

Having absolutely no idea in which direction she should begin, Angela left the front brick walkway of the town house that stretched from stoop to street, with thoughts that perhaps while visiting the most prominent portions of the city, she would meet up with Damian Dunsely. Perhaps if she openly confronted him with her knowledge that he was not a true friend to Royce and told him that she knew of his plans to ruin the duke, she could sway him from his purpose.

She had come up with this idea yesterday, and knew there were many loopholes in such a plan. Damian would claim her to be mad as a hatter and might tell Royce upon their next meeting. Such thoughts made her a little uncomfortable as her feet took her down the street. What if Royce called in the bet early because of her actions and freed her from his company? If she were forced to leave him now, how would she ever know if Damian carried out his foul plans?

By the time she turned the corner of the street, she was more confused than ever. If Royce had believed her and was making efforts this moment to protect himself from Damian's betrayal, she would not have to be going through this torment. *No, you would be back in your own time and far away from Royce St. James completely,* her conscience said. Even so, she would sacrifice any feelings she might have for Royce in order to save his life!

Paying little attention to her surroundings, Angela jumped back in startled surprise as a small, dark figure stepped from a building and clutched her forearm. Her first reaction was to jump back and jerk her arm free before calling for help or trying to run away to safety. There was little traffic on the streets, especially in this portion of Eaton Square, but Angela was no weak-kneed maid who would faint away at the first assault made to her person, if this is what her attacker believed! As she started to bolt away, she was halted in mid-stride by a feminine voice.

"I'm right sorry if I frightened ye, miss. I just be wanting to take a moment of yer time."

Looking closer, Angela realized that the form bundled beneath the tattered, dark cloak was the orange girl she had seen last night in the main saloon of the theater. "You!" Angela exclaimed in surprise. "What on earth are you about? You half-frightened the daylights out of me, jumping out like that and grabbing hold of my arm!"

The young woman's brown eyes sparkled as though that had been her intention, but her tone remained contrite as she said, "Oh, miss, I do be begging yer pardon. I didn't mean to be scaring ye, now that's fur sure!"

There was something about this young woman that kept Angela on her guard. She had seen many girls in her past with that same crafty look on their features, girls like herself who lived under Momma Leona's care or another Gypsy child of the street. Though she appeared apologetic at the moment, there was more to this creature than met the eye. Knowing that a young woman of simple means had no business in this part of the city and that she must have been waiting near the building with the hope of seeing her, Angela cautiously questioned, "What is it that you want from me?"

The girl's lightly freckled cheeks blushed.

"You remember me from the theater last night, then?"

Angela silently nodded.

"Have you told anyone what you saw?" The brown eyes with their flecks of yellow appraised her.

Angela caught on quickly enough. The young woman was afraid that Angela was going to turn her in for stealing the gentleman's wallet. "I didn't tell anyone, and I promise you that I won't say a word. You have nothing to worry about from me."

The young woman seemed surprised by Angela's ready answer, and her face once again became suspicious. "And why would ye be keeping me secret?" She hadn't even told her about her ailing mother and her three little brothers at home that she had to help support, as she had planned. She looked Angela over from head to toe, taking in the fine material of her gown and cloak. From her past experiences, the rich women were the worst sort. If they could accuse one of their own sex who had simple means, and especially a girl from Fleet Street, as a thief, they usually did not hesitate. "What's in it fur ye by keeping yer mouth shut?"

Angela did not answer immediately, but instead she asked her own question, "What's your name?"

347

"Why do you want to know?" The young woman's pointy little chin rose a notch.

"Well, for one thing, I like to know to whom I am speaking." Angela's smile widened into a grin. This girl was like most of the girls who lived under Momma Leona's care, and she reminded her a lot of herself before she had met Royce St. James.

Wondering now if she had made a terrible mistake in seeking this young woman out, the girl shuffled her feet and eventually confessed, "I am called Myra, but if ye intend to go to the theater and tell Mr. Mutely on me, he won't know which one of his orange girls yer talking about. He knows me by another name!" Again, the sparkle was in her eyes as Myra believed herself to have outsmarted this young woman.

"Well, Myra, I'll tell you why I am not going to tell anyone what I saw you do last night, and especially not this Mr. Mutely." The girl stood silent, waiting to hear what Angela had to say. "The truth is, I was like you only several months ago. The only reason I saw you steal that gentleman's purse was because I used to do the same thing!" Angela had nothing to lose by telling her this and hoped to put the young woman at her ease.

"Yer daft if ye think fur one minute that I be believing a single word of that as the truth!" Myra took a step backward, wondering what game this rich woman was wanting to play with her. She had seen this young woman on the arm of the Duke of Westfield; that is how she had found her, after asking around for the duke's house in London. Listening to the woman in her finery declaring that she had been a thief was difficult for the streetwise Myra to believe!

Angela read the mistrust on the other's features, and with another small smile, she added, "The first night I met Royce St. James, I was attempting to relieve his friend of his purse!"

Myra took a closer look at the young woman standing next to her. Something in her tone told her she was telling the truth. "And ye got caught?" The brown eyes enlarged with the question.

Angela nodded her dark head and the other women let out a woosh of breath. "Can ye be beating that? I'm surprised ye ain't sitting yer arse this minute in a Newgate cell!" But then upon reflection, she added, "I be guessing as how yer so beautiful, the duke and his friend didn't have the heart to bring ye before the magistrate!"

Some women have all the luck, Myra thought and some of us have none! Instead of sending this woman to Newgate, the Duke of Westfield had lavished her with beautiful clothes and made her his mistress. Another would have found herself lying on her back for the turnkeys at Newgate!

"I certainly didn't look anything like I do now that evening when I tried to steal Lord Dunsely's purse!" Looking down at the material of her velvet gown, she added, "I was anything but beautiful that night!"

"Yer telling the truth when ye say that it were Lord Dunsely that ye tried to relieve of his purse?" Myra's eyes remained brown saucers in her impish face.

"Do you know him?" Angela was taken aback.

"Know him? Why, all the orange girls at Covent Gardens knows Lord Dunsely. Meself, I never took up with the likes of him. I be hearing he has some strange ways with women, as well as men. I heard tell of him having both together, if ye be knowing what I mean? Anyways, I got meself a right smart lad by the name of Tommy, who comes around now and then. Whenever he's in need of a woman, he seeks me out.

"There was some talk not long back about Lord Dunsely taking part in some strange rituals in the church near the palace. Not that I be knowing any of this fur sure, and if ye repeat a word and take me name as the one doing the telling, I'll be swearing that yer insane! I was told by a girl called

Betsy, who ain't no longer working at the Gardens. She up and run off with her boy-friend after a Fleet Street wedding. Betsy claimed that she went to one of these dark rites with Lord Dunsely. She said an orgy took place and that the priests claimed they were sacrificing a virgin. But Betsy said they only stripped the girl down and dragged her into the underground part of the church where they hold such affairs. They tied her hand and foot across a slab of marble and then each priest had a go at her. The only sacrificing they were about was with their willy-rods, if ye be knowing what I mean."

"Do other people know about this? Do others know that Dunsely participates in such affairs?" Angela was a little surprised at the girl's revelations. This did not sound like the type of man that Royce St. James would call his friend!

Myra fiercely shook her head, her fiery red curls bouncing about. "Betsy told me that Lord Dunsely would not hesitate to si-lence her by cutting her throat if word ever got out and he suspected that it was her who was spreading it about."

"I wonder what other secrets he has," An-gela murmured, more for herself than for the other's benefit.

The brown eyes instantly filled with suspi-cion. "How come yer so keen on knowing about Lord Dunsely anyway? I thought ye and the duke had something goin' on." Perhaps she had made a mistake in telling this young woman what she had heard about Lord Dunsely. She might run straight to Dunsely and tell him all that she had said! Tommy was always saying that she talked too much!

"Have you had any breakfast?" asked Angela instead of answering the question. Feeling around in her skirt pocket, her fingers touched upon the few coins she had slipped in there before leaving the town house. Perhaps by befriending Myra, she would be able to gain her help in some plan to save Royce from Dunsely's evil intent.

"I don't be usually eating early in the day," Myra confessed, not adding that her first meal of the day was usually after she had lifted a purse or gained some other item valuable enough to barter for a loaf of bread.

"Well, come along, Myra, and I will buy us a pastry while I tell you about my interest in Lord Dunsely." She had nothing to lose by telling this woman about her need to prove that Dunsely was going to betray Royce. There was the slim chance that Myra would be able to give her a suggestion or two on where to begin her search.

Twenty-one

The two young women became fast friends soon after Myra's initial distrust of Angela wore off. By midafternoon, the young women had promised to meet again on the following day. Myra assured Angela, that she would find out all she could about Dunsely and the whereabouts of Hampsteed Castle.

As soon as Angela mentioned that the proof of Damian's deceit was reportedly at Hampsteed Castle, Myra had jumped at the opportunity to accompany her on this venture. "Lordy, Angela, I ain't never been inside a real castle before! I swear if ye let me go along with ye, I won't be no trouble at all! I know I can help!"

"If we can even get inside." Angela was relieved by the young woman's offer to accompany her. She had not allowed herself the time to think about going there, but what could be the harm? Going to the castle might prove the solution to all of her worries. That is, if they could make their way inside the castle and, once inside, find whatever proof was supposed to be there!

"Oh, I'm sure that we will be able to get in," Myra said confidently. "I just be wondering how we will find the proof. The inside of a castle is awfully big!"

Angela agreed with her, but now that she had assistance, she was determined to find the evidence of Dunsely's treachery and bring her discovery before Royce. It was the only way to prove to him that Damian was not his true friend as he foolishly supposed!

Before they parted company, Angela pulled the few remaining coins from her pocket and placed them in Myra's hand. "I know it's not much, but take it to help out at home." Tomorrow she would try and bring a bit more. Then perhaps Myra would not have to take so many chances stealing. It would be horrible if the girl got caught and was sent to prison. Angela knew that she herself had been lucky to have escaped the hated bars of Newgate. She knew that this young woman would not be so lucky if caught lifting a man's wallet. The chances of a gentleman like Royce St. James being there were slim to none!

"Drat it all, I don't be having a thing to give ye in return for yer coins!" Myra had

had few friends in her lifetime and had never taken up with another woman as quickly as she had with Angela. Going through the pockets of her dark wool gown and her thin cloak, she wished that she had something to give Angela to show her that she valued the friendship that they had formed this day. "The only thing that I have is one of these damn things that Tommy gave me last night." She held out her hand. In her palm was something that looked like sausage casing, except there was a bright red length of ribbon entwined around the edge.

"What on earth is that?" Angela peered closer at the girl's hand.

Myra giggled aloud. "Tommy calls it a sheath. It's when ye lay with yer man. He wears it over his cock!"

"You mean that's a condom?" Angela's gaze rose from the girl's palm to her lively features.

Myra's grin faded somewhat. She had never heard that word. "All I know is what Tommy told me. He said he bought it at a shop in St. Martin's Lane. He says it's made out of sheep gut and that the little ribbon is supposed to be tied around yer man's balls." The grin was back and wider than ever.

"He uses them for birth control?" Angela had not even imagined that the people in the eighteenth century were aware of condoms and birth control.

"Tommy said his friend Randy told him that some gents use them to keep from getting diseases from the whores along Southwark. The only thing that I be knowing about birth control is what me mum let on when she was speaking with the midwife, Mrs. Bothworth. I be guessing as how the old lady was right, 'cause after me mum's third boy, she feed me dad the juice of a honeysuckle in his mug of ale for thirty-seven days straight. After that, there weren't anymore little nippers running around our old shack.

"Me mum was surely relieved. Now that little Ben is getting on, she can take him along with her when she's needed to help clean the tooth drawer's front room. His place ain't far from where me mum and dad live. Old Tam Livingston's wife refuses to clean away the blood and mess when Tam has had a busy day, so it's up to me mum. Right thankful she is for the ha'penny she brings home, with me dad not having worked going on four or five years."

Angela was beginning to realize how hard life was for the poor people in London in this century. She wished she could do something more to help this young woman and her family. Perhaps she could talk to Royce and he would have a few suggestions. Getting back to the subject of the condoms, she responded, "Tommy's friend is right, Myra. Those things will help to prevent diseases."

Myra was about to ask how the other woman knew so much, but then remembered her crazy story about being from another time and another London! She wasn't sure whether she believed Angela or not, but she would go along with her. "Well, Tommy swears that he won't use one of them again. He says he can't feel everything he's a mind to." Myra grinned again, remembering the experience she and her lover had had the night before with one of the sheaths. "The truth to tell, Angela, I rather liked that little red ribbon! It tickled in just the right spot!"

This girl was outrageous, Angela thought and couldn't suppress a grin.

"Here, ye take this sheath, Angela." The girl pressed it into Angela's palm. "Tommy gave this extra one to me, but said he wouldn't wear one again, so I don't know what I will do with it anyway." Myra would not take the sheath back when Angela tried to refuse, and waited for her to drop it into her cloak pocket. Perhaps the duke would enjoy it better than Tommy, Myra decided.

After promising to meet again tomorrow morning, the women parted.

* * *

The many lit chandeliers and the candelabrum on each table enveloped the dining room at Eastbury's in a haze of yellow light. Earlier, upon entering Eastbury's and glancing around at the colorfully bedecked men and women, Angela had felt a little uncomfortable in her simple blue silk gown, which boasted a thin veil of silver tissue as an overskirt and was adorned with silver beads on the bodice. She had swept her hair up and had captured her tumbling curls with a silver comb. She and Royce were the only couple in the establishment who were not wigged. The ladies wore tall wigs which were decorated with ribbons, blossoms, fruit, exotic feathers, or flowers. Extravagant farthingales and panniers were displayed, and many of the colorful gowns had huge trains. Angela remembered from Mrs. Booth's tutelage that the longer the train, the richer the wearer.

Unlike Royce, who wore an elegant black frock coat and breeches, and a richly embroidered waistcoat in maroon and gray, the rest of the gentlemen in Eastbury's dazzled the eye with glittering gold and silver buttons on their coats, and diamond buckles on their shoes. Rainbow-colored, embroidered waistcoats covered fine linen shirts trimmed with lace and ruffles. Silk handkerchiefs dangled from huge pockets. Diamond-hilted swords swung at their waists. Most wore flamboyant hats upon their powdered perukes, and they carried canes with long, colorful tassels.

As Angela finished her meal and looked across the table she shared with Royce, she thought him the most handsome man in the establishment, with his somber dress and the glitter of his diamond-stud earring catching the reflection of the candlelight. As his gaze locked with her own, his lips curved into a sensual smile.

Setting his plate aside, his hand reached across the table to rest over her own. "You are the most beautiful woman here tonight, Angela. I must admit that Blade Devereux, though a bit odd, has a keen eye for fashion. I swear, by the envious looks being thrown in your direction, half the women at Eastbury's will be seeking out your dressmaker tomorrow morning."

"I am sure that Blade will be pleased with more business, for all of his complaining." Angela smiled warmly at Royce.

"Would you care to dance?" Royce invited, his hand tightening as he glimpsed the sparkle in her sapphire blue eyes. "Or, if you like, Eastbury's has two cardrooms; you could try your luck at a game of whist, quinze, or loo."

The thought of Royce St. James holding

her in his arms and dancing her across a ballroom floor was more than enough temptation for Angela. Mrs. Booth had taught her the basic steps to the latest dances of the century, and she was more than willing to spend the rest of the evening being held in his strong embrace. "I would love to dance, Royce," she responded.

Stepping to her side, he drew her up and murmured against her smooth cheek, "It will be my pleasure, sweetheart."

In the dancing saloon, a small orchestra was set up in an alcove across the room, and the music flowed as couples swirled in a colorful display across the dance floor.

Angela felt as though she was in a fairy tale as Royce swept her onto the dance floor, then glided her through the steps to the music. With his strong arms enfolding her, the music drew them together, and Angela was aware only of him.

Capturing both her hands to his heart, he said softly, "If only this dance would draw to its finish, sweet, then you and I could make haste back to the town house."

Angela's teasing smile caught his eye as she whispered in return, "And what would we do there to wile away the time, your Grace?"

A low groan escaped Royce's throat at her teasing. Feeling the light brush of her shapely hip, he wanted little more than to pull her against his length, and allow her to feel the proof of his intentions.

Angela was as willing to finish with the dance and leave Eastbury's to return to his town house. Their attraction for one another made it difficult for them to be overlong in the company of others. But forced to go through the motions to complete the dance, she smiled prettily to those around them, who watched the couple's every moment. Her shimmering blue eyes, with their passionate depths, held only her partner's gaze.

Royce sighed at the finish of the dance. "One more of those knowing looks, madam, and I swear to you that I would not have been held accountable for my actions." He boldly kissed her lips. "Let that hold you until we reach the carriage." He grinned down at her and glimpsed the bright flush in her cheeks. She was like a breath of spring air, Royce thought to himself. So unlike all the other women that he had known.

As the couple started through the saloon's doorway, they were halted by the sound of Royce's name being called aloud. "Well damn, if it isn't you, Royce, old chap. I was told by Geoffrey Billings that you were at Eastbury's with the most ravishing creature in all of London on your arm, and of course, I came immediately to see for myself." The coal black eyes of Damian Dunsely went from Royce St. James to the woman at his side. Before a word could be spoken by either, Damian whistled low under his breath. "I dare say, Geoffrey was not mistaken, old fellow!" His glance took in Angela from the crown of her dark curls to the tips of her tiny slippers peeking out from beneath her skirts.

"We were just leaving," Royce coolly responded. This was the last person he had wanted to see this evening. He clenched the muscle in his jaw as he watched his friend gazing intently at Angela. He had never been jealous of other men looking upon his female companions in the past. In fact, he had enjoyed flaunting his latest lady before his friends. He knew, though, that he was jealous now and he desired only to get Angela out of Eastbury's and back to his town house.

"Just leaving?" Damian looked askance at his friend. He wondered what was ailing him this evening. Royce was never in a rush to leave a gaming house, especially when he was escorting a beauty such as this. "Well, at least you can make the introductions, Royce. Surely you did not plan to whisk away such a perfect beauty before I even learn her name?"

Angela had recognized Damian Dunsely,

even though he was wearing a powdered pe-ruke with long curls. Nor was she surprised to see him loudly dressed in two tones of pink. His coat was a dark pink, shot through with silk; his satin waistcoat and breeches were a lighter pink. The outfit was set off by pink satin shoes with large pearl buckles. He looked the part of a silly fop, not the conniving backstabber she knew him to be!

"My companion's name is Angela," relented Royce. Taking hold of Angela's elbow, he attempted to step past Damian, hoping that Angela had not recognized him.

"Well, damn, Royce, if you're not in a rush this evening!" Damian halted them again. "Etiquette dictates that I, in turn, introduce myself; if you will not grant me the boon, I must take it upon myself." With a flourishing bow which made Angela wonder what kept his wig on straight, Damian bent a courtly knee as he stated loudly enough for all those around them to hear, "I am Lord Dunsely, madam, and more than pleased am I to be at your service, either day or night!" He rose to his full height with a wide grin upon his lightly powdered face.

Angela's features remained impassive, but she responded sweetly, "Of course you are." Turning to Royce, she bestowed upon him a warm smile. "If you are ready to go, Royce,

I believe I left my cloak near the front door."

Damian, as well as those standing around him, felt the snub. As the couple left, Damian's black eyes glittered with a piercing chill as he stared at their retreating backs. Who was she to treat him in such a manner, and in front of his friends? he questioned. He would have to find out more about her at the first opportunity.

Turning to those silently watching, he pasted on a smile. "For a beauty she is certainly lacking in the social graces!" He laughed and several of his companions joined in. Eventually they retired into the cardroom.

It was not until the couple was alone in their bedchamber, Angela sitting before the dressing-table mirror, taking the pins from her hair, that Royce broached the subject of Damian Dunsely. Standing behind her, he studied her reflection in the mirror as she brushed out her dark glistening curls. "You said nothing to Damian of the bet, nor did you reveal your identity to him," he said in a low voice.

His words were put more as a question, and gazing back at him through the mirror, Angela set the brush aside. "Then are you ready to call the bet in, Royce?"

Reaching out, Royce placed both hands

upon her shoulders. "In truth, I am not, but your manner toward Damian surprised me." The last thing in the world he wanted was to call in the bet and release Angela from his charge, but he was curious about her treatment of his friend. He had expected her to declare herself and end the bet, but instead she had insulted Damian before a roomful of his peers and said nothing about the wager.

"Why should my manner surprise you? I have told you that the man is your enemy. Whether you believe me or not, I cannot find it within myself to be civil to such a one as Lord Dunsely." Angela rose from the stool and turned to face Royce.

Royce's hands dropped to his sides as she turned to him. He had no desire to fight with her. He knew that her blasted dream had set off this distrust of Damian, but it appeared that nothing he could say would change her mind. The only thing he wanted was more time with her. If she were no longer in a hurry to call in the bet and leave him, why should he bring about the event sooner than the appointed date? That date loomed threateningly close; too close for his peace of mind, Royce thought as he pulled Angela toward him. For a few lingering minutes, he tempted her senses with an assault of heated kisses.

Angela moaned softly as he released her. Smiling, he turned her around and silently unlaced the ties at the back of her gown. "Why don't you make yourself ready for bed, sweet, and I'll draw back the bed-covers."

He certainly would not receive any arguments from Angela. Her flushed body was anticipating his touch. As she watched him silently pull off his shirt and throw it over the back of a chair before he stepped to the bed, her hungry gaze devoured his naked flesh.

Before pulling back the coverlet, Royce took up her discarded cloak from that afternoon, which had been thrown over the foot of the bed. As he laid it across the chair with his shirt, something fell to the floor from the pocket. Bending, he picked up the small object, his gaze shifting back to Angela questioningly. "Why do you have this in your cloak pocket?"

"Oh that," Angela grinned. "The girl I told you about, Myra, she gave it to me."

"And why would this girl give you something like this?" A dark winged brow rose in question.

"I guess that was all she had to give away at the time." Angela stepped out of her gown and now stood before Royce in only her shift. "I gave her the few coins I had in my pocket. I suppose she felt the need to give me something in return."

" 'Tis a strange gift for her to be giving."

"If you knew Myra, maybe you wouldn't think it so strange," Angela reflected. "She said that her sweetheart didn't enjoy them, and she wouldn't be needing it." Before she could halt the words, she asked, "Perhaps you would like to try it?" She felt her body trembling slightly as she stood before him and waited for his response.

"Perhaps," he grinned. "If you would like to put it on me."

Angela had never expected this. As she looked up into his handsome features, the air seemed sensuously electrified. "I have never done such a thing before," she murmured softly.

"I would not have expected you to have." The grin remained.

Looking at his broad chest, she slowly nodded her head. In the span of time in which the couple had been intimate, usually it was Royce who had initiated their love play. Now Angela stood before him rather nervously, not quite sure what she should do next.

At heart she was such an innocent, for all of her outspoken ways, Royce thought as he glimpsed a flush gracing her cheeks in the dimly lit chamber. "I guess it would be much easier if I undress."

Angela swallowed hard as she nodded her head, and he began to relieve himself of his breeches, stockings, and shoes. Lord, he was breathtakingly handsome, she thought as he completed his disrobing and stood before her entirely nude. Beautiful . . . powerful . . . manly . . . and entirely hers.

Royce felt his manhood enlarging, and with each second that she lingered in her appraisal of him, he felt hot blood surging and swelling his shaft. God above, he thought, what would he do when she finally touched him?

Swallowing nervously, Angela's blue gaze took in his growing manhood. Taking a single step toward him, she held out a shaky hand for the sheath.

His breathing was shallow as he gave her the sheath. It dangled from her slender fingers by its little red ribbon.

Every portion of Angela's body tingled with heated gooseflesh. The points of her full, firm breasts strained against the thin fabric of her shift. The exotic feel of the satin brushing against the hardened nubs sent fire racing through her loins. She could not tear her eyes away from the jutting, magnificent length of him. She dared not look into his face for fear of the passion she would read in his handsome features, knowing with a single glance that she would melt on the spot! Instead, she drew in a ragged breath. With another step she was close enough to touch him, close enough to feel the heat radiating from his naked flesh.

With hands clenched at his sides, Royce anxiously awaited her first caress. With the simple brush of her fingertips against his manhood, Royce felt the surging of hot blood as his lance extended to an even grater degree. As her fingers encircled his thickness, he felt the softness of the sheath as she began to slip it over the sensitive, velvet head. His first reaction was to reach down and help her, but as he glimpsed her concentration and effort, he stilled himself. He groaned as her small hands gently fondled his testicles as she endeavored to tie the ribbon about his scrotum.

Afterwards, Angela took a single step back and viewed her handiwork. Royce also looked down, and as a wide grin settled over his features, his eyes rose to meet Angela's.

"I guess the sheath isn't the right size," Angela said. The phrase "one size fits all" certainly didn't apply in this instance!

"I don't believe they come any larger than this." A touch of humor was in Royce's voice as he looked down. The sheath now bore several rips on the sides. The ribbon was tied in a little bow at the base of his shaft and was the only thing to have survived of the sheath.

Myra had made no mention of this happening to her boyfriend Tommy, Angela thought, a little confused by the outcome.

The seriousness which crossed her features struck Royce as funny. With a deep-throated chuckle, he reached out and drew her to him, gathering her in his embrace. Trying not to lose sight of the moment, he brushed back the thick length of hair which had fallen over her cheek, its fullness lying over her shoulder and covering one breast. "What say you, my sweet, that we dispose of this damn thing?" He ached to lose himself within the soft folds of her woman's flesh, and feeling the lush outlines of her shape beneath the satin shift, he felt the pulsing of blood rushing fiercely through his loins.

Angela nodded her head as she felt the hard contours of his body as he held her in his arms. Within seconds, she was naked, as Royce pulled the shift over her head with little hindrance. Her nude body brushed up against his naked length, and with the contact, her senses spiraled out of control; so on fire was she for him at this moment!

Lowering his head, Royce sampled the parted lips, and as her arms entwined around his neck, he lifted her up into his arms and carried her to the bed. Placing her upon the silken sheets, for a moment his gaze swept her bountiful curves. Lord, his body was starving for hers! He ached to plunge into her softness and to lose himself forever in the passionate bounty that awaited him! Before stretching out beside her on the bed, he tore away the sheath, but the little red ribbon remained.

The couple came together in a ravenous joining of bodies, lips hungrily clasping as they sought to sate their passions. Royce parted Angela's thighs and settled himself atop her. The brush of the swollen tip of his manhood against her moist opening caused her to gasp for breath. As his hard, veined length began to slowly press into her tight passage, she opened to him, her body shifting a small bit, her legs rising to settle fully around his hips.

Royce felt the power of his manhood as she gave herself fully to him. His hungry mouth rained kisses over her face and down the slender contours of her throat; his tongue tasted of her sweetness as he licked a path to the fullness of her tempting breasts. God, this woman drove him wild! He wanted only to feel and taste more of her as he never seemed to get enough! Cupping his hand around her full buttocks, he plunged deeper into her welcoming depths.

The feel of her tightness contracting around his swollen lance set off a rhythm of slow, undulating motion.

Shudder after shudder coursed over Angela's sensitive body as her flesh was attuned to his every caress, his every inch, his every kiss. The satin ribbon lightly caressed her cleft, causing sensory overload.

When fulfillment came, it was earth shattering. As he plunged into her one last time, she clutched his shoulders, her body rising up to meet his, her head thrown back, and his name springing from her lips. Trembling shudders of rapture caught and held her for endless moments, all feelings and emotions centering within the depths of her womanhood as the glorious eruption of passion's flame burst into a ricocheting climax.

It took every ounce of will power that Royce possessed not to follow her climax with his own. As he looked down into her passion-filled features, he wanted her to ride out the tempest to its fullest. When he sensed her descent, her body's sweet trembling diminishing, he allowed himself to be swept into the spinning vortex of satisfaction, and when he did, he was amply rewarded. As his seed pumped through his loins, his trusts becoming harder, her cries filled the chamber as she was carried along to the culmination of his fiery climax.

Their lips joined breathlessly. In shared silence, their heartbeats slowed, and Royce, holding Angela tenderly in his embrace, whispered huskily, "I will never let you leave me, Gypsy angel."

But Angela was already asleep.

Twenty-two

With the breaking of dawn, as the pink-hued breath of morning descended upon the Tudor town house in Eaton Square, Royce leaned upon an elbow and feathered light kisses across the bridge of Angela's nose and sleep-crested eyelids. "Wake up, Angela," he whispered softly against her cheek. "I have a surprise that I want to show you."

Drowsily Angela was pulled from the clutches of a deep sleep. "What is it, Royce?" she questioned. As her eyes opened, she noticed that a candle had been lit next to the bedside and Royce was already fully dressed. "Is something wrong?" She sat up, fear gripping her heart. Her first thoughts were that Damian had betrayed him and he had gotten word and was about to flee.

Panic was easily read upon her sleepy features, and Royce bent to kiss her soft lips. "Nothing is wrong, sweetheart. I thought that you would like to get dressed and take a ride with me through the park. I have an early morning business engagement."

A ride through the park. She instantly fell back against the soft pillows, her eyes closing as she tried to regain that peaceful state of earlier moments.

"Oh no, you don't, sleepy head. I want you to accompany me this morning."

"What was that you were saying about a surprise?" she questioned, eyes closed still.

"As soon as you get dressed and go with me to the stables, you'll see for yourself. I have already laid out your riding habit, love." He was being relentless. "All you have to do is stand up; I'll do the rest."

A small grin settled over her lips. "Are you going to dress me then, your Grace?"

"With the greatest of pleasure. I am your willing servant, my Lady." His reply was loud and lusty as he swept away the silk sheet and his silver gaze hungrily devoured her smooth curves.

"You are very wicked to pull me from my sleep, Royce." Angela glimpsed the passion which had leapt into his eyes. "Why don't we wait until later in the morning for that surprise?" She stretched like a tempting feline and put forth her own invitation. As thoughts of the night before came vividly to mind, her own eyes filled with desire.

Royce was not made of stone, nor was he lost to the seductive display of her charms. Bending again, he gathered her against his chest, his mouth slanting over hers. The kiss was heady and rewarding. It would have been so easy to stretch out on the bed next to her, but his resolve was firm. Desiring to see the pleasure in her eyes when she received the gift he had purchased for her the day before, he resisted with a superhuman strength. Pulling her along with him from the bed, he stood her before him. "Now get dressed, sweet, and I promise that this evening I will make that little body of yours purr as it never has before." God, for the rest of the morning, he would be imagining her naked. He would be hard-pressed to get any business done!

"Even more so than last night?" Angela smiled sweetly as she reached for her clothes.

That remark almost toppled Royce's resolve. Their love play of the night before filled his mind. He forced himself to draw in deep breaths of air as he kept his hands behind his back, not daring to allow himself the pleasure of touching her again until she was fully clothed.

Shortly the couple left the chamber hand in hand; the duke dressed in the usual somber black and his lady wearing an emerald green riding habit with a saucy feathered hat angled upon her head.

The carriage house was situated to one side behind the town house. As the couple neared the stable area, Angela spied the pretty, dapple-gray mare with her expensive saddle and bridle. A young man, his back to the advancing pair, held the reins, and as they drew closer, Royce released Angela's hand.

"This is the surprise that I mentioned earlier, Angela. The mare's name is Gypsy." As she looked at him, he added, "I didn't make it up, I swear it. The name came with her."

"Oh, Royce, she is lovely, and I love her name! Is she truly mine?" It was not the expensive gift that made her blue eyes sparkle with happiness, but the fact that he had purchased her any gift at all! This told her more than any words that he did care for her!

"Indeed, she is all yours, love. The young man at her side is her former owner. He has agreed most generously to spend a few days here at the town house in order for Gypsy to settle herself in comfortably."

Barely had the words left Royce's mouth before Angela threw herself into his strong arms and hugged him tightly to her breasts. With a smile of adoration, she looked up into his silver eyes and whispered brokenly, "Thank you so much, Royce." No one had ever given her anything of value, and Royce St. James had already given her so much. She knew now that it would be much harder than she had ever dreamed when she would have to leave him and return to her own time.

Gazing down into her blue eyes, Royce glimpsed the teary mist that filled them and quickly set about lightening her mood. "Come, sweeting. If we are going for that ride through the park, we must be about it shortly, or I will be late for my meeting." His hand settled upon the small of her back as he turned her around and started her toward the mare.

As Royce stepped away from her side to gain his own mount, the young man holding Gypsy's reins turned and faced Angela. Hurrying toward the mare, as she glimpsed Royce mounting his stallion, she said in low tones, "What are you doing here, Stephan?"

Helping her mount up, the young Gypsy man's jet eyes took in her surprise. "I told you that night when we danced before the campfire that I would come for you if you did not return."

"You came here to London to find me?" Angela asked in amazement. Quickly her blue eyes glanced in Royce's direction to see if he were paying any attention. She had forgotten all about the Gypsy tribe living in the forest on the Westfield property. After that night, when she had made love to Royce beneath a starlit sky, all thoughts had been swept from her mind except those of Royce St. James! She had not given a second thought to Stephan's promise to come for her if she did not return!

"Are you ready to leave, Angela?" Royce called out, noticing that the young man was still holding the mare's reins and that Angela looked distracted.

Instantly Angela's attention turned from Stephan to Royce, and she forced a warm smile to settle over her lips. "I can't wait to try Gypsy, Royce," she answered. Bending to gather the reins from Stephan's hands, she said quietly, "As soon as I return to the town house, we will talk."

There was something in the young man's gaze that told her that he would be waiting for her when she did return. Kicking the mare's sides, Angela cursed the fates that ruled her life. Royce might understand her befriending a poor orange girl from Covent Gardens, but she did not think he would take too kindly to a handsome, young Gypsy man showing up on his doorstep and imposing a claim because of his and Angela's past friendship!

The couple directed their mounts toward Green Park for their early morning ride. The park was a vast acreage of grass and trees that had been added to the Royal Park by Charles II, and thus replaced St. James's Park as the fashionable airing spot of London. At this time of the morning, there were few riders about, the upper crust more prone to horse-and-carriage rides in the late afternoon, when they could show themselves off in the latest fashions.

The chill morning air was invigorating and helped to clear Angela's head, but the more she thought about Stephan being at the town house, the more worries beset her. Why did he follow her to London? What did he want from her? He had been suspicious and wary of her up until that night when she had danced with him. Surely that night could not have brought about such a change in him!

"You and Gypsy are well-suited," Royce called as he watched the spirited little mare prancing daintily out in front of his stallion. With Angela's full green riding skirts draped over the beast's flanks, rider and animal were a picture to behold!

"She is wonderful, Royce. I don't know how I will ever be able to thank you enough." The little mare handled like a dream, sensitive to Angela's every movement of hand.

"I'm sure that you will be able to think of something, sweet." Royce grinned, well-pleased that she enjoyed his gift. Since their arrival in London, she had not mentioned leaving him again. Last night at Eastbury's, when she had insulted Damian and had not mentioned the bet, furthered his hope that he was winning her heart. "It was quite a stroke of fortune that brought Gypsy's owner to our stables to enquire if I was interested in purchasing her."

Luck had little to do with it, Angela thought to herself, but then another thought hit her: what if this lovely little horse that she was riding so boldly through the park had been stolen! She did not remember seeing such a valuable animal in the Gypsy encampment on the Westfield property. How came Stephan to be in possession of such a creature?

The pleasant morning ride now became a worrisome ordeal for Angela as she cast apprehensive glances down each trail they ventured upon, fearing that at any moment a rider would approach them and claim knowledge of the mare's true ownership. She nodded her head in relieved agreement when Royce asked if she were ready to return to the town house.

As quickly as Royce left the house to attend to his affairs, Angela changed out of her riding habit and was hurrying downstairs and out to the carriage house. She would insist that Stephan accompany her to meet Myra. In this fashion, she could try and find out if Royce had purchased stolen property by buying the mare. If this proved to be the case, she would quickly send Stephan on his way with the horse in tow. She also intended on explaining to him that her feelings toward Royce St. James had drastically changed since last she had seen him. She had the pocket watch and felt assured that at any time she could send herself back to her own time. All she had to do was first prove Damian Dunsely for the scoundrel he was!

Stephan was waiting for her near the front walk of the town house, and the minute she left the front door, he stepped to her side. His handsome features looked her over with appreciation as a generous smile drew back his lips.

"I have to meet a friend this morning. If you would like to come along, we can talk." Angela remembered how handsome she had thought him in his Gypsy garb. Viewing him in his short waist jacket and breeches, she could not deny that he held the power to easily draw a female eye. It would be hard for anyone to recognize him for the Gypsy he was; only his olive complexion and sparkling black eyes gave a clue. She was thankful that Royce had not recognized him from the night they had danced at camp.

"I would love nothing better than to accompany you to meet your friend, Angela." His dark eyes danced with bold, devil-may-care lights as he fell into step next to her.

As they started down the street, Angela pulled her cloak about her. She had remembered the dance the two of them had shared before the Gypsy campfire. She also remembered how this young man had held her tightly against his lithe, hard body.

"Where did you get the mare, Stephan?" she asked, hoping to keep their conversation impersonal.

"My brother Sergi found us camped in the forest on the Westfield property. The mare belonged to him. He had traded his wagon to a horse trader for her, and I, in turn, traded him two of the nags that my father and I owned. Sergi believes he is the better horse trader, but the price the duke paid for Gypsy was worth more than all the horses combined in our camp!"

"How did you manage that?" Angela

looked at the young man levelly. "And how did you find me here in London?"

A wide grin graced his face. His daring looks held a boyish appeal that was hard to resist. "That night when we danced before the fire, I knew that there was something between us that could not be seen, but only felt. Old Zela saw it, too. She told me the next day that you were linked to my future and that I should go and find you. One of the servants at the Hall told me that you were in the city. Once I had the mare in my possession, it was not hard to find the house belonging to the duke. I approached his groomsman with the offer of buying the mare. Once the duke agreed and seemed well-pleased with the price, I volunteered to settle Gypsy into her new surroundings."

Angela's head was swimming as she listened to his confession. He had been misled about his future linked to hers! She had been sent back in time for the sole purpose of saving Royce from being executed. She was in this century for only a short time, then she would return to her own time period. Looking into this young man's dark eyes, which were so filled with hope, she hated to shatter his dreams, but there was no helping it.

"Many things have changed since I saw you last, Stephan," she began. As he watched her closely, she drew in a deep breath before continuing. "The duke and I . . . I mean Royce and I . . ." There was no way out except to tell him the truth. "You see, Stephan, I no longer wish to flee Royce. I care a great deal for him." She did not explain about leaving this time period shortly, but she was not lying about her feelings for Royce. "I am sorry, Stephan, that you came all this way for nothing."

As they walked along, Stephan remained silent. When he spoke once more, she was blessed with his radiant smile. "The duke is a *gorgio* and you are of the Rom. I will stay here in London for a while longer and see what happens."

So now he believed her to be one of the Rom! Angela thought. Her people were known for optimistic views, but she wondered if Stephan was taking it too far. "As you wish," Angela said.

"Who is this friend that we are going to meet?" Stephan questioned blithely. As far as he was concerned, fate ruled the way of the world, and if Angela was the woman meant for him, he would have her in the end!

Angela could not help smiling; he certainly was a charmer, there was no doubt about that! "She's an orange girl at Covent

Garden. I met her at the theater, and she promised to meet me this morning."

Seconds later, Angela spied Myra's red hair flaming beneath the morning sunlight, and with a wide smile, she waved her to their side. "Myra, this is Stephan," she introduced when the girl reached them. "He is an old friend of mine."

Myra's hazel eyes traveled over Stephan with curiosity. "An old friend?" Myra asked, then remembered what Angela had told her yesterday about being from the future. Did this mean that this young man was also from another century? She eyed him boldly from head to toe; she certainly wouldn't complain if these two wanted to take her back with them!

Angela knew what the other girl was thinking and quickly set her straight. "We have been friends only a few months. I met Stephan on Royce's estate." She did not elaborate.

"It be a right nice pleasure to meet ye, Stephan." Myra smiled sweetly, her eyes flashing with interest.

"The pleasure is all mine, Miss Myra." Stephan, in return, bestowed upon her a warm smile.

Angela was glad that she had brought Stephan along with her. Maybe Myra could take his mind off his unrequited feelings.

The best cure for a broken heart was a new-found love, but as she watched the pair conversing as though they already were good friends, she wondered if Stephan would ever truly know a broken heart. He was so care-free and easy of nature, it would take quite a woman to make a real dent upon his heart.

"Did you find out anything about Hampsteed Castle?" she asked, drawing Myra's attention away from Stephan.

"I have me friends working on that. As soon as they be finding out what we need to know, I'll tell ye. I'm also trying to find out more about Lord Dunsely."

"Well, just be careful, Myra. Damian seems capable of anything."

Stephan looked mystified. "May I be of any help?" he offered, thinking that he could enter into Angela's good graces.

"No, thank you," Angela answered quickly, not wanting to involve anyone else in this venture. It was enough that Myra was involved, she thought; she didn't need to involve anyone else!

Myra looked at the other young woman as though she had totally taken leave of her senses. Why would she refuse such a handsome young man? There was no telling what they would have to do to steal the evidence from the castle.

"Sure, ye can help, if ye have a mind to," contradicted Myra. As Angela glared at her, she stated boldly, "Why don't ye be going back to yer duke's house now, Angela. Stephan can be walking me back to Fleet Street, and I'll fill him in on what we're about. When I learn anything, I'll be sure and send ye word."

Angela had hoped not to involve Stephan, but now that looked impossible, given Myra's stubbornness. "Oh, all right, but as soon as you hear anything, let me know, Myra."

"She can be sending word through me, Angela," Stephan offered generously, his wide smile beaming upon Myra, and bringing a flush to her cheeks. As he saw Angela's worried frown, he added, "I'm sure that the duke will not mind me staying on at the town house for a while. I am paying for my keep, what with helping his grooms-man to take care of the stables and the horses."

Myra appeared pleased at the prospect of this young man becoming the intermediary between her and Angela. She would have to see him each day, and if she played her cards right, perhaps she could meet him in the evenings, too. She would work harder on finding the information that Angela wanted to know, and with each little tidbit, she would be rewarded with a visit to Stephan!

There was little that Angela could say. The two were intent upon taking matters into their own hands. She just hoped they knew what they were getting themselves into!

Twenty-three

The remainder of the week passed by uneventfully for Angela as she awaited word from Myra, brought to her daily by Stephan. Each afternoon she sought out the young Gypsy man near the stables, under the pretext of visiting her newly acquired mare. Stephan appeared pleased by her visits, but his news was the same each day: Myra and her friends had not discovered the information that they needed to know about the castle. With each visit, Stephan gave assurances that she should not worry; he would be seeing Myra again that evening and surely she would know more soon.

On Saturday Royce took Angela to the horse races at Newmarket, and there, amidst much drinking and gambling, some of the finest horseflesh in the whole of England was wagered upon at the Newmarket tracks.

It was here that Angela came face to face with Damian Dunsely.

"Well, Royce old man, I see that you still have your little Gypsy in tow!" Escorting Belinda Thompson to the track, Damian had spied Royce and the woman shortly after their arrival. Now, coming up behind the couple where they stood off to the side of the track's railing, it was evident by his words that he had figured out who Royce's companion at Eastbury's had been. The scathing glance he bestowed upon Angela was intended to insult as he raked her with his coal black eyes. The bewigged, fashionably dressed young woman clutching his arm snickered slyly as she allowed Angela only the slightest glance before her hungry gaze turned upon Royce.

Feeling Royce stiffening at her side, Angela wondered why this woman appeared starved for the sight of Royce. She then launched her own verbal assault. "And you, Lord Dunsely; are you here at Newmarket to race Raven Boy one last time before you lose him to Royce?"

Nothing Angela said could have angered Damian Dunsely more! His pale features beneath his powdered periwig turned as scarlet as his waistcoat and vest. His ebony eyes filled with hatred as he glared at her and Royce. Tightening his hold upon Belinda's arm, he said seethingly, "The time limit of the bet is not up yet! Raven Boy still belongs to me!"

"But surely not for long. As you can plainly see, Royce is already the winner of the wager!" Angela smiled sweetly in the face of his contained fury. She twirled her umbrella of waxed silk with a gloved hand in a very ladylike gesture, her radiant smile bestowed upon the woman at his side.

Damian's fist clenched and unclenched at his side, but wise enough to control his emotions, he only sneered down at her before he turned to Royce. "Perhaps we can meet at White's or Almack's during the week for a round or two of loo. I am sure Belinda would be willing to play the gracious hostess to us afterwards at her apartments." Before the blond beauty could say anything, Damian had turned upon the heel of his scarlet shoe. Pulling her along, he strode off to join another small group who had turned out for the races.

Damian's words left Angela feeling hollow inside as she realized their full meaning. Her glance followed the couple where they stood with a group of onlookers, as her gaze nervously returned to Royce. "Damian's friend is beautiful, Royce. Do you know her well?"

There had been something in the woman's

eyes when she had looked at Royce that told Angela more than any words he might say. For the first time in her life Angela felt pure jealousy.

Royce could have gladly strangled Damian for bringing Belinda around him and Angela. But hoping to put Angela at ease, he looked down and replied, "Belinda's beauty holds little comparison to yours, sweet. I knew her a long time ago; she means nothing to me now." These words were the truth. He had ended their relationship not long after he had left Angela at the Hall. He had been put off by Belinda's pouting ways, but had bestowed upon her a large settlement and had arranged for her to remain in her apartments for the time being. He wished her well and hoped that she would find someone to take his place.

"You don't intend on going with Damian to visit her, do you?" Angela's voice was low as she tried to remain calm, but she could not help the childlike edge to her tone.

Royce smiled down at her, his hand tightening over hers. "No, love, I will never return to Belinda's apartments. Damian knows this well: he was talking because you prick him so sharply. He hates to lose anything, and especially he hates to lose to me!" His smile widened boyishly as he pulled Angela closer to his side, then turned toward the track, where the first race of the day was about to begin.

If only Royce could see that Damian more than hated to lose to him; he hated everything about Royce St. James, Angela thought. The day had been ruined for her. As she absently watched the horse race, she told herself that the only way to make Royce face the truth about Damian Dunsely was to gather whatever proof she could from Hampsteed Castle!

The following morning Angela awoke feeling queasy and lightheaded. Under Royce's instruction and ever-watchful eye, she stayed abed for most of that morning. The following day, after Royce left the town house and she finished dressing, as she approached the breakfast tray which had been brought to her chambers, she was attacked by a nausea that forced her to lie abed with a dampened cloth covering her eyes until the upset slowly withdrew.

It was late afternoon before she was able to venture out to the stables, and as Stephan approached her, his manner was as light and carefree. "Good news, Angela, Myra has learned about the castle and the best way for us to gain entrance. She said that you should be ready early in the morning. The castle is a distance outside of London, so it might take us some time to get there. A friend of hers has a small dray wagon; he's a brewer and won't be needing it tomorrow, so has agreed to let us borrow it. Myra said that she will bring us some clothes to change into."

Angela wished that she had talked to the girl, so that she could have learned more of the specifics. "You know you don't have to come along with us, Stephan," Angela said, giving the young man an out. "You could leave this afternoon to return to your own people."

"After everything that Myra has told me about this Lord Dunsely, I wouldn't miss going along, Angela. Anyway, you two might need me once you're inside the castle." His smile was wide with anticipation of tomorrow's adventure. Besides, he wasn't ready to leave London. He wanted to make sure that Angela stayed out of harm's way, but there was something about that cheeky girl called Myra that intrigued him!

Thankfully, Royce left the town house early the following morning. In no way did Angela want him to know of her plans, for she knew with certainty that he would forbid her to go.

Though she felt her stomach roiling

again as she began to dress, she wisely averted her eyes from the breakfast tray. The sight or smell of the food beneath the silver lid was enough to cause her to rush to the commode and splash her face with cold water from the pitcher resting next to the bowl.

As she left the house and started down the brick walkway, Stephan stepped out from behind the hedge and took up beside her. "Myra is waiting down the street for us," he informed her. There was an excited air about him this morning that bespoke of his love for life and adventure.

"What be ailing ye, Angela?" Myra asked when first greeting her friends.

"It's nothing. I've felt a bit queasy in the stomach the past few mornings; it will leave as the morning passes." Angela climbed to the seat of the wagon with Stephan's help.

Myra and Stephan exchanged glances, but neither commented. "Here, throw this cloak over yer gown till we get somewhere where ye can change out of that fancy gown." Myra climbed into the back of the wagon which had several barrels strapped along its wooden sides, allowing Stephan to take over the driving. Tossing a torn and dirty cloak to Angela, she added, "It were the best I could do. The gown is a sight better than the cloak."

Angela glanced at the dark woolen dress that the other girl had bundled on the bed of the wagon at her side. She doubted that its condition was much better than the cloak she was holding. It was strange how quickly she had become accustomed to finer things. The gowns that Royce had given her had become a part of her everyday life. Only months ago she had worn rags not much better than these that Myra was presenting to her now. She was in no position to argue about something as silly as a foul-smelling cloak and a scratchy wool dress. If they could find the information at Hampsteed Castle that the tabloid had mentioned, she could save Royce's life and also the future Westfields' inheritance! She was not sure what the three of them would be up against, but she knew that they had to succeed!

Leaving the area of Eaton Square, Stephan directed the tired-looking horse outside of the city. As soon as they were on a less-traveled street, the wagon pulled to halt along the dirt road. Angela stepped from the wagon, and behind the cover of trees, she changed into the baggy serviceable dress which had seen much better days.

Climbing back onto the wagon seat, Myra handed her a piece of leather and instructed her to tie back her long hair. "When we reach the castle, we're to tell the gatekeeper that we're delivering ale for the brewer. That's what them barrels are for; but in truth most are empty. I don't think old Jeb Cooper trusted me that much—"Take me wagon but not me ale!"

"If everything goes right, I am sure that Royce will be very generous to him for the loan of his wagon and barrels," Angela said.

"That be just what old Jeb's acounting on!" Myra laughed. "Once we get to the rear of the castle, we'll go through the kitchen and store the barrels in the cellar. That's where Stephan, with all them fine muscles, will come in." Myra boldly winked at the young man as he turned in the seat to grin at her. "From there, we're on our own, and we'd best make haste in finding whatever it is that proves Lord Dunsely is evil!"

Angela could only pray that things would go as easily as Myra had planned. For the remainder of the journey, she remained quiet as Stephan whistled a lively Gypsy tune, and in between bouts of humming and laughing, he lustfully sang an entertaining song to Myra, who clung to his every gesture.

The couple had taken a liking to each other faster than Angela had anticipated. She surreptitiously watched Myra tracing a finger along Stephan's collar and brushing back a wayward strand of dark hair that had fallen from the leather thong that held his hair back.

It was midafternoon when the small dray wagon turned down the winding, dusty road which would lead them to Hampsteed Castle. The castle loomed starkly in the distance. The impregnable stone walls filled Angela's heart with a trepidation that left her clutching tightly to the side of the wagon. Swallowing nervously, she stated, "It looks big, doesn't it?"

Myra laughed aloud and Stephan grinned. "What did ye expect, girl?" she said. "Hampsteed Castle belongs to the Earl of Shrifrey. He is away from England. There is only a small staff who remain at the castle, but ye can be betting that when the old earl returns, he brings with him a houseful! They say he is a regular fop and loves nothing better than to pass the time at Hampsteed Castle by holding fox hunts and fancy balls. Now would a chap like that live in a small castle?"

Angela couldn't help but smile at Myra's witticism. As the wagon passed over the drawbridge and started through the open gates, a lone sentry waved them on toward the main keep without a question to their intent.

"I were told that those here at the castle were a lazy lot. With the earl away, they don't be expecting any trouble, so close to London and all." The first part of the journey was now behind them, and it had been easier than even Myra had imagined.

As Stephan pulled the wagon toward the servants' entrance, the three watched for any sign of servants or serfs. There was little activity taking place within the castle grounds at this time of the afternoon. The only sounds were the hawks in the mews and the dogs growling among themselves in the kennels.

Angela sighed with relief as Stephan jumped from the wagon and helped the two women down. She had expected token resistance to their arrival. As Stephan began to unload several of the barrels from the back of the wagon, Myra motioned for Angela to remain near the wagon as she disappeared through the kitchen door. Soon she returned with a wide grin upon her pixie face, and Angela realized that now their only obstacle was finding the evidence of Dunsely's betrayal.

"There is only one old woman in the kitchen. She said that at this time of the day, most of the servants are in their rooms taking a nap. Can ye be imagining what the old earl would have to say about that!" Myra giggled as she took a barrel and rolled it toward the kitchen door.

Within fifteen minutes, most of the barrels were sitting outside the kitchen door. Without a word from the old woman, who was nodding off in a chair before the open hearth, Myra led the way through the kitchen to the ale room, which the woman had pointed out earlier.

While Stephan slowly began to drag the barrels into the ale room, grunting as though the barrels were filled to the brim, Angela and Myra made their way down a long hallway and up a flight of stairs, which brought them into the large common room.

Looking around, Angela was at a complete loss. How on earth were they ever going to discover what they needed. They didn't even have a hint as to what they were looking for!

Myra did not waste the precious time allotted them with such worrisome thoughts. She quickly set about snooping through every little nook and cranny that the large, open room possessed. Not a drawer did she leave unopened, nor a vase did she not turn upside down. Even the tapestries and pictures hanging upon the stone walls were subject to scrutiny as she looked behind them.

Angela joined her in the search, and soon both women looked nervous and strained. "I guess we should go up them stairs," Myra ventured, pointing to the staircase near the hallway.

As they reached the first-floor landing, the sound of music was heard from the second floor. With a little wink thrown back over her shoulder, Myra boldly climbed onward.

Following the sound of the music down the hallway of the second floor, the young women halted outside a closed door. Taking a deep breath, it was Angela who pushed the door open slightly and peered inside. Surprise etched her features as she saw, sitting on a small window seat, a slim-figured woman playing a psaltery, her slender fingers running over the strings and her eyes closed tightly. She looked as though she was deep in meditation.

Myra nudged Angela out of the way so she, too, could get a look. With a grin, she excitedly motioned Angela to enter the room with her; then she very quietly closed the door.

The woman played on, but sensing she was being watched, the music of the psaltery died. Her eyes opened and she saw the pair of intruders.

For a tremulous minute, no one said a word as the three young women looked questioningly at one another. The woman finally stepped away from the instrument, and with graceful movements, she approached the intruders. "Are you here with word from Damian?"

The words were spoken barely louder than a whisper and certainly surprised the two women. Myra was the first to react to the frail creature in white. "Aye, mistress, Lord Dunsely sent us here to the castle." She turned toward Angela and gave her a bold wink.

"You must come in then. Come over here by the window and be quiet, or they will catch the two of you." The reed-slender figure glided across the room and laid a hand upon each girl's wrist. Her flesh was so fair that Angela could see her blue veins.

"Before who catches us? We saw no one in the hallway." Nor had they seen anyone about the entire castle, besides the old woman in the kitchen, Angela thought. Looking at the pale woman with the deep-set black eyes, she wondered if she were mad. Were they wasting valuable time here? But Angela remembered that the young woman had mentioned Damian.

Myra nudged Angela sharply in the ribs and followed the woman across the room and toward the window. "Sure, we'll come along with ye," agreed the redhead. With a scolding look, she warned Angela to follow along.

After the pale young woman sat down on

403

the window seat and spread out her white taffeta skirts, she asked, "Did you bring me another letter from Damian?" The afternoon sunlight filtered through the leaded glass and made the woman appear even younger than Angela had believed her.

Angela caught on to Myra's game quickly enough, and it was she who questioned, "Lord Dunsely sends you letters here?"

"Of course Damian sends me letters, silly! Who else would send me a message through the two of you?" There was a touch of concern in her dark eyes as she looked closer at the pair of women. " 'Tis strange that Damian has never sent messages through any other women in the past. But then, it has been two weeks since last I heard from my darling love." Their dress was so plain, it was easy for her to believe that the two women were only messengers.

"He writes you often?" Angela questioned. Myra gave her a cautionary look to go slowly.

A wan smile settled over the woman's pale lips. "As often as possible we are in contact with one another, but if Father ever found out, it would mean the end of everything!" The woman's eyes filled with fear, and she scanned the room again to make sure that they were indeed alone.

"So, yer father doesn't be liking his Lordship, hmm?" Myra asked.

"Oh, you both are as silly as can be!" The woman's smile grew friendlier, as though it had been some time she had talked to another woman. "Father loves Damian, of course. After all, he is his son!"

What was going on here? Angela wondered. Like Myra, she was surprised by the woman's strange reply. She had thought she had stumbled upon Damian's lover, but this woman was only his sister. "But I thought you said that you loved Lord Dunsely?"

"Did he tell you that he loves me?" The woman looked from one woman to the other, and without a glance between them, both Myra and Angela nodded their heads. "Then you can see why Father cannot find out that Damian knows my whereabouts. Father sent me here to Hampsteed Castle after finding Damian and myself together at the manor house. In his last letter, Damian said that he has a plan for Father, so that I will be free of him. He told me about another plan, but swore me in his letters not to tell a soul!"

"A plan?" Angela softly repeated. This was it! Damian must have told her in his letters about his plans to ruin Royce! Her blue gaze traveled the room as she wondered where this woman would keep her corre-

405

spondence with her brother. Angela felt her stomach turn over with what such a thought implied, but she would not let herself dwell upon that now. She had to find out where those letters were!

"I imagine you saved every one of Lord Dunsely's letters," she said. "Why, when my own sweetheart sent me a pretty card with verses of poetry inside, I kept it in my most secret place!"

"As I do my own sweetheart's!" the girl responded in a dreamy voice.

"Perhaps you would like to show us how much his Lordship cares about you. By showing us how many letters he has sent you, we will be able to tell how true his love is." Angela said anything that might help her find those letters.

At last Myra appeared to understand what she was about. "Aye, if you show the letters to us, we will be able to tell the other girls that Lord Dunsely has a sweetheart."

The young woman was not overly sharp-witted, and after only a few seconds of indecision, she rose from the window seat and motioned them to follow her to the hearth. "They are hidden here behind this brick." She reached out a slender hand and pried out one brick.

Angela's breath clutched in her throat as she glimpsed a stack of white envelopes in the small crevice behind the brick. Just as the woman would have drawn the letters out for their viewing, the crash of the chamber door being thrown back against its hinges held the three young women immobile before the fireplace. Before anyone could react, a powerfully large man charged into the room growling and snarling!

Twenty-four

"Now, wait just one minute!" Angela shouted as the pale young woman fainted. The man paid little heed to the young woman, but started in the direction of the intruders. Angela tried to put some distance between them by running behind a chair and table. "We weren't doing any harm—just a little visit with the lady!"

The large man bored down upon her, knocking the table and chair aside with a swat from his powerful fist, and as Angela tried to lunge for the open door, he leaped after her, grabbing hold of her wrist and dragging her back to his side.

Without a thought to the man's size, Angela began to fight off her attacker. A few seconds later, Myra had thrown herself upon the giant's back, and he made circles around the room, fighting off Angela's small fists which were beating his chest and face and

Myra's fists which were battering his head. He swore viciously as he reached up and behind him and grabbed hold of Myra by the scruff of her dress; as though she weighed little more than a kitten, he held her in midair and shook her with a heavy hand until she stopped struggling. Snatching Angela with the other hand, the two women's efforts to overcome the brute were soon over.

The pale woman's guard was the most awesome brute Angela had ever encountered. Grabbing both her hands in one of his, he dragged her out the chamber door, Myra still being held off her feet. Carrying both women down the winding stairs and through the lower hallway, he did not relax his grip until he reached the deepest portion of the keep. He then released his hold when he shoved both young women into a dank chamber that was plainly some sort of prison. "You two whores will stay in here until I get word to his Lordship that you were in the Lady Camelle's chamber! His lordship will know what to do with you!" He slammed the heavy door and the rattle of a key could be heard from the other side as he locked the portal.

Angela groaned aloud as she sank to the stone floor, her back leaning against the chilled wall as she clutched a hand to her roiling midsection. Lord God, what had she gotten the pair of them into? She felt ill, and as she looked around the dimly lit cell, her upset intensified by the filth and stench in the chamber.

"I'd be saying that come around this time next year, yer going to be having a little nipper sucking at yer breast," Myra casually threw over her shoulder as she glanced at Angela sitting on the floor of the cell. The young thief was pushing her shoulder against the stout door to try its strength.

"What?" Angela thought she had heard the other incorrectly, and drawing in a deep breath, she attempted to bring some calm into her desperate situation.

"I've seen it often enough in the past from me own mum. Ye got yerself caught, girl—yer going to have a babe. That's why ye've been sick in the mornings of late."

"A baby? I can't. . . . It's not possible!" Angela remembered all the mornings lately that she awakened feeling ill. *Morning sickness!* The two words hit her full force. "This can't be happening!" she moaned as she closed her eyes and leaned back against the wall of the cell. She couldn't be pregnant! Her life was complicated enough without her having to worry about a baby!

"I remember me own mum saying those very same words when she got caught with me little brother Ben." Myra grinned widely with remembrance. "But not believing that yer caught don't be making a change of things!"

Drawing deep breaths of air into her lungs, Angela tried to turn her thoughts from her possible pregnancy. "We have to do something to get out of here!" she said as she watched Myra climbing up on a wooden crate that had been in the corner of the cell. The girl was standing on the crate on tiptoe and was peering out the sliver of a window.

"My thoughts exactly," Myra returned.

Myra took everything lightly enough, Angela thought. Here they were, in a stinking cell in the bowels of the castle, and that hulking brute had sworn that he was going to send word to his Lordship, whoever that might be! What if it were Damian Dunsely, she thought with dread. If Damian were to find out that she was at Hampsteed Castle talking to his sister, he would keep her prisoner until she was old and gray—if he allowed her to live that long! What had the woman upstairs said about him having some plan for her father so that he could not interfere in their lives again. A shudder shook her as she realized how very dangerous Damian Dunsely could be. If they had had another moment or two alone with the woman upstairs, perhaps they could have

411

had a chance to get the letters and prove Damian for what he was! But how would she ever be able to do that now? Her thoughts went to Royce, and she wondered if he would ever find out what happened to her. Would he realize how much she loved him, or would he just believe she had left him without word and returned to her people? Now that she was locked in a prison cell, she could admit that she loved Royce. She loved him with all of her heart, and she was going to have his baby. Tears formed in her eyes and slowly trailed down her cheeks.

Stepping away from the crate and the window, Myra glimpsed the despair in Angela's face, and she tried to cheer her up. "Here, ye might want to read these while we try to come up with some plan to get ourselves out of this damn cell!" Throwing the bundle of letters tied neatly with a little blue ribbon into Angela's lap, she went back to the door and jiggled the latch one more time.

"You got the letters from behind the brick? But how did you do it? I mean, when did you have the time?" Angela brushed away the moisture in her eyes, and sitting up straighter against the stone wall, she grabbed the letters and quickly began to untie the ribbon.

"While you were fighting off that hulk upstairs and that stupid woman fell to the floor in a faint, I pushed the brick away and put that bundle into me pocket. I be hoping that they be the proof ye were talking about. If we ever get out of here, I don't want to be having to come back and try again! I've seen enough of the inside of a castle to last me a lifetime!"

With her belly now feeling better, Angela made her way over to the crate beneath the small window, and sitting down, she began to read through the letters. At the finish of the first letter, her gaze rose upward, and she saw Myra standing nearby as though waiting to hear about the contents. "The woman upstairs is Camelle. She and Damian are brother and sister by the same father, who will, according to the letter from Damian, soon be having an accident, and then Camelle will be able to live under her brother's charge, with no one to interfere with their lives."

"Does he say anything about yer duke?" Myra's brown eyes were large with amazement as she wondered how anyone could plot out the death of their own father. Damian Dunsely surely must be evil, and his sister must be insane!

"He doesn't say anything about Royce. Most of his writings are about his love for Camelle, but I know there must be something in one of these." She looked down at the rest of the envelopes in her lap, feeling certain that this had to be the proof that the tabloids spoke about. Camelle must have left the letters behind the brick, and someone in the twentieth century must have found them where they had been hidden for years.

"It all sounds pretty queer to me! I knew that Lord Dunsely was strange, but for him to love his own sister just ain't right!"

"He says here that after his mother's death he was sent to the Earl of Chester. He didn't set eyes on his half sister until her coming out. She was sent to London for her coming-out season, and Damian claims that when he first glimpsed her coming down the grand staircase at the Countess of Wesley's house, he fell in love with her right on the spot!"

"Like I said, they're queer in the head!" Myra replied. In the next instant, she was waving for Angela to hide the letters in her skirt pocket and to remain quiet.

Someone was at the door of the cell, and after shoving the bundle of letters into the pocket of her woolen dress, Angela stepped to Myra's side, both women staring at the stout oak door with apprehension. Had his Lordship arrived at the castle, or was it the large man coming to do them more ill?

The loud creaking sound of the cell door being pushed open was the only sound in the stark cell. The two young women stood against the stone wall, clutched tightly to each other's hands, and stared at the cell door. A dark head peered into the cell, and Stephan's tall figure stepped into the chamber.

"I thought that you two might be somewhere down here. I heard that clubfooted barbarian yelling at the old woman out in the kitchen that he had caught two women upstairs in some woman's chamber."

"Stephan!" both women cried in relief, but it was Myra who ran across the space of the cell and threw her arms around the young Gypsy man's neck. "I knew ye wouldn't be letting us down! Why, I was just telling Angela that ye would be coming to our rescue most any minute now! Isn't that the truth of it, Angela?" Myra's brown eyes sparkled with sheer joy, but Angela glimpsed no remorse for the bold lie that had just left her lips.

"Did the old lady tell him that we came to the castle with you?" Angela worried now that the hue and cry would be sounded.

"That old crone can't be remembering a thing from one minute to the next!" Stephan laughed, tightening his embrace around Myra and hugging her back. "Right now we had best get our hides out of here before he comes back."

"He claimed that he was sending for someone; he didn't mention a name, only 'his Lordship.' I don't know if he meant Damian or his father," Angela said.

"It could be Lord Dunsely. After he left the kitchen, I heard the old lady mumbling to herself about the guard not being loyal to the old earl. But we can speak on it later. We must leave." Stephan clutched Myra's hand in his own before starting toward the cell door.

Angela was only a step or two behind as the three silently and cautiously left the cell and made their way back toward the kitchen. They could hear more activity within the castle, but with luck aiding them, they did not run into anyone until they regained the large kitchen.

The old woman swung around from the worktable, and squinting, she peered in their direction, "Be that ye, Hannah? Come on over here and chop up these onions for this eve's stew."

"Besides being a touch senile, she must be blind and deaf too!" Stephan whispered. Grinning, he pulled Myra toward the kitchen door.

"Don't ye be running away when there's work to be done, girl!" the old woman shouted at their retreating backs. "When the earl returns, he's going to be hearing about yer lazy ways! Yer good for nothing besides flirting with sentries and avoiding honest work!"

"Hurry, the both of you, and climb into one of the empty barrels in the back of the wagon." Stephan gave each young woman a hand up as his dark eyes searched the area behind the kitchen for any sign of a servant approaching. "Stay quiet," he hissed after making sure that the lids of the two barrels were loosely laid atop, so that the women could breathe. Climbing on top of the wagon seat, Stephan slowly began to direct the old nag back toward the drawbridge.

Most of the servants had awakened from their nap, and as Stephan passed an old retainer with a pail of milk in each hand, he nodded his head and with a smile bid him good day. Apparently the brute inside had not realized that the women had escaped, and no word of caution had been sent to the front gate. The sentry waved the wagon and Stephan onward, not giving a second thought that the two women who had entered the castle earlier with the ale deliverer were no longer at his side.

Some minutes passed before the two women peered from beneath the barrel lids and Stephan assured them that it was safe.

"That was a close call back there!" Myra said, laughing and jumping out of the barrel, then climbing over the wagon seat to sit next to Stephan. "Stephan, how did ye open that cell door?"

"I've already told you, love, I'm a Gypsy. There isn't anything that I can't open when I set my mind to it!" His rich laughter filled their ears.

As soon as Angela climbed out of the barrel, she sat upon the floor of the wagon. Leaning her back against the wood-frame seat, she pulled the stack of letters from her pocket and began to read as Myra and Stephan chatted away.

It was the second-to-last letter which had what she was looking for:

My dearest Camelle,

I promise you that it will not be much longer before we are together. This very day I sent replies to the Marquis of Tullsbardine and Lord Dunmore's brother, who are heavily involved in the Jacobite cause. They have agreed to falsify the necessary papers to implicate the Duke of Westfield in their scheme to place James Stuart on the throne. For them the promise of gold, when I gain Royce St. James's lands and title, is an excellent inducement! Do not worry, my love. We shall not have to bear this separation much longer. My heart yearns for your very sight, and when I become the Duke of Westfield, you, Camelle, shall become my duchess! With Father out of the way, the documents to claim him not your legal sire will be easy enough to have drawn up!

As ever, I long to be at your side.

Damian

The letter was signed with both Damian Dunsely's signature and seal. Angela held the proof needed to save Royce's life in the palm of her hand! Tears came to her eyes, and looking at her dear friends who had risked all to help her, she smiled tremulously. "It's here. All the proof needed is right here. Royce will have to believe me now!" she told them.

The evening sun was setting when Stephan directed the dray wagon down the London streets toward Eaton Square. Angela did not stop along the way to change back into her fashionable gown but remained in the scratchy woolen gown and tattered cloak.

The town house was ablaze with light when the wagon halted in front of the brick walkway and Angela jumped to the ground. After expressing her thanks one last time to Stephan and Myra, she turned from the wagon. Stephan would drive Myra to Fleet Street, where they would return the wagon to its owner; later, Stephan would return to the town house.

Now that Angela held the proof in her hand, she found herself reluctant to rush into the town house and reveal everything to Royce. She knew that the end of their relationship would follow close on the heels of Damian Dunsely's denouncement. She would no longer have any reason to stay in this time period. With the thought, her hand absently went to her belly. Thoughts of being pregnant with Royce St. James's child did not bring about any resolution. She knew that she could not stay in this century because the shame that would be cast upon an unwed woman with child was even greater in this time than it was in her own. Thousands of women in 1994 found themselves pregnant and without a husband to give the babe a name or support.

Momma Leona would not be happy with her arriving back in their camp pregnant, but with time the Gypsy woman would relent. In a few years, she would have another child to teach the fine art of thievery! The thought made Angela feel ill, and brushing away the tears that instantly filled her eyes, she started to the front door of the town house.

As Angela's hand set upon the doorknob, the door swung wide and Royce St. James stood in the foyer looking out at her, his handsome features scowling as his silver gaze traveled over her from head to toe. "Where have you been, Angela?" His tone held none of the usual warmth that he used while addressing her. He sounded much like the Royce St. James that she had met that night when he had taken her to Westfield Hall.

Angela couldn't speak, knowing what she must look like in her frayed clothes, but swallowing hard, she braced herself. She had nothing to be sorry for! "I went out to Hampsteed Castle."

"Why did you go there and why are you dressed like that?" She reminded him, as she stared up at him with large, hollow-looking eyes, of the Gypsy waif that he had brought into his home months ago!

"May we talk in your study, Royce?" Angela felt uncomfortable standing in the foyer, where all the servants could be privy to their conversation.

Royce had been on his way out to begin a search for Angela when he had pulled the door open to find her standing on the front stoop. Arriving back at the town house that afternoon and finding her missing, he had feared the worst: that she had fled him and returned to her people. Looking at her now, he tried to calm himself. Realizing that there was more to the day's happenings than she had revealed and glimpsing the manner in which she looked about, he turned without saying a word and led the way to his study.

Royce did not speak until Angela had followed him into the room and closed the door behind her. Now sitting behind his desk, his silver gaze held her. "Why did you leave the town house without a footman? Mrs. Cambridge said that this is not the first time this has happened, but she has not mentioned it because you always arrive back at the town house before me."

Anger flashed over her, but she kept a tight rein on herself. He didn't have to concern himself much longer; she would be out of his life soon enough! Without saying a word in her own defense, Angela reached over and set the letter in front of him.

"What is this?" A dark brow rose in question, and as Royce turned the letter over, he noticed Damian's seal on the outside.

"Have no fear, your Grace, you will hear no more Gypsy lies. Everything is in the letter. There is no need for me to say anything further."

Angela felt drained. The day had been dangerous and exhausting, and her reception at the town house was nothing as she had anticipated. As Royce's glance lowered from her to the letter, she sank down into a chair.

After opening the envelope and drawing the letter out, Royce studied the letter. At first his features registered disbelief, but as he scanned further and recognized Damian's seal, the eyes which rose back up to Angela were a stormy gray. "Where did you find this?" He slipped the letter back in the envelope and laid it down upon his desk as though it were a viper.

"At Hampsteed Castle."

"But how could you have known that such a letter would be at the castle?" Royce was more than a little confused.

"The tabloid. I told you that night when you thought I was dreaming that the tabloid told about Damian's betrayal. It also mentioned that the proof of his deceit had been found at Hampsteed Castle." Angela could see by his steady regard that he still did not fully believe her. "There are more letters, and in some Damian tells of his evil plans for his own father. Camelle is his sister."

"I know who Camelle is," Royce said softly. He still could not accept that she was telling him the truth. There had to be a reasonable explanation for all of this besides the crazy story she was telling him about being from another century. But looking from her to the letter lying in front of him, he could not imagine how she could have known to find Damian's letters at Hampsteed Castle unless she had gained the knowledge from someone.

There was so much at stake here, he could not think straight. He had to get word to Damian's father about his son's plans for him, then he had to go to the King to clear himself of any charges that might come against him. Damian's letter would clearly convince anyone of his own innocence. But paramount in his thoughts was the fact that there was nothing to hold Angela at his side. The bet no longer stood; she was free to leave him at any time! "I must attend to this now, Angela." He rose to his feet, his hand clutching the letter. "Do not leave the town house. I will be back as soon as possible." With that, he left her alone in the study.

He had made no mention of believing her. He had left the town house as though upon his return they would carry on as usual! Tears sprang into her eyes and rolled down her cheeks. Nothing would ever be the same again! He would never think of her as anything more than the Gypsy brat he had taken out to the Hall that night so long ago! In a daze, she rose from the chair and left the study, tears blinding her as she climbed the stairs to her chamber.

There was nothing left for her here!

Royce had proven that by leaving her without so much as acknowledging his belief in her or their relationship. She felt her heart breaking in two. What relationship? He had never declared his feelings for her. He thought little more of her than he had any one of his previous mistresses. The image of the overblown blonde upon Damian's arm that day at Newmarket came to mind and intensified her weeping.

He didn't love her as she loved him, and for her foolishness, she would be forced to pay the ultimate price! She was going to have Royce St. James's child! Through her tear-blurred vision, she glimpsed a foil-covered box in the middle of the bed. Sitting on the edge of the mattress, she pushed the lid aside. Within lay the gown that Blade had been commissioned to fashion for her, the gown Royce wanted her to wear to court! Her hand reached out and tenderly caressed the violet-blue taffeta which matched her eyes exactly. She would never wear this beautiful gown, she thought as she stepped away from the bed and went to her wardrobe. Bending to the farthest corner, she pulled out the small box that contained her hair coins and jewelry. With an indrawn breath, she pulled forth the pocket watch that had brought her there.

Twenty-five

Looking down at the pocket watch, Angela pressed the clasp on the side and the lid popped open. Silently she read the same inscription she had read that evening as she lay near the edge of the pond: *Hold in your palm, set both hands to twelve. Move the small hand backward or forward if you desire the world at your feet. Your fate shall be set by the time of the watch. Close the lid and push the button.*

Her fate had been set all right! She had come to this time and saved Royce St. James from death, only to return to her own time carrying his child and with no hope for her future or the future of the child. There were no guarantees in this life, she reminded herself. She had tasted the lifestyle of the rich, which was more than most of her people could claim to have done! Now reality had caught up to her, and as she stood looking down at the pocket watch in her hand, she knew that the only steps for her were those that would lead her back to Momma Leona and the children. With the old Gypsy woman, she would have a roof over her head for herself and child, and this was more than she had been promised in the eighteenth century!

All she had to do was set the hands, she goaded herself. Set the hands and push the button and leave all those that she had grown to care about, especially the man she loved! The temptation was great, but with a strong will, she slipped the watch into her skirt pocket. She would tell Stephan good-bye, at least.

Going to her bureau, she gathered up some gold coins that Royce had given her yesterday afternoon. She would make sure that Stephan got the money to Myra to pay the ale man for the use of his wagon. Whatever was left over, perhaps the orange girl would be able to make a better life for herself.

Leaving the bedchamber, she made her way downstairs and out to the stables. Stephan had just arrived back from Fleet Street. Making her way to the back of the stables, where Stephan and the groomsman had the single room which they shared as their sleeping quarters, Angela softly knocked upon the door.

It was Stephan who opened the door, and glimpsing the paleness of Angela's features, he took hold of her arm without question. Pulling her into the room, he waited for her to sit on the edge of the bed before he spoke. Myra had told him earlier, when he had driven her home, about the child that Angela was to have, and at this moment he worried that something was wrong. "You are as pale as the ghost my grandfather claims is his father, that stalks our camp of an evening when there is a wet moon." His smile was warm as he added, "I also saw the ghost of my great-grandfather. That is how I know what he looks like."

Angela felt like weeping, but with a strong will, she kept herself from falling to pieces in front of him. "I have come to tell you goodbye, Stephan, and to give you this to give to Myra." She held out the lace handkerchief in which she had tied the gold coins.

"Where will you go, Rawnie?" The dark eyes held her with all the love that he felt in his heart for her.

"I have told you many times that I am not called Rawnie. I am as you and our people." Angela felt a catch in her throat and had to lower her eyes to her lap in order to continue with what she had to do.

"You will always remain a great lady to me. Now, tell me where you will go, and I will follow. Did your duke not welcome the news that you brought him? Was he not

428

pleased to know that you risked your life to see him kept safe from the evil that his friend would visit upon him?"

Stephan had bent down on his knees in front of her, and reaching out, Angela took his hands into her own. "No one can come with me, Stephan. I must return to my life alone." What was between herself and Royce she would not speak of.

"Then do not return to this time in the future that makes you unhappy. Stay here with me, Angela, and everyday I will make sure that your heart knows only joy. We are alike, you and I. We will live each day to its fullest and we will raise our children to love life and to feel blessed that they are of the Rom."

Tears formed in Angela's violet eyes, and absently her hand left his and touched her belly.

"I know of the child. Myra told me, and I would claim it as my own." There was hope in the ebony eyes as they watched her; hope and a promise.

Sadly Angela shook her head, "I love Royce, Stephan." This was the first time these words left her lips, and tears rolled down her cheeks with the confession.

Reaching out a tanned finger, Stephan smiled through the sharp pang that pierced his heart. "Your duke loves you also, Angela. I have seen it in his eyes when they look in

429

your direction. He needs more time to realize it, though."

Stephan would have begged her to come away with him, but something in the blue eyes that looked into his own told him that this could never be. She held a love for her duke that was all encompassing, the type of love that his old grandmother had held for his grandfather. When her husband had died, she had still been a young woman, but she had never taken another man to her pallet, though she had lived to be an old lady. She had loved too deeply to ever love again, and with an inner sense, he knew that Angela loved her duke in this same fashion.

Angela wished that Stephan's words were the truth, but she knew better. Royce St. James had never admitted any strong feelings of affection for her. Even in his study, his only concern had been the letter she had presented to him. Other than ordering her to remain at the town house, he had shown little concern for her. "You are wrong, Stephan." She rose to her feet. "Royce does not love me." Starting to the door, she turned and looked back at him one last time before turning and leaving the stables.

* * *

Staring down at the pocket watch in her hand once again, Angela saw that the small hand was still set upon the ten, where she had set it that night near the pond. With a ragged breath, she moved the hand to twelve and snapped the lid closed. Without allowing herself a moment to think of the outcome, only knowing that her love for Royce St. James was unrequited, she closed her eyes tightly and pushed the small button on the side of the pocket watch.

Standing in the center of the bedchamber, Angela slowly opened her eyes as she felt nothing happening. Her first thought was that she had done something wrong—she had not set the hands right or pushed the button correctly. Soon, however, only a few feet in front of her, she glimpsed a spectrum of light, barely visible at first, but slowly taking shape and form. The outline was that of a man.

She took several steps backward, her eyes wide with amazement. The solid upper portion of a man appeared before her eyes, then the lower portion of his body took shape, until standing whole before her was the little man from whom she had stolen the pocket watch.

"You! What . . . what are you doing here? I thought that by setting the hands back on the watch, I would be returned to my own time!" Angela gasped, not believing that he stood before her. *No more possible than for her to be traveling through time!* her inner conscience silently reminded.

The little man took a minute to straighten out his black suit with its silk tie. Before speaking, he held out his hand and revealed a pocket watch that matched the one she was holding. "I have been searching the centuries for you, Angela."

"You know my name?" This was insane! Here she was in the eighteenth century, talking to a little man from the twentieth who had appeared in a spectrum of light!

"If course. I tried to find you in 1994. That watch you hold is most valuable. I went out to the park where your guardian, Momma Leona lives, but by the time I arrived, you had already vanished. I must say, the woman was in a high temper at your disappearance, though I can't say that I blame you in the least."

"But I must return!" Angela sat down upon the edge of the bed, feeling overwrought.

"What will you be returning to, Angela?" The little man's eyes looked at her as though he possessed the knowledge of the universe. "The future holds little besides hardship for you. You belong in this time."

"I have nothing here," Angela whispered softly.

Wisely the little man nodded his head. "Your arrival in this century has changed the history books. The Duke of Westfield's name will never be mentioned with those Jacobites who were disloyal to the Crown. Do you not think that if you share your heart with the duke, he will in return share his with you?"

Great teardrops formed in her eyes as she shook her head. "But you don't understand! What if Royce turns me out?" She thought of life in 1745 for an unwed mother.

"Would you have given your heart to a man such as that? Trust in your heart, Angela. Trust in your own heart." With this he stepped to her side and eased the pocket watch out of her hand. "I am called Guardian. If you need me, I will come." With the click of a button on the side of one of the watches, he vanished as quickly as he had appeared.

Brushing the tears away from her eyes, Angela looked around the room, still not believing that he had been there. His words resounded in her brain: *Trust in your heart, Angela. Trust in your heart.*

By the time that Royce returned to the town house, the hour had grown late and the fire in their bedchamber had burned down to dim embers. His gaze was first drawn to the great bed in the center of the room, where he expected to find Angela, but noticing the coverlet still drawn upon the bed, his eyes quickly searched the room. With a small sigh he noticed her curled up in a chair upon the hearth.

Silently he made his way to the fireplace. Before turning to Angela, he bent down and stoked up the fire, placing a log upon the coals. As the wood caught fire, he turned and looked into the most beautiful blue eyes he had ever seen. "You waited up for me. I am sorry that I took so long, sweet."

"I thought that we should talk, Royce." For the past few hours, Angela had worried herself almost sick about what he would say if she told him that she loved him and that she was carrying his child. The little man had told her to trust in her own heart, but how could she do that when she had never been able to fully trust anything in her entire life!

"I agree, love. There is much that must be said." Royce drew her out of the chair, and sitting down, he pulled her onto his lap. She wore only her shift. "I know that I have been a fool where you are concerned, and I ask this minute that you forgive me."

Looking into the silver-gray eyes that were gazing upon her, Angela softly asked, shaking her head without understanding, "What would you have me forgive, Royce?"

Even this minute, when she could declare him the biggest fool in the whole of England, she was tender of heart. "Upon our first meeting, I treated you unkindly and did not give you a proper chance to explain yourself. I felt you were lying and did not allow you the slightest benefit of a doubt."

Angela had forgotten that Royce had not believed her to be from another century, so worried was she that she was pregnant and her fate and that of her child rested solely upon the feelings that he had never expressed for her. "Then you believe that I am not from this time?"

He searched her face before he slowly nodded his dark head. "I believe everything that you have ever told me. I believe that in the future there will be carriages without horses and there are such things as airplanes, though you have not described these things to me. I believe that you knew before meeting me that Damian would betray me and that the proof would be found in Hampsteed Castle. I must believe this, for there is no other explanation for your finding the letters that Damian wrote to Camelle."

"Oh" was Angela's only response. She had hoped that he was going to declare his undying love for her.

Pressing his lips to her forehead, Royce drew in another deep breath. "There is another reason for my believing what you have told me, love." His words were softly spoken, and something in their depths held Angela still in his arms. "I had a long wait this evening for Granville: he was at the palace giving counsel to the King. But during my wait, I realized what you must have risked to gain these letters at Hampsteed Castle, and I also realized why you did it." As she would have spoken then, he pressed a finger over her lips. "I know your reasons, and I can't say that if I were in your place, I would not have done the same."

"And what reason is this, your Grace?" Angela could not imagine what he was getting at.

"I am talking about the love that you hold for me. That is why you risked all to prove me innocent of Damian's charges, even though I was so stubborn I would not believe you."

Angela had not expected this. Looking upon him, she was warmed by the smile that had settled over his lips, but a spark of her old rebellion straightened her spine. "And what makes you believe that what I feel for you is love?"

His grip upon her tightened. When he had been in Granville's study waiting, letter in hand, it had struck Royce that he was hopelessly in love with his Gypsy brat. As he had sat there, he had had time to recapture in memory everything that had happened between himself and Angela. Realizing how unfair he had been to her since their first meeting, he had finally come to the decision that it must be her love for him that had kept her at his side and had led her into the very face of danger in order to save him! Now, looking down upon her, he wondered if this had been wishful thinking on his part. "Perhaps I was mistaken, Angela, but I had hoped—"

"What was it that you had hoped, Royce?" she interrupted as she felt the unsteady beat of her heart.

What did he have to lose by proclaiming his feelings? he asked himself. He could only lose if he remained quiet as he had thus far. His hand reached up and lightly caressed her soft cheek. Inwardly he prayed that she would understand. "I know that after everything I have put you through, I am unworthy to claim your love, but I had hoped you would take pity on this heart of mine, Angela. I love you more than life itself, and if able, I would take back all of the hurt and cruelty that I have inflicted. I offer unto you, if only you will stand at my side: my heart, my protection, and my name."

Sheer, marvelous joy sang within Angela's heart and coursed throughout her every vein! Royce St. James had declared his love for her and was offering her his name! The child growing within her would not know the hardship of life she had suffered and would have a father that would provide protection and care, and she would have the man of her heart, the man that she loved! Tears made a path down her cheeks as a tremulous smile touched her lips. "You truly love me, Royce?"

"I certainly do, madam, more than anything I have ever known in this life!" He took heart as he glimpsed the smile and the sparkling happiness that glowed from her eyes.

"I love you, too, Royce!" She threw her slender arms around his neck. "The guardian told me that if I needed him he would come, and I am sure that I could go back to my rightful time, but oh, Royce, I want to stay here with you forever!"

He believed her, even though what she said made little sense. To him, she had made her choice to remain because of her love for him! Pulling her to him, his lips covered hers.

No more needed to be said. He carried

her over to the large bed in the center of the chamber, and sometime, in the early hours of the dawn, as they both lay sated and wrapped within each other's arms, Angela whispered the news that he would soon become a father.

The following day, dressed in the rich violet-blue taffeta gown with its embroidered trim and long train, Angela arrived at court upon the arm of Royce St. James. The Duke of Westfield had arranged that morning for the banns to be posted in announcement of their marriage.

The court of George II was full, and as Angela looked around, she glimpsed Damian Dunsely making his way to their side. Her hand automatically tightened upon Royce's arm, and as his hand covered hers, the slight pressure told her that she had nothing to fear.

"I am surprised to find you here at court, Royce." Damian looked disdainfully at Angela. "I have been summoned to court this day and have a meeting later with the ministry." His chest swelled with pride.

A knowing smile settled over Angela's lips, and as Damian cast a glance upon her beauty, the anger he held for his friend rekindled. Even here at court, the Duke of

Westfield thought he could flaunt his latest mistress, a woman who should belong to him! Yes, lately he had been dwelling over the fact that the night she had attempted to steal his wallet, he should have kept the wench for himself! Turning back to Royce, he also noticed that his friend was looking at him rather strangely.

Royce held only contempt for Damian Dunsely. He knew well what Damian would face later in the day. The ministry would condemn him for his plans to murder his own father and for his plans to involve the Duke of Westfield in the Jacobite plot against their King. Damian would not be so smug when he found that the tables had been turned on him.

"Well, Royce, old man, I guess that the year is almost up." With those standing close by and listening to their conversation, Damian appeared to gloat, a thin smirk pulling back his lips, as it took Royce a minute to realize what he was talking about. "The bet is all but up, but I fear that you have come out the loser in our game this time! Your Gypsy whore is definitely no lady!"

Royce could hear women tittering behind fans and men chuckling. At the same time, he could feel Angela draw back as though she had been physically slapped. Without a second thought, his powerful fist smashed into Damian's vile mouth. His enemy collapsed to the floor, spitting teeth and blood.

"Hear me well, Damian, for I will say this only one time in front of these witnesses." His stormy gaze circled all those standing around, and many a head lowered in his glare. "The next time you besmirch the woman I love and will claim as my wife, my second will seek you out. And be forewarned that on the dueling field I will be aiming for your heart!" Turning back to Angela, he took her arm and stepped away from the man upon the floor.

"Was that wise, Royce?" Angela wondered as she glanced over her shoulder and watched Damian rising from the floor. She still worried that he could cause them some evil.

"Do not worry, love. There shall be no next time for Damian. When the ministry gets done with him, he will be lucky if he escapes the scaffold." Pressing his hand once again over hers, he looked deeply into her blue eyes. "Have I told you today how much I adore you, my Gypsy angel?"

A warm smile settled over her lips as she trusted fully in his protection. "Aye, your Grace, you have told me, but I don't think that I will ever tire of hearing the words!"

Epilogue

"Gad, Angela, isn't he the most handsome man ye ever did set yer eyes on? I still can't believe that he's mine!"

Angela smiled knowingly and absently nodded her dark head as she looked upon the two men standing at a distance, her gaze holding full upon her husband and the little dark-haired girl that he was holding in his strong arms. "Absolutely the most handsome man alive," she replied softly.

"Stephan is hoping that our child will be a little girl, too. He told me so last night after ye and the duke left the camp to return to the Hall." Myra was grinning widely as she patted the rounded swell of her belly. The child would be born during the winter months, and Angela had promised Myra that she would be there for her. "I'm so happy that ye will be the one to help me deliver, and I won't be having that old hag Zela

bending over me when me time comes!"
Myra added, thankful that they would not be
wandering over the countryside, but would
be encamped here in the Westfield forest
when the baby arrived.

"I hope that you and Stephan will be as
happy as Royce and I have been with Angel."
It had been two years now since Angela and
Royce had wed, and not a day's passing of
that time had she regretted. She never wished
to set the hands of time to that day when she
had followed the little, dapper man down the
London streets and had stolen the tiny box
from his pocket. Fate had brought her to this
century, and love held her here.

"Why don't we join our handsome men?"
she asked Myra, and together they approached the men who stood admiring the
new horse that Stephan had recently acquired.

Royce turned in Angela's direction, his
gaze, as ever, filled with love. The baby in his
arms pointed excitedly to the horse, and in
her lilting little voice, she tried to say *pony*.

Royce St. James was certainly the family
man now, Angela thought as he drew her to
his side with a hand around her waist. Perhaps this evening, with Angel tucked away
in her bed, would be the time to tell him
that he was once again to become a father.
As she felt his tender strength encircling
her, Angela knew true love.

If you enjoyed *Time's Angel* and would like a free bookmark, please send a SASE to Kathleen Drymon in care of Zebra Books, 475 Park Avenue South, New York, NY 10016.

SURRENDER TO THE SPLENDOR OF THE ROMANCES OF F. ROSANNE BITTNER!

DANA RANSOM'S RED-HOT HEARTFIRES!

ALEXANDRA'S ECSTASY   (2773, $3.75)

Alexandra had known Tucker for all her seventeen years, but all at once she realized her childhood friend was the man capable of tempting her to leave innocence behind!

LIAR'S PROMISE   (2881, $4.25)

Kathryn Mallory's sincere questions about her father's ship to the disreputable Captain Brady Rogan were met with mocking indifference. Then he noticed her trim waist, angelic face and Kathryn won the wrong kind of attention!

LOVE'S GLORIOUS GAMBLE   (2497, $3.75)

Nothing could match the true thrill that coursed through Gloria Daniels when she first spotted the gambler, Sterling Caulder. Experiencing his embrace, feeling his lips against hers would be a risk, but she was willing to chance it all!

WILD, SAVAGE LOVE   (3055, $4.25)

Evangeline, set free from Indians, discovered liberty had its price to pay when her uncle sold her into marriage to Royce Tanner. Dreaming of her return to the people she loved, she vowed never to submit to her husband's caress.

WILD WYOMING LOVE   (3427, $4.25)

Lucille Blessing had no time for the new marshal Sam Zachary. His mocking and arrogant manner grated her nerves, yet she longed to ease the tension she knew he held inside. She knew that if he wanted her, she could never say no!

Available wherever paperbacks are sold, or order direct from the Publisher. Send cover price plus 50¢ per copy for mailing and handling to Penguin USA, P.O. Box 999, c/o Dept. 17109, Bergenfield, NJ 07621. Residents of New York and Tennessee must include sales tax. DO NOT SEND CASH.